SHAKEDOWN

SHAKE DOWN

JOEL GOLDMAN

PINNACLE BOOKS
Kensington Publishing Corp.
www.kensingtonbooks.com

PINNACLE BOOKS are published by

Kensington Publishing Corp.
850 Third Avenue
New York, NY 10022

All Kensington titles, imprints, and distributed lines are available at special quantity discounts for bulk purchases for sales promotions, premiums, fund-raising, educational, or institutional use. Special book excerpts or customized printings can also be created to fit specific needs. For details, write or phone the office of the Kensington special sales manager: Kensington Publishing Corp., 850 Third Avenue, New York, NY 10022, attn: Special Sales Department; phone 1-800-221-2647.

This book is a work of fiction. Names, characters, businesses, organizations, places, events, and incidents either are the product of the author's imagination or are used fictitiously. Any resemblance to actual persons, living or dead, events, or locales is entirely coincidental.

ISBN-13: 978-0-7860-1610-5
ISBN-10: 0-7860-1610-8

First printing: April 2008

10 9 8 7 6 5 4 3 2 1

Printed in the United States of America

*For Dorothy Bodker, of blessed memory, and
Stanley Bodker*

ACKNOWLEDGMENTS

Humans have always struggled to divine the truth using everything from tea leaves to torture to separate fact from fiction. Recent research in this field was very helpful to me in writing this book. I first learned about Professor Paul Ekman and the Facial Action Coding System in Malcolm Gladwell's book *Blink*. Dr. Ekman's book *Telling Lies* explains more fully how a lie catcher can recognize deceit. I learned about additional brain research on lying in an article by Yaling Yang and others titled *Prefrontal White Matter in Pathological Liars*, published in 2005 in the *British Journal of Psychiatry*. *USA Today* reported on June 27, 2006, about the use of MRIs to detect lies. *Time* magazine reported in its July 17, 2006 issue about prosopagnosia or facial blindness.

I also benefited from Steven D. Levitt and Stephen J. Dubner's book, *Freakonomics*, which describes a drug-selling gang's finances, including the importance of paying funeral benefits for those killed while doing the gang's business. Dr. Levitt expanded on this research in a 1998 paper, entitled *An Economic Analysis of a Drug-Selling Gang's Finances*, published by the National Bureau of Economic Research.

Murray Rhodes and Gilbert Castro shared with me the history of the Argentine Mine in Kansas City, Kansas. Steve Gershon answered questions about income taxes. I thank them all for their assistance.

I was privileged to participate in the FBI Citizens' Academy in Kansas City. I learned a great deal about the difficult work the FBI does and was greatly impressed by the integrity, commitment, and passion of the men and women who serve that agency. I thank them and remind them that this book is a work of fiction. I really was paying attention in class.

Thanks, as always, to my agent, Meredith Bernstein, for her friendship and guidance. Thanks also to my editor, Audrey LaFehr, for her work in making this a better book.

Nothing in my life would be as rich without my wife, Hildy, and our children, Aaron, Daniel, and Michele. Thanks to them for going along for this ride.

Chapter One

Marcellus Pearson counted out three thousand dollars, wrapped the short stack of cash with a rubber band, and handed the money to Oleta Phillips, a narrow-shouldered woman with razor lips. He covered her hand with his, her hard knuckles like pitted marbles against his palm, and rolled her arm over, studying the needle tracks running from the crook of her elbow like drunken sutures stitched into her coffee-colored skin.

"You stayin' clean, Oleta?" he asked.

"Tryin' to," she said, pulling her hand away.

"That's good, real good. Sorry 'bout your boy. He was family."

Oleta looked at him, opening her mouth, then thinking better of it, not asking him what kind of family put a fifteen-year-old boy on a corner, his pockets full of crack, so he could get killed over just whose corner was it anyway. She was afraid to ask Marcellus, the way he watched her with his own dead eyes. And she was flush with shame, knowing that she might have saved her boy if she had cared more about him than her next fix. It was too late by the time she realized how important her son was to her.

"Funeral costs and a little somethin' extra, this being a hard time and all."

Oleta nodded, knowing Marcellus was paying for her son's funeral and her silence, damning herself for taking the money, taking it anyway.

Marcellus's girlfriend, Jalise Williams, came down the stairs into the front room where he did his business, wobbling on four-inch heels. Barely out of her teens, she carried their son, Keyshon, on her hip, the boy old enough to walk but glad to be in his mother's arms. A short-legged honey-colored dog followed after her.

"Put him down," Marcellus told her. "Boy can't spend his life bein' carried around by his momma. Ask Oleta, here. She know. She raised her boy right."

Oleta looked at Jalise. The crack dealer's whore, she thought. Girl's ass hanging out of shorts that was too short, her tits squeezed out of a tube top wouldn't cover nothin' if nothin' was all the girl had, wearing enough bling to buy a house. They the ones somebody ought to be collecting death benefits on, she thought, saying nothing.

"He be walkin' enough," Jalise said, ignoring Oleta. "I'm goin' out."

Marcellus didn't argue. Jalise took better care of the boy than he would have, changing diapers he wouldn't touch, keeping herself and the kid out of the way and out of his business. Girl had a fine ass. That was enough.

"You go on," he told Oleta. "Put that money away, hear. And stay clean."

Marcellus smiled to himself as Oleta opened the screen door, letting herself out, knowing that she wouldn't stay clean, not now, not after burying her boy. She'd be high by the time it got dark, broke a week later, selling her ass again, the money he'd handed her back in his pocket.

It was Monday, late September; there'd be a few days still warm like today, but the nights were going cold. Not much color in the trees, the leaves mostly brown and blowing up and down the street like they was lost, same as Oleta.

Her family gathered around her on the front porch like it was Christmas, whispering to her, "Wuhju get?" Oleta, her head down, answered in a quiet voice, flies buzzing around them. Her brother, a heavyset man, yanked at his pants, shooing away the flies with the back of his hand, telling the others it was more than Condre Smith got when his boy got hisself killed last year, saying that Marcellus sure knows what it costs to live and die.

Rondell and DeMarcus Winston leaned against the porch rail, tipping their heads at Marcellus to let him know that the family was satisfied. They were Marcellus's enforcers—hard-muscled, cold-blooded brothers, seventeen and eighteen years old, three killings between them. If Marcellus decided to hit back for the boy's death, the Winston brothers would do the hitting.

Marcellus was twenty-three, a high school dropout running the crack trade in Quindaro, a rundown quadrant in northeast Kansas City, Kansas. Of all the money Marcellus paid out to run his business, funeral benefits were the smartest. It sent a message: We take care of our own. His people understood that. They needed to feel valued and he set the price.

A fan hanging from the ceiling in the front room stirred heavy air stale with Chinese takeout that had been left to rot in open boxes on the kitchen table. The dog stole one, racing into the front room, its snout deep in the container, wrestling for crumbs. Marcellus cursed the dog, kicking the box out of its mouth; the dog scampered out of the room, out of his reach.

An old twenty-seven-inch television sat in the corner, rabbit-ears antenna not helping to make the picture clear. He kept the plasma screen with its high-definition cable in the upstairs bedroom.

Marcellus's mother lived across the street, cooking the crack. He stored his inventory in the basement of the one-room church next door to his mother's house. The pastor rented the space to Marcellus, and the rent was paid in protection.

For thirty years, Kansas City, Kansas, had been the disrespected punch line to jokes told by people living south in Johnson County or east, across the state line, in Kansas City, Missouri. Now, the city had turned the corner, merging with Wyandotte County into a unified government, landing a NASCAR track that triggered an economic boom. The city had shed its stepchild image, the conversation changing from getting out to getting in.

But nothing had changed in Quindaro. Too many people didn't have jobs and a lot of those that did still couldn't pay the rent. Boys joined gangs and quit school. Girls got pregnant and followed the boys into the street. The economy ran on drugs, not NASCAR, not strip malls and subdivisions with walkout basements, not anything, Marcellus bragged to his people, that wouldn't kill you or thrill you.

Marcellus stuck to crack despite the growing competition from meth, on top of the heat he got from Javy Ordonez and his bunch, pushing out of Argentine and into Quindaro. Rondell Winston had warned him that they were losing money, giving him a hard time a couple of days ago.

"That cracker, Bodie—what's his name?" Rondell had asked.

"Name of Bodie Grant. I know who he is. White boy over in Raytown. Got so many tats, hardly see any white on the boy."

"He peddlin' meth in our territory," Rondell had told Marcellus. "It's bad for bidness. We gotta git in it or git they asses outta here. Mebbe both."

"That shit is a real mess," Marcellus said. "People all the time blowin' their own selves up just cookin' the shit. No way my momma gonna jack wit no fuckin' meth."

"Shit, man," Rondell said. "Javy Ordonez picking us off our street corners and Bodie Grant bringin' his shit into our motherfuckin' backyard. Things gonna get real tight around here we don't do somethin'."

Marcellus had already talked to his supplier about it, the supplier tellin' him nothing lasts forever, like he don't already know that. Marcellus said how he busted his nuts every day keeping the lid on, the supplier saying keep on busting while he could.

Marcellus told his supplier that if Javy Ordonez and Bodie Grant took him down, the supplier could kiss good-bye the money Marcellus been paying for his product and the extra to keep the cops off his back. The supplier said competition was good for everybody, said get back to the street while he was still walking on the green side instead of lyin' under the brown side, letting Marcellus know he on his own.

"I know what I know," Marcellus said. "Ain't gonna do no fuckin' meth."

"Can't keep pretendin' Javy and Bodie Grant ain't squeezin' our ass. Wuhju gonna do 'bout it?" Rondell asked, stepping up in Marcellus's face.

The way Rondell asked the question was more important to Marcellus than the question, Rondell telling Marcellus maybe he'd do somethin' 'bout it if Marcellus didn't. That's the way it always was, Marcellus thought to himself. Somebody always watchin, askin' wuhju gonna do 'bout some shit, waitin' for his turn to make hisself head nigga. Best way to cool that shit was to give Rondell someone else to take a few swings at, calm his ass down.

"You and DeMarcus go see Mr. Tattoos-Up-His-Ass Bodie Grant, mess wit his mind a little bit, tellum peddle his shit some other place."

"What about Javy?"

Marcellus gave Rondell a flat, street stare. "Let him know what's what. I don't care what shit he puts on the street long as he keep it out of Quindaro. Tell him take his shit back to Argentine."

"I'm all about that," Rondell said, satisfied for the moment, coming back that night, his chest puffed up like he'd gotten laid for the first time, telling Marcellus he and DeMarcus done delivered the messages.

Marcellus had started out like Oleta's son, standing on a corner, selling rocks. He made a name for himself when he killed a soldier from a rival Hispanic gang. The soldier had thirty pounds on Marcellus and a gun under his shirt. One day he shoved the gun in Marcellus's eyes and grabbed him by the balls, telling Marcellus it was his corner and to take his skinny black ass home.

Marcellus waited until it was dark before he came back and hid in an alley with a baseball bat. When the soldier walked past, Marcellus stepped out behind him, swinging the bat like he was in a slow-pitch cage. The soldier was dead when he hit the ground, Marcellus's gang calling him Barry motherfuckin' Bonds. That was six years ago, a couple of lifetimes in the crack business. He'd survived by taking care of his own and doing business with the right people.

His strategy had paid off when the cops came crashing through the front door of his house two weeks ago. He was ready, watching TV in bed with Jalise and Keyshon, the only shit in the house belonging to the dog. The cops kicked them out while they searched, saying they had a fugitive warrant for some cat named Darrell. The next day, when the Winston brothers asked what had happened, Marcellus told them it waddn't nothing.

Then Oleta's boy got hisself shot the day after Rondell and DeMarcus delivered their messages. Marcellus suspected the shooting was either Javy's or Bodie's way of answering back, though, in some ways, it didn't matter who did it.

What mattered was what his people thought happened and what he was going to do about it. If Marcellus didn't hit back at someone, they would think he was weak or afraid. Worse, they would think he didn't value them. As soon as that happened, they'd want someone else to tell them what to do. Marcellus shook his head, knowing he had to do something even if it was wrong. He walked to the screen door, tapping on the wire mesh.

"Gitcho asses inna house," he told the Winston brothers.

Chapter Two

Latrell Kelly blinked, ducking his head from the sun, his eyes stinging. He'd slept in the cave again and the daylight was painful. The night before, he'd watched from the shadows on his back stoop while the Winston brothers took turns with some girl in his backyard, the bitch hollering, Rondell smacking her till she shut up. Latrell was mad, seeing his mother taking that beating instead of the girl.

He'd lived in his house more than half of his thirty-two years. The closest thing to a father he ever knew was Johnny McDonald, the man who used to own the house. Johnny sold dope and pimped his mother out, sometimes slapping her, sometimes him, sometimes both of them, until Latrell buried Johnny and his mother in the basement.

He was fifteen then, doing odd jobs at the rail yard in Argentine when he wasn't in school, eventually hiring on full-time after he graduated. Now he worked as a file clerk in the terminal building. He had paid off the taxes Johnny owed on the house with money Johnny had stuffed under the mattress where his mother had earned her share, and then kept the rest for groceries. When he wasn't working, he kept up his house and yard and tried not to think about his mother.

Then Marcellus come along, him and his girlfriend, Jalise, and their little boy, moving in right behind him, the three of them making it so Latrell couldn't stop thinking about Johnny McDonald and his mother and him when he was the same age as the boy, until he had a hard time telling the dead from the living. The whole neighborhood knew Marcellus was dealing dope but nobody did nothing about it. The more Latrell couldn't put them out of his mind, the closer he got to making things right. The Winston brothers waling on that girl in his backyard was it. He couldn't take any more.

Growing up, he was a small, soft boy, easy prey for bullies, gangs, and any kid looking for someone to pick on who wouldn't fight back. The cave, a remnant of a mining operation, had saved him. He'd stumbled onto the entrance one day after work while walking in the woods not far from the rail yard. It was nothing more than a seam in a rock wall till he pulled down some bigger rocks, learning how to put them back so no one who didn't know about it could tell it was anything.

After that, Latrell spent his spare time exploring the inside with a flashlight, storing batteries and candles on a rock shelf, comfortable in the shadows. Most of the cave was underwater, his hideaway confined to a series of chambers ending on a rocky beach. He never did know how far the water went or how deep it was, only that it was so black there was no bottom and no end.

Johnny McDonald had had a pair of .45 caliber Marine pistols and some night-vision goggles he stole off a guy at a gun show, that and the cash under the mattress Latrell's inheritance. When he was old enough, Latrell went to a range and learned how to shoot the .45s. Then he'd practice in the cave wearing the night-vision goggles, dry firing 'cause he was afraid of ricochets, ready in case he had to make things right again one day, same as he had with Johnny and his mother.

A few years ago, some kids out canoeing had found their way into the cave from a small lake and gotten lost, making a big deal about spending the night in the cave like they was gonna die. He read about it in the paper, the article calling the cave the Argentine Mine and saying it covered thirty-four acres underground. The county promised to seal it up before anyone else got lost and they did just that except they never did find Latrell's way in.

He spent several nights in the cave imagining how, late at night, he would walk through the front door of Marcellus's house and kill everyone inside. He could do it. Soft, shy, quiet Latrell, stronger than any of them, could kill them all. He'd practiced and practiced. It wouldn't be hard. It would be a good thing. He replayed the scene over and over in his mind, opening his eyes to find that nothing had changed until simply imagining wasn't enough.

On the day he first decided to do it, he changed his mind when he saw the camera installed on the utility pole down the street from Marcellus's house. He had seen men climb those poles before at the rail yard. He knew the kind of tools they carried, the kind of work they did, and how they did it. The man on the pole never touched his tools, the tool belt slapping against his right thigh like it didn't belong. The man was some kind of cop, maybe even FBI, he decided, not caring so long as they got rid of Marcellus. So he waited.

Latrell thought it was all going to be over a week later when the police raided Marcellus's house, until he realized that no one had been arrested. He didn't understand—first the camera, then the raid, then nothing. Still, he had waited two more weeks until last night, listening and watching Rondell and DeMarcus mess with that girl who could have been his momma.

The FBI had failed him. The police had failed him. What was he supposed to do? They left him no choice. If he didn't make it right, he'd keep seeing his mother in every woman's face. He'd have no peace. His eyes adjusted to the sun and he headed for home where he'd wait for dark, when it would finally be time.

Latrell drove past Marcellus's house. Oleta Phillips, her fat brother Rodney, and some more of her people were out in front, Oleta looking half dead, Rodney grinning. He'd heard that Oleta's boy got hisself shot on a corner belong to Marcellus. She must've come to collect.

Oleta reminded Latrell of his momma more than Jalise did; Oleta was so thin that the light passed right through her. His momma had lived on dope her whole miserable life, paying for it with her legs spread, coming on to him right after he killed Johnny, saying he had to take care of her now that Johnny was dead. He told her no, shoving her away. She came back at him, throwing her arms around him, rubbing against him, begging.

He snapped her neck like it was nothing. She was already dead to him. He just made it real. Latrell dug Johnny's hole in the basement floor a little deeper and laid her on top of him, the washer and dryer covering the grave.

He slowed down, looking at Oleta again. He was right. She did have his momma's face.

It started to rain late in the day, the storm growing into a steady pounding after midnight. A good sign, Latrell thought. It would be like taking a walk in the cave.

He'd been in Marcellus's house once or twice years ago. It had a shotgun layout: front door, front room, kitchen, and out the back; two bedrooms and a bath were down the hall on the second floor, stairs to the left as you come into the house.

Latrell had watched the lights turn on and off for weeks, figuring out which bedroom Marcellus used and where the

Winston brothers flopped. He'd seen people coming and going enough to know that Marcellus did his business in the front room. That's where he'd find Marcellus and the Winston brothers if he was lucky. If he wasn't lucky, he'd find them anyway.

Afterward, he knew the police would question him just as they would everyone else in the neighborhood. He would answer their questions. Be polite, smile as he lied to them. He could do that, he knew, better than anyone.

Rummaging through his dark house, Latrell found a pair of galoshes, pulling them over his shoes, not wanting to leave muddy footprints on Marcellus's floor the cops could trace back to him. He'd thought of everything. He stuck the gun in the waistband of his pants, slipped on the goggles, pulled on a pair of latex gloves, and stepped outside into the storm.

Chapter Three

I was alone in my office, lights off, door closed, cradling a cold cup of coffee. It was past midnight, everyone else long gone except for the new security guard who knocked at my door on the half hour, last time reminding me not to take any files from the building without signing them out.

"I've been an FBI agent almost as long as you've been alive," I told him.

"I know that, Agent Davis. Regulations say I'm supposed to make sure, that's all," he said. "Get that light for you?"

I shook my head. "Call me Jack."

"Yes sir, Agent Davis."

A storm blew outside, the rain hitting the window without making a sound against the insulated glass. I leaned back in my chair outside the reach of the pale-blue glow from my computer monitor. I kept to the dark so I couldn't see myself shake.

The tremors started in my belly, galloped up my neck, and spilled into my arms and head like they were excavating fault lines. I didn't shake all the time. Tonight, it had been every ten or fifteen minutes, usually only for a few seconds, except for one stretch that lasted two minutes by my watch.

It had started two months ago, right after my future former wife Joy moved out. It was a few twitches at first, not enough to send me to a doctor, slowly getting worse, taking off in the last week. I could go for hours without so much as a hiccup. Other times, like now, I kept the door closed. I'd gotten a few looks, but no questions, from the agents on my squad. That's the way it had to be until I shut Marcellus Pearson down, which I would do when our surveillance warrant expired in four days. I could wait that long to find out what was happening to me.

I was watching the feed from the surveillance camera I'd installed two and a half weeks earlier in the front room of Marcellus's house. The camera was in the ceiling fan, giving me a 360-degree view, and with a microphone that could capture a fart.

Marcellus's crack operation was good enough to make him Entrepreneur of the Year, except he didn't have anything to show for it besides the usual pimped-out ride, tattoos, and bling. He could have lost his money in the stock market, given it to charity, or funded retirement plans for his enforcers, the Winston brothers. Or, he could be fronting for someone.

I ran the Violent Crime squad in the FBI's Kansas City regional office and there was no criminal enterprise more violent than drugs. Marcellus had been operating in Kansas City, Kansas, for a long time. No one bothered him. People who did woke up dead. I intended to bother his ass right out of business before I shook myself into an early retirement. We had already mounted a camera on a utility pole down the street, but we needed eyes inside the crack house.

A month ago, I asked Marty Grisnik, head of Robbery and Homicide for the Kansas City, Kansas, police department, for his help serving a fugitive warrant. I'd met him a year ago at one of the interagency events put on to foster cooperation between federal and local law enforcement. We hadn't worked a case together, but we drank enough that night to make up for it, and had traded a couple of favors since then. I gave him Marcellus's address, not telling him that the warrant was phony and that I was going to use it so I could get inside the house and install a surveillance camera.

"FBI has its own fugitive warrants team, Jack. Why do you want my help?"

Grisnik had a linebacker's build and looked uncomfortable in a suit, like he'd rather be on the field roaming for someone to hit. Near my age, he worked harder than I did to keep a muscled edge. We were in his cramped office on the fifth floor of the police department headquarters on Seventh Street, Grisnik rocking back in his swivel chair. I stood, keeping a tight grip on the arched back of a chair in case I started to shake.

"The guy we're after, Darrell Johnson, is hooked up with one of our undercover people. If we don't get him, we don't want him tipped off that the FBI is chasing him. Works better if he thinks it's you guys."

"But you want to go through the door, not us?"

I took a breath, glancing over his shoulder at the view to the east out his window. The Intercity Viaduct stretched over an area called the West Bottoms for its close proximity to the Missouri River. The Viaduct and the West Bottoms connected the two Kansas Cities, the highway a concrete artery, the Bottoms muscle and ligaments made of old warehouses, new businesses, and reborn bars. From Grisnik's window I could also see a thin slice of the Missouri coming down from the north, then bending east on its way to St. Louis. The FBI building stood on a bluff on the southwest edge of downtown Kansas City, Missouri, part of a string of office towers running north to the river.

"That's right. I need your people for backup. And I'd like to borrow one of your uniforms."

Grisnik pecked away at his computer, sending an e-mail, double-checking my warrant to make certain he got the address right. He smiled, waiting for a response, his silence code for telling me I was full of shit and he was about to prove it.

"The Bureau appreciates your cooperation. If we get him, you get the credit. If we don't, nobody will know or care."

I didn't tell Grisnik about the surveillance camera because I suspected that Marcellus had some KCK cops in his pocket. That would go a long way in explaining how he had stayed in business for so long. If I were right, Marcellus would get word of our raid and clean house so that we wouldn't have any reason to arrest him. That was fine with me. All I wanted was to get him out of the house long enough to install the camera. I wasn't ready to lock him up.

Grisnik's computer binged, signaling that he'd received a reply to his e-mail. I couldn't see his monitor to read it, though that wasn't necessary.

"This would play a little better if you worked homeland security into it somewhere along the way," Grisnik said.

"Do I need to?"

"Wouldn't smell any sweeter if you did. This address belongs to Marcellus Pearson. Says here Marcellus is a suspected drug dealer. Bet you didn't know that. And no one named Darrell Johnson shows up on the list of his known associates. You want me to run a quick check on your fugitive?"

"I'd rather you didn't."

"We got our own fugitive squad and we got our own drug squad. You ought to be talking to them, not me. Since you aren't, makes me think you've got a reason I'm not going to like."

"I do."

"This isn't my idea of cooperation, Jack. You coming to

me for help and not telling me what I need to know, especially if it involves this department."

"Operational constraints. It's better for everyone."

"Better for you, maybe," Grisnik said. "Puts my ass in a sling if this blows up."

"It won't blow up."

"You can't keep something like this a secret."

"I don't intend for it to be a secret."

Grisnik nodded, his eyes softening as he understood what I needed. He held the warrant to the halogen lamp on his desk as if he was checking a fifty-dollar bill to see if it was counterfeit. He slid it back toward me with a reluctant grunt.

"You'll need a name tag for your uniform. You want one that says Jack Davis or you want me to pick on somebody else?"

"Any name will do as long as it isn't mine."

Chapter Four

In my world, only liars, drunks, and the guilty shake uncontrollably. If Ben Yates, the Special Agent in charge of the Kansas City office, caught me doing "Shake it up, baby," I'd be on the shelf before I got to "Twist and Shout." So I worked late and kept my door closed.

I'd been an agent since I gave the army the tour of duty I'd promised in return for my college education. I'd worked in FBI offices all over the country, picked Kansas City for my last stop since it was where Joy and I wanted to live when the Bureau retired me in five years when I turned fifty-five.

It wasn't just a job. It was who I was—the right guy, doing the right job for the right reasons. I could never give it up, especially after our son Kevin was killed almost twenty years ago when I didn't do my job. They'd have to take the badge from me. I owed that much to Kevin.

I wasn't ready to deal with the possible causes of the shaking—brain tumor, Parkinson's, MS, ALS, or some other equally grim alphabetical practical joke. I played with images of Muhammad Ali shuffling like an old man, not floating like a butterfly, his face a mask, or of Lou Gehrig telling a packed Yankee Stadium that he was the luckiest man alive. Whatever it was, I didn't feel lucky. Every time I shook, I offered whatever it was a deal. Just go away, no questions asked. So far, there were no takers.

The late shift was a good place to hide, and I was in no hurry to go home. When Joy moved out, she left me a note saying she had tried to tell me what was wrong with our marriage ever since Kevin died but I never heard her. I called her cell, told her I was ready to listen. "Too late," she said. "Now you can be with Kate Scranton." I told her again that there was nothing between Kate and me; she's a jury consultant, helps me with some cases. That's it. It was Joy's turn not to listen.

Our other child, Wendy, inherited the enthusiasm, wit, and determination that I'd found in Joy when I first fell in love with her. After Kevin died, Wendy hid it away, replacing it with fear of the dark, of being left alone, and, most of all, of being taken from us.

She had a stuffed animal, a monkey that she slept with every night after we lost Kevin. I made up a song that made her laugh, a rare occurrence in those days.

I had a little monkey girl.
She climbed a tree just like a squirrel.
And when she got up to the top,
She held her breath until she popped.

And when she got back on the ground,
She wore a smile and not a frown.
She's always glad, she's never sad
Because she has a goofy dad!

Wendy loved the song, changed her stuffed animal's name from Pickles to Monkey Girl, and insisted we create a secret code in case someone kidnapped her. She'd use the code to tell us that she was okay and that I should come find her.

"That's a great idea," I told her. "Very smart for a little girl."

"You know Monkey Girl?"

"Sure. We're great pals."

"When the kidnappers put me on the phone so you know that I'm still alive, I'll tell you to say happy birthday to Monkey Girl. That way you'll know I'm okay."

"How do you know that's what kidnappers do?"

"I heard you talking to your friends from work. One of them said that's what always happens except the man that took Kevin didn't do it the right way."

I wanted to tell her that there was no such thing as a right way to kidnap someone, but she was holding onto that certainty like a lifeline, convinced she would be kidnapped and hoping her abductor would do a better job of it than had Kevin's. I pulled her onto my lap, hugged her fiercely against my chest.

"Then you better hang onto Monkey Girl. I'd hate for her to miss out on her birthday party."

Wendy had her own survival scars, growing up in a house where her brother's ghost and her parents' wars made certain that she never felt safe and secure. It was a breeding ground for her mother's alcoholism, a disease Wendy flirted with through drugs.

She lived in a state of perpetual rebound between bad choices and second chances. I was her spotter, ready to catch her when she fell and pat her on the back when she pulled herself up again, saved by an eternal flame inside her that gave her strength and gave me hope.

Her first stab at college lasted six weeks.

"It's not for me," she told me over the phone. "All the sorority debs, the jocks. That's not me. And this college town is dead."

"It's not the people or the place," I told her. "It's you. You've got to deal with that no matter where you are or what you do."

"I know," she sighed. "Just not here and now."

"Stay in school and mom and I will support you. Drop out and you're on your own."

"Fair enough. Front me the first few months and I'll pay you back?"

"Deal."

And she did, working, taking occasional classes until she discovered she liked the action in the commodities market. She landed a job at the Kansas City Board of Trade working for a broker, studying for her trading license. Along the way to getting her head on straight, she did two stints in rehab and I helped her get two possession busts expunged.

"You'll always have to be careful," I told her. "Staying straight and sober is like working without a net."

"Except I've got a net. You," she said, and kissed my cheek.

Wendy more or less lived alone, the less being Colby Hudson, one of the agents on my squad. I wasn't surprised when she got involved with him. Kids repeat more of their parents' mistakes than they avoid, sometimes seeking them out. It was enough to make me shake.

Five seconds and the latest shaking stopped. I timed it. No one noticed. No one said "what the hell was that"? Ben Yates didn't get out of his warm bed in the middle of the thunderstorm to shove a claim for disability in front of me, telling me where to sign and saying that he was sorry I missed my full pension by a lousy five years.

I checked my computer monitor. The Winston brothers hadn't noticed, either. DeMarcus Winston was taking inventory, bags of crack spread out on the card table Marcellus used as a desk. A TV so old it had a rabbit-ears antenna sat in one corner, an episode of *Buffy the Vampire Slayer* keeping Rondell from helping his brother.

Using the arrow keys on the computer, I zoomed out, adjusting the focus on the camera. I picked up the image from the TV and the trail of smoke rising from the joint Rondell held between his lips.

The storm intensified, playing hell with the transmission, filling the audio with static when an explosion of thunder and lightning rocked the neighborhood, causing the lights to flicker on and off in the crack house. When the lights came back on, Rondell was staring at himself on the TV screen where Buffy had been a moment before. The electrically charged air had scrambled the signal from the camera, causing the TV to pick it up as a live broadcast.

Rondell stubbed out his joint, stepped closer to the TV, and motioned DeMarcus to join him. I adjusted the camera to give me a wide view of them as they watched themselves on the TV, waving like kids playing a game in a mirror, watching as they waved back at themselves, their faces scrunched, mystified. My face was as twisted as my gut. They'd lost a rerun. I was about to lose a case.

I had enough evidence to nail Marcellus, but I didn't have what I really wanted—the identity of his supplier and a line on his money. Watching the Winston brothers watch themselves, I realized that Marcellus would be in the wind the instant he discovered the camera. I hated to shut the operation down, but I had no choice. Maybe I could persuade Marcellus to roll over.

I had a SWAT team on standby. I picked up my cell phone to call Troy Clark, the team leader, and send them in when Rondell threw a blanket over the television, his voice now sharp and clear.

"Ain't no motherfuckin' vampire killer gonna spy on us."

"Which one of you the vampire?" Marcellus asked, stepping into the picture.

I wasn't breathing, but I wasn't shaking. I punched Troy's speed dial.

DeMarcus explained, pointing to the television. "We on the box. Rondell covered it up so's nobody can see what we doin."

Troy answered on the first ring. "You aren't going to believe this," I told him.

Marcellus pulled the blanket off the television, jostling the rabbit-ears antenna enough to restore *Buffy* just as the credits rolled.

"Yo, dogs," Marcellus said, "just count the shit; don't be smokin' it, too."

I started breathing and shaking. Troy interrupted both.

"Believe what, Jack?"

"Nothing," I managed, the shakes adding a quick stutter to my voice. "Call you later."

I hung up the phone as the lights in the house went out again. There was no thunder or lightning this time, just Marcellus shouting "what the fuck?" the answer coming in a burst of gunfire. I called Troy back as I ran for my car, the sounds of additional gunfire echoing behind me.

Chapter Five

Latrell found the utility box on the side of Marcellus's house, flipped the switch cutting off the electricity, and vaulted the porch rail, the tired wooden planks sagging under his weight. The gun in one hand, he yanked open the front door. He was invisible in the dark, though he could easily see inside the house, the goggles painting everyone in a green haze. The Winston brothers, shaking the television like it was a vending machine that had eaten their quarters, ignored him; Marcellus shouted "what the fuck?" like it mattered.

Latrell assumed the firing position, just as he did on the range. Marcellus and the Winston brothers were nothing more than targets hanging from a wire. He pulled the trigger again and again and again, the inside of the house glowing with gunfire.

He saw the bodies where they'd fallen, Marcellus on his back in the middle of the room, the Winston brothers piled against one another in the corner next to the television. Latrell knelt on the floor, collecting his spent shells, sliding them into his pocket.

He cocked his head at the sound of the whimpering child upstairs suddenly gone silent, imagining Jalise covering his mouth with her hand. Though she had always left Latrell alone and the boy had never even chased a ball into his yard, Marcellus had ruined them. If he let them live, Jalise would end up like his momma, her boy growing up like Latrell. That would be wrong. Things had to be put right.

Latrell rose, slipping on the bloody floor, catching himself against the stair rail. He took the steps one at a time. There was no need to hurry. It was happening exactly as he imagined it would. He found them hiding in a closet.

Afterward, he went out the back door, standing on the concrete patio, the rain in his eyes. Blinking, he looked down at his feet. His galoshes were splattered with blood, the coppery smell all over him. He peeled them off, turned them inside out, stuffing one on each hip inside his belt.

Latrell held his hands up, squinting. They were steady. He put one hand on his chest, his heart barely registering.

All he wanted to do was go home, until he saw Oleta Phillips standing beneath a tree on the side of Marcellus's backyard, staring at him through the driving rain. The tree's limbs drooped in surrender to the summer's drought, yellowed leaves scattered around the trunk. Her thin dress was soaked and matted against her bony frame, arms hanging at her sides, one hand clutching a wad of cash.

He didn't know whether she'd seen him go inside Marcellus's house, but she'd seen him come out and that was all that mattered. She didn't move as he approached her.

"Thank you," she said.

Latrell didn't know what to say. He studied Oleta's face, seeing her, then his mother, then Jalise, then all of them. He raised his hands to her throat, tightening his grip, feeling the bones in her neck crumble, twenty-dollar bills dropping from her hand, mixing with the dead leaves.

Chapter Six

Police cars, lights flashing, had formed a barricade at each end of Marcellus's block by the time I arrived. Overhead, a helicopter swept the neighborhood with a spotlight. The SWAT team had taken up position on either side of the crack house. I flashed my badge at a KCK police sergeant who let me through the line. Every house except Marcellus's was lit up, people watching from covered porches, some standing in the rain. Troy Clark emerged from the shadows on one side of the house.

"What do we got?" I asked him.

Troy had grown up in Quindaro and flirted with gangs until his grandmother set him straight, telling him he was too strong and too smart to die young for some fool weaker and dumber than he was. In his late thirties, pushing six feet and chiseled, he was tough, stubborn, and ambitious, a combination that could make you dead or make you famous.

Troy wasn't afraid of death, and he didn't care about being famous. What he cared about was my job, the SAC's job, and the director's job, all of which he made clear he intended to have before he was through. He didn't hesitate to second-guess me and was right more often than I cared to admit. I didn't like him, but I respected him even though his stubborn streak occasionally blossomed into an outbreak of hysterical blindness.

"Door was open. I had a look inside. Three dead. I'm guessing it's Marcellus and the Winston brothers."

"Anybody else?"

"Don't know yet. We haven't gone in."

"You think the shooter is still in there?"

"No way to tell from out here."

I looked up and down the block. "Why is his house the only one without power?"

"It's got power. There's a utility box on the side of the house. We were going to turn the power off, go in with night vision in case the shooter decided to stick around. No reason to make us easy targets. But somebody had already turned the power off."

I nodded, understanding the tactical dilemma. "The shooter cut the power and killed them in the dark. Probably wore night-vision goggles, too. Means he can see you as easily as you can see him. If he stuck around."

"I think the shooter knew." Troy said.

"Knew what?"

"About the surveillance camera in the ceiling fan."

"Based on what?" I asked.

"It fits. Gives him a reason to cut the power."

"Maybe. Go see if anyone else is home. But go easy. No good guys die tonight."

I didn't want to discuss Troy's theory until I knew more about what had happened, especially if Troy was right. There was only one way the killer could have known about the camera in the ceiling fan. He had to have a source inside my investigation or, worse, he had to be someone on my team.

Flushing out a bad agent was one of the hardest things to do, especially in the middle of a case that was taking every waking hour. Besides, the odds were heavily against the leak coming from my squad or anyone else at the Bureau. Not that they were all saints. It just rarely happened.

I had begun making a list of plausible theories on my way to the scene, ignoring the pressure rising in my chest and throat. I knew that it would continue to build until the shaking started, releasing the tension like opening a relief valve. I pulled over a block from the scene, cut the engine, and let it happen, my eyes closed, bracing myself against the steering wheel as if I'd been punched in the gut.

The shakes tapered off and I started the car, focusing again on the gunshots I'd heard. The obvious explanation was that the shootings were drug related, that the killer worked for a competitor, or unhappy business partner, of Marcellus Pearson—maybe even the supplier I was after.

That option faded as I considered Troy's suggestion of a leak. I ran through mental pictures of my agents, unable to imagine any of them selling out. Troy pulled double duty, working the SWAT team and my squad. All I had to do was look at him. There was no artifice, just dedication, even if it was more to his career than to the squad. Jim Day, Lani Haywood, and Ammara Iverson were so loyal they almost apologized for taking their paychecks.

Colby Hudson, my daughter's boyfriend, was the last member of the team, the only one I hadn't recruited for the squad. He was the lone holdover from the team my predecessor had assembled. All agents rotated through different assignments—organized crime, antiterror, and the rest. Colby had managed to stay on the drug squad, making a career working undercover. His newest best friend was Javy Ordonez, Marcellus's number-one competitor for control of the neighborhood crack market. Colby looked the part, hair long and face scruffy. I trusted him with everything except my daughter.

One of Marcellus's corner kids named Tony Phillips had been shot in a drive-by a few days ago. Maybe one of Javy's people had done it. Maybe tonight's shootings were the next round in a gang war. I needed to talk with Colby, who was the one member of my squad who wouldn't be at the crime scene. Wearing a jacket with FBI printed on the back was not the secret of success for an undercover agent.

I found no weaknesses, no reason for suspicion, in my team. If there was a leak, it had to have come from outside the Bureau. That would be even harder to track down.

I silently recited the list of possible sources, including the cops who had tipped Marcellus about my phony search warrant, the utility company, the federal judge who issued the surveillance order, the judge's law clerk who did the research that convinced the judge he could issue the order, and the judge's secretary who typed it. I could round them all up and make them take polygraph tests—if I lived in another country and if I wanted to waste my time.

The lights came on in the house. Troy found me again.

"All clear. Two more dead in the upstairs bedroom. Jalise Williams and her boy."

"Keyshon."

"They were hiding in the closet. She was shielding the boy with her body. The killer shot right through her, killed both of them."

I was supposed to care about all the victims equally, caring the most about catching their killer, but I couldn't. Marcellus and the Winston brothers were garbage waiting to be thrown out. That didn't mean they deserved to be murdered or that they didn't count or that I would be any less determined to find out who was guilty of their murders. It meant that I wouldn't mourn them the way I did Jalise and Keyshon.

Jalise's story was sadly familiar: broken home, sexually abused as a kid. She had dropped out of school and hooked up with Marcellus, her version of *Rescue Me*. Wendy had me to watch her back. Jalise had Marcellus to drag her down. There weren't many retired crack dealers. I had watched the surveillance tapes enough to know she stayed out of his business. That didn't make her innocent, but it put her in an outer circle where people had a right to expect an occasional break.

Keyshon was different, deserved better. He hadn't made any of his parents' bad choices, but their decisions cost him his life. I knew what that was like. I lost my son when he was six years old. Both boys could have been saved but for the mistakes their parents made.

Joy started drinking the day we buried Kevin. I let it go, blaming me, not her, hoping she'd come out of it, unable to ease her pain or mine. We hadn't forgiven ourselves or reconciled, settling instead for a silently shared burden.

Both Jalise and I had failed to save our sons. That Jalise wouldn't suffer the way my wife and I had was no consolation. I would hear their voices, mothers and sons, long after I caught Keyshon's killer.

I asked Troy, "If the killer was after Marcellus, why kill the woman and the boy? The house is dark. They're hiding in the closet. Odds are they didn't see the killer and couldn't identify him."

"Maybe she was the target," Troy said.

"What do you mean?"

"The shooter had to assume that Marcellus and the Winstons were armed and a threat to him. Makes sense that he put them down. But he put three rounds point-blank into a woman and child hiding in a closet who couldn't have hurt him if they'd have tried."

"Jalise Williams was nineteen. She wasn't involved in Marcellus's business. Who'd want to kill her?"

"Maybe she had something going on the side. Maybe the killer didn't figure Marcellus would be home and took Jalise and the boy out to punish him for something."

I rolled my eyes. "That's the best you can do?"

Troy shrugged. "Why kill her and the kid? You got me.

All I know is that's why we get the big money—to figure out crazy shit like this."

The helicopter started another circle, rotors thumping, its searchlight spraying the dark. My squad and what seemed like half the Kansas City, KS, police department stood in loose clusters in the street waiting for orders.

"Get out of that flak jacket and start a door-to-door canvass."

"Jack, it's a quintuple murder. KCKPD will claim jurisdiction."

"Tell them we've got it because of our ongoing drug investigation. Don't hurt their feelings, but make sure they know this is our case."

I waited until the crime scene investigators gave me the all clear, then walked up the steps, stood on the porch, imagining the killer standing there less than an hour earlier and wondering what went through someone's mind in the instant before he slaughtered five people. If Marcellus had been the target and the rest merely collateral damage, I could picture a cool, methodical professional. Check his weapon, take a deep breath, get it over with, and get out, no survivors, no loose ends. If Jalise had been the target, I saw someone filled with rage, the kind of fury that propelled the killer to empty his weapon into a defenseless woman trying to save her child. I could imagine what the killer thought and felt but not what he looked like. I had learned a long time ago not to trust the face.

I stared through the open front door, preferring to study the scene while the rest of my squad started with the neighbors. I knew that the good people outnumbered the bad on these streets, but that didn't mean they trusted the cops enough to tell us what they'd seen.

Even if someone came forward, I knew it wouldn't be enough. Eyewitnesses were among the least reliable sources of evidence about a crime. People never experience an event the same way. Fear, anger and excitement distort recollection as much as differences in eyesight and hearing. Psychological factors load eyewitness testimony with bias and unreliability.

For me, that was the beauty of the crime scene. It didn't have a face that hid the truth. It had no hidden agenda. It hadn't just had a fight at home or too many drinks after work. It didn't want to be interviewed on Court TV and it wasn't trying to cover up. It wasn't afraid of the cops, it wasn't out to screw us over, and it wasn't smarter than us. It was what it was and it never lied.

Chapter Seven

When I was assigned to the Dallas office, we lived in a new subdivision that must have been landscaped with a steamroller, it was so flat. Half the families that lived on our block were with the Bureau, some of the agents buying their houses from the agent they were replacing, knowing they would sell it to their replacement a few years down the road. We knew each other's spouses, kids, and dogs. Everyone looked out for everyone else, watching each other's houses when someone was away for the weekend. The level terrain and the absence of trees more than eight feet tall made it easy to see everything.

We were watchers, noticers, detail people. Something strange, someone new, something that didn't look or feel right, we picked up on it. It was what we were trained to do.

Frank Tyler lived three houses down from us. He was a computer programmer, worked out of his house, jogged every morning, waved to me when I drove Kevin and Wendy to school. Every year he dragged his Weber grill to the end of the street for the Fourth of July block party, grilling hot dogs and making balloon animals for the kids.

I must have seen his face a thousand times. Brown, welcoming eyes pinched at the corners; they always seemed to me to be from laughter and sun. A once-broken nose, crooked enough to make his face slightly off-kilter in an interesting sort of way. His mouth was full, his smile quick and easy. He wore his dark hair in a casual cut, angling across his forehead. That's all I saw. It wasn't enough.

Joy always picked the kids up from school. One day, she had car trouble. Frank worked at home and she asked if she could borrow his car. He told her that he had some errands to run and would be happy to swing by the school and pick up the kids. Wendy had Girl Scouts that afternoon. Kevin was the only one who would be coming home. She called the school to let them know that Frank would pick him up.

When Frank didn't come back, Joy called the school. They told her that Frank had been there, shown identification, and signed the form confirming that he was taking Kevin as she had authorized. One of the teachers remembered seeing Kevin get in the car with Frank.

Worried, Joy went to Frank's house, knocked, and went in when she found the door unlocked. She walked through the house, stopping in the den, where she found stacks of child pornography on a coffee table. That's when she called me.

Today it's called an Amber Alert. Back then we didn't have a name for it. We didn't need one. All agents dropped what they were doing to find Kevin. The Dallas police scoured the streets. A highway patrolman spotted Tyler's car southbound on I-35 between Austin and San Marcos a few hours after he'd taken Kevin. The chase lasted thirteen minutes. It ended when Tyler ran over spikes the patrol had spread across the interstate to puncture his tires, the car swerving into the concrete median barrier. I was in a helicopter heading for the scene when Tyler shot Kevin and then put the gun under his chin, blowing up the face that had fooled me.

I thought about Kevin each time I stepped into a crime scene, promising him I would get it right this time, that I wouldn't let him down and be deceived again by a friendly smile, an anguished cry, a poker face, or any of the other masks people wore.

I learned to trust hard facts, lab work, and the polygraph. My jury consultant friend, Kate Scranton, was different. She was all about behavioral clues—leakage, she called it—the face more than the body, the heart more than the mind. I wanted proof beyond a reasonable doubt. She wanted the truth, saying they weren't always the same thing.

I stood in the doorway, absorbing the scene, letting the dead and the details talk to me, comparing the images with the hours of surveillance tape I had watched. I recognized the card table Marcellus used to conduct his business and the Louisville Slugger standing in the corner that had earned him his reputation. Plastic sandwich bags containing crack were scattered across the table's vinyl surface, all of it probably worth less than ten thousand dollars on the street. It may have been enough to kill five people for, but at least for this killer, it wasn't enough to steal after they were dead. That didn't mean the murders weren't about drugs. It only meant that the murders weren't about *these* drugs.

The walls were bare. No pictures, no mirrors, no clocks. The hardwood floors were warped, a dimension I couldn't see on the video; an upturned box of Chinese leftovers sat in one corner, a trail of fried rice littered across the floor. The only other furniture was two folding canvas chairs. This was a place of business, not a home, the old television in the corner the only concession to comfort.

The bodies rested in pools of blood beneath where they'd fallen. I'd let the crime scene specialists find the bullets, calculate the trajectories pre- and post-entry, but it wasn't hard to pin down the basics.

Marcellus was on his back, his shoes less than five feet

from the door, closer than the Winston brothers by several feet, the difference enough to make him the first victim the killer had confronted. That fit with me hearing him yell "what the fuck?" the instant before I heard gunfire. The entry wounds on Marcellus's body were in his gut and chest, the volume of blood indicating that at least one bullet had hit an artery, probably causing him to bleed to death.

The Winston brothers were slumped on the floor on either side of the television. Rondell had taken a round in the belly and a round in the groin. DeMarcus was hit in the left thigh and the neck.

A professional would have put all his rounds in the killing zone—the center chest, making sure with a final round in the back of the head after his targets were down. This looked like the work of an amateur who had gotten lucky, except amateurs weren't likely to use night-vision goggles. That wasn't the only mixed message.

The killer was organized, turning off the power, using night-vision goggles, picking up his shell casings. Organized killers were the most difficult to catch because they left so little evidence at the scene.

But then there were the bloody footprints. The killer had stepped in Marcellus's blood, leaving dark red footsteps going up the stairs. He'd stepped in the blood a second time, leaving another set of footprints from Marcellus' body to the back of the house. I couldn't be certain about which set of footprints came first, but my sequence made the most sense. Kill these three, then do Jalise and Keyshon, then out the back door.

I followed the second set of prints through the kitchen and turned on the back porch light. The rain had washed out any other footprints, though I hoped the crime scene people would find trace amounts of blood in the concrete. I walked back to the stairs, reassessing a killer who had been good enough to shoot three men in the dark and who had been organized but careless enough not to wipe his feet.

Someone on the SWAT team had also stepped in the blood, proving that it was easy to do. His ridged boot prints were easily distinguished from the flat, rounded prints left by the killer. There were a few partial prints that were clear enough to indicate the surface of the sole. It didn't have a pattern like an athletic shoe and it didn't have the smooth, even appearance of leather shoes. And it was wider than a normal shoe, like it was made by something that had been slipped over a shoe. Maybe the killer had worn galoshes so he wouldn't get his shoes wet in the rain or bloody in the house.

I hesitated before going upstairs, turning toward the front door, conjuring the killer as he entered the house, testing another assumption I'd made. There had been only one killer. If there had been more, there likely would have been another set of footprints that didn't match those left by the SWAT team.

The smell of blood and bodies hit me as I climbed the stairs. It had been there all along, but I'd been too focused on the scene to notice. It was a too familiar stench, but I never got used to it. My stomach was churning as much from the pungent odor as the anticipation of what I would find in the bedroom.

The clothes hanging in the closet had been swept to either side like a parted curtain, exposing where Jalise Williams had been hiding. She was on her knees, bent over her child, the back of her head a pulpy mess, with two more entry wounds in the middle of her back. Keyshon's hand was wrapped tightly in his mother's hair, the rest of him hidden.

I crouched next to her, my chest trembling, the shakes waiting to be let loose and wanting to touch the boy's hand. I searched for a glimpse of his face, finding it buried against his mother's neck, and wondered in a fanciful moment if our two sons—hers and mine—would somehow find each other on the other side. Mine was not a conscious faith, born of study and contemplation. I had more hope than belief that pain and suffering and good deeds would be rewarded in some afterlife. I accepted the notion of free will but had seen enough to doubt the wisdom of a God who had bestowed it. I didn't wonder whether pure evil existed. I had seen it first-hand. I pulled back, the mother cradling her child evidence enough of what had happened.

The rest of the room was a mess, clothes lying on the floor where they'd been dropped, bed unmade, makeup and jewelry littering the dresser lining the wall opposite the bed. The disarray was natural, the product of people who never cleaned up after themselves. It wasn't the result of the killer tossing the room in search of something.

The jewelry looked real, though I was no judge. The last diamond I'd bought was for Joy's engagement ring twenty-eight years ago. Like the drugs left on the card table down-stairs, there was enough jewelry worth taking even if it wasn't enough to kill for.

I reminded myself that this was a crack house. I'd found the drugs and jewelry. Now it was time to look for the guns and money. I tried a series of deep breaths to stifle the shakes, glad that it worked for the moment.

Using a pen to pull open drawers without leaving finger-prints or disturbing those already there, I did a quick and dirty search of the bedroom and bathroom. I found a few hundred dollars in cash, not the stacks of twenties I would have expected. That didn't mean money wasn't hidden else-where in the house or that the killer hadn't found it in the bedroom and decided it was the one thing worth stealing.

The guns were hidden behind a panel in the bathroom wall. A couple of sawed-off shotguns, three 9mm Smith & Wessons, and enough ammunition to make a point. It wasn't exactly an arsenal, but it was more than one man needed to protect hearth and home. The serial numbers on the weapons had been filed off, making them untraceable and worth more than the drugs or jewelry to someone in the business of killing people. They would have been easy to find and easy to steal.

My search was interrupted by a whimpering sound coming from beneath the bed. I lifted the blanket draped over the foot of the bed, finding a dog, its paws covering its nose, peeking at me. I scooped the dog up, examining the honey-colored, curly-haired mutt, guessing its weight at around fifteen pounds, confirming that it was a she. The dog licked my face and peed, the shower just missing my pants.

"You go, girl," I told the dog, setting her down and checking her collar, reading the name on the tag. "Stick with me until we find a new home for you, Ruby."

The dog followed me back down the stairs. I picked her up so that she wouldn't step in the blood, and took her outside. The rain had stopped. The yellow patio light faded to black at the edge of the concrete slab. The dog ran toward a tree on the side of the yard, disappearing in the darkness. I heard her scampering back and forth until she found a suitable spot, quiet as she relieved herself once more. Satisfied, she trotted back to me, jumping up and planting wet paws on my leg. I reached down to pet her, finding a twenty-dollar bill matted against her wet coat.

I peered into the night outside the ring of patio light, unable to see anything more than the outline of a tree. Lights were on in houses on either side and in the houses that backed up to these. It was the middle of the night, but no one was asleep. In spite of all the lights, deep pockets of darkness remained, black boundaries cutting people off from one another. The helicopter closed for another pass.

The killer hadn't stolen the drugs or jewelry that had been left in plain sight or taken the guns he could have easily found. He'd left bloody footprints leading out the back door onto the patio, his trail disappearing either because of the rain or because he'd removed whatever he'd been wearing over his shoes. Now Ruby, the newly orphaned dog, had retrieved a twenty-dollar bill from Marcellus's backyard. A bone, I would have believed. A double sawbuck required a leap of faith I was in no mood to take.

I retraced Ruby's route, wet, spongy ground squishing beneath my shoes as I approached the tree, the shakes starting their drumbeat in my torso. My eyesight adjusted to the darkness enough that I could see clumps of twenty-dollar bills scattered amidst fallen leaves. I guessed there was at least a couple of thousand dollars, maybe more, lying on the ground. Maybe enough to steal. Maybe enough to kill five people for. Then why leave it out in the rain? Ruby had followed me, nosing the money, pawing at it.

The police helicopter hovered overhead, capturing me in a cone of blinding light. I shielded my eyes, squinting past the tree, catching a glimpse of a silhouetted figure running away, a fleeting sense of recognition washed out by a shouted command from behind to stay where I was. I recognized Troy Clark's voice over the din of the chopper, wondering why he would give me such an order. Then I knew why. He didn't recognize me. I was bent over at the waist, my face buried against my knees, shaking so badly I could barely stand.

Chapter Eight

Latrell was smoothing Oleta's hair when he heard the sirens. He cradled the back of her head with one hand, massaging the tangled strands of hair clotted around her face and unraveling knots with the other as he lay her head gently onto the plastic tarp lying on the basement floor.

Oleta's features were smooth, her dark skin fading to a dingy gray. Any pain she may have felt when he crushed her throat had passed without leaving a furrow in her brow or a grimace in her cheeks. Latrell had released her from that pain as surely as he had released her from whatever torment had brought her to that place in the middle of the night, in the rain, beneath that tree, as if she had been waiting for him. Maybe she'd come there to die, he thought, and that's why she had thanked him.

It didn't matter to Latrell any more than it mattered that he'd killed her. She was as dead as his mother, as dead as Jalise. They were all the same. Finished with her hair, he brushed out the wrinkles in her dress, his hands and heart as steady as when he'd walked out of Marcellus's house.

He cocked his ear toward the window well near the top of

the basement wall. The rain beat against the glass, a weak accompaniment to the wailing police cars rushing toward the neighborhood. Latrell listened, calculating how long it would be before someone with a badge knocked on his door asking whether he'd seen or heard anything unusual in the house behind his.

The police would block off the streets, sneak up on Marcellus's house like they were making a surprise attack, uncertain of who or what they would find inside. Once they knew, they'd start searching for witnesses. He had plenty of time. No reason to hurry. After they were gone, he'd bury Oleta in the basement.

Tomorrow Latrell would take the gun, goggles, and bloody galoshes to the cave and everything would be right. Until then, all he had to do was be smart. He could do that.

He unlaced his shoes, peeled off each layer of his clothes until he was naked. He tucked one edge of the tarp under her body, rolling her over, wrapping her inside the plastic, and securing it with duct tape until she was mummified.

The basement was dark, damp from a leak along the base of the west wall, with water trickling into a drain in the center of the concrete floor. A washtub sat on a stand, a faucet sticking out from the wall. Latrell connected a garden hose to the faucet, turned the water on strong enough to wash the floor but not loud enough to be heard, and rinsed his feet before he went back upstairs.

He showered, nearly scalding himself with hot water, scrubbing hard. Afterward he changed into boxers and a ratty black T-shirt he slept in, padding downstairs to wait in the kitchen. When the police came, he'd tell them that he'd been asleep, the storm mixing with his dreams. He'd say he woke to the sirens, turned on his lights, and was unable to fall back asleep, like everyone else.

He repeated it again and again, the soundtrack to the image he saw when he closed his eyes: he was standing at his front door, rubbing his chin, answering the cop's questions, tired but polite, believing the story he told. Latrell sat in a chair at his kitchen table and waited, nodding his head with the repeated rhythm of what he would say, what he decided was true, what he would make them believe.

The window from his kitchen gave him a view of the back of Marcellus's house. The porch light came on. A man came out the back door carrying a dog. Sat the dog on the ground. Stood still and quiet. The dog disappeared, then came back. The man bent down to the dog, then followed the dog into the shadows where Latrell couldn't see them, though he knew where they were.

He heard the helicopter, felt the wash of the rotors breaking against his house, and blinked when the spotlight lit the backyard like it was Yankee Stadium. The man he'd seen was in the center of the spotlight, bent over. Even from where he was watching, Latrell could tell that there was something wrong with the man, like he'd had a seizure. The cops surrounded him, one of them taking him away. Latrell went back to his kitchen chair and waited.

Soon the doorbell rang. He listened, counting until the chimes had sounded five times. He shouldn't be in a hurry to answer and he wasn't.

He looked out the keyhole at a square-shouldered white man, the man's dark eyes staring back at him as if he could see inside the house. A tall black woman stood at his side, her eyes studying the windows as if Latrell might jump out of one. Both of them wore navy windbreakers, FBI stenciled in yellow letters over their hearts. He smiled. He'd been right, after all. The man on the utility pole had been FBI.

Latrell eased the door open, leaving the chain latched to the frame, cautious as he should be, looking at them without saying anything, rubbing his chin. Just as they expected he would.

"Sorry to bother you," the woman said. "I'm Agent Iverson. This is Agent Day. We're with the FBI."

Ammara Iverson and Jim Day held up their badges and IDs. Latrell took his time, comparing the faces on the IDs to the two people at his door. He didn't doubt who they were, but it was important to take his time. He nodded, unlatching the chain and opening the door, still not talking.

"Something happened at the house behind yours tonight," the woman said. "We're going door-to-door. Trying to find out if anyone heard anything unusual, maybe saw something, heard something."

Latrell shook his head, answering slowly. "Only thing I heard was the storm. Kept me up at first, but I finally fell asleep. Next thing I heard is the sirens. Now I can't get back to sleep."

This time it was Agent Day who nodded. "You know who lives in the house behind you?"

"Marcellus and his people. I know him but I don't know him. You understand what I'm saying."

"You know what Marcellus had going on at his house?" Iverson asked.

"Everybody knows he deals crack," Latrell answered. "But like I said, I know him but I don't know him. That's what I'm sayin'."

"You do any business with him?" Iverson asked.

"No way," Latrell answered. "I don't want nothing to do with that shit. I got a job. I got a house. I don't need no trouble."

"You ever have any trouble with Marcellus?" Agent Day asked.

Latrell shook his head. "I stay out of his business and he don't bother me."

"Good for you," Day said with a tight smile. "How about the other people in the neighborhood? You know anybody had a reason to come after Marcellus?"

"Nobody except you and the cops," Latrell answered.

"And I'm glad you finally got around to it. Hope you put him away."

"We won't have to," the woman said. "Someone beat us to it."

Latrell looked at them, his breathing steady. "Marcellus? He's dead?"

"Yeah," the woman said. "He's dead."

"It don't matter."

"How's that?" she asked.

"There'll be someone else dealin' that shit tomorrow afternoon. That's why."

"Mattered to Marcellus and it matters to us," Ammara Iverson said. "You know Marcellus's girlfriend?"

"Seen her around, that's all. Her and her kid."

"You know anyone might want to hurt either one of them?"

Latrell took a shallow breath, shaking his head again. "You saying they dead, too?"

"Both of them. Rondell and DeMarcus Winston, also," she said. "You sure you didn't hear anything? They lived right behind you."

"Wish now I did," Latrell said. "That's not right. Kill all those people. Don't care what they did. That's not right."

Ammara Iverson handed him a card. "No, it isn't. You think of anything that might be important, give us a call."

Jim Day also handed Latrell his card. "We need your name, sir. Just to complete our report. And where you work. If you don't mind."

"Latrell Kelly. I work at the rail yard in Argentine, in the terminal building. And I don't mind."

Chapter Nine

I felt Troy's hand on my back, heard him ask if I was okay, saw him wave off the chopper as I turned my head skyward. Time got lost, seconds confused for minutes, moments for lifetimes. The involuntary muscle contractions that had folded me in half let go, allowing me to stand, clutching my sides, still shaking. I tried to talk, but words strangled in my throat and finally escaped in a stutter.

"I'm fine, just peachy," I managed.

Troy cupped my elbow in his palm, guiding me past a gauntlet including my team and at least a dozen KCK cops, fresh contractions contorting my steps like I was a drunken puppet. Jim Day nodded, his chin tapping against his barrel chest, his massive arms hanging against his sides. Lani Haywood bit her lower lip. Ammara Iverson fought back tears. Marty Grisnik, my police department coconspirator on the fugitive warrant, was at the end of the receiving line, shaking his head like he should have known better.

"There's an ambulance on the street," Troy said as we cleared the crowd. "We'll have the paramedics take a look at you."

"Forget it. This will pass. Just let me catch my breath."

I stopped in the darkened strip of ground between Marcellus's house and the house to the north, easing Troy's grip with my free hand. I tried the deep breathing again. The tremors were fading. I didn't know whether the breathing was helping or whether the shaking had ended on its own.

"What's going on, Jack?"

I looked at Troy, the worry obvious in his wrinkled brow and narrowed eyes. Some things were easy even for me to read in a man's face.

I took another breath. "I've been having some shaking on and off for the last couple of months. It comes and goes but tonight it's mostly been coming."

"That was more than shaking. You were like an old man who fell and couldn't get up."

The shakes and the stuttering were nothing new, but this was the first time I'd lost complete control of my body. Something inside me had snapped like a mousetrap and I couldn't stand up until the spring was reset. I didn't want to speculate about it until I knew what I was talking about.

"I must have gotten excited when I found all that cash lying around."

"Bullshit, Jack! What's the doctor tell you?"

"Haven't been. Too busy with this case."

"Busy, hell! You're going to get your butt in a doctor's office when the sun comes up if I have to handcuff you and take you there myself. I ought to take you to the nearest ER right now."

I smiled, put my hand on his arm. "I can handle this, Troy. I was waiting to get it checked out until we took Marcellus down. The timetable has changed after tonight. Let's catch whoever did this and then I'll get checked out. Probably nothing a couple of weeks on a beach won't cure."

"Jack, you need to find out what's wrong with you. We can run this case until you're ready to come back."

I didn't know what was causing me to shake, but I had figured out that the longer I worked and the less I slept, the more I shook. I also knew that if I walked away now, my chances of getting back to this case or any case weren't good. FBI agents don't do anything involuntarily—especially shake uncontrollably. I didn't have a hobby, a wife, or a mistress, no matter what Joy thought about Kate and me. Ex-agents do a lot of things. They become private investigators, security consultants, or suicide statistics. I wasn't interested in any of those options. I looked at my watch.

"It's almost three o'clock in the morning. I'll go back to the office, get some sleep on my couch, and I'll be fine. You wrap things up here. Bag the cash I found and start thinking about why someone would leave a few grand lying under a tree that money doesn't grow on. We'll have a team meeting at six. I want reports on the neighborhood canvass and preliminary forensics by then. Have someone pull all the surveillance video from the camera on the utility pole and the one inside the house. I want names put to faces."

Troy looked at me, his face blank, unimpressed. "Jack, you've got to see a doctor. Now. Today."

"I will. As soon as we find whoever killed the people inside that house. Am I clear, Agent Clark?"

Troy backed up a step. "Clear."

The regional FBI office was located at Fourteenth and Summit on the west side of downtown Kansas City, Missouri. It was the first new regional office built after 9/11, and the lockdown security measures were reflected in its remote location on the far side of the downtown interstate loop, the high wrought-iron fence encircling the rectangular two-story building, and the armed guard at the entrance to the parking lot.

The offices were laid out like an ordinary civilian corporation except for the crime lab, the body shop, the armory, and the room where agents practiced with a simulator how not to kill innocent bystanders during gunfights with the bad guys. The interrogation rooms were another upgrade over the civilian model. The emphasis was on efficiency and duty—gray carpet, off-white walls, any color of furniture as long as it was blond or black, pictures of presidents and FBI directors on the walls, and one wall reserved to honor the memory of fallen agents with their photographs.

Field agents and law-enforcement personnel on loan from other agencies worked in bull pens filled with modular cubicles. A life-sized cardboard cutout of John Wayne in full cowboy regalia complete with six-guns and chaps kept a lookout at the end of one corridor. The corner offices were reserved for upper brass, the one with the best view overlooking the confluence of the Missouri and Kansas rivers belonging to Ben Yates, Special Agent in Charge of the Kansas City office.

Yates had been in Kansas City for six months, none of them happy. Like all other agents, he rotated through different offices. The lucky ones, including me, were able to choose our final posting, someplace we'd like to live after we retired. Yates was from New Jersey, had worked in Los Angeles, New York, and overseas. He made no secret of the fact that Kansas City was not on the glamour itinerary he'd mapped out, that he'd serve his time here, move on, and never look back.

Yates was married to the manual and fond of telling us to lean forward, a fitness freak who kept a log of his body fat. I didn't know how much body fat I had, only that it was more than I had the day before. Yates was ten years younger than me, taller, and didn't need glasses like I did to study crime scene photographs.

He rode us about our statistics—cases opened, cases closed, conviction rates. I didn't care about the numbers. I cared about the victims. My only worry was getting it right for them. One case meant nothing to another unless a person, not a statistic, linked them.

When Yates rattled on about bringing closure to the families of murder victims, I wanted to puke. I knew better. Long prison terms, life without parole, even the death penalty, whether the courts or the criminals carried it out like Frank Tyler had, wouldn't heal the holes in our hearts. Some wounds never closed. But killers could be caught. That was what I did. One case at a time.

I had called Yates on my way back to headquarters. His voice was sharp, his questions quick and pointed; he wasn't groggy from sleeping, as I would have been. I left out the part about my shaking. Now that I'd had my debut before God and everybody, I'd have to tell Yates before he heard about it from someone else, but I wanted to do it in person, hopefully without special effects.

Troy woke me just before six. We set up shop in a large conference room. One wall was lined with dry-erase boards, another housed flat-screen monitors linked to network, cable, and satellite feeds when they weren't being used for in-house presentations or video conferences. Modular tables were laid out around the perimeter in a rectangular donut.

We were working with limited information since the preliminary forensics reports weren't back. Troy posted the names of the victims on one of the dry-erase boards, adding names of their known associates, competitors, and enemies to the rapidly expanding universe of people to be tracked down, interviewed, and ruled in or out as suspects. I thought again about Troy's speculation that Jalise Williams may have been the real target. We'd have to dig into the lives of all the victims to be certain of anything.

Ammara Iverson sketched a rough schematic of the neighborhood on another board, noting the houses they'd been to in the search for witnesses and the ones that warranted a second visit. Lani Haywood and Jim Day were studying the surveillance videotape, isolating freeze frames of people for whom we would need names and alibis.

I took a moment from studying the crime scene photographs to watch them work. They did their jobs with unhurried efficiency, making certain they didn't miss anything. I waited until I made eye contact with each of them, offering a half smile and tilt of my head to reassure them I was okay and in charge.

I played with my pen beneath the table, hands shaking, testing my condition by repeatedly putting the cap on and then taking it off. I thought that if I could master the pen, I could get through the day. So far, the pen was winning.

"Ammara, what did you get from the neighbors?" I asked.

She finished her drawing, gathered her notes, and gave me a straight-ahead look. She was lean and muscular, a tribute to her days playing college volleyball, tall enough to rise above the net, strong enough to spike the ball right through the opposition. She wore her hair tightly cut, almost buzzed, against her brown skin, her jeans and T-shirt hanging on her lean frame with a casual elegance.

"Big surprise. No one saw or heard anything. They might even be telling the truth. It was raining pretty hard. Lots of thunder and lightning. Plus it was the middle of the night. No reason to be looking out their windows."

"Did you talk to the people who lived on either side and behind Marcellus?"

She turned to the drawing of Marcellus's block and the one immediately behind his to the west.

"LaDonna Simpson lives by herself on the south side. She'll be eighty-one tomorrow. Goes to bed at eight o'clock. Slept through everything, which makes sense since she's mostly deaf. Only reason she answered the door was that she'd gotten up to go to the bathroom when we came knocking. Wayne Miller has the house on the north side. He wasn't home."

"Where was he?"

"In jail. Bad checks. His girlfriend is staying there. Her name is Tarla Hicks. She was out partying. Came home after the shooting was over. Girl was so high I don't know how she found her way home."

"What about the house that backs up to Marcellus? The lights were on when I was in the backyard."

"Belongs to Latrell Kelly. Works at the railroad terminal in Argentine. Said everyone in the neighborhood knew what Marcellus was about. Said he stayed out of Marcellus's business and never had any trouble with him. Said the storm woke him but he didn't get out of bed until he heard the sirens. Guy's no help."

"Did you check him out?"

"Yeah. Port Authority confirms his employment. Supervisor says he's quiet, does his job, shows up on time. No problems. No arrests, no convictions. A couple of traffic tickets. That's it."

"Dig deeper on him. I don't want to wake up one day and see his neighbors on television saying how he always seemed so quiet before he started killing everybody in sight. And expand the canvass to cover a block in every direction from Marcellus's house. Put together profiles of the residents. We may not find an eyewitness, but we might find someone who has heard something since the shootings that could help us. And see what you can find out about Jalise Williams. Was she cheating on Marcellus? Did someone wish she was?"

"I'm on it," Ammara said.

"Okay, people," I said. "What do we got?"

"Five dead and nothing else," Troy answered.

"Nothing else is right. It's daylight and we're falling behind. Keep digging."

Chapter Ten

Colby Hudson appeared in the doorway of the conference room at seven o'clock, his beleaguered appearance stopping everyone. He looked like he'd spent the night in the rain, his long hair matted and tangled, shirt clinging to his body, the bottom of his jeans streaked with mud. He was thirty-three but his pale complexion, red-rimmed eyes, and worn appearance made him look five years older, the price of working undercover.

That made him seven years older than my daughter Wendy in human years and at least eleven years older in FBI years. Either way, the age difference made me nervous, though that wasn't the only thing that bothered me about their relationship. Colby delivered great intelligence that had led to a number of important arrests. That didn't make him right for my daughter. Not because there was no one good enough for Wendy, though I had my doubts. It was because he liked undercover work too much. Living on the edge, pretending to be someone and something he wasn't for as long as he had, can make it hard for a man to remember who he really is, or worse, the myth becomes the reality.

Working undercover didn't mean that Colby lived with the drug dealers we investigated. Every contact he had was supposed to be monitored by a backup team. Every operation was tightly regulated. There was no freelancing. Most of the time, that worked. Agents could play the role and leave it behind when they went home at night. A few forgot the difference, forgot who they were.

I may have felt differently about their relationship if Colby was working undercover on something other than drugs. Wendy had started smoking dope when she was a freshman in high school, graduating to cocaine and pills by her senior year before we put her in a program. She got clean, relapsed, and was arrested twice for possession. The second program stuck and she'd stayed sober ever since. Dating Colby put her too close to her old life.

I'd made the mistake of telling Wendy of my concerns. She told me she was cured. I told her there was no cure. She said that I needed to let go. Then she told Colby what I had said and the temperature between Colby and me turned cold and stayed that way.

"That a new outfit?" Lani Haywood asked him.

Lani was a fifteen-year veteran, just tall enough to qualify for the Bureau but more than tough enough to stay. She had matured from sleek and fast to middleweight and steadfast, her senses of fashion and humor still intact.

"Business casual," Colby answered.

He dropped his lanky frame in a chair opposite me, swiveling it around and straddling it, arms draped over the back, fingers nervously tapping the upholstery. He had the same no-sleep aura the rest of us did, only he was that way all the time. The rest of us only got the dead man's glow when five people were murdered in the middle of the night.

"You look like you haven't been home in a while," I said, calmly laying the pen and cap side by side on the table. I put my hands in my lap, hoping they'd stay there. He had his own place but spent as many nights as he could at Wendy's. I didn't like it, not because I was a prude, but because it would be too easy for the people he dealt with to track him back to Wendy. I had raised that issue with Wendy as well, getting the phone slammed in my ear for my efforts. He turned away for an instant, making a crooked smile, not taking the bait.

"Last night was a good night not to go home. Just ask Marcellus Pearson," he said.

"I didn't get the chance. Your buddy, Javy Ordonez, know what went down?"

"He got word a couple of hours after it happened."

"How'd he take it?"

"Not well. I was with him in the back room of this club on Central. One of his guys comes in, whispers in his ear. Javy tried hard to stay cool but he damn near pinched a loaf in his shorts."

"Any chance he set it up?"

"If he did, he put on a helluva show. Said good night and hit the street. Told his people to stay loose but not to go home. You ask me, he was afraid that whoever did Marcellus would come looking for him next."

"Were you wired?"

He looked away for an instant. "No."

"You went in alone without a backup team to monitor you?"

"Wasn't time. Javy called. Said he needed to talk about the buy I've been setting up with him. Said it had to be now."

There were a lot of things wrong with what Colby had done, none of which I wanted to deal with at the moment.

"Makes you his alibi for the murders."

Colby leaned forward. "I'm telling you, Jack, he was so scared he needed a diaper, not an alibi."

"That was almost four hours ago. Where've you been since then?"

"Talking to people. You know the kid that was shot on the corner in Quindaro the other day?"

"Name of Tony Phillips. Worked for Marcellus," Troy Clark said.

"Right," Colby said. "Javy had the kid popped. Gave the job to one of his new boys, Luis Alvarez."

"Why would Javy take the chance of starting a war with Marcellus?" I asked.

"Are you kidding me?" Colby asked. "Those two guys are like North and South Korea. They been staring at each so long, every now and then one of them has to make sure he's still got the balls he thinks he has."

"Marcellus sent the Winston brothers to hit back for the Phillips kid. We've got that on the surveillance tape from the camera in the ceiling fan," I said.

"Rondell and DeMarcus caught up to Luis," Colby said. "Beat the shit out of him, left him for dead. Only he didn't die. He's in the ICU at Providence. If he lives, we may be able to make a deal with him, put a case together against Javy for capital murder. With Marcellus and Javy both out of the picture, we might have to find another line of work."

"What if Javy was putting on a show for you?" I asked. "What if this all started with Luis Alvarez shooting Tony Phillips? Javy flexes his pecs so Marcellus retaliates. Javy decides to win the war the quick and dirty way."

Colby shook his head. "Javy's not a good enough actor to turn white, which he did when he heard what went down. If he set it up, he'd have been cool. With Marcellus and the Winston brothers gone, there'd be no one left to challenge him. No one with the balls or the backing. He'd have been pouring shots of cold Grey Goose for everyone."

"Where does that leave us?" I asked.

"Looking for someone Javy Ordonez was afraid of—someone with the balls and the backing," Colby said.

"Could be Bodie Grant," Jim Day said. "We don't have much on him. Just Rondell and Marcellus talking about him on the surveillance tapes. The guy is supposedly doing business with Javy Ordonez. We haven't had a chance to run any of that down yet."

"What about Bodie Grant?" I asked Colby. "Javy say anything about him."

Colby shook his head. "Not much. Just enough to figure out they're probably working together. Javy wants what Bodie is selling and Bodie wants Javy's market. The two of them probably figure to give Marcellus a run for Quindaro."

"If you ask me," Troy said, "we should be looking for someone who knew about the camera in the ceiling fan. The killer doesn't turn off the power to the house, we get the whole thing on tape. I don't believe in that much luck, good or bad."

"That's a small club," Colby said.

"Not so small," I said. "Not when you count all the people besides the five of us who could have known even if they shouldn't have known."

"I'm not saying there was a leak," Troy said, "or, that if there was, it was one of us. No way do I believe that. It's not a perfect theory, but it does explain the lights going out. You can't ignore the possibility."

"That's just one piece of what happened," I said. "Colby says that Javy Ordonez was pushing Marcellus, maybe with help from Bodie Grant. The tapes corroborate that. We don't know what Marcellus was doing with his money. We got a killer that thought part of this thing through, but not everything, and who may not have been after Marcellus at all. Jalise Williams could have been the target and the others just collateral damage. Either way, the killer left behind enough of a mess that says he's either a sloppy pro or a lucky amateur."

"Bottom line?" Colby said.

"It's an hour later and we still don't know shit," I said.

"Is that what you are going to put in your report?" Ben Yates asked.

He was wearing a dark navy suit, fresh white shirt, and pale blue tie. Same outfit every politician in Washington wore. He was standing just inside the conference room door, listening quietly.

A quick tremor shot through my upper body like a burst of static electricity, followed by two more in rapid succession, each lasting a few seconds and impossible to miss. Colby's eyes went wide, mouthing a question he held back. I shot a glance at Troy, catching him making eye contact with Yates, who answered with a barely perceptible nod.

Yates cleared his throat. "Jack, I'd like to have a word with you."

I picked up the crime scene photos and waved them at the whiteboards. "We're pretty busy right now. I'll stop by as soon as we get a fix on the preliminary forensics and I've got my people back out in the field."

"Now would be better."

Troy was halfway to the door, Jim Day, Lani Haywood, and Ammara Iverson in close formation behind him. Colby hadn't moved.

"Looks like I didn't get the memo," he said.

I dropped the photos on the table, not believing that Troy had gone to Yates behind my back. I understood why, or at least why he would say he did it, that it was for my own good, the good of the squad, and that it was in the best interests of the case—the rationales of every loyal mutineer.

"Makes two of us."

"You okay?" he asked.

"Never better. By the way, I haven't said anything to Wendy about the shaking."

Colby stood. "Don't worry, Jack. Your name doesn't come up much, anyway."

Ben stayed where he was, across the room, eyeing me like a suspect, waiting for me to confess. I didn't want it to happen, not like this, not now. I tried deep breathing, tried gripping the table with one hand, the front of my chair with the other. I even tried pinching the inside of my thigh. Nothing worked. I was tumbling inside, about to blow. Powerless, I gave in, closed my eyes, and let it happen, bending forward in my chair, my chest tight against my thighs, grunting and cursing. The one surprise was how relieved I was, how it almost felt good.

"Two minutes," Ben said when the shaking stopped.

I was breathing like I'd just woken from a bad dream. "Thanks, but I'm not keeping track."

"You should have told me."

"It was personal."

"Nothing is personal if it affects the job."

"I'm doing my job."

"There's something wrong with you. You don't know what it is and you don't know whether it puts you, your team, or your case at risk. From what I understand happened in the field and from what I've just seen, all three are likely. I'm not your mother or your father. I can't make you eat your vegetables, get enough sleep, or go to the doctor. But I'm not going to let you take chances with our people and our mission. I won't tolerate that."

"Troy didn't waste any time telling you, did he?"

"Troy understands our mission. I'm not certain you do."

I wasn't moving but the ground beneath me was. "I'll see a doctor, today if I can find one. In the meantime, I've got five dead bodies and I've got to get back to work."

Yates sat in the chair Colby had used, his voice quiet but unyielding.

"This isn't about you, Jack. You're a good agent, one of the best we've got. Go find out what's wrong. Do what you have to do. Take all the time you need. We'll handle this case."

I looked at him. His eyes were steady and calm. His mouth closed. There was no give. No room for debate.

"You're right. I should have told you."

"Would have come out the same way. You know that. I'll need your gun and your credentials."

"I'm on sick leave. Why are you treating me like I'm under investigation?"

"You're not under investigation."

"Then why do you want my credentials and my gun?"

"Don't make this harder than it is, Jack."

"Then make it easy. Let me do my job."

"That's the point, Jack. Right now you can't do your job and we don't know why. Until we do, I need your badge and your gun. Talk to Anita in HR on your way out. She's got some disability forms for you to sign."

"So that's it. You think I'm having a breakdown, that I can't be trusted?"

I let the time pass waiting for Yates to answer. When he didn't, I pulled my gun from the holster on my hip, put it in his outstretched palm along with my ID and badge, and made my way to the door, turning back toward him.

"Who's got my squad now? Troy?"

Yates didn't hesitate. "He'll do a good job."

Chapter Eleven

The only doctor I'd seen in the six years I'd been in Kansas City was the one the Bureau used for our annual physical. Nice guy. Soft touch when he checked my prostate but not much personality.

No matter what they said about physician-patient privilege, I wasn't taking a chance with someone on the FBI's payroll. I needed a doctor who could tell me what was wrong, fix it, and get me back to work, and I didn't want someone who might have the same fit of self-serving conscience that had put me on the shelf and Troy Clark in charge of my squad.

Joy had a doctor for each limb, organ, and hemisphere of the brain, enough to start her own hospital. None of them were able to save the part of her that died with Kevin. I didn't have any more confidence in them than she did.

The rest of my close friends, the ones I would normally confide in, were people that worked for the Bureau. That world had always been enough for me. Now I was on the outside looking in.

That left Kate Scranton. I was always careful when I denied Joy's accusations that I was having an affair with Kate, repeating that there was nothing going on. I couldn't tell her that Kate had touched my heart in a way I never thought would happen again. It didn't matter that I had never acted on my feelings and that I only suspected that Kate felt the same way. Feeling the way I did was betrayal enough.

I had reconciled myself to the way things were with Joy, accepting it as penance for having let her and Kevin down. When she left me, I realized that we had both served out our sentences.

Kate had just returned from a lengthy jury trial in which former executives of an energy company were accused of looting it and misleading investors, resulting in a bankruptcy that had wiped out thousands of jobs and retirement accounts and billions in shareholder equity. I hadn't seen her since Joy moved out, though we'd talked on the phone while Kate was away. She knew about Joy but not about my shaking, unless she could feel it over the phone.

I met her a year ago when she was working with a lawyer defending a pharmacist who was accused of dealing in black-market painkillers. The case hinged on the credibility of the government's informer. I sat through the whole trial not just because it was my case but because of her.

At first, I told myself it was because she was so good at what she did. She scanned everyone in the courtroom like her eyes were bar-code readers, whispering advice to the defense attorney about jurors and witnesses. A case I thought was airtight unraveled before my eyes, collapsing completely when our star witness was caught lying on the stand. Everyone in the courtroom was watching the witness stammer and stutter. I couldn't take my eyes off Kate, her satisfied smile saying *gotcha*.

She had an angular face and lithe body with long ebony hair, fair skin, and blue eyes. She was tall, like me, smarter than me; her smiles came more easily than mine.

It was at that moment that she got me, though I didn't tell her when I asked her to lunch the week after the trial, saying only that I wanted to learn more about what she did. I'd never been unfaithful to Joy and had never thought I could be until I met Kate.

We ate at D'Bronx Deli on Thirty-ninth Street, gorging on their special pizza that had more than everything on it. We ran through the mutual background check. I told her about Wendy and Colby Hudson. Kate's reaction hit home.

"And you wish they weren't seeing each other."

"What can I say?"

"You didn't have to say anything. Your face did all the talking."

Kate was forty-one, divorced from her husband, Alan, after a fifteen-year marriage she described as a war of attrition. The one thing they agreed on was each other's talent. They were both psychologists. Alan conducted mock-jury trials, using the results to craft questionnaires for the real jurors. She knew of no one better. Congratulating themselves on being mature adults, they agreed that their business relationship as jury consultants would survive their divorce. Her father, Dr. Henry Scranton, had started the firm and she and Alan were his partners. Alan, Kate said, had regretted the divorce the moment the ink was dry on the decree, but she knew it was the right decision.

Her thirteen-year-old son, Brian, split time between his parents. Her sister, Patty, was the poster child for happily married soccer moms, always nagging Kate to quit her job, patch things up with Alan, and provide their son a more stable home. Her father agreed on everything except quitting her job.

"How do you do it?" I asked her.

"Do what?"

"Get it so right in the courtroom."

"It's how my father raised me."

"Not good enough."

Kate shoved the leftover scraps of olives, pepperoni, anchovies, and onions into a small mound, scooped them into her mouth, chewing and then smiling.

"My father is an expert in the Facial Action Coding System," she explained.

"I was absent that day in school."

"It's a catalog of over three thousand facial expressions people make every day. A psychologist, Paul Ekman, developed the system. The majority of our facial expressions are involuntary. They flash by in milliseconds, too fast for most people to even see them. But they are there. You can videotape someone and break down their expressions frame by frame."

"I thought the eyes were the windows into the soul."

"Very romantic, but the eyes are cloudy windows at best. Facial expressions can reveal whether someone is cheating on their spouse or their taxes or whether their heart is filled with mercy or murder, if you can put their expressions in the right context."

We debated whether that was true, matching our experiences. I told her about Kevin. She eased back in her chair.

"It wasn't your fault," she explained. "You didn't know what to look for."

"That's not an excuse. My job is to know what to look for."

"Even so, it's hard to see beneath the surface. My earliest memories of my father are of him staring at me, taking notes, staring some more, studying my every move and mood. While other kids played outside, I played face flash cards with my father, every card a different facial expression. I had to tell him what emotion the person was expressing."

"I bet he gave you ice cream when you got them right."

"Chocolate, and a lot of it. He discovered that I had an unusual aptitude for recognizing micro facial expressions in, literally, the blink of an eye. I was eight when my mother died. I grew up as my father's research subject. Eventually I became his assistant and then his partner."

"So, you're like a mind reader."

"No. A mind reader works Las Vegas lounges, her name lit up on the bottom of the casino marquee, pulling silver dollars out of customers' ears, making them admit they've never met before telling the audience the names of everyone the customer slept with in high school."

I was still a skeptic. "No ESP either, huh?"

"Not a drop. And I don't bend spoons just by looking at them and I don't see dead people."

"What do you see?"

"I see people's smiles, frowns, raised eyebrows, and flared nostrils. I see their flickering eyes, quivering cheeks, laugh lines, crow's feet, and wrinkles."

"So do I. Everyone does."

"Except I see more. I see the involuntary, uncontrollable, soul-stripping micro expressions that lay people open like an autopsy."

There was more resignation than bragging in her voice.

"What's that like?"

"It depends on who I'm looking at. I see things people don't want me to see. It's great for business but it's hell on relationships. There are times when I'm grateful for my skill and there are times when I wish I had cataracts."

I took a chance. "What do you see in my face?"

She hesitated, setting her fork down, folding her arms across her chest, a half smile creeping out of the corner of her mouth.

"Well, Agent Davis, I can tell whether you just want to have lunch or whether you want to take the rest of the day and the night off."

"Which is it?" I asked, stunned to hear her say what I was thinking.

Kate laughed. "You're married. It doesn't matter what we want since lunch is the only thing that we can have."

I liked that she laid it out so there was no misunderstanding. And I liked that she said it didn't matter what *we* wanted, not that it didn't matter what *I* wanted. We both understood why she was right.

I found excuses for more lunches, always on the pretext of talking about a case I was working on, asking her advice about how to read suspects and witnesses. I would never trust myself when it came to reading faces after what happened to Kevin, but I loved listening to her talk. We let our lunches linger and wander, often coming back to the similarities between what we did. I caught bad guys. She caught lies. We both feared that we would be deceived by the guilty and fail the innocent.

We argued about the polygraph. I trusted it. She didn't.

"The polygraph measures the response of the body's limbic system, which controls emotion. It assumes that someone telling a lie will experience an involuntary increase in heart rate, pulse, temperature, breathing, all of which are controlled by the limbic system," she said. "But a pathological liar can beat the polygraph."

"How?"

"Wrong question. They answer is they lie. The right question is why aren't their lies detected."

"You're going to tell me."

"Of course. It's my obligation to show you the errors of your ways," Kate said with a grin. "A psychologist at the University of Southern California did a study on the brains of liars. It's not conclusive, but it is interesting. He found that liars average 22 percent more white matter in the prefrontal cortex of their brains and 14 percent less gray matter."

"So what?"

"The gray matter contains neurons, which are the brain's

networking material. Think of neurons like telephone wires that connect phones. And neurons link the prefrontal cortex to the limbic system. The fewer neurons someone has, the fewer connections there are to the limbic system. Pathological liars get away with lying because they don't show any nervousness. They are genetically designed to lie."

"But you can see it in their faces?"

"A psychopath or a natural liar is hard for anyone to catch. A psychopath doesn't care about anything, so why get emotional? A natural liar, or someone who is trained to deceive, like actors or trial lawyers, they can be just as hard to figure out. The rest of us are a lot easier because micro facial expressions are almost impossible to control."

"Aren't they tied to emotions just like heart rate and breathing, which the polygraph measures?"

"You're right, but people can learn to regulate their breathing and their heart rate. They can't do that with micro expressions. And the polygraph is so unreliable no court will allow the results into evidence."

"No court will allow a videotape of a defendant's micro facial expressions into evidence either."

"I don't need them admitted into evidence. I just need to see them."

"How can you be so certain what each expression means?"

"Facial expressions are universal in type and meaning across all cultures and ethnic groups," she said.

"Show me the one that says you're a liar."

"That's not how it works. Facial expressions, especially micro expressions, are clues. Someone pretends to be angry, but their face says they are afraid. They should be devastated but a smile lasting a fraction of a second shoots out of the corner of their mouth. I look for inconsistencies, asymmetries, things that don't fit."

"Like the dog that didn't bark."

"Exactly. If you know what to look for, they are the closest things to money in the bank for a lie catcher."

"Well, then. I better not lie to you."

"Not unless you want to get caught," she said, her grin firmly in place.

Chapter Twelve

I needed sleep more than I needed a doctor. It took me thirty minutes to get home, detouring around construction on I-35 to my house in Overland Park, a suburb on the Kansas side of the state line that bisects Kansas City.

The house looked like it always had from the outside—a boxy two-story with a two-car garage, beige stucco, short trees, and shorter grass. Walking inside, finding it almost empty after I agreed that Joy could take whatever furniture she wanted while the lawyers worked out the rest of the property settlement, it reminded me of a house whose owners I had arrested for selling dope to their kids' friends. They held an estate sale to raise money so they could pay their lawyers. I took a tour when it was over. Everything worth having was gone, the picked-over remnants all that remained. They went to jail for a long time.

My dining room was empty; my beer-stained easy chair and ring-marked end table sat alone in the den, ruts in the carpet where the cherrywood entertainment center had stood. There was no kitchen table, just a pair of stools with their white paint chipped by careless heels, tucked under the black granite lip of the island anchored in the middle of the room. The walls were scarred with holes where pictures had hung. The drapes had been stripped from bare windows and my footsteps echoed off hardwood floors.

Joy left me the nineteen-inch TV with a built-in DVR she kept in the kitchen to watch the *Today Show* and to tape soaps, along with a futon that I moved from the basement into the master bedroom. Looking around, I missed the comfortable familiarity from the furnishings of a bad marriage. This was my new normal.

I woke up in the late afternoon to an undercurrent of tremors—sensations, I called them—shakes in the making. I showered, nicked my chin shaving and shaking at the same time, and then left Kate a message that I needed to talk to her.

I flipped on the early news in time to see a report on the murders. Adrian Williams was the spokeswoman for our office, a polished fashion plate who knew how to feed the media beast. She recited what little was known, made the usual comments about an ongoing investigation, and appealed to the public for patience and help.

By now, I knew the preliminary forensics report would be finished. The number of shots fired, the estimated distance between shooter and victims, the number and quality of fingerprints—all that and more would have been laid out for my squad. A more detailed rundown on the neighborhood canvass, together with the list of known associates, would have yielded a chart of people to interview, priorities flagged with a red check alongside their names.

I tried watching the rest of the news but couldn't concentrate on the latest fistfight between dueling county commissioners or the postseason prospects for the Royals and the early odds on the Chiefs breaking their Super Bowl drought. I didn't care about the coming changes in the weather or the latest triumph of the station's Problem Solvers.

I cared about Keyshon Williams, imagining the paramedics unraveling the boy's fingers from his mother's hair and picturing the coroner laying his arms alongside his body in preparation for removing, weighing, and measuring his vital organs. I already knew the cause of Keyshon's death, but the person who had caused it was still upright and breathing. I couldn't live with that.

I called Ammara Iverson, remembering the tears in her eyes when Troy Clark led me out of Marcellus's backyard. I hoped her soft spot hadn't hardened.

"Hey, Ammara. I just saw Adrian on the news."

"Girl looked good too, I bet."

"Like a million damn dollars of taxpayer money."

Her laugh came from deep in her throat, full and honest. I liked the sound.

"How are you doing, Jack? Feeling any better?"

"Yeah. I got some sleep. I'll find a doctor tomorrow and get this thing figured out."

"That's great."

"Listen, what did CSI come up with?"

She lowered her voice. "I'm sorry, Jack. I can't help you with that."

"Can't help me? What does that mean? I'm taking some time off. I didn't go over to the other side."

"It's not my decision. Troy and Ben Yates sat us down, told us how it would be. Said any leaks and somebody's going to get their ass kicked."

"I'm not a reporter, you know."

"Troy made a special point that we weren't supposed to talk to you about the investigation."

I was standing in the kitchen and slid onto one of the stools. "Why me?"

I heard her breathing, deciding what to say. "Troy said that since we don't know what's wrong with you or how stable you are right now, we can't evaluate the risk of keeping you in the loop. I'm sorry, Jack."

I was scared I had a brain tumor or a fatal disease. Troy just thought I was crazy. I wasn't sure which was worse. I didn't know what to say, so I didn't say anything.

"You still there, Jack?" Ammara asked.

"Yeah, I'm here. Listen, we never had this conversation, okay?"

"Sure. Take care of yourself."

Troy had pushed me to do the right thing, to take myself out, to get help. If I'd been shot or run over or just had a bad cold, he would have told me the same thing. If I had refused, he would have passed it off as admirable stubbornness and devotion to the job. Instead, when he found me shaking uncontrollably under the tree in Marcellus's backyard, he saw a security risk, someone no longer to be trusted.

Troy couldn't let go of the possibility that someone on our squad or close to it had leaked the existence of the surveillance camera to whoever was responsible for the murders. If he were right, he wouldn't trust anyone, least of all me.

I spun Troy's scenario until it snagged on something I had felt but not been able to pin down since I first saw the cash lying on the ground. I'd caught a glimpse of someone running away from the scene, vaguely familiar but not clear enough to identify in the dark.

Colby Hudson fit the profile, as did thousands of other men in Kansas City. Except Colby had shown up in the morning looking like he'd run a marathon in the storm after having an unauthorized, unsupervised, unrecorded meeting with Javy Ordonez at the same time five people were executed, possibly on Javy's instructions.

I went over the timing in my mind, suddenly realizing that I had been wrong when I told Colby that he was Javy's alibi, a statement Colby hadn't denied. Colby had said that Javy learned about the murders a couple of hours after they happened while the two of them were at an after-hours club. I was in Marcellus's backyard less than an hour after the shootings. Colby could have been the person I had seen running away and still made it to his meeting with Javy. He could even have been the person who told Javy that Marcellus was dead. If so, there was only one way he could have known that.

I worried that my suspicions were feeding off my feelings about Colby's relationship with Wendy and Troy's leak paranoia. I didn't like it, but that didn't mean I was wrong. If I was right, Wendy could be caught in the middle. I called her, treading softly.

"Buy you dinner?"

"Dad, are you okay? Colby said you weren't feeling well."

In spite of everything that had happened, Wendy was still my girl and I was still her dad. I felt it every time we talked.

"I thought you guys didn't talk about me."

"Says who?"

"Says Colby. What else did he tell you?"

"Just that you were shaking a lot. What's going on?"

"Probably nothing. I'm taking some time off until I get it checked out. How about dinner? I'm buying."

"Sorry, Dad. I can't make it. Colby is thinking about buying a new house. He wants me to go look at it tonight."

"A new house? Really. Where?"

"In Lions Gate. He says he can get a good deal on it."

"He better. There's nothing in there for less than three-quarters of a million. Where's he getting that kind of money?"

"He's made some good investments and he's getting a good deal on it."

I hoped that he'd bought stock in Google when it was cheap. I didn't care how good a deal he was getting or where he found the money as long as the deal was clean.

"Well, good for him. Listen, I'm taking a few days off. How about lunch tomorrow?"

"Dad, I haven't eaten lunch since I started this job last spring, you know that. Are you sure you're okay?"

No commodity traders or their assistants ate lunch while the market was open. After a week on the job, Wendy told me she liked the chaotic atmosphere of fortunes being made and lost in a split second, saying it was like walking a tightrope with your eyes closed, "sort of like living with you and Mom." She specialized in dark humor that made her hurt as much as it made her laugh. She was living proof of the old saw that what didn't kill you made you stronger.

"I'm sure I'm okay. Sorry, honey. We hardly get to see one another. I've got the time for a change and thought I'd give it a try."

"I could do an early breakfast."

"Great. How about seven-thirty at Classic Cup on the Plaza?"

"Perfect."

"Have you talked to your mother lately?"

"Are you kidding? At least three times today and it's still light out."

"Did you tell her anything?"

"About what?"

"About what Colby said. You know, about me shaking."

"She asked about you so I told her. I didn't think it was a secret."

"I didn't say it was a secret, sweetheart."

Wendy let out an exasperated sigh. "You two are amazing. You're going to screw up being divorced as much as you screwed up being married. You're perfect for each other."

"Yeah. A match made in heaven. Listen, instead of breakfast, maybe you, Colby, and I can have dinner tomorrow night."

"Are you sure?"

"Absolutely."

"I'll check with him. I'd like that."

I had never asked Wendy to bring Colby anywhere, including to dinner. She couldn't keep the happiness out of her voice. I was glad that she didn't ask me why I had made the invitation. She wouldn't have liked the reasons.

Chapter Thirteen

With Troy's gag order, I was reduced to relying on the media to keep up with my case. I knew that press coverage was often sketchy and slanted, whipsawed by selective leaks and pressure to goose ratings with sensational stories, but it was all I had for the moment. My DVR allowed simultaneous recording of two stations. I set it to tape the news broadcasts on two of the local network affiliates that had built their audiences with ceaseless coverage of grisly crime.

The murders were a big enough story to warrant team coverage. The station I'd been watching was still working its way through its roster. One reporter had just finished interviewing Marcellus's mother when I hung up the phone, the woman dissolving in tears when asked how she felt after discovering that her son was one of the victims. I wondered who she'd be crying for when we searched her house, as we certainly would before the sun set. She had cooked both his dinner and his crack and would end up serving time that should have been his.

The camera cut to another reporter standing in front of three people, turning to them for comment, the name of each appearing on the screen as they answered the reporter's questions. LaDonna Simpson, the white-haired, elderly neighbor who lived next door clicked her tongue in regret about the decline of a neighborhood she'd lived in for over fifty years. Tarla Hicks, the girlfriend of the jailed neighbor on the other side of the house, posed for the camera like she was auditioning for the pole position at a strip joint, describing the Winston brothers as good dudes she'd partied with in the past and would miss.

Latrell Kelly, who lived in the house directly behind the victims, was the last one to be interviewed. He had round shoulders, a pudgy middle, and a soft voice. Ammara's description of him had been dead-on. Mass murderers came in all shapes and sizes. Meek and mild didn't rule anyone out. I turned up the volume when the reporter asked Latrell what upset him most about what had happened, keeping the microphone close to his mouth to make him heard.

"That little boy," Latrell said. "Nobody takes care of a little boy, you see what happens."

It wasn't a confession. It was a reminder, his words pricking the dull ache I carried for my dead son. The reporter threw it back to the anchors, who nodded somberly and promised to stick with the story, telling viewers to stay tuned for Triple Action Weather with ESP Doppler and the latest from the RV show. I turned off the TV as the phone rang. Kate's name popped up on the caller ID.

"Welcome home."

"Thanks. I haven't had time to unpack," she said. "What's up?"

"I need your advice on something. Wendy already turned me down for dinner. I'm hoping you won't make me zero for two. I can only take so much rejection in one day."

"Second choice has never sounded so good. How about one of those soulless chain restaurants that you suburbanites find so sophisticated?"

"You mean like IHOP?"

"I have visions of a Belgian waffle with my name written on it in whipped cream."

"There's one at 119th and Metcalf. I'll call ahead and have them reserve our usual booth. I should warn you that the violin players are off tonight."

"We'll make our own music. I'll see you in an hour."

After Joy moved out and filed for divorce, my phone conversations with Kate had edged into a new intimacy, both of us saying that we missed the other and looked forward to being together again. There was no heavy breathing, no suggestive questions about what she was wearing, just a quiet acknowledgment that things had changed. She was on the road, in the middle of a trial. I was here, in the middle of an investigation, both of us feeling the pressure of getting it right. If this was to be our first date, neither of us had said so. I arrived ten minutes early, found a booth along the windows facing 119th Street, and took deep breaths every few minutes, hoping that would keep the shakes off the table.

Kate was on time, stopping for a moment inside the door until she caught my wave from across the restaurant. She was wearing her dark hair pulled back in a tight ponytail, a lime green tank top under a black jacket and jeans. A tremor shook both of us as we embraced. She pulled back and searched my face for an explanation.

"This isn't about one of your cases, is it? This is about you."

"Let's at least order our waffles first."

"Why? Are you afraid I'll lose my appetite?"

"You live downtown. I'd hate to make you drive all the way out here and then cheat you out of your waffle. We'll eat. Then we'll talk."

She kept her eyes on me while we ordered. It was like

being x-rayed. The tremors were humming just under my skin, waiting for their cue. The waitress left and they took center stage doing a one-minute number that rivaled the latest hip-hop moves. I tried to talk as I shook, my words garbled in a strangled stutter.

Kate studied me like I was a test subject. "How long has this been going on?"

I shrugged and took a deep breath. The tremors became distant ripples, my voice tripping over them until they faded.

"Like this, about a week. It started a couple of months ago, low key at first but lately it's been picking up steam."

"Have you been to a doctor?"

"No. Didn't think I need to until now. I'm off duty until I can walk and chew gum at the same time without shaking. I was hoping you'd know a doctor I could see."

"The University of Kansas Hospital has a movement disorder clinic. I'd start there. You said the symptoms started two months ago. That's when Joy left, isn't it?"

"You think there's a connection?"

The waitress delivered our waffles. Kate paid no attention.

"It's possible. Stress aggravates everything, including movement disorders. And, there are a lot of those to choose from, like Parkinson's, ALS, MS, myoclonus, dystonia, Tourettes, and tics. The psychology journals I read usually have a few articles each year about them, but it doesn't come up in my jury work, so I'm not a student."

"It's more annoying than anything else," I said.

"Are you lying to both of us or just yourself?"

"Meaning?"

"Meaning that ordering a mocha at Starbucks and the barista doesn't stir the chocolate so you end up with a latte on top and a layer of chocolate on the bottom that drips on your chin when you try to get it out—that's annoying. Loss of control over your body, which, by the way, is an apt metaphor for losing control over your life, together with worrying whether you'll lose your job are definitely more than annoying. And, if they aren't, fear of dying beats annoying any day of the week."

I leaned back in the booth. "Which of the wrinkles in my face told you that?"

"All of them. Your eyes are wide, your brow is raised, and your lips are set on full-time quiver—classic expressions of fear. I'd bet you'd rather bust down a door blindfolded than shake and not know why."

My reflection in the window was a poker face.

"It's your micro expressions, Jack. You can't see them. They come and go in a flash when you talk about the shaking. If it makes you feel any better, I'm probably the only one you know who can see them. How long have you been off work?"

"About twelve hours."

"Your idea?"

I shook my head and told her about the murders, about my backyard breakdown, Troy's suspicions about a leak on the squad, and my suspicions of Colby. I told her more than I would ever have told Joy and more than Troy would have wanted me to tell anyone. She listened closely, asking just enough questions to flesh out the details.

"What makes you suspicious about Colby Hudson?"

"Nothing solid. Just loose threads and gut feelings."

"I thought you were the *Dragnet* version of FBI agents, the kind who only wants the facts and leaves the intuitive stuff to more sensitive types like me."

"I believe in what I can prove—whose blood, whose fingerprints, what motive, means, and opportunity. That's what puts criminals away. Not a wink and a nod that no one can see. But I've been cut off from the real evidence. Suspicion is all I've got left."

"Why not let it go? Let Troy and the rest of your team work it out."

"Two reasons. I can't get that boy, Keyshon, out of my mind."

"Don't confuse him with your son. Nothing you do or don't do will change what happened to either of them."

"That doesn't pay the debt."

"Jack, you aren't responsible for what happened to your son or that boy. The man who killed your son was a classic psychopath. No one, including me, could have seen him coming. It's no different with Keyshon."

"Kevin was my son. That makes me responsible."

"Keyshon wasn't your son. You didn't even know him."

"I knew enough. I knew that he was living in that house. I was watching it every day, putting my case ahead of him. I left him there to take his chances with people who'd buy, sell, or kill you for drugs, money, or sport. It's like one of the neighbors said on the news."

"What's that?"

"Nobody takes care of a little boy, you see what happens."

Kate folded her arms across her chest, grinning. "You're a throwback, you know that? One man, standing up, alone. It's brave, righteous, and sexy. But if you shoulder that much weight, you'll shake yourself into a million little pieces."

"I don't suppose you'd be interested in putting me back together again?"

"Maybe," she said with another smile. "I've never been big on jigsaw puzzles, but you might be worth the effort. You said there were two reasons. What's the second one?"

"Wendy is pretty serious about Colby. If I'm right about him, she could get caught in the middle. Troy will feel bad if that happens, but he won't let it get in his way."

"And you will?"

I straightened, put my hands on the table, looking at her hard. "I already lost one child. I won't lose another."

Kate nodded. "What if you're not the right one to save her? What if your dislike of Colby, your resentment at being forced out, and your anxiety about whatever is wrong with you makes you the wrong one? What if the best thing for Wendy is someone with a clear head?"

She had touched all the bases, just as Troy had. I gave her the same answer as I had about Kevin.

"I'm her father. It's that simple."

She reached across the table, taking my hand, her skin warm, melding with mine. "What can I do?"

"You've done a lot already. You drove out here and listened to me while letting a perfectly good waffle turn cold. You warned me not to do what we both know I'm going to do anyway. And you told me who to see about my problem. I can't think of anything else unless you want to pick up the check."

She took a twenty-dollar bill from her purse and put it on the table.

"My pleasure. You've got enough on your plate. Your marriage is over and, even if that's a good thing for us, you've got to deal with that before you can move on. You're still blaming yourself for your son's death and you're scared for your daughter. Plus, you've got to find out what's making you shake."

"That's supposed to make me feel better?"

"At least you know what's in front of you and, like G.I. Joe says, knowing is half the battle. Here's the real kicker. You won't have ballistics and forensics, DNA, wiretaps, and all the other bricks and mortar you've always surrounded yourself with. You're in my world now. You want to get through this, you'll have to work the people."

Chapter Fourteen

I woke with mild, morning shakes. They rose from my belly into my throat as I rolled out of bed, an internal wake-up call. I'd gotten used to it, like they were as much a part of me as my arms, legs, and heart, their absence more notable than their presence.

I took Kate's advice and called the movement disorder clinic at the Kansas University Hospital. It was a large teaching hospital located at Thirty-ninth and Rainbow, just inside the Kansas side of the state line with Missouri. I'd been in the ER and up on the floors to talk with victims and suspects, but I hadn't been a patient there or in any other hospital since I tried to catch a hockey puck with my chin when I was in high school. The receptionist transferred my call to the person handling new patient intakes, who questioned me for fifteen minutes before asking which doctor I wanted to see.

"The one who can make this go away," I told her in a halting voice. I'd found that talking about my symptoms made them worse. It was a lesson in modesty my mother would have appreciated.

"We cannot promise that you will get better." Her disclaimer had the flat, rote familiarity of being read from a script.

"Okay, then give me the one who won't make it any worse."

"We cannot promise that you will not get worse."

I almost told her to give me the doctor with a sense of humor since she obviously didn't have one, but didn't want her to tell me that they couldn't promise to laugh at my jokes.

"Okay. How about the doctor who can see me the soonest?"

"Dr. Fitzpatrick has an opening November twenty-fifth."

"That's not for two months."

"It is our next available appointment. I can put you down for that date and add you to a waiting list in case we get a cancellation."

"Do you get many cancellations?"

"No. Should I confirm your appointment and put you on our list?"

"No place I'd rather be."

The prospect of waiting two months to see a doctor was a joke that didn't make me laugh. It was one more thing I couldn't control. The only thing I could control was how I dealt with it. I took a quick inventory.

Apart from the shakes, I felt fine. My appetite was good enough that I hadn't lost the extra five pounds around my waist. When I jogged in the morning, my knees didn't hurt any worse than they had when I turned fifty a few months ago. My dark hair was turning sandy but wasn't falling out. And, I wasn't having dizzy spells like other people I'd heard of who turned out to have brain tumors. I shook. That was it. How bad could it be? Not bad, I decided. I kept repeating that, waiting for it to sink in.

I thought about the case and what Kate had said, that I

had to work the people. That had always been part of my job even if I didn't trust my ability to read beneath the surface to decipher people's inner demons. I relied on the facts, the evidence, to cross-check against what I guessed about human nature. That approach had served me well. I'd never repeated the mistake I'd made with Kevin. If I were going to live in Kate's world without my tools, I'd need to learn how to use hers. I called to ask if I could borrow them.

"Teach me to read micro expressions," I told her.

"Good morning. I had a lovely time last night and I appreciate that you thanked me for me buying dinner, although I expected more than a good-night kiss in the parking lot for my investment."

It had been an awkward moment when I walked Kate to her car. She leaned into me, hands behind my neck pulling me toward her, and kissed me, her mouth open and urgent. Joy and I had been married twenty-eight years and had dated two years before that. I hadn't kissed another woman like that since I was a teenager. Even though my marriage was over and I'd fantasized about being with Kate, she caught me by surprise. My reflexive fidelity to my future former wife made me clumsier than when I groped Sue Ellen Thorpe in a darkened hallway during a junior high school dance. I mumbled something about being tired and went home alone.

"Give me another chance. I start slow but I finish strong."

"Good to know. Maybe we can even harness your shaking for a higher and better use somewhere besides the IHOP parking lot. Now what were you saying about micro expressions?"

I'd appreciated her directness the first time we'd had lunch, when she told me that it didn't matter what we wanted, we couldn't have it, not then. Things were different now and her frank sexual banter was another reminder that it was time for me to move on. I didn't know if she'd been like this when she was married. I didn't know anything about the relationships she may have had since she was divorced five years ago. I only knew that I wanted her and that, by some unlikely alignment of the planets, she wanted me.

I tried to remember whether I had ever felt that way about Joy, believed that I must have, but couldn't summon the memories. We'd driven our love for each other into the ground, leaving it cold and hard.

"I want to go to the college of facial knowledge."

"Classes start this weekend. They run Friday night to Monday morning."

"How about an advance session? I'm having dinner tonight with Wendy and Colby Hudson. If he flares his nostrils, I need to know whether he's lying or just has allergies."

"You want to learn how to read micro expressions by tonight? What are you, drunk? This isn't some parlor trick you can learn to do in one easy lesson. Could you teach me how to kick in a door, plant a wiretap, or work undercover before lunch?"

"Not a chance."

"Exactly. So stop being stupid. I'm offering you a weekend of personal instruction and you're about to blow it, big-time."

"Personal instruction?"

"Very personal."

"So today is not a good day for a quickie course?" I asked, finally getting into the flow.

"Today, no, but hold onto that option. I do have another idea, which happens to be a good one. I'll join you for dinner and interpret afterward."

I was never good at waiting, letting a case come to me, depending on a drug dealer, embezzler, or terrorist to do me a favor by screwing up. I got in my car, a two-year-old Chevy Impala, and drove back to Marcellus's neighborhood. There was a chance that my squad would be canvassing the neighborhood again and following up on leads. I didn't want to put any of them in a tough spot, forcing them to report to Troy that I had been nosing around. I decided to tour the surrounding blocks first for any sign of my people. If the streets were empty, I'd take a shot at the neighbors.

A KCK patrol car and an unmarked Crown Victoria were parked in front of a house three blocks to the west of where Keyshon, his father, mother, and the Winston brothers had been killed. Two uniformed cops were milling around in the front yard. I slowed down when I saw Marty Grisnik standing on the sidewalk talking to a heavyset black man nearly as tall as he was. Grisnik glanced at me and then barked something to one of his officers, who flagged me down, motioning me to the curb.

Grisnik walked slowly to my car. He bent down, his broad frame cutting off the sun and the cool morning breeze coming through my open window.

"You lost?" he asked me.

"If I was, I'm found."

Grisnik examined the length of my car, running his hand across the paint. "Not much of a ride for an FBI agent."

"It's paid for."

"Good thing, too. Last time I saw you, I wouldn't have given much for your chances of getting a car loan. You doing all right?"

"No complaints that count."

"I hear they put you on the shelf."

"Just temporary."

"That why no one over there can remember your name when I called looking for you? Had to talk to someone in human resources just to find out that you were on leave. After your performance the other night, it wasn't hard to figure out what happened."

The law-enforcement community is a small one, smaller

since 9/11. We were all told to put aside the petty jealousies and resentments that fed the stereotypes local cops and feds had of each other and learn to play nice. For the most part, we had succeeded. One of the unintended consequences of those closer relationships and better communications was that it was harder than ever to keep a secret.

"Out of sight, out of mind. You didn't have your officer flag me down to inquire about my health. What do you want?"

"Do me a favor, get out of the car. I'm too old to stay bent over like this. I stay down here much longer and my officers will need a crowbar to get me to stand up straight."

Grisnik stepped back, giving me room to open the car door. Up close, he wasn't old. He was a powerhouse, a point he made by putting me in his shadow.

"When you asked for my help with your fugitive warrant, you didn't want to tell me what was going down," he said. "I got that. I didn't like it, but I got it. But you gave me your word that your case, whatever it was, wouldn't blow up. Next thing I know, five people are dead. That's not blown up. That's a goddamn explosion."

"We had no way of knowing that was going to happen."

He started to jab his finger at me. I blocked him with my palm, firmly pushing his hand away, letting him know that he couldn't treat me like a suspect or a rookie cop, no matter how angry he was. He took a breath, keeping his voice low, his words clipped.

"That doesn't mean squat to me or the people who are dead. Three men, a woman, and a child were murdered in my city. I take that personally."

"You could have shut Marcellus Pearson down any time you wanted. If you had done your job, he and the Winston brothers would be in jail. Jalise Williams and her son would be alive. I don't have to listen to you blame me for what happened to them."

My chin bobbed, my voice trembled, and my eyes squeezed

shut as I finished my self-defense. Grisnik gave me some room, letting me settle. I waved my hand.

"Don't worry," I told him. "I'm not going to foam at the mouth."

"Good. That's what happens to a dog with rabies. Back when I was on patrol, I had to shoot a rabid dog one time to keep him off a little kid. Tore me up to shoot that dog. I'd feel almost as bad if I had to shoot you."

"I'm touched. So why didn't you bust Marcellus?"

"I work Robbery and Homicide, not drugs. Our drug squad did bust him, more than once. Sometimes the house was clean, like he knew we were coming. Other times, we had problems with the arrests. Prosecutor wouldn't take the case or the judge would throw out the evidence."

"That's why we went after him and why I couldn't bring you into the loop."

"I know that. What I don't get is why the FBI doesn't want my help catching whoever killed those people."

"Troy Clark told you he didn't want your help?"

" 'Course he didn't tell me that. Said the exact opposite. Told me how he'd be leaning on me all the way. Then when I offered to send one of my detectives over to work with him, he said he'd get back to me. Hasn't happened."

I defended Troy—another act of reflexive loyalty. "You know how these cases are. No one goes home, no one sleeps or eats. Give him some time. He'll get back to you."

Grisnik snorted, shook his head. "Then I hear that they showed you the curb, said you were unstable. Now I find you roaming around a few blocks from where the murders took place and I ask myself what you are doing over here since I'm guessing you don't have friends or relatives in the neighborhood."

Grisnik wanted the same thing I did—information. I knew my reasons. His were obvious. This was his turf and he didn't like being shut out.

"Not a one."

"Makes me wonder whether everyone at the FBI is an idiot or an asshole," he said. "Which do you think it is?"

"One doesn't rule the other out," I told him.

That made him laugh. He wiped the sweat off his face. "There's someone I'd like you to meet."

I followed him to the man he'd been talking with when I drove up.

"Jack Davis, say hello to Rodney Jensen." Rodney and I shook hands. "Mr. Davis is with the FBI. Tell him what you told me."

Rodney turned his jowly face to me, hiked up his pants, resting his thumbs inside his suspenders. "My sister gone missing."

I looked at Grisnik, who nodded at me. "What's your sister's name?" I asked.

"Oleta Phillips."

Chapter Fifteen

"Tell Agent Davis when it was you last saw your sister."

Rodney Jensen pulled at both of his chins. "Day before yesterday. We was all standin' outside where Marcellus and them stay at. Oleta, she went to see Marcellus on account of her boy, Tony, gettin' hisself killed. Boy worked for Marcellus, and Marcellus, he done the right thing. Give Oleta three thousand dollars—funeral benefits, he called it."

"Tell Agent Davis what kind of bills Marcellus gave your sister," Grisnik said.

"All twenties. I seen 'em."

"You seen the money since?"

"No, sir. I ain't seen the money and I ain't seen my sister."

"What makes you think she's missing instead of just off on her own?" Grisnik asked.

"She don't got no off on her own. She stays with me. She ain't been home in two nights."

"Do you have a picture of your sister?"

"Might have one in the house."

"See if you can find it and then you go with the officers. They'll take you downtown so one of our detectives can get the rest of your information," Grisnik told him. "Let's go for a ride," he said to me. "I'll drive."

The Crown Vic was clean, but lived in, the upholstery faded and coffee-stained, the faint smell of cigarettes hanging in the air. The two-way radio hummed with calls to be answered. Grisnik ignored them, easing the car from the curb, letting it glide down the street barely above idle.

"Troy Clark came from here," he said when he turned east at the first cross street.

"That's right. You, too?"

He gave me a sideways grin. "No. I grew up in Strawberry Hill. Not too many Croatians lived in Quindaro. They had their neighborhood and we had ours, us and the Poles and the Lithuanians, even a few Dutch. It was real nice until they cut it in half with I-70. Some called it the Canyon after that but we still call it Strawberry Hill. It's finally coming back, like a lot of the rest of the city."

"Except for Quindaro."

"Doesn't help when people like Troy Clark turn their backs."

"If you mean he shouldn't freeze you out of the investigation because you both grew up here, you can forget it. That's not the way Troy thinks."

"How does he think?"

"He thinks about the case, how to pull it together. All he wants is to do it right and get it right."

"Even if he shits all over you?"

I thought about Grisnik's question, though I knew the answer. "Yeah, even if he shits all over me."

Grisnik turned north. We were skirting around Marcellus's block. The streets were quiet.

"I know why you pulled that scam with the fugitive warrant," Grisnik said.

I didn't answer. If he knew, he'd tell me. I'd learn more by letting him.

"You figure someone in my department was taking money from Marcellus. Could have been me. Could have been those two officers. Could have been the whole goddamn department. But you didn't care who it was so long as word got back to Marcellus. That way he'd be ready for you when you showed up with that phony warrant. That's why you wanted our cops to back you up. The more cops knew about the warrant, the more likely someone would tell Marcellus."

We were doing the dance, giving a little to get a little, hoping to get a lot more. There was no reason not to play.

"I put a camera in the ceiling fan in the front room."

"So you got the killer on tape?"

"Lights went out just before the shooting started."

"That's real handy. Makes you wonder if the killer knew about the camera."

"That it does."

"Anyone outside of your squad know about the camera?" Grisnik asked.

"Hard to say."

"Looks like you and me might have the same problem."

"And I didn't think we had anything in common."

He parked the car at the next corner.

"There it is," he said. "That's the corner where Oleta Phillips's son got shot last week. Marcellus and Javy Ordonez have been fighting over that corner a long time."

"We're pretty certain Javy is responsible; he had one of his guys, Luis Alvarez, do it."

"How certain?" Grisnik asked.

"Certain enough that I can't tell you how certain without compromising my people. Marcellus sent the Winston brothers to balance the books. Alvarez is in the ICU at Providence. If he makes it, you can fight with the Justice Department over who gets him first."

"Why are you telling me this when Troy Clark won't give me the time of day?"

"I'm not Troy. The cash I found under the tree in Marcellus's backyard—you think that's the money Marcellus gave Oleta?"

"Seems likely," Grisnik said. "Especially now that Oleta has disappeared."

"Where does that leave you?"

"Leaves me with a missing mother and her murdered son. I think both of those cases are related to Marcellus and his people getting killed. If Javy ordered the hit, the murders could be the next round in a gang war. Maybe Oleta saw something she shouldn't have seen. She could have run off or maybe we'll find her body dumped out in the woods. Make my job a lot easier if the FBI would share some information with me, but they won't because they don't trust us."

Grisnik put the car in drive, continuing his lazy tour. I thought about what he'd said, weighing my options.

"What do you want from me?"

"Help. If you suspect somebody in my department of being on Marcellus's payroll, I want their names."

I shook my head. "We weren't investigating your department. We didn't have any names."

"You've got surveillance tapes. Let me see them. I may recognize someone."

"Even if I wanted to, you forget that I'm on the disabled list."

"You must have at least one friend left at the Bureau."

"Like you said, they've forgotten my name."

Grisnik squared around. "You've been there too long not to have someone who will talk to you."

I thought of Ammara Iverson. She had said no the first time. That didn't mean she wouldn't change her mind.

"There may be one person."

"Give it a try. And, remember, I may be able to help you."

"How could you help me?"

"I don't know why you're touring our many fine attractions this morning, but I don't think you're looking to buy a new house. So I'd say you're working the case on your own. As a general rule, that's a bad idea. One of my detectives did that, I'd fire his ass."

"But I'm not one of your detectives."

"Which is a good thing for me. This gate can swing both ways, Jack. If I'm right about the death of Tony Phillips and the disappearance of his mother, I'm likely to learn things that will be helpful to you. Find out what you can, share it with me, and I'll give you what I come up with."

I looked away. I had defended Troy out of loyalty to him and the Bureau. That was more than the by-product of my training. It was the way I saw the world. I had never cheated on Joy even when our marriage existed in name only. I had taken a vow. She had released me from it when she left and filed for divorce. Troy was my colleague, the Bureau was my life. I wasn't ready to turn my back on them, even if they could only see me over their shoulders. I turned toward Grisnik.

"I told you about Luis Alvarez. That's the best I can do."

Grisnik pulled to the curb again, this time in the middle of the block down the street from Marcellus's house.

"Why? Because those people are your friends? Because the FBI is your mother, father, wife, and mistress who'd never treat you wrong so you can't treat them wrong? I'm not asking you to do anything you're not already doing."

"What do you mean?"

"They cut you loose. Maybe because you've got the shakes. Maybe because you're unstable. Or maybe because they blame you for those people getting killed. Hell, I don't know. But I know this. You're already acting like a free agent, working the case on your own, telling me about Luis Alvarez. What do you think the FBI is going to do if they find out what you're doing? Give you a fucking medal and your job back? Give me a break."

"I've got my reasons for being here."

Grisnik let out a sigh. "I'm sure you do. Why don't you tell them?" he said, pointing to a dark sedan that rounded the corner in the next block. A man and woman got out and walked up to the first house on the corner. Even at this distance, I recognized two members of my squad, Jim Day and Lani Heywood.

"Go on," Grisnik said. "Get out of my car. Tell your friends that you're snooping around on your day off and that you'll let them know if you find out anything important."

Kate's words reverberated in my head: *work the people.* I had to work myself first. I had told myself that I wanted to avoid seeing the people on my squad because I didn't want to put them in a difficult situation. That was only partly true. The rest of the truth gave me reason to shake. I didn't want them to know what I was doing because I didn't trust them.

"Maybe later. Let's get out of here."

Chapter Sixteen

My father was a salesman who preached that life was all about opening doors. The ones you could open yourself were the easiest, he said. All it took was guts. The hard ones were the ones someone else had to open for you because people won't let you in if they don't trust you. It didn't matter what his product line was—plumbing supplies, corrugated boxes, or anything else he could buy right and sell smart—he always told me that he was selling the same thing. Trust.

That's all I had to offer to Ammara Iverson. Troy Clark had told her not to trust me. That didn't mean she didn't, only that she was following orders by refusing to talk with me about the investigation. I had to give her a reason to disobey and open her door. I called her cell phone.

"Yes," she said.

Her voice was quiet but hurried. I didn't have to ask to know that I'd caught her at a bad time.

"It's Jack. Call me on my cell when you can talk privately. It's important."

I had no place to go and nothing to do when I got there so I drove around, waiting for Ammara to call. I cruised south on Seventh Street, east on Central, winding my way across a bridge that took me back in to Kansas City, Missouri, past Kemper Arena, a modernistic white elephant relegated to tractor pulls after the Sprint Arena opened on the south edge of downtown.

I crept along Liberty Street, turning east on the Twelfth Street Bridge, which rose above old redbrick warehouses now converted to Halloween haunted houses whose faded logos advertising furniture and hardware were now obscured by three-story skulls with gaping, bloody mouths. Halloween was five weeks away, but it was never too early to be scared to death.

I continued across Twelfth Street, wandering south on Broadway into the Crossroads District where the warehouses had become art galleries and studios, lofts and restaurants that drew large crowds the first Friday of each month. Broadway carried me past Union Station and the Liberty Memorial, a towering obelisk remembering the victims and veterans of World War I, and south to the Country Club Plaza shopping district in midtown.

I left Brooks Brothers, Abercrombie & Fitch, and The Sharper Image in my rearview mirror, going farther south, where I passed the mansions on Ward Parkway. I turned west on Fifty-ninth Street, across State Line Road, and back into Kansas. More mansions flashed by in an enclave called Mission Hills.

In the space of thirty minutes, I'd gone from ghetto to grandeur, without destination or purpose. I didn't know what to do with myself and I began to shake, my hands locked on the steering wheel, my chin jackknifing against my chest. I pulled into a church parking lot, stopping the car while waiting for the spasms to ease. A sign announced that I'd crossed into Prairie Village, another of the ubiquitous suburbs that ran together like colors bleeding from cheap madras. My phone rang as I caught my breath.

"Jack, it's Ammara. What's so important?"

She was all business, careful and brisk. There would be no dance. I wouldn't ask any questions, so she wouldn't have to refuse to answer. I'd give without asking for anything in return, banking the information I gave her for a future payback.

"Marcellus Pearson gave Oleta Phillips three thousand dollars as funeral benefits after her son, Tony, was killed. She's probably on the surveillance videotape. Find out if she's ever been arrested. Check her fingerprints against any prints on the cash I found in Marcellus's backyard."

"Why?"

"Because Oleta has disappeared. If that's her money, she may have seen the killer. If she did, she's either hiding or dead. You need to find out which it is."

"How do you know she's disappeared?"

"Her brother told me."

"Jack, what are you doing talking to her brother? Don't tell me you're working this case on your own! Ben Yates will have your head and Troy will give it to him."

"Relax. I don't have anything else to do. I was bored so I took a drive. I ran into Marty Grisnik."

"He's the KCK detective."

"Right."

"I remember seeing him the other night at the scene. He was not having a good time."

"He doesn't like being cut out."

"I don't blame him, but I'm not the one with the scissors. What's the story with Oleta and her brother?"

"The brother's name is Rodney Jensen. Oleta lives with him. He called in a missing-person report after she didn't come home for the second night in a row."

"Grisnik runs Robbery and Homicide. What's he doing making a house call on a missing-person report?"

"He thinks Oleta's disappearance is related to the murder

of her son, Tony, the kid who got shot on the corner last week. I just happened to drive by Rodney's house while he and Grisnik were out on the sidewalk. Grisnik saw me and flagged me down. He wanted to know what was going on with our investigation. I told him I was out of it. He introduced me to Rodney and Rodney told me about his sister. So I'm telling you."

"Why aren't you telling Troy?"

"Because Troy might get the wrong impression and think I was freelancing. If he did, I'd probably never get back to work and I wouldn't be able to tell you anything else that Grisnik might share with me the next time we run into each other. I was hoping that you'd follow up on the lead and leave me out of it."

Ammara waited before responding, doing her own calculus. I knew the numbers she was crunching, trying to decide if an FBI agent who might be unstable, who was on medical leave for an unexplained disorder that made him shake like a ride at Six Flags and who had been booted out of the inner circle, qualified as a confidential source whose information she could rely on and whose identity she could protect. Plus, she had to factor in Marty Grisnik.

"What's Grisnik's stake in this?" she asked.

"Two things, I said. He wants anything that will help him with the shooting of Tony Phillips and the disappearance of Oleta Phillips. And he wants to know if we've got proof that any of his people were taking money from Marcellus."

"He and Troy, they both got the same bug up their ass. I don't like thinking that someone on our squad is bent. It changes the way I see all of us. Sometimes I don't even trust myself."

"We don't get to choose what happens," I told her. "Only what we do about it. Maybe Grisnik could get a look at the surveillance videotapes. I doubt that any cops would have shown up in uniform, but he might recognize someone who shouldn't have been there."

"I don't know if Troy would go for that."

"It's going to take a long time to ID everyone on those tapes. Tell him that Grisnik can help. Just don't tell Troy it was my idea."

"Makes sense. I'll see what I can do."

"Thanks."

"And Jack," she said. "You get anything else, let me know. I'll keep it between the two of us."

With nothing else to do until I met Wendy and Colby for dinner, I went to the Bullet Hole, a private shooting range located in a low-slung building that is bigger than it looks from the street. The owners spent their money to make certain it was safe, not gorgeous. The walls and floor are the same off-white, the showcases are all nicked wood and scratched glass filled with polished handguns. Wall-to-wall gun racks brim with rifles and shotguns. The staff is devoted to the members, their guns, and the Second Amendment.

My personal weapon is a Glock 23 .40 caliber semi-automatic. It's as close to perfectly balanced as any gun I've carried, fits neatly on my hip, and feels like part of me when I hold it in my hand. It's slightly smaller than the original model, so some people call it the mini-Glock, but there's nothing mini about it. I use it because it has the knockdown power that can make the difference in a life-or-death situation.

I've pulled my gun many times, fired it enough to know how I and it perform under real conditions, and hit enough people to know that I'd rather not. Real conditions had changed for me. I had to find out whether I could shoot and shake at the same time.

I bought a box of PowRball bullets. Each round has an

expanding jacketed bullet with a polymer ball in the bullet cavity. The soft-point cap promotes controlled expansion of the bullet, resulting in a classic mushroom shape that dumps all the available energy into the target. I knew all that because I'd read it on their website and I'd seen what happens when one of their bullets hits a flesh-and-blood target instead of one made of paper.

The range is half a flight down from the main floor and consists of a series of shooting stations separated by partitions. I set my gun and ammo on the ledge in front of my shooting station. I was the only one on the range, which suited me just fine. If I was going to fall apart again, I didn't want another audience.

Guns are unforgiving weapons. They carry out the errors committed by the person firing them without apology or regret. They will jam or misfire if you don't treat them with the care and respect they require. Their accuracy depends on a number of factors—range, wind, and angle to name a few. The steadiness of the shooter, more than any other factor, determines whether he hits his target. A firm grip and a controlled trigger pull are essential.

I went through my routine, making certain the gun was unloaded, checking the sight, loading the magazine, planting my feet, squaring my body, and gripping the gun with both hands. I measured my breaths, staying calm and focused. Still and steady, I fired, emptying the thirteen-shot magazine. I reloaded it and repeated the process a second time, then a third, locking my concentration on the gun, the trigger, and the target.

The pistol jumped slightly in my hand as I fired each round, the very manageable recoil another user-friendly feature of the Glock. After each round, I came back to my starting position and fired again. The blue smoke and smell of cordite were as reassuring as the bunched holes ripped in the center of the silhouetted target.

I started shaking when I tried to reload the magazine a fourth time. I clasped a bullet between my thumb and forefinger, repeatedly smacking it against the magazine like I was tapping out incomprehensible Morse code. The round slipped from my hand, landing on the rubber mat at my feet, followed by three more rounds before I laid the gun on the ledge next to a ballpoint pen someone had left there.

I picked up the pen, pulled the cap off, and tried to replace it, unable to make that happen, either. The harder I tried, the worse I shook, the tremors rebounding into my midsection until the muscles in my abdomen contracted like a snapped slingshot, yanking my head to my knees and leaving me grunting and gasping.

I raised my head. There were no witnesses except for the target hanging from a wire thirty feet away. I scooped the bullets off the floor and left.

Back in my car, I felt the butt of the gun cut into my waist, the barrel pressing hard against my hip. A gun was just one of the things I put on each day. All of a sudden, it didn't fit. It was like a pebble rolling around inside my shoe. I couldn't imagine not carrying it. The only thing worse was what might happen if I had to use it. There were too many things that could go wrong, none of which the gun would forgive.

Chapter Seventeen

There was no doubt that Wendy was her mother's daughter. They shared the same silky, honey-colored hair, strong chin, intoxicating green eyes, and full-face smile.

A psychologist at the drug treatment facility said that Wendy felt guilty for having stayed after school the day Kevin was taken, believing she could have saved him had she been there. The shrink said that she compounded her guilt by blaming herself for the disintegration of our marriage, punishing herself further by making choices she knew would turn out poorly. It was the only explanation that could make us feel worse and it did.

Through it all, she still loved us. That counted for a lot, even when she accused me of not doing enough to help her mother, even after we tried counseling, rehab, and AA. Some things, I once told her, can't be fixed, and her mother had decided that she was one of them. "Not good enough," Wendy had said. "You love her, you fix her, like you fixed me." I did but I couldn't, telling Wendy she fixed herself. Then I didn't love Joy anymore and I stopped trying. Two more things I regretted but couldn't change.

Wendy met Colby Hudson last December at a holiday party for agents, staff, and their families, telling me later that she thought he was cute and edgy.

"Don't date an agent," I told her. "Especially that one."

"Why not and why not him?"

"Because you might fall in love with him, decide to get married, and end up spending the rest of your life unpacking your suitcase and hoping he comes home vertical and sober. That's a tough way to live, especially for someone with your history. A lot of agents and their spouses can't hack it. But Colby is the kind of guy who ups the ante. If he's edgy, it's because he lives on the edge. You don't want to be holding on when he falls off, and I've seen enough guys like him to know that sooner or later that's where he's headed."

"I'm not you and I'm not Mom. I don't give up. If he falls, I'll catch him."

"And who will catch you?"

"You," she said with the wide-eyed smile that never failed to open my heart.

Dinner was at Fortune Wok, a Chinese restaurant in a strip center at 143rd and Metcalf in Overland Park. Five years earlier, the owners would have been serving wontons in the middle of a cow pasture. Now they were stoking the appetite of the latest wave of suburban migration for everything wok roasted.

There were too many cities on both sides of the state line for me to keep up. There were forty-plus burgs in five counties, each with a budget and a city council dedicated to high growth, low crime, and good times. Overland Park was one of the biggest, cramming farmland down its throat and regurgitating rooftops so fast that it wouldn't be long until Denver was just down the street.

Lions Gate, the subdivision where Colby was house hunting, bordered the strip center. I was early, so I drove through its manicured streets, past the clubhouse and the villas on the golf course. I remembered a friend who decided to sell his house and downsize to a villa only to discover that a villa was half the house for twice the money. The houses in Lions Gate were bigger and more expensive than the villas, proving that size mattered but not as much as money. There were no Chevy Impalas in anybody's driveway.

I circled back to the restaurant, parked, and stopped short of the entrance when I saw Colby sitting in a Lexus two cars down from mine. I tapped on the passenger-side window and let myself in. He was on his cell phone.

"It's nothing, man. I just needed some air. Call you later," he said to whomever he was talking to, flipping the phone shut. "Don't you knock?" he asked without looking at me.

"I tapped."

"Next time, knock and wait. The people I talk to don't want anyone listening. They play close attention to everything, including the background noise. They know I'm in my car, they hear the door open, and then they start asking a shitload of questions about who opened the door, who got in the car; who got out of the car, how come I let someone get in the car with me while I'm on the phone with them. Crazy shit like that."

"You should get one of those Do Not Disturb signs the hotels use and hang it on your rearview mirror. Maybe get a bumper sticker that says 'Undercover FBI Agent driving car he can't afford.'"

Colby looked at me and grinned, running his hand across his freshly shaved chin. He'd washed the red out of his eyes with sleep or Visine and was wearing crisp jeans and a black, short-sleeved polo. With his hair brushed back, he was indistinguishable from the thousands of other doctors, lawyers, and accountants who were living large.

"You remember that case we had last spring, the one

where the stockbroker husband made a career move to peddling dope and the wife called us and turned him in after she caught him cheating on her?"

"Yeah. Thomas and Jill Rice. He went away and the wife got an emergency divorce."

"And," Colby said, laughing and shaking his head, "the wife called the office a few weeks ago and I took the call. Said how much she appreciated that we got rid of her husband for her. Then she says that she got his Lexus in the divorce settlement and did I know anyone at the Bureau who'd be interested in it, that it was her way of showing her gratitude. I told her I'd be interested but I couldn't afford it. So she says, 'you don't know my price.'"

"She make you a good deal?"

"A helluva deal. Says she doesn't care about the money. She just wants her ex to know that she sold his car to an FBI agent for next to nothing."

"Love is a beautiful thing."

"It's better looking than you think. I go over to her house to pick up the car and she says her ex was so pissed off that I was buying the car that she's decided to do the same thing with her house, really make the poor bastard suffer. Says she's leaving town and wants that to be her going-away present to him. So I figure, what the hell. Even with what's she's asking, it'll stretch me, but I figure I can flip it, sell it to someone else, and make a bundle. I just came from her house. It's a done deal."

"Sounds like you can't lose."

He brushed the soft leather seat with the palm of his hand. "Like you said. Love is a beautiful thing." He studied me, losing the grin. "You doing okay, Jack?"

"Yeah. Swell. I'm going to see a doctor at KU Hospital. He'll adjust my vertical and horizontal holds and I'll be good as new. How's it going with the Marcellus Pearson case?"

Colby shrugged, looked away. "The usual grind. Run the forensics, run the family, friends, and neighbors. Line up the known bad guys and listen to their bullshit alibis. Hope somebody snitches so we can all declare victory and go home."

Colby had told me more than once that he thought Ben Yates was a tightass and that Troy was so straight you could stick him through a keyhole. Ammara would struggle with breaking the rules. Colby would look for the chance. I decided to push him, make him decide whether to talk to me about the case.

"Did we pick up Marcellus's mother?"

"Yeah."

"Get anything from her?"

"Just a lot of crying about her baby."

"Who's Troy looking at? Javy Ordonez? Bodie Grant? Is he still obsessing about a leak from our squad?"

Colby put his hands on the steering wheel, sliding them slowly around its circumference and looking at the instrument panel like it was the first time he'd seen it. His arms tensed, as if he'd rather be fighting the wheel around a hairpin curve than answer my questions. A horn blared behind us, making both of us jump. Colby glanced in his rearview mirror, a smile creasing his face. I turned around to see Wendy waving from her car. Colby waved back, opening his door. I reached for his arm. He pulled away.

"Look, Jack. I can't talk about it."

"Why not?"

"Orders. Ben Yates put the lid on it. Troy has him shitting in his pants that there might be a leak, that someone at the Bureau might be involved."

"I'm not exactly an outsider."

"You are now. People think you cracked up. No one expects you to come back."

"Do I look crazy to you?"

My words came out in a staccato rhythm, tripping over another round of tremors.

"Face it, Jack. You're not right. Stay out of the case before you make things worse for everyone."

Chapter Eighteen

I hadn't told Wendy that I'd invited Kate to join us for dinner because I didn't know how. Though Wendy accepted that our marriage was over, she was loyal to her mother and protective enough of me that she'd welcome a new person in my life with the same open arms she would extend to a carrier of the avian flu.

Joy had told Wendy that I was having an affair with Kate well before we separated. Wendy confronted me and I told her it wasn't so, explaining that ours was strictly a professional relationship. Wendy pushed harder, educating me about emotional affairs that stopped short of sexual intimacy but were equally destructive of marriages.

I had more trouble denying that because I fit the profile, remembering again how I'd reacted to Kate when I first saw her in the courtroom and how the word *intimate* so accurately described the lunches, conversations, and thoughts we'd shared since then. I fell back on a strict interpretation of my marital vows, telling Wendy that whatever our marriage was, it was still a marriage. When Joy finally left me, I realized how weak my defense had been. Joy was the one who'd been honest and courageous enough to walk away.

Watching Wendy and Colby embrace on the sidewalk, I knew I had to tell her that Kate was joining us. She wouldn't need to read my micro expressions to know that I was lying if I told her that Kate's presence was a coincidence.

"Honey, can I talk to you for a minute before we go inside?" She looked at me, then at Colby, raising her eyebrows. "Alone. It will only take a minute."

Colby nodded and went inside.

"What's up, Dad?"

"I'm really glad we're having dinner together."

"Me too, but I don't think you have to keep that a secret from Colby."

My mouth felt dry and my gut started to quiver. Wendy hadn't seen me shake. I didn't want to frighten her, but I couldn't shut the tremors down.

"Listen, I should have told you sooner," I began, my voice turning to gargles, my chest, shoulders, and arms wobbling.

"Dad, what's the matter? Is this what Colby was talking about?"

She hugged me, easy at first, then fiercely as if she were doing battle with my demons. The shaking passed and she let go.

"It's okay, really. I've got an appointment with a specialist at KU Hospital."

"When?"

She made it a demand, not a question.

"Couple of months. That's as soon as they could get me in unless they get a cancellation."

"Well, that is bullshit!"

"Bullshit it may be, but it's all they were serving."

"Thanks for telling me. I'm going with you to see the doctor."

"You don't have to do that, honey."

"Yes, I do. You stood by me all these years when I stepped in one bucket after another. You may not need me to go to the doctor with you, but I need me to go with you."

I couldn't help but smile. There comes a time in the lives of parents and children when their roles reverse, when the child becomes the parent. We had a long way to go before that happened. For now, we would take care of one another.

"I'd like that. But that's not what I wanted to talk about."

She folded her arms, took a step back, her mouth tight. "Is it about you and Mom?"

I shook my head. "No. Relax. It's nothing so dramatic. I invited a friend of mine to join us for dinner. I should have told you sooner but it was kind of last minute. I just didn't want you to be surprised."

She brightened, smiling and grabbing my wrists. "That's okay. Who is it?"

The door to the restaurant opened. A familiar voice said, "There you are. I've been waiting inside. I was afraid I was at the wrong place at the wrong time."

Kate stood five feet away. Colby was a step behind, looking over her shoulder. The bell had rung and I couldn't stop the chime. I held Wendy's arm, not certain whether she'd attack, retreat, or fall down.

"Sweetheart, say hello to Kate Scranton," I said.

Wendy stared at Kate, then at me, her mouth changing shapes as she searched for the words she wanted to use. Her eyes filled. She blinked, turning her head away from Kate, looking at me with wide and pained eyes.

"What world are you living in, Dad? How could you do this to Mom and me?"

Before I could answer, she was gone, speed walking to her car without looking back. Colby followed, stopping long enough to ask what had happened.

"What the hell was that about?" he asked.

"I invited Kate Scranton to dinner without telling Wendy in advance."

"So?"

"So, Wendy's mother told her that Kate and I are having an affair."

Colby looked at Kate. "Her? I just met her inside. No wonder she was cross-examining me. You'd have thought she was the mother of the bride, not the stepmother."

His multiple wedding references threw me. Was it possible that in one sentence he had said not only were he and Wendy getting married but that he believed that Kate and I were also getting married? If so, I had the answer to Wendy's question. I was living in the Twilight Zone.

"And," Colby continued, "somehow you thought it would be a good idea to make an ambush introduction of your girlfriend to your daughter before your divorce is final? Man, your brain must be shaking worse than your body. Like I said, you're not right. Stay out of our case and stay away from Wendy."

Colby thumped my chest with his index finger to make the point. On another day, I might have grabbed his hand and broken his finger. Instead, I watched both of them leave, not moving until I felt Kate alongside me.

"When I was a kid," I said, "my buddies and I were convinced that we could cause a train wreck by leaving a penny on the rail, like that was enough to make the whole train jump the tracks. We were so certain it would work we didn't have the nerve to try. Now I know what it feels like to cause a train wreck."

Kate put her hand on my shoulder. "It's not that bad."

"You're right. A real train wreck would have been better."

"C'mon. You made a mistake. You should have told her that you had invited me, but you didn't. If I was her, I'd be angry, too. Wendy'll calm down and when she does, you'll apologize."

"She'll never believe we weren't having an affair."

"Maybe not. She'll have to reconcile herself to the past, whatever she believes about it. Then, she'll have to get used to the future."

"You think that will be any easier?"

"Depends on how she feels about us having an affair," she said, kissing me softly.

Her kiss was filled with promise. I made her one of my own.

"By the way," I said, "Colby says that you were you cross-examining him like the stepmother of the bride. What was that all about?"

Kate gave me a sly smile. "Well, I didn't think he'd talk to me if he saw me only as a jury consultant, which is how I assumed you would introduce me. I had to put him at ease as quickly as I could. I knew he wouldn't discuss the murders, but I thought I'd be on safe ground talking about buying a house."

"And?"

"And I recognized him from your description and introduced myself. I told him I was a friend of yours, that you had invited me to join the three of you for dinner, and that Wendy had mentioned to you that he was considering buying a house out here. He couldn't wait to tell me about the woman who had turned in her husband and how she was making him such a good deal."

"That's what he told me. He thought the whole story was very funny."

"Really. For such a funny story, he's a pretty worried secret agent."

"Undercover agent."

"Undercover agents are all about secrets. I caught a flash of his hidden face in between his grins. I don't know if it's buying this house, but he's losing sleep over something."

Chapter Nineteen

Kate wanted to try the wok-roasted shrimp and scallops. I wanted to chase after Wendy, apologize, explain, and warn her again about Colby.

"What's your purpose?" she asked me.

I crimped a scallop between my chopsticks. "She's my daughter. I've got to protect her. Or haven't you been listening?"

"How do you think that would work out?" Kate asked.

"She's upset, but I can calm her down and get through to her."

"Doubtful. When someone is that angry, they can't hear much of anything, especially an apology. Try combining a premature apology with a warning that she should run away from the man she loves and you violate one of life's basic rules."

"What's that?"

"When you're in a hole, quit digging," Kate answered.

"How certain are you that Colby is worried about this house?"

"Pretty certain. Like I've told you, context is everything.

He only displayed the micro expressions when he talked about the house."

"What did the expressions look like?" I asked.

"His upper eyelids were raised and his lower eyelids were tense. His eyebrows were slightly raised and bunched together. We call it a fear eyebrow."

"He told me that the house was a stretch for him even at the price he was paying, but he figured he could flip it to another buyer and make money on the deal if it turned out that he couldn't afford it. Maybe that's why he was so nervous."

"Now you're the one defending him," Kate said. "Nervous, worried, and afraid are variations on a theme, a matter of intensity. If he was truly afraid, his jaw would have dropped open and he would have stretched his lips horizontally back toward his ears. He was past nervous, definitely worried, and not far from being really afraid."

"How could he keep that much emotion under wraps?"

Kate shrugged. "He's used to hiding his true self. That's what an undercover agent does. It's hard to know from a single micro expression how intense the emotion is. He might be more afraid than I thought."

"I'll check it out in the morning."

"How?"

I sat back in my chair. "I'll check the county's records on the ownership and appraisal of the house, then I'll talk to the wife. The husband is doing his time at the federal penitentiary in Leavenworth. I'll drive up and see him. Shake the bushes, see what comes crawling out."

"At your peril."

"I know. Colby will find out what I'm doing, tell Wendy, and my hole will keep getting deeper."

"You could walk away."

"You know I can't."

"I do."

"Am I wrong?"

"To love your daughter? To want to protect her from a man that may have crossed to the dark side? No one would argue with that," Kate said.

"But . . ."

"But, sometimes you have to get out of the way. The hard part is knowing when."

"I'll get out of the way when I know that she's safe."

"That's not wrong but it's likely to be tricky, maybe dangerous. Because of his undercover work, Colby is used to living with violence and betrayal. Someone like that gets into a tough spot, they're capable of doing almost anything. I saw a piece of him that he keeps hidden and it frightens me."

"Then I'm not wrong."

"No, you aren't."

The wok-roasted shrimp and scallops were delicious. I did a better job of saying good night in the parking lot than I did at IHOP.

"Don't forget that your class on micro expressions starts Friday night. You have the potential to be a very good student," Kate said, slipping out of my arms. "I've got to go home and finish preparing for a client presentation in the morning."

"This is Wednesday. What am I supposed to do until then?"

"Get a dog," she said.

I knew where to find one. That is, if Marcellus Pearson's dog hadn't run away in the nearly forty-eight hours since her owner had been murdered. The last trace of sunlight was being chased out of the western sky when I headed back to Quindaro to look for Ruby. I hoped she was as good at surviving on the streets as she was at retrieving twenty-dollar bills.

I doubted that any FBI agents would still be going door-to-door, but if they were, I'd explain that I was looking for the dog, not wanting to leave her on her own or at the mercy of animal control. It was a thin story but I practiced saying it with a straight face and a mild case of the shakes.

Half a dozen young black men were clustered in the driveway of a house on the corner of Marcellus's block, two of them playing basketball, battling for position beneath a hoop without a net, the others smoking and joking. The game of one-on-one stopped when I drove by and parked in front of Marcellus's house.

One of the players held the ball on his hip, staring at me as I got out of my car. He was wearing shorts and was stripped to the waist, his ripped torso and shaved head glistening beneath the streetlight at the edge of the driveway. Someone snatched a towel from the ground, trading it to him for the ball. The player wiped the sweat off his body and handed the towel to another member of the group without taking his eyes off me. Nature abhors a vacuum, and the one left by Marcellus's death was no exception.

We sized each other up from a distance, wordlessly agreeing that we were neither afraid nor impressed, content to stay out of the other's business for now. If I came closer, he'd feel compelled to test me, something I didn't need.

I gave him a slight nod, letting him know that I got it, that I was on his turf and that he was graciously allowing me to be there. He shot the ball at the other player, hitting him in the gut, picking up their game again.

The crime scene tape that had been stretched across the front porch of Marcellus's house was gone, only a few remnants clinging to the corner posts, the inside and outside of the house wrapped in shadows. I wondered whether Marcellus had owned the house. If someone else owned it, they might wash the blood off the floor and walls and rent it to someone who didn't know or care what had gone down inside.

If that didn't happen, Quindaro would eventually claim it. Young kids would break in to see where the bodies had fallen. Drug dealers and gangbangers would turn it into a free-trade zone to be shared with rats. The weeds would grow tall, the roof would leak, the concrete would crack, and the foundation would sag. The city would place liens on it for unpaid taxes, fine the unknown and absent owner for code violations, and let the property deteriorate, telling whoever complained that the city didn't have the money to fix it up or tear it down. The people who'd lived there had died in an instant. The house would take longer.

I found the light switch in the front room. The warped hardwood floor had purpled where blood had been left to soak into the planks. Except for the bodies that had been removed, it was otherwise just as I had seen it two nights ago.

I walked through the house again, stopping in the kitchen, at the top of the stairs, and in the bedrooms, imagining Keyshon eating his breakfast, taking a bath, and sleeping as his mother checked on him one last time before she went to bed. The clothes still hung in the closet where I'd found him clutched in his mother's arms, more dried blood the only testimony to what had happened in that small, dim space. His mother was dead. His father was dead. It was as if he'd never lived. There was no one to remember him.

That's why I was there. To make certain someone did.

Chapter Twenty

The dog wasn't in the house or in the backyard. I stood beneath the tree where Ruby had found the money, the ground now hard and rutted, turning in a slow circumference to get a sense of who and what could have been seen that night. The houses on either side were dark.

LaDonna Simpson, elderly and deaf, had probably gone to bed. Wayne Miller was still in jail, his girlfriend Tarla Hicks most likely out on the town. A light was on in the back of Latrell Kelly's house, though I didn't see anyone moving through the half-open drapes.

Using the tree as twelve o'clock, Latrell's house was at eleven o'clock. The figure I'd seen, or thought I'd seen, running away was headed on a bearing at one o'clock, a path that would have taken him between the two houses to the north of Latrell's. The backyards of those houses weren't fenced.

I did a quick inventory. Neither Marcellus's nor Wayne Miller's backyards were enclosed. LaDonna Simpson's and Latrell Kelly's were. The man had run away from the scene and away from the fences, choosing the path of least resistance.

I walked the route I assumed the man would have taken, rousing dogs that patrolled their patches of turf from behind chain link or at the end of sturdy ropes. Most of them were big and aggressive—Dobermans, rottweilers, or a mix. None of them were friendly. I thought back to Monday night, not recalling the sound of barking, realizing that the helicopter would have drowned out the dogs' noise. Whoever had been running away had cut his escape quite close. If I hadn't wandered into Marcellus's backyard, the helicopter's searchlight may have found him.

I stopped on the sidewalk in front of Latrell's house. The dogs had quieted, the low hum of late-season cicadas filling the void. A third of the moon hung in the sky, cool light on a cool night, the seasons shifting from summer to fall, an easy passage marked by hard dying.

The house next door to his would have blocked Latrell's view to the north, making it impossible for him to have seen the fleeing man. Though he had told Ammara Iverson that he was asleep at the time the murders were committed, he would have been awakened by the sirens, as was everyone else in the neighborhood. Someone should have seen the man. I hoped that the follow-up canvassing had produced a witness that made him real.

My hope triggered another memory, one of omission, the kind that made me instinctively distrust every eyewitness I'd ever interrogated. I was looking for evidence of someone who may have committed the murders or been a witness to them; someone who might have seen Oleta Phillips standing beneath the tree, her hands bunched around bundles of twenty-dollar bills; someone who may have killed her for what she'd seen, not for the money she held. There was possibly no one more important to the investigation of these crimes and yet I hadn't breathed a word of his possible existence to my squad.

I knew all the excuses and explanations. People get so excited or traumatized by a crime that they often forget details, not knowing what they know until they have time for reflection or until a skilled interrogator walks them through the moment frame by frame. Even then, such recovered memories are often tainted by time, bias, or the witnesses' own suggestibility.

I was one of those people the night of the murders, not only a witness to the mysterious fleeing man but a participant in my own sideline drama of shakes, shudders, and convulsions. My memory could be real or it could be pure confabulation. It meant nothing by itself, though it could lead to everything.

Not all leads are created equal. They are appraised based on the credibility of the source. At the moment, I had less credibility than a politician swearing he did not have sex with that woman. The surest way to make certain my lead about the fleeing man was ignored was to tell my squad what I thought I might have seen.

I started to walk back to my car when I heard a muffled, high-pitched bark, more like a burst of rapid-fire yaps. The front door to Latrell's house was open, a splash of light marking Ruby's swift flight down the front steps to where I stood. She planted her front paws on my leg, her tail wagging fast enough to fall off, her joy at seeing me expressed in the puddle she deposited at my feet.

I scratched behind her ears and hoisted her to eye level. She rewarded me with a lick on my cheek and a playful swipe at my nose. I put her down and she immediately rolled on her back, legs spread so I could rub her belly.

"She act like she's your dog."

I'd been so preoccupied with the dog and Latrell had been so quiet in his approach that I didn't realize he was there until he spoke. He was a half a head shorter than me, round-shouldered, and soft, just as he'd appeared on TV.

Despite his innocuous looks and the clean pass Ammara had given him, I knew better than to dismiss him as a suspect. Most murder victims know their killer. Neighbors always qualify. He lived close enough to Marcellus to have shot everyone and gone home before Ammara rang his doorbell. If anything, his easy innocence should give me pause. I'd learned that lesson with Kevin's killer.

"We met the other night. I found her hiding under Marcellus Pearson's bed."

"You a cop?"

"Jack Davis. FBI."

"Lemme see some ID."

"I'm not here on official business."

"You're standing out here in front of my house tellin' me you're FBI. Show me some ID."

He was asking, polite, not demanding, more curious than defensive. I showed him my driver's license.

He handed it back to me. "That's not an FBI ID."

"I'm taking some time off."

"They take your ID when you go on vacation?"

Same tone. Just trying to understand. No offense intended or taken. I started to shake, so I bent down to pet the dog, hoping to break the rhythm or distract Latrell's attention. Neither worked.

"Why you shaking?"

I stood, letting the spasm pass, taking a breath. "I don't know."

"That why you don't have your FBI ID anymore?"

I tried half a smile. "Yeah. Hard to catch the bad guys when I shake."

"But you say you were here the other night?"

I wasn't certain how I'd lost control of the situation, letting him question me, but I didn't mind. He'd already been interviewed, maybe more than once. He'd want to ask his own questions before he'd consider answering any of mine.

"I was."

"Hey, were you the guy in the backyard?"

I nodded.

"At first, I thought you musta been the one that did it, the way the cops surrounded you. Then I saw how one of them helped you and the rest of them just stood there. Didn't look like they was arresting you or nothing."

"You saw all that?"

"Watched from my kitchen, out the back window. One of them walked you out like there was something wrong with you. All them dead bodies make you start shaking?"

I shook my head and smiled again. "Nope. But that's when the people I work with caught me shaking."

Latrell laughed. "I guess that's how come you on vacation and don't have any FBI ID."

"You're right about that."

"So what you doing outside my house?"

"I was looking for this dog, for Ruby. I got worried that she didn't have anyone to take care of her. Looks like I was wrong."

"Couldn't leave her on the street. Them Dobermans and rottweilers eat her for breakfast if they get half a chance."

"Well, you did the right thing, taking her in."

He didn't say anything for a minute, looking at me, then at the dog.

"You want her?"

I did. Not only because Kate had told me to get a dog, at least until Friday, and not because I was living alone in a house too big and empty for one person. I pictured Keyshon playing with the dog. Then I imagined Kevin playing with a dog we never had. Ruby linked those images, softened them for me. Still, I couldn't take the dog from Latrell.

"She's yours. You're taking care of her."

"Only 'cause no one else would. I keep a neat house. That is not a neat dog. Wasn't raised right. Not her fault. You take her."

He was wearing shorts and a T-shirt, both looking like they'd just been pressed. I noticed his yard for the first time. Even in the dark, I could see that it was neatly mowed, the grass next to the sidewalk and steps cleanly edged. A row of close-cropped shrubs ran beneath the front windows, concrete flowerpots filled and blooming atop the stairs leading to his door.

"You keep a nice-looking place. You own or rent?"

Latrell stood a couple of inches taller. "It's mine."

"Good for you. How long have you owned it?"

"A while."

"You're pretty young to have been able to buy a house."

"My momma left me some money."

I studied his empty face. If there were another story hidden beneath it, someone else would have to dig it up.

"Any idea who owns Marcellus's house?"

He shook his head. "Not my business."

Ruby jumped up, bracing herself against my leg again.

"You're sure you don't want to keep her?" I asked him.

"I didn't want nothing to happen to her, but I can't have a dog messing up my house. You don't take her, I got to do something with her."

"Okay. If you're sure."

"Sure enough I'll let you buy the dog food I got for her. Wait here."

He went inside, returning a moment later with a bag of Science Diet and a dish with separate bowls for food and water.

"I don't have a leash," Latrell said, handing me the supplies.

"Thanks. Will this cover it?" I handed him two twenties. He folded the bills between his fingers.

"Close enough," he said with a grin. "You saving me money. That dog eats, too," he said, turning back toward his house.

I called to him. "You know, I'm sure you've been over this with other agents, but I'd like to ask you a few questions about the other night."

He stopped, looking back at me. "How come? They took your ID. What you got to do with it now?"

I shrugged. "Hard to stop being what I am."

He nodded, arms at his side, relaxed. "I got that. What you want to know?"

"I'll make it easy. Give me the short version. What you saw, what you heard."

"It's like I told them other agents. I was asleep until I heard the sirens. Then I come downstairs into the kitchen, looked out my back window. Everything was over by then, I guess. All I seen was you and then the rest of them come get you. That's all."

I rubbed my chin, thinking about what he said. This was how memories were shaped. The witness didn't see or doesn't remember. The cop prods the witness's memory with a suggestion that blossoms into a fact. If the witness is a suspect, the memories can become a trap.

"There may have been a couple of other people in the backyard or close by, maybe standing near that big tree where you saw me—a woman and a man. The man may have been running away just when I came out of Marcellus's back door."

"I didn't see anyone like that. I only saw you. And that was after."

"The man may have been the killer or he may have seen what happened. You sure you didn't see anybody running away?"

Latrell didn't hesitate, shaking his head. "Didn't see nobody running away. You ask the other people live around here?"

If Latrell were the killer, he would have jumped on the fleeing man, letting us chase a ghost, unless he thought I was trying to catch him with a lie about a witness that didn't exist. His unforced answer said he was either innocent or brilliant.

"I'm sure the other agents did. Somebody always sees something. You know a woman named Oleta Phillips?"

"I know who she is and I seen her around, but I don't know her to talk to her."

"You see her that night?"

He shook his head again. "Like I told you, I didn't see nobody besides you and the rest of the police and FBI. They already come talk to me. You can ask them."

"No need. That's what they told me before I went on leave. It's just that sometimes people remember things later on that they don't remember the first time they are asked. The mind is funny like that. Happens to me, too. You think of anything else, you call the FBI. Ask for Ammara Iverson."

I handed him one of my business cards, jotting down Ammara's name.

"I'll do that," he said. "You take care of that dog."

"Don't worry. Hey, you know, I saw you on television, on the news."

"Is that right?" Latrell asked, smiling.

"Yeah. You said something that really hit home with me."

"I did?"

"The reporter asked you for your reaction to the shootings and you said that's what happens when no one takes care of a little boy."

He tilted his head and narrowed his eyes. "What's that to you?"

"It's my whole life. I made that mistake with my son and I lost him."

He nodded, his face softening, his soft voice almost a whisper. "Then you know it's true," he said.

Chapter Twenty-one

Latrell watched the FBI agent drive away, glad to be shed of the dog. He felt responsible for having orphaned the mutt and meant it when he told the agent that he wanted to protect the dog from the bigger, stronger predators in the neighborhood. The dog, smaller and weaker, wasn't to blame for having been abandoned. Nonetheless, he didn't like cleaning up after the dog, which had left her messes all over his house. If the agent hadn't taken the dog, he would have gotten rid of her, one way or the other.

He wasn't certain what to make of the man who said he was FBI except he wasn't working because he shook too much except there he was on Latrell's street looking for that dog and oh, by the way, he says do you mind if I ask you some questions like did he see a woman out back of Marcellus's house and did he know Oleta Phillips. Only reason Latrell believed he was FBI was because of seeing him come out of Marcellus's back door that night and the way everyone treated him when he seized up.

The other agents hadn't asked him about a man running away or a woman. The woman was Oleta. He knew that but he didn't know who the man was, if there was a man. He wouldn't be tricked into remembering something, that was for sure.

The agent told him someone always sees something. Latrell didn't doubt that. Oleta had seen him. He went over everything from the time he stepped out of his house until the time he stepped back in, carrying Oleta over his shoulder. He was certain that no one else had seen him.

Yet the agent knew about the woman, asked him straight up did he know Oleta. Why would he do that? Then Latrell remembered the money she was carrying. He figured Marcellus had given it to her for her son being killed. It was blood money and he wanted no part of it. He took Oleta because she'd seen him. Didn't matter that she thanked him. What mattered was that she'd seen him. That, and when he looked at her, he saw his mother. Saw his mother even now just thinking about her. How many times, he wondered, do you have to kill someone before they stay dead?

The agent had found the money under the tree. That's how the agent must have found out about Oleta. He was smart not to have taken the money. That would have made sense to the FBI—someone killing Oleta for the money. Leaving it on the ground, that was the smart play. Maybe they found her fingerprints on the money. That's how come they knew it was her. He was smart not to have even touched it.

Then there was story the agent told him about losing his son. Latrell knew a good lie when he told one, knew how important it was to feel it when he told it because a person could see the feeling in him. No feeling and it was just words. He felt it when the agent talked about his son; he saw the cloud in the agent's eyes.

Why, he wondered, would the agent tell him about his son? Was it to make him feel sorry for the agent so FBI man could trick him? Was it because the agent knew about his mother and the men and Oleta and Jalise and everything else? The questions made his head spin, leaving him with only one certainty. This man who said he was an FBI agent, who came looking for a dog and who shook too much and asked too many questions, was dangerous.

Latrell went back inside and took off his shoes. He began in the kitchen, down on hands and knees, scrubbing the floor, countertops, and tables. Moving into the living room, he swept the hardwood floor, vacuumed the area rug, pulled out the sofa cushions, vacuumed them and the sofa, and wiped down the small bookcase filled with his alphabetized CD and DVD collections, double- and triple-checking that they were all in order.

The two bedrooms and bath upstairs were next, even though he hadn't allowed the dog on the second floor. He changed the sheets on his bed, turned the mattress, scoured the bathroom, and waxed the hardwood floors until his face reflected back at him. By three a.m., he had cleaned up after the dog for the last time.

Exhausted, he fell into bed. Latrell had planned to go to the cave tonight to make certain that everything was in order there as well, but he had to be at work in five hours and he was too tired. He'd go tomorrow night, probably sleep there in case any more FBI agents came knocking.

As he was falling asleep, he replayed his conversation with the agent. No doubt about it, the agent had suspected nothing. Latrell would have been able to tell. Still, it bothered him that they kept coming back to talk with him. Maybe they would leave him alone if he remembered something. Maybe the man the agent said had been seen running away. But not the woman. Definitely not the woman.

Chapter Twenty-two

Joy's car was parked in front of my house when Ruby and I got home. It was a Hyundai Sonata. We were basic-transportation people, not flashy-car people. There was a crease in the front fender from a too-close encounter she'd had with the center post in the garage. It had prompted one of the last fights we had had about her drinking before she left. "You don't have to be a drunk to hit the garage," she had shouted at me. "No, but it makes it a lot easier," I had shouted back. By the end, we were shouting people, not talking people.

She still had a key to the house. I hadn't changed the locks. It wore me out to see her car there.

Ruby flew through the door from the garage into the house like she knew she was home, finding Joy in the kitchen before I did.

"Well, who are you?" I heard Joy ask. "Aren't you the gorgeous dog?"

I found them on the floor, Joy cross-legged, Ruby lapping at her face.

"It didn't take you long to replace me, did it?" she said

with a laugh, cuffing Ruby, who instantly rolled over on her back and offered up her belly.

Joy stood, brushing the wrinkles from her jeans. The lines in her face seemed to have softened and the gloom in her eyes was gone, a flicker of life taking its place. I hadn't seen her since we'd separated, all of our communications passing through our lawyers or our daughter. I wasn't certain, but her hair looked shorter, shaped differently, and colored a shade lighter.

"The dog and I are just friends," I said. "You look different—in a good way."

She smiled at my compliment. "Thank you, I think."

We looked at each other, not talking, the dog racing in and out of each room, back to the kitchen, doing circles around us.

"So," she said.

"So."

"Thanks for not changing the locks."

"Wasn't necessary. What's the occasion? Something you need to pick up?"

Joy swept her hair behind her ears with both hands, turning her head to the side, then releasing her hair. It was a gesture she'd used as long as I'd known her, a prelude to an unpleasant conversation.

"Wendy called. She's pretty upset."

I let out a long breath, the reason for Joy's visit now clear. "I know. I really blew it, inviting Kate to dinner without giving Wendy any advance warning."

Joy's mouth opened wide, her eyebrows rising off the charts. "Tell me you're kidding? You didn't really do that."

It was my turn to be surprised. "I wish I was. I thought that's why you were here, to tell me what a lousy father I am."

She chewed her lower lip, arms crossed over her chest.

"Nothing is easy with you, Jack. Wendy didn't say a word about Kate. That's not why she called."

I felt the fool again, heat rising in my neck. "Then what?"

The shaking started as the words left my mouth. I bent over, cursing between clenched teeth, waiting for the contraction to release me. Joy kept her distance, turning away until I could stand. When she looked at me again, her eyes were wet.

"That," she said.

"It will pass."

"From the looks of it, like a kidney stone."

I caught my breath and laughed, not able to remember the last time she'd told a joke. "I see that you've been practicing your stand-up routine."

"Actually, I've been practicing my sobriety routine. Fifty days as of today. My AA counselor gave me a gold star."

The last time she'd tried AA, she stayed sober for a record 148 days, falling off the wagon on Kevin's birthday. That was three years ago. The binge that followed wiped out that record with a vengeance. I was stunned but cautious, having seen her go down this road before.

"That's great. One day at a time, right?"

"First thing they teach you."

"Well, good for you. Keep it up."

She stuck her hands in her jeans pockets. "I intend to. How long have you been like this?"

"A couple of months, but I'm not like this all the time. Sometimes, it's nothing more than a shiver and I can go long stretches without anything happening."

"Long stretches meaning like days or hours?"

I hesitated a moment, not wanting to concede. "Hours."

"What are we going to do about you?"

"You don't have to do anything. I've got an appointment

at KU Hospital. They'll give me a pill or a shot or something and I'll be as good as new."

"In November. Wendy told me. I'm certain she wasn't pleased that you invited Kate to dinner, but all she could talk about was that you needed to see a doctor right away and what were she and I going to do about it. Those people at KU will give you the runaround, the once-over, and tell you to take it easy after making you wait two months for the privilege."

Joy had tried every doctor and medical center in every city we'd lived in for every malady she'd had or thought she'd had. She didn't like any of them because she didn't like what they told her: quit drinking. KU Hospital was no exception, though I couldn't remember who she'd seen there or why. On the plus side, she knew practically every doctor in town.

"They've got a good movement disorder clinic. I'm on the cancellation list. I'll probably get in to see someone sooner than two months."

"No, you won't. I checked. You are number sixty-three on the waiting list. A lot of people have to die if you are going to get in before November."

"What do you mean you checked?" I asked, my voice rising with my irritation.

"Calm down, Jack. Wendy was so upset. I had to do something. I called the clinic and told them I was your wife, which I still am, legally, that is."

I looked at my watch. It was nine-thirty, three hours since I'd seen Wendy.

"You're telling me the clinic is open at night?"

"As a matter of fact, it isn't. But I got a hold of the chief neurology resident and browbeat him into having the appointment secretary call me back. She was very nice about the whole thing, but said there was nothing she could do about your appointment. Even said you were lucky to have a wife like me. I spared her the details."

"You are unbelievable!" My annoyance was giving way to grudging admiration.

"I didn't use to think so. Now, I'm willing to consider the possibility."

Her purse was on the kitchen counter. She opened it and handed me a slip of paper.

"What's this?"

"Your schedule. I made an appointment for you to see Dr. Carl Winters. He's the best neurologist in town according to his wife, who's in my AA group. You'll see him on Monday morning at ten. He's in the St. Luke's Medical Building. He wants you to have an MRI of your entire spine, with and without contrast media, and an MRI of your brain before he sees you. You'll get the MRIs done by the radiology group he uses. They've got offices all over town. There's one in Overland Park and one on the Plaza next to the library. Take your pick, but you've got to let them know in the morning. They are working you in as a favor to Dr. Winters, so don't get pissy if you have to wait a few minutes. Wendy will go with you on Monday but she and I decided that you can get the films done by yourself."

I didn't know what to say. I had misjudged both Wendy and Joy. That was nothing to be proud of. I'd spent the last two months feeling isolated and alone when I could have avoided both.

I took another deep breath. "Thank you."

Joy smiled, picking up the dog. "You're welcome. Where'd you get this cute little cockapoo?"

"Cocka what?"

"You bought a dog and you don't even know what breed she is? Honestly, how do you get through the day? She's a cockapoo—half cocker spaniel and half poodle. What did you think she was?"

"A mutt that was orphaned after everyone she lived with was murdered Monday night."

She set Ruby on the floor. The dog sat at her feet.

"Oh, my. That was your case, wasn't it?"

"The operative word is *was*. I was at the scene when Troy Clark caught me in one of my shakedowns. He went to Ben Yates before I had a chance to explain to Yates that I wasn't crazy or dying and could still do my job while I got this shaking thing figured out. The next thing I know, Yates put me on medical leave and gave my squad to Troy."

She pushed her lips out in a pout. "Quit acting like Troy tattled on you. He probably told you to see a doctor and you refused. Am I right?"

I shrugged. "More or less."

"Well then, you didn't leave him any choice. So how did you end up with the dog?"

"I found her hiding under a bed in the house where the murders took place. I went back there tonight looking for her."

"Men," she said with a wry grin, "are incapable of being alone."

"Living alone wasn't my choice."

The familiar weariness rippled across her face. "You were living alone for years without knowing it, Jack. We both were. I just made it official."

The old battle lines reappeared. The veins in her neck popped to the surface. The muscles in my shoulders tightened and my gut began to quiver.

"I'm sorry. I shouldn't have said that," I told her.

"Well, at least you're sorry. That's something."

"Thanks again for going to all the trouble with the doctor appointments."

Joy tucked her purse under her arm. "I did it for Wendy. As long as we have a daughter, we're still a family. But eventually you'll have to learn to take care of yourself. I won't be around forever to look after you."

The dog and I followed her to the front door. Ruby whimpered until Joy bent low, cupping the dog's face in her hands.

"You want to know something funny?" she asked, nuzzling the dog.

"Sure."

"One of the people in my AA group had one of these dogs. She was moving to an apartment that didn't allow pets and asked me if I wanted hers. I don't know what made me say yes, but I did. Her name is Roxy. She's white with a dirty-blond streak down her back, not apricot like Ruby. Otherwise, they could be sisters. We never had a dog while we were together. What are the odds we'd each end up with a dog, let alone the same breed?"

"I wouldn't bet on us."

"Then you'd lose," she said, giving Ruby a final pat on the head.

She was halfway down the walk when she turned around. I was still holding the door open, watching her go.

"Do one thing for me," she said.

"Sure. What's that?"

"Whatever happens with you and Kate, don't force Wendy to be part of it."

It wasn't a cheap shot, but I felt it below the belt. I retreated to the kitchen, Ruby at my side. The message light was flashing on the telephone. I pushed the button and listened as my lawyer told me that the final hearing on our divorce was scheduled for a week from today.

"At least I was right about one thing," I said to the dog. "I wouldn't bet on us."

Chapter Twenty-three

Ruby slept alongside my futon, waking me while it was still dark. I fumbled with the light, assuming she wanted to go out. I was wrong. She'd already gone. Inside. A lot. I cleaned up after her, wondering if I'd made a bad decision to take in a dog that wasn't housebroken and that I'd have to leave alone most of the day.

I played back the local newscasts I had recorded and scanned the newspaper for additional information on the investigation into the drug house murders. It was all a rehash of the first reports. The Bureau had cut off the flow of information, reducing its public comments to the standard blather about an ongoing investigation and appeals for anyone with knowledge of the crimes to call the TIPS hotline.

Sifting through the mail, I saw a flier for a place called Pete & Mac's, which described itself as a pet resort that offered day care for dogs. They had a facility on Eighty-seventh Street in Lenexa that opened at seven. By seven-fifteen, I'd signed Ruby up for a week of day care and obedience training, grooming included. She went with her pet attendant, tail wagging, without a backward glance at me, proving that she was charmingly indiscriminate with her affections.

One of the staff helped load my car with a kennel for Ruby to sleep in and enough food, treats, and toys to last a lifetime. I left, realizing that my dog now had a higher standard of living than I did.

I stopped at a restaurant that offered free Wi-Fi access. Using my laptop, I logged on to the website for the County Treasurer's office and searched for records of property owned by Jill Rice, Thomas Rice, or both. It only took a few keystrokes to find the records on the house Colby Hudson was buying.

The house was titled to Jill Rice. Last year, the county appraised it at $850,000. The property taxes were $12,427. I couldn't figure out how Colby could afford the taxes, let alone the purchase price, no matter how much Jill Rice discounted it for the pleasure of pissing off her ex-husband.

There was no mortgage on the house. The only lien was in Thomas Rice's name. While the details of the lien were not explained, there was a link to the Register of Deeds office. I clicked on the link and a page appeared explaining that Mr. Rice's lien was pursuant to a Property Settlement Agreement, the terms of which could be found at yet another link. I followed the electronic trail, landing at the website of the Clerk of the District Court, where I was able to find and read the agreement. I was pleased at how easy it was to find until I realized that the terms of my own divorce would join the public record in less than a week's time.

Thomas Rice had a lien for half the net proceeds from the sale of the house. It was the same deal that Joy and I had made. The legalese was painfully familiar. The sale had to be conducted in a commercially reasonable manner, including advance notice to Thomas Rice, and the house had to be sold for fair market value.

Colby wasn't just buying a house. He was buying a lawsuit if the price was too far below market. It was possible that he didn't know the terms of the Rices' agreement. I could tell him and deal with the fallout from explaining how I knew. Or, I could keep my mouth shut until I knew just how bad a deal he was making. That was the right call, perhaps the only one I had made so far.

Since the agreement required that Thomas Rice be given notice of the sale before it occurred, I decided to talk with him before I spoke with his ex-wife. He would have less reason to hold back information and he might be more willing to keep our conversation private.

I looked at my watch. It was eight-thirty. I could be in Leavenworth, Kansas, in less than an hour. I knew from past trips that visiting hours were from eight in the morning to three in the afternoon every day except Wednesday and Thursday. Inmates were given twenty-four visitor points per month. Each hour of visits cost one point. Each inmate had an approved visitor list. If you weren't on it, it didn't matter what day of the week it was or how many points the inmate had left for that month.

Today was Thursday. Even if I waited until tomorrow, I still wouldn't be on Rice's visitor list and I had no idea if he would be willing to use any of his points to talk with me. Normally, I wouldn't care about any of that since the visitor rules didn't apply to law-enforcement personnel. But the visitation rules did apply to me because, without my FBI credentials, I was one of the unwashed, unknown, and unwanted.

My cell phone rang as I was considering how long it would take me to get arrested, convicted, and sentenced to Leavenworth just so I could have a conversation with Thomas Rice. A television show had already tested that scheme, one brother getting himself sent inside to break out his innocent brother before they were both killed. I doubted that my version would do well enough in the ratings to last through sweeps week.

"Nice call on the cash," Ammara Iverson said.

"You found Oleta Phillips's fingerprints?"

"On a couple of the bills so far, a thumb and index finger. It will take a while to check all of the money. Three thousand dollars in twenties is a lot of twenties."

"A hundred and fifty, to be exact," I said. "Who had her prints?"

"KCKPD. She'd been picked up a few times for soliciting prostitution plus she had a couple of misdemeanor possession busts."

"What about the videotapes? Will Troy let Grisnik have a look?"

"He said we should do our own analysis first. Ben Yates is going to ask the KCK chief for a set of photographs for comparison."

"Grisnik won't like that. I get the impression he's trying to keep this quiet."

"Troy doesn't care what Grisnik likes. He's not taking a chance on anybody. If it will make Grisnik feel any better, tell him that I reviewed the tapes. I didn't see anybody who looked like a cop."

"I'm sure that will be a great comfort to him, since everyone knows that all cops look alike, especially when they're out of uniform."

"You know what I mean," she said. "Cops carry themselves differently. Same as we do. Doesn't matter what we're wearing. That's what makes undercover so hard. You have to learn to be someone else."

She was right. I wanted to ask Ammara about the results of the neighborhood canvass, find out if anyone had reported seeing someone leaving the scene, but I didn't want it to be about me.

"Did any of the neighbors see Oleta that night?"

"If they did, they aren't saying. We went back to her brother. He said the last time he saw her was when Marcellus gave her the money. We haven't found anyone who admits seeing her after that. That was about twelve hours before the murders."

"Did the neighbors see anyone else, maybe someone hanging around after the murders like an arsonist that likes to watch the fire?"

"I've got to tell you, Jack. You're the only one anybody saw. LaDonna Simpson, Latrell Kelly, a few others. They all saw what happened to you in the backyard, but that's all they saw."

"I'm glad I put on such a good show for them. Did you take another look at Latrell Kelly?"

"Yeah, and there's nothing to see. None of the neighbors have anything bad to say about him. He even brings his charcoal cooker whenever they have a block party."

"Say that again."

"I said they have block parties during the summer. He cooks the hot dogs. You think that makes him a suspect?"

If I told her yes and explained why, she'd agree that I was too close to this case to be of any use. "Remember what they taught you at Quantico," I said. "Keep an open mind until the statute of limitations expires."

"I'll do that. In the meantime, things have gotten real tight around here since you left. Troy is having all of us take polygraphs to make certain no one leaked anything about the surveillance camera inside the house. They're bringing in someone from D.C. to run the tests. You'll probably have to take one, too."

"When?"

"Tomorrow. Troy set them up on the hour. He's going first at eight o'clock. I'm on for nine, Colby is at ten; Jim and

Lani are at eleven and twelve. I'm surprised he hasn't called you yet."

"Maybe he wants to rule everyone else in or out before he gives me a turn."

"Why would he do that?"

"Who knows? Maybe he thinks it couldn't have been me since it was my show or maybe he thinks it had to be me because that would explain why I was shaking so badly. Either way, it would make sense for him to leave me for last."

"I hate taking a polygraph," she said.

"We have to take one every year just to make certain we're still good guys. I thought you'd be used to it by now."

"I don't know," she said, sighing. "Those guys always make me feel like I'm guilty of something even if I don't know what it is."

"That's what they get paid to do. Did you tell Marty Grisnik that you found Oleta's fingerprints on the money?"

"That's Troy's call. I just report the news. How about you? Grisnik tell you anything else I should know?"

"I haven't talked to him."

"It would be convenient if you did," she said.

"Yes, it would."

Ammara didn't know it, but she had just shown me how to break into the federal penitentiary. I didn't know if I could be convicted for trying. Like all criminals, I knew that it wouldn't matter unless I got caught.

Chapter Twenty-four

"You want me to take you where?" Marty Grisnik asked.

I was on my cell phone, still at the restaurant. "Leavenworth. The federal penitentiary."

"That good-looking Chevy of yours broke down?"

"Runs like a dream, but your big Crown Vic will make a much better impression on the warden."

"Why would I want to take you to Leavenworth?"

"To make a new friend."

"I don't like the friends I have. I don't need any new ones," Grisnik said.

"You might like this one."

"This friend of yours know anything about Oleta Phillips and her boy?"

"Doubtful."

"Then I'm not going."

"But he might know someone who does."

"Who is it and what do you think he knows?"

"I'll tell you on the drive over. And I've got something else for you. It turns out I do still have a friend at the Bureau. I'll park in the city lot behind the federal courthouse. You can pick me up on the corner of Seventh and Ann in half an hour."

"I'm going to quit taking your phone calls," Grisnik said.

"Won't help. I'll sleep on your doorstep, follow you to work, and wait outside your office."

"I may leave you in Leavenworth."

"I'll pack a toothbrush. There's one other thing."

I could hear Grisnik grinding his teeth over the phone. "What?"

"You still have that phony ID you loaned me when I served the fugitive warrant at Marcellus Pearson's house?"

"I've got it locked up in my desk drawer. I'd burn it except I'm afraid I'll be accused of destroying evidence."

"Good. Bring it with you."

"What for?"

"They won't let just anyone into that prison."

"The easiest way is to take I-29 North to Platte City, then pick up Highway 92 and take it straight into Leavenworth," I told Grisnik.

He'd hung his suit jacket in the backseat, rolled his sleeves, and put the air conditioning on high. He furrowed his eyes and set his jaw like he wanted to pimp-slap me.

"You don't think I know how to get to Leavenworth?"

"I'm sure you do. I'm just saying that's the best way to go."

"You gonna tell me how to tie my shoes and brush my teeth?"

"I don't care about your shoes or your teeth. Do whatever you want with them."

Grisnik goosed the Crown Vic into the traffic on the Inter-city Viaduct, catching I-70 East, then cut over to I-29 North.

"Happy?" he asked.

We were on the Paseo Bridge crossing the Missouri

River. A casino built on a floating barge was docked below, tight against the riverbank, its garish pink, red, and yellow neon lights reflecting off the cloudy water, the promise of something for nothing dragged down by a swift current and then drowned in mud and silt. Though it was still early, the parking lot was half full, gamblers anxious to roll the dice on the rent money. I envied them. My odds were longer and my stakes were higher.

"As a pig in shit," I said.

"Now tell me again why I'm driving you to Leavenworth."

"I told you. There's someone there I want to talk to."

"Why don't you talk to him by yourself?"

"I had to turn in my FBI credentials when they put me on medical leave. The Bureau frowns on freelancing."

"So you have to make an appointment like every other visitor—that whole thing they do there with the visitor lists and the points."

"Exactly. And today isn't a regular visiting day. So I need you to get me inside."

"But that's not enough. You want me to help you impersonate a police officer, too."

"No. I want you to help me do my job so I can help you do yours. Think of it as a back-scratching, gate-swinging-both-ways road trip. You know as well as I do that the prison keeps records of every visitor. Doesn't matter if it's family or feds. I'd rather keep this one off the radar for now."

Grisnik didn't respond for a few minutes, finally shaking his head like he would regret his decision. "We want to see an inmate, always works better to let the warden know we're coming."

"Call him."

Grisnik reached in his pocket, flipping open his cell phone. "I'll need a name."

"Thomas Rice. Went up a few months ago on a drug charge."

"I remember hearing about that case. Wife turned him in, right?"

"That's the guy."

"Why do you want to talk to him?"

"The wife is selling the house."

"You in the market?"

"No," I told him. "Someone else is who can't afford it."

"This person in the market or just interested in this house?"

"Just this one. Already signed the contract. The wife ended up with the house when they got divorced. The husband gets half the sale proceeds, but the wife has to give him notice of the sale and the price has to be fair market. The buyer says she's selling the house to him for peanuts just to piss off her ex."

"Why do you care?"

I didn't answer, letting him work it out. His eyes narrowed, then widened.

"The buyer is one of your people?" he asked me.

"Yeah."

"You think the buyer came by the money the wrong way?"

"I don't think that his rich grandmother died or that he won the lottery. He can't afford it even if she's giving it away. The property taxes are more than twelve grand a year."

Grisnik asked, "Even if you're right, what's that got to do with my case?"

"Maybe nothing. Or maybe the money is coming from somebody who needed to wash some cash or pay off a favor."

"Marcellus Pearson?"

"More likely whoever put the hit on Marcellus, if that's what happened."

"I'd put the early money on Javy Ordonez. He and Marcellus have been scuffling for a long time," Grisnik said.

"Could have been him. Could have been Bodie Grant."

"That jerk-off from Raytown?"

"You know about him?" I asked.

"What do you think, Jack? That I spend all my time writing traffic tickets and waiting for you to call?"

I laughed. "No, I guess not. We think Bodie and Javy may have decided to go into business together. Getting rid of Marcellus could have been their first joint venture."

Grisnik said, "I talked to one of our detectives that works drugs."

"You and I both know someone in your department was tipping Marcellus. You think that was a good idea?"

"I've known him a long time. If he's dirty, we're all dirty. He told me that he didn't think Javy or Bodie were smart enough or ballsy enough alone to pull this kind of shit but that together, they might talk themselves into it."

"Maybe," I said, "but I think it's someone else, someone further up the food chain. As much business as Marcellus was doing, he didn't live like he had much money. Someone else was getting fat off his action. That's who I was after."

"And you think that's who could have taken out Marcellus and his people?"

"Makes the most sense to me. Maybe Marcellus had a silent partner who decided to renegotiate his contract."

"Doesn't add up to a pass for your home buyer."

"No, it doesn't."

"You said you had something for me on my case," Grisnik said. "What is it?"

"Marcellus gave Oleta Phillips three thousand in twenties twelve hours before he was shot. I found three thousand in twenties in Marcellus's backyard an hour after he was shot. Oleta's fingerprints were on the money."

"That friend you still have tell you about the fingerprints?"

"This morning. She thought it would be convenient if I

ran into you. Seems she has this idea that you might tell me something she'd like to know."

Grisnik nodded, smiling. "I can see how she might think that. I might send her the ballistics on the bullets the coroner dug out of Tony Phillips. Let her check them against the ones that killed Marcellus."

"Her name is Ammara Iverson."

"I like that name," he said. "Is she a good enough friend to get me the surveillance videos?"

"Not yet, but Ben Yates, our SAC, is going to ask your chief for pictures of everyone on your force so he can cross-check them against the video."

Grisnik laughed. "I can't wait for that turd to blossom. The chief will ask Yates if he's got any proof that one or more of his officers are dirty. If Yates does, the chief might cooperate as to those people but he'll never let the entire force be painted with that brush. Yates has to know that."

"If he doesn't, I'm sure your chief will educate him. In any event, Ammara said she reviewed the tapes and didn't see anybody who looked like a cop."

Grisnik shook his head. "A cop looks like anybody else when he's out of uniform."

I thought about what Ammara had said and realized that I agreed with her. I could pick an FBI agent out of a crowd. "You saying you can't tell when someone has been on the job?"

"I guess you're right. Usually I can. I guess if Ammara didn't see anyone who looked like a cop on the tapes, I should feel better. So how come I don't?"

"Because you're like me. You don't trust people because of how they look."

"Amen to that. You still think someone at the FBI leaked word of the surveillance camera in the house so that the killer would have known to cut off the electricity?"

"Troy Clark does. He's having everyone take a polygraph tomorrow."

"Including your home buyer?"

"Yeah."

"I take it you'd like to know about the home buyer before the polygraph exam."

"That would be a good thing."

"Same question. Why do you care?"

"I've got other interests I'm trying to protect."

"Yours?"

I shook my head. "No, but it's personal. Leave it at that."

"You have any proof your home buyer is dirty?"

"Only that it seems strange that he would buy a house at a bargain price that used to be owned by a guy we busted. Other than that, I've got nothing."

"Just one of those gut feelings cops on TV always get?"

"More like the gut fear real cops get," I said.

"Who's the buyer?"

"I'd rather not say until I've got something hard to work with."

"Suppose Thomas Rice gives up his name?"

"That would qualify."

Grisnik had the warden's number stored in his cell phone. Their conversation was brief. He hung up and pulled a KCKPD ID from his shirt pocket, tossing it in my lap. I was about to become Detective John Funkhouser again.

"How about the neighborhood canvass?" Grisnik asked. "Any eyewitnesses?"

I decided to bounce my memory off him. He'd interviewed enough witnesses to gauge how my story would play.

"Not so far. There is one person who may have seen something."

"What?"

"Someone, probably male, running from the scene."

"When?"

"After I got there. He could have been watching from the backyard of one of the houses nearby. If he were, he would have had a view of the rear of Marcellus's house. The tree where I found the money was roughly in a line between where this guy would have been standing and the back door."

"Who saw him?" Grisnik asked.

I let out a long breath, looked at Grisnik, then looked away, staring at the highway. "I did. Maybe. I'm not sure. That's when I started shaking."

Grisnik grunted. "I don't like eyewitnesses," he said.

"Me either."

"Only thing worse is a lineup. Just read a report that said seventy-seven thousand people go to trial each year because someone picks them out of a lineup. Study said that eyewitnesses get it right in a lineup only about fifty percent of the time. Then they looked at two hundred people who were convicted and later exonerated based on DNA evidence. An eyewitness had identified one hundred and fifty of them, usually in a lineup."

"Numbers like that, the guy I saw, probably not even worth mentioning," I said.

"Probably not."

"Unless I could prove who it was and that person turned out to know something about your case and mine."

"All that shaking, Jack, and you are still a clear thinker."

Chapter Twenty-five

"Tell me more about Thomas Rice," Grisnik said.

We drove past Kansas City International Airport. The Platte City exit was only a few more miles north.

"Rice sold insurance, stocks, bonds—any kind of investment you wanted. Had his own company, a one-man operation. A buddy of his did outplacement consulting. One of his big clients offered early retirement to its employees with at least twenty years of service. A lot of them took the deal, which meant they had profit-sharing accounts they had to roll over."

"Rice's buddy hooked him up with the retirees?"

"It was a sweet deal for Rice. Most of these people didn't know their ass from third base when it came to investing. The stock market was hot so anyone with a series-seven license and a computer looked like a genius."

"Market cooled off," Grisnik said.

"It's called a correction."

"I remember. I got corrected right up my ass. Put my retirement off by at least five years."

"Same thing happened to Rice's clients. Except they

hired a lawyer who told them she could get their money back because Rice put them all in high-risk, high-tech stocks that were inappropriate for their retirement plans. They sued Rice and won."

"Didn't he have insurance that paid the claims?"

"Yeah, but he lost his licenses to sell investments and insurance."

"So he couldn't think of anything else to do except sell drugs?"

"I guess he thought it was just like anything else. Buy low and sell high. He knew someone who knew someone and—boom—he was an instant coke dealer. Really got into the lifestyle, using and selling, got himself a girlfriend. The wife found out and turned him in. Told us that for better or worse didn't include criminal and stupid. He pled and it was all over pretty fast. His entire career as a drug kingpin lasted all of about eight months."

"What kind of a deal did the U.S. Attorney make with him?"

"Five years and forfeiture of everything traceable to the money he made selling drugs plus cooperation on other investigations."

"Which left him with what?"

"A lot. His house was already paid off before he started his life of crime."

"That all the feds got?"

"Rice helped us make cases against a couple of small-time dealers. Didn't make much of a dent in the traffic."

"How was the wife able to hold on to the house?" Grisnik asked.

"Before the lawsuits were filed, he put it in his wife's name, same for his car, a Lexus. We couldn't tie her to the drug money, either, so she got to keep it."

"Was it your case?"

"They were all my cases since I ran the squad, but I wasn't directly involved with this one," I said.

"Who was?"

The question threw me. I hadn't thought about it until Grisnik asked me.

"I assigned two people to every case, rotated the assignments so everybody worked with everybody. Troy Clark and Ammara Iverson ran this one."

"Either one of them house hunting?"

"Nope."

"You have squad meetings, talk about all your cases?" Grisnik asked.

"Sure. Same routine as every law-enforcement agency in the world."

"So your home buyer would have known all about the Rice case. No problem looking at the file, knowing what's what."

"Of course."

"Any reason for your home buyer to have had contact with Rice or his wife while the case was going on?"

There it was. Grisnik was a smart cop. He kept asking the right questions, tugging and tickling a problem until a door opened. Colby Hudson wouldn't have known anything more about the Rice case than we had discussed at our squad meetings. He wasn't an investigator on the case; he wasn't a witness at the trial. He wouldn't have had any reason to meet or talk to either Thomas or Jill Rice. Neither did I.

Yet Colby claimed that Jill Rice had called the Bureau out of the blue to offer her husband's car for sale and that he just happened to have taken the call. The house was next. If she had called anyone, it would have been Troy Clark or Ammara Iverson. Even if Colby had taken the call, she would have asked for someone she knew, not offered a sweetheart deal to a stranger.

"No good reason," I said.

"That's what I don't get," Grisnik said.

"What's that?"

"Even the ones who should know better almost never do."

* * *

It doesn't take long for prison to leave its mark. For some, it's ragged tattoos and rippled biceps. For others, it's shoulders stooped in surrender or backs stiffened in defiance. For Thomas Rice, it was his bleak face with its pale and sagging skin.

He was average height and heavy, probably going around two-fifty until he started eating on the prison meal plan. Down by at least fifty pounds, he had a loose wattle beneath his chin, his clothes hanging on him like sheets hung out to dry.

The visiting room was as washed out as he was—vanilla floor tile worn dull, walls painted off-white, scuffed and stained; and fluorescent ceiling light with more glow than any inmate had. Stand Rice against the wall and he was more pillar than person. Still a salesman, he summoned old habits, pumping our hands with a firm grip as he struggled to make a connection between his new life and us.

"I'm Tom Rice," he said, fumbling with his hands like he didn't know what to do with them. "But I guess you guys know that. I mean you're here to see me. I don't get many visitors. Not that I mind, you know. A lot of guys, they've got family come up here all the time. My wife, she, well, we're divorced. No kids. So, there's really no one who's likely to make the trip, you know what I mean. Hey, I'm sorry. I know I'm rambling, but I don't get the chance . . . much . . . anymore . . ."

"To work a room," I said.

He brightened, laughed. "Yeah, I guess so. Curse of the salesman, huh?"

Grisnik hadn't asked for an interrogation room. There was no need since visitors weren't allowed on Thursday. We had the place to ourselves except for the guards and the video cameras.

I grinned and nodded. "Got to sell yourself before you can sell anything else."

"That's the truth," he said, gathering himself, his hands clasped at his belt line, rocking slightly on his heels. "Now what can I do for you gentlemen?"

"I'm Detective Funkhouser. This is Detective Grisnik. We're with the Kansas City, Kansas, police department. We'd like to ask you a few questions."

We showed him our IDs and he pointed at two empty chairs, taking one for himself.

"Knock yourself out. I promised to cooperate with the FBI and you can see what a good deal that turned out to be," he said, smiling and waving at the cameras.

"Actually, we're more interested in real estate," I said.

"Real estate. Really?" He leaned back in his chair, keeping his distance. "I never did any real estate deals. Just stocks, bonds, and insurance."

"And cocaine."

"Yes, Detective Funkhouser. I am a bad man. I sold cocaine and I cheated on my wife. She caught me, cleaned me out in the divorce, and here I am. I never was certain whether she was angrier about the drugs or the adultery."

"Ever sort that one out?"

He shook his head. "Not really. The money was good and I needed it. My wife could spend money in her sleep. She had no appreciation for the risks I took for her, for us. I was entitled to a few perks. You'd think she'd have cut me some slack."

"Hard to figure some women," I said. "So ungrateful."

He leaned forward, studying me. "I know you're pulling my chain. You think I'm just a self-centered shit who blames everyone else for my problems."

"You should feel right at home in prison."

"Okay, Detective. The only thing I've got left to sell is bullshit and you aren't buying. So what do you want?"

"Your ex-wife has something to sell. Your car and your

house and she's letting them go for a lot less than they are worth. What do you know about that?"

Rice studied me some more, turning toward Grisnik, who stared back at him, his face a mask, not giving Rice a clue about how to answer my question.

"This is a federal penitentiary," he said quietly. "I'm here because I violated federal law, not state law. My problems are federal, all the way around. My wife, my car, and my house are all in Johnson County. I've got nothing to do with anyone or anything in Kansas City, Kansas, or Wyandotte County."

"Actually, Wyandotte County and Kansas City, Kansas, are the same thing. The county and the city were consolidated a few years ago," I said. "And it doesn't matter to me where you and your wife live. I still want to know why she's taking a bath on your house and car."

"Thanks for the civics lesson," he said, his voice low but hard. "My wife got the car and the house in our divorce. What she does with them is none of my business or yours."

"Your wife says she's selling them on the cheap to piss you off. I'm wondering how that's working out for you?"

Rice hung his head, shaking it, chuckling at the floor, another mood swing. I couldn't tell which ones were real and which ones were for show. He straightened in his chair, his drooping face a fresh shade of gray.

"You can't help me with this."

"I can't help you if you don't tell me about it. Once I know what's going on, you'd be surprised what I can do."

He stood and took a short tour of the visiting room, hands clamped under his arms, and came back to his chair, rubbing the edge of the hard plastic mold with his fingers.

"It's like I told you," he said, letting out a long breath. "She got the house and the car in the divorce. What she does with them is up to her."

"You're right about the car, but not the house. According to your divorce settlement, she has to notify you of the sale of the house, which has to be for a fair price, and you get half the money. She's screwing your lights out and you're rolling over like she still has you by the short hairs. What's up with that?"

He bit his lower lip and pulled on the flap of skin dangling from his chin as if he was trying to distract himself with self-inflicted pain.

"What do you think I'm going to do, Detective? Start jumping up and down, call her a miserable cunt, and say something that will make you happy? Then in a day or two, I'm on my way to the shower and two overgrown guys with serious steroid habits come up to me, throw their arms around me, and one of them says how's it hanging, bro, while the other one sticks a sharpened spoon between my ribs. No thanks, Detective. I was stupid enough to land my sorry ass in this joint. That doesn't mean I'm not smart enough to get out of here alive."

"You don't have to jump up and down. Just tell me what's going on and I can help you, keep you safe."

Rice laughed. It was high pitched, nervous, and afraid. "Trust me, Detective Funkhouser, you don't mean shit in here. I'm done talking." He marched to the door and banged on it. "Guard! Guard!"

The door opened. The guard swung it wide. Rice was almost gone when I took my last pass at him.

"Hey, Tom. The guy who's buying your car and your house, you think he's just fucking you or does he get to fuck your wife as part of the bargain?"

His neck and face shot full with blood as he ran at me. The guard grabbed his wrist, wrapped it around his back, kicked his legs out from under him, and put him on the floor before he'd taken two steps. Two more guards materialized, one of them putting a knee in his back, the other poised over him with a Taser. Rice managed to lift his head.

"You son of a bitch!"

He spit at me as one of the guards stepped on his head, pressing his cheek hard against the floor.

"You're right about that," Grisnik said.

Chapter Twenty-six

I was fine until we got back to Grisnik's car. He didn't say a word while I shook myself out. I didn't understand how I could hold myself together during an interrogation and crumble five minutes later. Whatever the reason, I was grateful it had worked out that way, although it was a measure of the change in my life that I even had such a thing to be thankful for.

"When I was growing up, we had rugs all over our house, no wall-to-wall carpet. My mother always said that was for the rich folks who lived in Johnson County," Grisnik said after I settled down. "She used to hang the rugs up outside and beat the hell out of them to get rid of the dirt. The way you shake, you remind me how she made those rugs flop every time she cleaned house."

The prison was fading in the rearview mirror, the town passing by in a blur as we headed back to the highway. I wasn't paying attention to either.

"You have a remarkably soothing bedside manner. I bet you're a real hit at executions."

"Hey, man," Grisnik said, one hand raised in self-defense. "What do you want me to say? It is what it is."

"Don't say anything. I'm not putting on a show and I don't need any reviews of my performance."

He rubbed his jaw, trying to expunge the embarrassment from his red face. "You're right. I didn't mean anything by it. It's just hard to watch and not feel something for you. I was just trying to keep it light."

"Light is good. If it makes you feel any better, these shakes don't hurt even if it looks like they do."

Grisnik gave me a quick turn of his head, his natural color restored, one eyebrow raised like I couldn't be serious. "If it doesn't hurt, why do you make those faces and grunt like you been kicked in the balls?"

"I get all caught up inside, like I'm locked in a clinch and can't let go. The facial expressions and the sound effects just happen. I can't control any of it."

He nodded his head, not doubting me this time. I was in a netherworld, unable to explain to myself or anyone else what was happening to me. If people were uncomfortable, I could understand that even if I couldn't do anything about it. But the last thing I wanted was pity, and Grisnik hadn't offered any. I was glad when he changed the subject.

"What'd you think of Rice's performance?"

"The guy was all over the place," I said. "Nervous, friendly, sad, tough, scared, pissed. He went through enough personality changes I thought he was auditioning for the lead in *The Three Faces of Eve*."

"Could be he was all those things. Prison messes a man up."

"What about his face? How'd you read him? Was it for real or an act or some of both?" I asked.

"Shit, man," Grisnik said. "I start out believing they're all liars, everyone one of them. Rice was no different. He was definitely playing us at the beginning. At the end, when you suggested his wife was cheating on him, he was one seriously pissed-off fat man."

"Yeah, but was he telling the truth about being afraid? All that crap about I couldn't help him because he was in a federal prison and I was just a city cop. You suppose he was trying to tell me something?"

"Like what?"

"He said his problems are federal, all the way around. Maybe he's not just afraid of his fellow inmates. Maybe he's afraid of someone on my side of the aisle," I said.

"Like your FBI agent who is buying his house and his car and who you want Rice to believe is also boning his ex-wife."

"That's one way to read it," I said. "My squad has put a lot of people away. It wouldn't be hard to make a connection with one of them, buy a favor now, and pay for it later. Make Rice's shower-room nightmare come true."

We were crossing the Missouri River again, passing from Kansas back into Missouri, the Platte City water tower announcing our arrival. The highway and the river ran roughly parallel the rest of the way back to Kansas City, though we wouldn't see the river again until it turned east for its last leg across Missouri, where it would disappear into the Mississippi River just outside St. Louis.

"Could happen that way," Grisnik said. "But it takes time to set something like that up. Hard to keep the circle of knowledge small. More people you have to bring in to get it done, the more likely it is that someone talks to someone, buys his own favor, or gets paid back the same way as Rice. Inmates keep killing each other, sooner or later the guards are bound to notice."

"You have another explanation?" I asked.

"Yeah, I do. By now, everyone on Rice's cellblock knows he had visitors today. The only visitors on Thursdays are cops and we don't make social calls. Inmates don't care what really happens when someone talks to us. They assume a guy like Rice snitches and they'll kill a snitch just for practice. Hell, just by coming to see him, you probably caused him more trouble than that poor slob can handle. I was him, I'd be afraid, too."

"What about his face? You think you can tell if someone is lying just by looking at their face?"

"We try to do that all the time," Grisnik said. "Doesn't mean we get it right, but we do it. Suspect acts scared, we assume it's because he's guilty. Doesn't answer our questions, looks the other way, licks his lips. All kinds of shit like that. First thing we say, the asshole is guilty, why else would he look like that?"

"What if he's cool about the whole thing? Smiles, chats you up, or has the perfect poker face."

"That's what the polygraph is for. Hard to beat the machine even if the courts won't let us tell the jury about it," Grisnik said.

"I don't know. I don't trust faces. People have too many masks. That's what bothers me about Rice. He had enough for everyone at a masquerade ball."

"Hold him up against what you do know. Ask yourself: what did he say that you can prove was the truth or a lie? Only thing he really told us is that it was none of our business what his wife did with the house and the car. He didn't admit or deny anything. All you did was scare him. I don't think we learned a damn thing."

"Rice isn't a career criminal," I said. "He screwed up bigtime, that's for sure. But he didn't grow up to be a cocaine dealer."

"But that's what he became, so what's your point?" Grisnik asked.

"Rice understands money. He's going to get half the proceeds from the sale of a house worth close to a million bucks if his wife sells it for what it's worth. He invests his share well and he's set when he gets out. She's about to take his future away from him. He ought to be a hell of a lot more scared and pissed about that than what he's going to tell his cellmate about why we came to see him. On top of which, he's a salesman. He's in the bullshit business. He'll come up with something to satisfy any suspicious inmates."

"Bottom line?"

"Rice has no reason not to talk to me unless someone has already gotten to him."

"You could check the visitor records. See who's been to see him," Grisnik said.

"I can't, but you can. I don't want Detective Funkhouser's good name to be dragged into this mess any more than it already has been," I said.

"I'm having a hard time thinking of a reason why I should. I'm the one who's going to have to explain about Detective Funkhouser, not you. Only reason I agreed to bring you up here was you promised that Rice could help me with my case. I didn't hear either one of you mention Oleta Phillips or her son."

"I didn't promise you anything. I said that Rice might know someone who knows something about Oleta. I'm not wrong yet. I know I'm working this case ass-backwards, but it's the only way I can go at it right now."

"How is that supposed to make me feel any better?" Grisnik asked.

"Try finding out who has been to see Rice since he's been in prison and find out if he called anyone after we left. That might make both of us feel a hell of a lot better."

Chapter Twenty-seven

Grisnik took the Fifth Street exit off I-70, a street that runs through the heart of Strawberry Hill. At the south end of Fifth, just after we came off the highway, there was a low-slung bar wearing a faded coat of red paint. Narrow windows offered a peek into a dimly lit interior while a dyspeptic neon sign over the door irregularly blinked its gospel of FREE BEER TOMORROW. Cars were parked at the curb, probably belonging to faithful customers who were hoping that today was the day. A sign bolted to the roof said it was Pete's Place.

Next to the bar was a restaurant, painted from the same can, a companion sign on its roof reading Pete's Other Place, the neon promise over its door pledging Good Eats. A barrel barbeque cooker sat on the sidewalk, the tangy smell of smoked sausage mixing with rising smoke. Grisnik slowed and rolled his window down, breathing deep. I followed his lead, the enticing smell convincing me that this was one promise Pete kept.

"In the early days, the whole area was covered with strawberry fields. That's where the name comes from. But I'll take the sausage any day. It's Pete's secret recipe. Kind of a Croatian kielbasa."

Post–World War II brick and stone houses with well-kept front porches; tidy, narrow yards; and single-car garages lined the steep hills that explained the other half of the name. Grisnik waved to a white-haired couple, the husband relaxing in a rocking chair on his porch, the wife tugging at weeds peeking through the concrete walk. They waved back, calling him by name.

"Petar and Maja Andrija, my godparents. They own the bar and the restaurant," he explained. "Their daughter, Tanja, runs the bar and their son, Nick, makes the sausage and the povitica."

"Sausage, I understand. What's povitica?"

"Croatian cake bread. Lots of different flavors, like chocolate, walnut—anything you can think of. Can't have a holiday or a party around here without it."

Farther north at the intersection of Fifth and Ann, a Catholic church framed in limestone stood on the corner, its steeple aimed at heaven, its painted-glass windows catching the fire of the early afternoon sun. A small herd of young children, dressed in parochial blue and white, chased a soccer ball across the fenced, paved playground affixed to the hip of the church.

"Let me guess," I said. "Your alma mater?"

Grisnik laughed. "My neighborhood, my people."

"What's next? The drive-in theater where you lost your virginity?"

"Nope. That would be the back room of the bar."

"The daughter?"

He grinned. "She had a way of looking at you that made you forget everything holy."

"But you didn't marry her."

Grisnik shook his head, the grin receding. "Oh, I asked Tanja enough times, starting when I was fifteen. She kept saying no, said she was moving to New York as soon as we graduated high school. I heard she got married, after that, nothing. Eventually I got married too, had a couple of kids, and got divorced. A few years ago, she shows up out of the blue, divorced, too. Went back to her maiden name. We tried it again, but it was nothing but memories for her. I guess she outgrew me."

"Sounds like you didn't outgrow her."

He didn't answer, looked at his watch, then back down the hill. I checked mine. It was almost one o'clock.

"You got time for the best sausage sandwich in the world?" Grisnik asked.

"I've got nothing but time."

We parked in front of Pete's Other Place. There were eight square wrought-iron tables with matching chairs, all of them empty, and a deli case filled with cold meats, salads, and loaves of povitica. A row of sausages hung above the counter like a curtain in front of a blackboard menu advertising stew, pasta, fish, salads, and sausage.

"Hey, Nicky," Grisnik said to the man behind the counter.

Nick Andrija stepped out to greet us. He was a slab of hard muscle with a shaved head, bulging arms, and pile-driver legs. I pegged him at five-eight, an easy one-ninety, none of it wasted. He gave Grisnik an easy grin, sharing it with me. They shook hands, clapping each other on the shoulder.

"Marty! How goes it, baby? Who's your friend?"

"Jack Davis, shake hands with Nicky Andrija, sausage master of Strawberry Hill."

"Hey, Nick," I said. "The sausage taste as good as it smells?"

"Better."

"Give us a couple with everything," Grisnik said.

"Two with peppers, onions, potatoes, and sauce coming at you," he said, leaving the counter for the grill on the sidewalk.

A double-wide doorway connected the bar and the restaurant. We took a table that gave us a straight-shot view to the other side. The two buildings were twins on the outside and the inside. The bar was positioned identically to the deli counter, a row of bar stools the only difference.

Nick returned with our sandwiches, which lived up to Pete's promise of good eats and Grisnik's claim that they were the world's greatest. We washed them down with cold soda.

Grisnik wiped his mouth and belched his satisfaction with our meal. "I gotta hit the head."

I glanced at the counter. Nick had disappeared somewhere in the back. I scraped the crumbs from my plate and drained the last of my soda, watching the traffic at the bar.

There was only one customer, his back to me and his head down as he leaned in close to the bartender, a shapely blonde. Her fingers toyed with his, their laughter drifting my way. The guy moved in to kiss her and she spun away, both of them laughing again at a familiar game. The guy shrugged, swiveled around, and slipped off his chair, looking up and directly at me. It was Colby Hudson.

It was one of those frozen moments. We were both running a thousand computations through our heads. If he was on the job, he couldn't acknowledge me without risking blowing his cover. I couldn't recall any references to Tanja, Nick, or their restaurant and bar in any of Colby's reports. It was possible, but unlikely, that a lead had developed in the last few days that brought him here, but his relationship with Tanja, whatever it was, was too intimate to be recent.

The situation was clear to me. Colby wasn't worried that I'd blow his cover. He was worried that I would tell Wendy he was cheating on her.

Colby made the call, smiling broadly at me, turning to the bartender, signaling me to join him at the bar. Tanja stepped around the bar, standing close to Colby. She was as Grisnik had promised. Calling her good looking, saying that she had a good figure, missed the point. Her allure was in the way she walked, like a lioness casually stalking prey, and the way she looked at you with her crystal blue eyes made you want to be caught.

There was a picture of her behind the bar outside a restaurant, the sign reading Mancero's. She was maybe ten years younger in the picture. The photograph wasn't a close-up, the focus more on the restaurant. Now in her late thirties, maybe early forties, she was a woman who'd gotten better, not older. She would attract younger guys like Colby or older guys like me just by breathing.

"Tanja, say hello to a friend of mine, Jack Davis."

I stood, taking the hand she offered me. It was warm and soft. She held my eyes with the politician's gift of making me feel like I was the only person in the room.

"Your brother makes a helluva sausage."

"It's all in the skin," she said, letting her hand slide reluctantly from mine. "That's what holds all the flavor together."

Colby said, "You can't beat their food."

"Looks that way," I said.

"A buddy of mine told me about this place," Colby said to me. "How'd you find it? It's not exactly in the Zagat guide."

He was smooth, treating our encounter like the most natural thing, admitting that we knew each other without acknowledging how. His purposeful ambiguity suggested that Tanja didn't know what he did for a living. That made sense. When you cheat, you keep a lot of secrets.

"Same as you—a friend of mine," I said.

"Well, I've got to get going," Colby said. "Catch you later."

Now there were two people in the bar, Tanja and me. I pointed to the photograph.

"I don't recognize the restaurant. Where is it?"

"New York. I used to be married to the owner."

"So you divorced him but kept the picture."

"Reminds me of the good times."

"You have a picture of Colby for when you're finished with him?"

Tanja laughed. "You're not shy, are you?"

"Doesn't pay. So, how long have you two been together?"

She shrugged, smiled again. "It's not like that. He drops by once a week, sometimes more often, sometimes less. He's a good guy. He makes me laugh."

"And you make his balls turn blue."

Her face hardened, her eyes grew flinty. "I don't think I like you."

"You wouldn't be the first."

Grisnik returned from the bathroom before either of us could draw blood.

"Tanja, honey," he said, one arm squeezing her around her waist. "I see you met Jack."

"You're the one who brought him in here?"

"Yeah, why?"

"Don't bring him back," she said, turning her back on both of us and retreating to the bar.

Grisnik stared at me. "What the hell was that about?"

"I'm not her type."

Grisnik's cell phone rang, ending the discussion. His expression turned cold as he listened and then asked the cop's automatic questions of who, what, when, where, and how. He hung up and snapped the phone into the cradle on his belt.

"What is it?" I asked.

"Javy Ordonez is dead."

Chapter Twenty-eight

"I'm betting against natural causes."

"Preliminary indications are that he died of brain inflammation," Grisnik said.

"Brain inflammation? What causes that?"

"Lot of things can do it: high fever, brain tumor, meningitis. But, in Javy's case, it was a bullet."

"Any chance he put it there?"

"Not unless he was a hell of a shot. The entry wound was in the back of his skull."

"Any witnesses?"

"Don't know yet. Garbageman found him when he was emptying a Dumpster."

"Makes sense. Garbage in, garbage out. Where did he find the body?"

"Down in Argentine. On the northern edge of the rail yard. There are some storage buildings that back up to a stretch of woods. The Dumpster was out back behind one of the buildings. Javy's car was parked next to it."

"Argentine is his neighborhood," I said.

"That's where he grew up, but it's not the only place he

does business. Mexican Americans have lived in Argentine ever since the 1920s when a lot of them came here to work for the railroad. In those days it was the Atchison, Topeka & Santa Fe. Burlington Northern bought them out in 1995."

"You're a railroad expert too?"

"I'm a cop and this is my town. It's my business to know. The federal government moved the Shawnee Indians here in the early 1800s. Toward the end of the century, a silver smelter was built on the reservation. Don't ask me what happened to the Indians. Whatever it was, it wasn't good."

"It usually wasn't."

"Anyway, the smelter kept growing and hiring people and the next thing you know, they had the town of Argentine. Lots of mining, too. Then the railroad saw a good thing and built a terminal here. The smelter went bust around 1900 and, not long after, Argentine became part of Kansas City, Kansas. The mines lasted a little longer, and then steel fabrication kept everyone employed who didn't work for the railroad like my old man did. If I hadn't become a cop, that's where I'd have ended up."

"Well, at least Javy died in his own backyard."

"Doesn't sound like it was his idea."

"You think his death is connected to Marcellus, Oleta, and the rest?" I asked.

"Shit happens. Sometimes it's the same shit. Some time's it's just a coincidence."

"If there is a connection, it could mean that someone is consolidating market share. We started the week with Marcellus Pearson butting heads with Javy Ordonez and Bodie Grant. Two out of those three are dead and it isn't Friday yet."

"Bodie could be trying to become the next Head Fred or avoiding becoming the next victim," Grisnik said.

"More likely the next victim. How far is a white boy from

Raytown going to get moving in on black and Hispanic gangs in Kansas City, Kansas?"

"Not very damn far. Seems more likely that someone is getting even."

"Or cleaning house," I said. "Like your mother beating her dirty rugs."

"Only we're the ones get to clean up the mess. I can drop you at your car or you can go along for the ride. Your call."

"Whose case is it?"

"Mine, at least so far. None of your people have showed up yet. Could be they're too busy buying cars and houses or they might just have their police scanner tuned to sports talk. You want to tag along, that's fine with me. Troy Clark shows up, he's likely to take a dim view of your secret identity as Detective Funkhouser."

"You're right about that. I don't suppose you could deputize me?"

"We quit doing that right after Wyatt Earp cleaned up Dodge City."

The smart choice was to let Grisnik drop me off and tell me what happened later. Troy would be on the scene before the body was removed, claiming that it was the Bureau's case, that it was related to their ongoing investigation of Marcellus Pearson's murder. It was the same argument I would have made.

He wouldn't be happy to see me there. It wouldn't matter that I wasn't breaking any laws. It was possible I wouldn't even be breaking any Bureau regulations. Grisnik had invited me and I had accepted his invitation. It was simple. Troy wouldn't see it that way. Neither would Ben Yates when Troy told him. Both Troy and Yates would see it as one more reason I shouldn't come back any time soon, if ever.

If I stayed away, the crime scene would be picked over, rolled over, and swept up by the time I got there on my own.

I wouldn't learn anything from the one source I trusted more than any other.

I liked unified theories of crimes, ones that captured a single perpetrator responsible for multiple crimes. But crime was rarely that neat. More often crimes and criminals overlapped, an investigation of one unintentionally leading to the resolution of another.

Javy's death could be part of a turf war that included the five drug house murders, the shooting of Tony Phillips, and the disappearance of his mother, Oleta, all the victims linked by drugs. Colby Hudson had said that Javy ordered the hit on Tony Phillips, making it tempting to tie Javy to the drug house, with Oleta somehow caught in the crossfire.

But the victims in Marcellus's house, Oleta Phillips, and Javy Ordonez had a different link—Latrell Kelly. He lived behind where the drug house victims died and where Oleta's money was found and he worked at the Argentine rail yard where Javy's body was found. Tony Phillips could have been a one-off, unrelated to the rest.

"I'll go along for the ride," I told Grisnik. "Troy Clark has a problem with that, I'll tell him you kidnapped me."

Grisnik laughed. "Kidnapping is a federal offense."

"Maybe Troy will arrest you instead of me."

He pulled away from Pete's Other Place, not bothering to turn on the red flashing light mounted in the driver's corner of the windshield or his siren. We weren't in that big of a hurry since there was nothing we could do to change what had happened.

Chapter Twenty-nine

"I've driven over this place on I-635," I said, as we approached the rail yard on Kansas Avenue, crossing Eighteenth Street. "The highway is like a bridge over a river of tracks and trains."

"More like one of the Great Lakes," Grisnik said. "The yard covers 780 acres. Eighteenth Street is the east end. It goes all the way west to Fifty-fifth. Kansas Avenue is the north end and the old Santa Fe main line makes the southern border. You could put the Chiefs and Royals stadiums out here and have room left over."

"I didn't know there was this much train traffic in Kansas City."

"Over a hundred trains a day. One of the biggest hump yards in the country. They do a lot of refueling and crew changes here, too."

Once inside the grounds, Grisnik navigated a series of unmarked roads without hesitation, pulling up in front of a row of three windowless one-story buildings made of steel siding with rusted overhead garage doors flanked by gravel driveways. Treetops marking the edge of the woods loomed over the flat roofs, faded red and yellow leaves matching the decayed steel.

Three patrol cars, two Crown Vics, and an ambulance were parked in a haphazard row in front of the first building. The uniformed officers were directing what little traffic there was, maintaining a secure perimeter. A detective was interviewing the garbageman, probably for the third or fourth time. The pace was slow, everyone careful to get it right.

"You found this place so easily, you must have been here before," I said to Grisnik.

"You can thank my old man for that. I grew up following him around down here. These buildings are used to store equipment. He was responsible for the inventory, making sure none of it grew legs and walked off. Burlington Northern spent a fortune upgrading the yard when they took over in ninety-five. Didn't bother with these. They are fifty years old if they're a day. My father used to say that the rats wanted to put them on the National Register of Historic Places so they couldn't be torn down."

The gravel drive wrapped around to the back of the storage buildings. It was firm enough that my footprints barely made a dent but soft enough to leave tire tracks. We followed the deep wide ruts left by the garbage truck.

I looked for tracks left by Javy's car. There was a vague imprint that stopped and started, partly obliterated by the garbage truck, the last stretch ending at Javy's Cadillac. If the killer had driven his own car, I didn't find any evidence of it. Its tire tracks could have been wiped out by the garbage truck or been so mixed with other tracks as to be unidentifiable.

The crime scene techs greeted Grisnik with a mock deferential bow. They'd had their look. It was our turn.

All four doors to Javy's car were open. Blood had soaked into the creamy leather of the driver's headrest, running down the back of the seat. More blood and bits of bone and tissue were splattered across the backseat, proof that the killer had been sitting behind Javy when he pulled the trigger.

It was likely the killer had caught some of the splatter, evidence that would be difficult to get rid of without burning his clothes and hosing himself down. That's what a careful killer would have done, though it amazed me how many criminals are caught because they are slobs.

There was also blood on the dash and the windshield. The glass was fractured in a spiderweb pattern caused by the impact of the bullet after it exited Javy's head, more proof that a large-caliber round had been used.

The rail yard location was out of the way and out of sight, indicating that Javy had either come to the scene with his killer or agreed to meet him. And Javy almost certainly knew the killer. Why else would he have made himself so vulnerable? I wondered if Latrell and Javy had crossed paths.

I was also willing to bet that Javy had come alone. If he'd brought backup, there would have been more bodies or, at least, signs of a struggle. That supported my assumption that the killer was someone whom Javy either felt safe with, like the harmless-looking Latrell, or was someone whose invitation to a meeting Javy couldn't refuse.

The passenger windows were tinted dark. If the garbageman had wondered why a Cadillac Escalade was parked next to the Dumpster and decided to look inside, he wouldn't have seen a thing.

The killer could have left the body inside the car, locked the doors, and walked away, perhaps giving him more time to escape or set up an alibi. Instead, he'd thrown Javy in the trash, making a statement and taking an unnecessary chance. Any contact he had with the body increased the chances that he'd leave evidence behind—body hair, fiber, or something else that could be traced back to him.

I wondered whether the killer had left the car doors locked. Even if the garbageman hadn't discovered the body, the car would eventually have drawn attention. Locking it wouldn't have delayed for long the discovery of what had happened inside. Still, it was a detail, the kind an organized killer would have remembered.

Like the person who'd committed the drug house murders, this killer was organized, careless, and angry. Maybe it was the same killer or maybe they were just kindred spirits, like separated-at-birth twins.

The area between the back of the storage building and the edge of the woods was a narrow stretch, a good part of which was taken up by the garbage truck. The back end of the truck was open, Javy's body lying facedown on a bed of garbage, his legs disappearing beneath the sweeper blade that compressed and crushed the trash, his arms cast out from his sides in a casual, indifferent pose.

I'd never seen Javy up close and in person, but I had watched him on surveillance video, heard his soft, high voice on audio, and studied still photographs of him. He was barely five-seven, probably went around one-fifty dressed and wet. It wouldn't have been hard for Latrell to lift him out of the car and drop him in the trash bin.

Some punks, like Marcellus, got to the top of their personal kingdoms because they were the biggest, strongest, meanest motherfuckers on the block. The ones like Javy, who lacked that physical prowess, made up for it in other ways. They were natural, charismatic leaders who compensated for their diminutive size by being more ruthless and clever than their larger counterparts. From what Colby had told me, that described Javy, though he wasn't a good enough politician to stop a bullet. None of them ever were.

Grisnik pointed to the forks extending from back of the truck. "Driver picks the Dumpster up, empties the container into the belly of the truck. Sweeper blade probably got hung up on Javy's legs and jammed."

"You are some kind of Renaissance cop," I told him. "A walking encyclopedia on Shawnee Indians, silver smelters, mining, railroads, Mexican immigration, and now the care and feeding of garbage trucks."

"Listen, Bureau Boy," Grisnik said. "You stay in one place doing one job long enough, there isn't much you don't see. You keep your ears and eyes open, read a book once in a while, and there isn't much you can't learn. Some of our best street bums have been ground up in these things after checking into a Dumpster they could of sworn was the Four Seasons."

I leaned in to get a closer look at the body. The back of Javy's head was flattened, caved in by the impact of the bullet. The back of Jalise Williams's head had looked the same way when I saw her body crouched in the closet. Grisnik shined a flashlight on Javy's skull.

"He never looked so good," Grisnik said.

"You knew him?" I asked.

"By sight, sound, and smell. We were pretty sure he was good for at least three murders, probably more if you count the ones he'd ordered done, but it was always the same old story. No one saw anything. No one knew anything. No one cared and even if they did, still no one saw or knew anything."

There was a door on the backside of the building. I tried the handle. It was locked. The dirt around the handle and the door jamb was undisturbed. There were no scrape marks on the threshold and no footprints leading to or from the door. The murderer hadn't come through the shed to meet Javy.

I walked around to the far side of the truck and stared into the woods. It was a mix of thick ground cover, vines, wild thorn bushes, saplings, and mature trees. A few empty beer bottles and fast-food wrappers were scattered along the edge of the brush. I could make out a faint, hard-packed trail crossing roughly parallel to where I was standing, a good ten feet back in the woods.

The grass along where I was standing hadn't been disturbed. None of the tree branches were broken and no clothing remnants had been snagged on the thorns.

"How far back do these woods go?" I asked Grisnik.

He was talking to another detective, his hand on his colleague's back. "Hang on a second," he said to me.

I walked along the edge of the woods to the west, keeping my eye on the trail. It bent toward the gravel drive running behind the storage sheds in a gradual arc, coming out across from the third storage building, about a hundred paces from the Dumpster where Javy's body had been found. The grass there was beaten down, nearly dead. Plastic rings from emptied six-packs, cigarette butts, and a wrinkled condom marked the end of the trail. Grisnik caught up to me.

"What did you want to know?" he asked me.

"I asked how far back these woods go."

He shook his head. "I'm not really sure."

"You mean there's something you don't know about your town and your people?"

"I'm a lot of things, Jack. But I'm not a Boy Scout. Never had much use for the great outdoors. Always stayed out of the woods."

"The killer could have walked through the woods and met Javy."

"Already thought of that. The crime scene techs did a sweep of the immediate vicinity. They're expanding the perimeter. So far, they haven't found anything."

"I think I'll take a stroll," I said and started down the path.

"Leave some bread crumbs so you don't get lost," Grisnik said. "I'm going to talk to the driver of the garbage truck."

I followed the path back to where I could see the Dumpster, the garbage truck, and the storage shed. I crouched close to the ground, not finding any sign that someone had stepped off the trail, though I was no more adept at following a trail in the woods than was Grisnik. The sound of an angry and familiar voice brought me to my feet.

"Jack! Where the hell are you?" Troy Clark materialized at the front of the garbage truck, hands on hips, scanning the woods, locking on to my position. "Get your ass over here!"

I've always prided myself on being a team player, following orders as well as giving them, respecting the rules and chains of command. Structure and discipline are both necessary features of the FBI and I had incorporated them in to my life. None of which meant that I was going to get my ass anywhere for Troy Clark. I pretended he was my future former wife and, therefore, pretended I didn't hear him as I retraced my route. He matched me stride for stride and was waiting when I emerged from the woods.

"What are you doing here?" Troy demanded.

"I'm taking a walk in the woods. What are you doing here?"

Troy screwed his face into a threat. I'd seen him use that face with suspects, sometimes with a gun pressed into their neck for emphasis. That he would try the look with me left me more amused than moved.

"Grisnik says you're with him. What were you doing? Hiding from me?"

"I've got no reason to hide from you."

"You're on leave. Medical leave. This isn't your case. Stay out of it."

"It's not your case, either. It's Grisnik's. He invited me to come along. I didn't want to hurt his feelings."

"We were—you were, for Christ's sake—investigating Javy Ordonez. Colby Hudson was babysitting him. That makes it our case."

"I'm not your audience. Grisnik will fight you over this

one. Then someone at Justice will have to get involved and the killer will be a long way down the road before you and Grisnik stop pissing at each other. Why not make nice and work the case together?"

Grisnik, accompanied by a crime scene tech, joined us before Troy could answer. The tech was sweating and smiling, holding a plastic evidence bag, a .45 caliber pistol hanging in the bottom.

"Tell him," Grisnik said to the tech.

The tech held the bag up like he'd just won first prize at the state fair. "We found it under another Dumpster about a quarter of a mile from here."

Chapter Thirty

"Grisnik," Troy said, "this case falls under the FBI's jurisdiction."

"I don't think so," Grisnik said, taking the plastic bag from the tech. "I let you get away with that on the drug house murders. But Javy Ordonez was a suspect in the shooting of Tony Phillips. Phillips's mother, Oleta, is missing. I'm handling both of those cases. The murder of Ordonez may be connected."

"We had Ordonez under surveillance. One of our undercover people was on him. That makes it our case."

"Your investigation, what was it for? Drugs?"

"Yeah, drugs. What's your point?" Troy asked.

"Cause Javy's drug-dealing days are done. He's nothing but a corpse now. Can't help you one damn bit with your case. It's my job to catch his killer. I find out anything that you boys may want to know, I'll be sure and tell you."

More cars arrived. Doors opened and were slammed closed. Troy smiled and waited. Ammara Iverson came around the corner of the storage shed accompanied by Josh

Ziegler, the U.S. Attorney, trailed by two of his junior lawyers.

Ziegler was born to the role, tall, with a square chin that matched his squared shoulders, dark blond hair, and ice blue eyes. He was appointed by the previous administration and was so good at his job that the current president kept him on even though they belonged to different political parties. Unlike a lot of U.S. Attorneys, he tried cases, leaving the job of managing the bureaucracy to his deputies. He guarded his turf like a Doberman in a junkyard.

"Troy," he said, without acknowledging Grisnik, "what's the story?"

"You're familiar with our ongoing investigation into drug trafficking in the greater metropolitan area."

"Of course I am. You're keeping me busy trying cases."

"Javy Ordonez was one of our prime targets. We've devoted considerable assets to making a case against him, including putting one of our undercover agents next to him. That's his Escalade, where he was shot to death, and that's the Dumpster where the killer dumped his body."

"Who found the body?"

"Driver of that garbage truck," Troy said, waving his hand at the truck, "when he unloaded the Dumpster."

Ziegler listened with his hands on his hips, his eyes boring in on Troy as if he were the only person within a hundred miles, the two of them having a private chat.

"Who was first on the scene?" he asked.

I'd seen this dance routine many times. In fact, I'd choreographed a few of them myself with Troy as my understudy. Troy knew that Grisnik would fight to hold on to this case. He'd already briefed Ziegler and the two of them were preparing to shuffle off to Buffalo with the case before Grisnik could gain any traction. Troy had been a good pupil. I should have been proud.

"KCKPD," Troy said. "Did a good job like they always

do. They've filled us in on the preliminaries. We're ready to run with it. Detective Grisnik here runs Robbery and Homicide. I believe he has a question about jurisdiction."

Ziegler turned his "ladies and gentlemen of the jury" smile on Grisnik and stuck his hand out. Grisnik hesitated but gave in, clasping hands for an instant before letting go.

"I don't blame you for wanting the case, Detective. It's why we get out of bed in the morning. Thanks for the good work your people did. We depend on them to get things under control in cases like this. It's the kind of cooperation the director likes to hear about."

"You be sure and tell him next time you see him," Grisnik said. "But this is about murder, not drugs. Javy was a dealer, but he's the victim, not the perp, and he's not the one that's going to be arrested and convicted. His killer is going to win that prize. No federal laws are in play. This is my case."

I half expected Grisnik to also tell Ziegler it was his town and his people, but he left that out. They stood a foot apart, waiting for the other to blink. Grisnik held his ground, subtly tightening his grip on the plastic bag containing the gun.

"Detective," Ziegler said, with the patience of a priest forgiving the wayward, "We know that Ordonez was engaged in interstate drug trafficking. Obviously, something went wrong in a deal or somebody got jealous or angry over territory or money. Whatever it was, there's no doubt that this case is about drugs, drugs that crossed state lines, and that makes it a federal case. Murder isn't the end of our case, it's just the latest development in our ongoing investigation. I talked to your D.A. on my way over here. He agrees with me. You can give him a call if you like."

Ziegler retrieved his cell phone from his jacket pocket, holding it in the palm of his outstretched hand. "Go ahead, Detective. It's number five on my speed dial if you can't remember the number."

Grisnik's eyes burned, his shoulders flaring back as he

unconsciously stuck out his chest. I knew the pose. It was the reflex when your own people slipped the knife between your shoulder blades. It's hard to tell which is worse—the shock, the pain, or the humiliation. To his credit, Grisnik didn't buckle, didn't let his shoulders sag in surrender, or otherwise acknowledge the bitterness of defeat.

"You'll want this," he said to Ziegler, handing him the plastic bag. "I'll have my people deliver a set of reports and all the forensics. You need anything else, give me a call."

Grisnik looked at me, giving me a brother's nod, telling me he'd just taken a walk in my shoes, then turned away and left. I didn't blame him for not asking me if I wanted a ride.

Chapter Thirty-one

The Argentine terminal was perched on a tower high above, and dead smack in, the center of the rail yard, with an expansive view of the surrounding roads, highways, businesses, hills, and homes that spread out from the yard like rings on a tree. Trains crawled along the miles of tracks like robotic serpents, each taking its turn, adhering to a careful, plodding routine that delighted Latrell Kelly. He tracked the movement of each train in the records that came across his desk, filing the manifests, inspection reports, route changes, and anything else his boss, the terminal manager, told him to put away in its proper place. It was, for him, the perfect job—creating and keeping order.

Latrell had a small desk in one corner, the surface made smaller by the stacks of paper piled on it, each sheet waiting to be put in its designated folder. The monotony of the job was soothing. The precision with which he maintained the perpetual paper flow comforted him.

Today Latrell's work neither soothed nor comforted him. He was tired from being up late the night before after giving Marcellus's dog to the FBI agent and he had been uneasy all day, fidgeting as if tiny, invisible insects were burrowing into his skin. The itching distracted him, making it difficult to concentrate. He was falling behind and the further behind he fell, the more he itched.

Then, after lunch, things got worse when everyone in the office gathered at the windows along the north wall. Curious, he joined them, watching as police cars and an ambulance, their emergency lights flashing, converged at the storage sheds on the northern edge of the yard, their sirens drowned out by the trains' ceaseless grinding and whistling.

The phone rang. A secretary answered, listened, and handed the phone to Latrell's boss, who muttered "shit," gave the phone back, and bolted for the stairs, bad knees and fifty extra pounds slowing him down.

Latrell pressed against the glass, wishing he had a better view. He saw the parade of cars stop in front of the storage sheds, saw people miniaturized by the distance pour out and disappear as they went around the sheds to the edge of the woods.

The entrance to the cave was a short distance from the storage sheds, an easy walk if you knew which trail to follow. The possibility that the cave was their destination inflamed the insects marching across his skin. Though he had camouflaged the entrance with a thick layer of deadfall, someone who knew what to look for might find it. Latrell didn't realize that he was holding his breath until he felt a hand on his shoulder, the secretary asking him if he was okay. He nodded and returned to his desk, afraid of attracting more attention.

A while later, the manager returned with four others, two of whom he recognized as the FBI agents who had knocked on his door after he'd put things right with Marcellus. The other agent, the one who had come looking for Marcellus's dog last night, wasn't part of the group. Latrell kept his head down, stealing a glance at them. No one looked his way.

He should have relaxed when his boss didn't summon him, saying that the agents wanted to ask him some questions, but he didn't. Instead, the itching got worse until his skin felt electrified. Latrell was clinging to the edges of his world, gathering them tightly around him, but he was losing his grip. Things should have been better after he'd killed Marcellus and the others, but they weren't.

Latrell ducked into the bathroom, closed the door to a stall, and sat, taking things apart, putting them back together in his mind, searching for what had gone wrong. Each time, he came back to the FBI agent, Jack Davis, he said his name was. Worried about Marcellus's dog. Standing outside his house waiting to trick him with that bullshit story about losing his son.

Latrell pinched his eyes closed, picturing himself in the cave, hidden deep under the surface, touching the special things he kept there, and screaming until his throat was raw. The image put him at ease. Get through the day, he told himself. Then he'd go to the cave and sort things out. Figure out what he had to do and do it. Put things right again.

The heat in Latrell's skin slowly cooled to a tingle, then faded. Settled, he returned to his desk, his face a placid mask. The FBI agents were huddled with his boss in the conference room, its interior glass wall giving him a clear view of what they were doing.

The secretary rapped lightly on the door, a bundle of rolled maps and enlarged aerial photographs under her arm. The manager let her in, directing her to spread the maps and photographs out on the table. The agents crowded around as she unrolled them, Latrell's boss pointing and nodding in response to the agents' questions. Twenty minutes later, they rolled up the maps and photographs. Each of the agents shook his boss's hand and they left, taking the documents with them.

Later, Latrell asked his boss what was going on. Found a

dead body in one of the Dumpsters back by the storage sheds, his boss told him. It's a rail yard, not a goddamn cemetery, his boss added, annoyed at anything that kept him from making sure the trains ran on time. Latrell should have been relieved, but he wasn't. He began to itch again.

Chapter Thirty-two

Ammara Iverson gave me a lift back to my car.

"That was slick," I said, as she drove away from the rail yard.

"You mean the Mutt and Jeff routine Troy and Ziegler did back there?"

"They were smooth, I'll give them that. You think Ziegler had really talked to the D.A.?"

"Ziegler never bluffs. Troy reached out to Ziegler as soon as we found out about Javy Ordonez. I was on the call with him."

"You think there's a connection?"

"Doesn't matter. Troy would have done the same thing. Ziegler, too. They're all in favor of cooperating with the local cops as long as they get to run the show."

"I get that. I don't care about the turf battle. I'm more interested in whether the cases are connected."

"Too soon to tell, but that gun the tech found makes things more interesting."

"How so?" I asked.

Ammara took a breath. "Remember, I didn't tell you any

of this. Ballistics says that a .45 caliber was used in the drug house murders. If this gun is a match, we may have our first real break."

"The .45 was standard military issue, marines mostly," I said.

"They aren't just for the military," she said. "Glock and Ruger both make .45s. So do some other manufacturers. They're great for self-protection. Lots of stopping power."

"If the gun they found was military issue, that could give us an angle to look at."

"Us," she said. "Not you."

I ignored her comment. "How about our squad? Anybody like the .45?"

Ammara turned toward me, smiling. "Nope. Everybody likes the .40 caliber, Glocks mostly, same as you."

"I'm not just talking about service weapons. What about personal guns?"

She bit her lower lip, shaking her head. "Troy asked all of us. No one said they had a .45, but I guess that doesn't prove anything, does it."

"Not much."

Ammara didn't argue, changing subjects instead. "You should let go of this case, Jack. Take care of yourself."

"That's what they tell me."

"I'm serious, Jack. You keep showing up like this, Troy will change the locks."

"How badly does Troy want to keep me out of the way?"

"Bad enough. You saw him today."

"Doesn't answer my question. I don't think it has anything to do with my health. I think that's a convenient excuse. He wants my squad on a permanent basis. Always has."

"I don't know. Troy has his way of seeing the world. It's not mine, but he's running the squad."

"Anything else new from your end besides the ballistics?" I asked.

"A few more dead ends. That kid, Luis Alvarez, the one who supposedly shot Tony Phillips and who the Winston brothers put in intensive care, he didn't make it. Never woke up."

"It's like they all decided to kill each other. Kind of like a suicide pact."

"Only difference," Ammara said, "people who make a suicide pact kill themselves, not one another."

"Has to be a last man standing. Anything else?"

She shrugged. "We talked to Jalise Williams's family and friends. No indication she was stepping out on Marcellus or doing anything else to make her a target."

"Well, that's not all bad. We keep eliminating enough possibilities, we'll be left with the answer, even if it doesn't make sense now."

"Maybe, but this thing with Javy Ordonez has Troy's balls in a bundle," Ammara said.

"Why? Because it doesn't fit with his theory that we've got a bad agent on our squad? The ballistics report doesn't, either."

"He's not telling us what he thinks."

"First rule—trust no one," I said.

"Second rule—eventually you have to trust someone. He can't do this on his own," she said.

"What about the polygraphs? Still on for tomorrow?"

"Yeah, except he's not going to ask you to take one."

"Why not?"

"The examiner told him that the results would be meaningless if you start shaking during the test."

"Lucky me. So how do you know what the examiner told Troy if Troy isn't talking to the squad?"

Ammara smiled, not taking her eyes from the road. "I don't like being shut out so I pay real close attention to my surroundings. Did you get anything else from Marty Grisnik?"

"He's going to call you for the ballistics on the gun used to kill Marcellus and company. He wants to compare it to the ballistics from the Tony Phillips shooting."

"They recover the gun in that shooting?"

"Grisnik didn't say, but they've got the rounds that killed the kid. They can compare those to the rounds we found at Marcellus's house."

"If the same gun was used in all three cases, that would be nice," Ammara said.

"Be more than nice. It would be sweet," I said. "But it wouldn't make any sense. Why throw the gun away where it was likely to be found after using it to pop Javy? Pretty sloppy."

"Wouldn't have been found if Javy's body hadn't jammed up the garbage truck. The gun would have ended up in the landfill along with Javy. More unlucky than sloppy."

"There's another angle. Latrell Kelly," I said.

"Mr. Cream Puff?"

"Yeah. He lived behind Marcellus and he works at the rail yard. See if you can find a connection between him and Javy. You ever been to a joint on Fifth Street in Kansas City, Kansas, called Pete's Other Place?"

"You mean that sausage place Colby's always talking about? He dragged me there once. Not my kind of food. I like to see dogs walking around, not on my plate stuffed inside an intestine."

I laughed. "Grisnik took me there for lunch today. I liked the sausage."

"You see any dogs?"

"Not a one. I did run into Colby. He was sitting at the bar," I said, my voice trailing off.

"And?" asked Ammara.

"And what?"

"And when someone's voice trails off, Special Agent

Davis, it implies they want to tell you something else but they prefer to be asked. That's and what."

It was my turn to laugh. "Well, I don't prefer to be asked, at least not at the moment."

We didn't say anything else until Ammara pulled alongside my car. I got out and then leaned back in the open window.

"You remember that case last spring, the one where the wife turned the ex-stockbroker husband in for dealing dope?"

Ammara laughed. "And for cheating on her. I think that's what killed the deal for him. Man, she wanted his nuts slow roasted."

"Guy's name was Thomas Rice."

"Right. The wife's name was Jill. What about them?"

"You and Troy handled that case."

"We did."

"You ever hear from the wife afterward? She ever call?"

Ammara pursed her lips and squinted her eyes, thinking before she spoke. "Last time I talked to her was when the judge sentenced her husband. What's this about, Jack?"

I smiled. "It's probably nothing, but I'd like to get a look at the file."

"Troy would kick your ass out the door."

"He doesn't have a boot big enough, but all the same, I'd rather no one know I was looking at it."

She thought for a minute, chewing her lip. "How much of the file you need?"

"Names and addresses of Rice's clients before he lost his license. Same for the people he gave up to the U.S. Attorney as part of his plea bargain. Plus any witness statements and all of Rice's financials."

"I can't take the file out of the building," Ammara said. "There would be a record of that and a lot of questions for me to answer if Troy finds out I gave it to you."

"You could make copies. Bring them out to the house."

She looked closely at me, narrowing her eyes, passing judgment. "If I had a dick, I'd say I was about to step on it," she said.

"Don't wear heels."

Chapter Thirty-three

I lowered the windows in my car, releasing the heat that had built up since morning. The day caught up to me like jackhammers pounding me from my insides out before I could start the engine. I fought the tremors with stiff arms clamped to the steering wheel, finally letting go, only to be whipped against the seat back, grunting like I'd been kicked. A woman walking through the parking lot stopped in front of my car, staring, hand to her heart, asking "are you okay?" I nodded and waved her off, though I imagined it was hard for her to tell where the shaking stopped and the nodding started. It was for me.

I'd become a display piece, a street performer, an oddity belonging at the state fair along with the two-headed cow, the bearded lady, and the tattooed man. I wasn't okay, but that wasn't her problem. It was mine. I didn't want her to ask me how I was doing. I wanted her to leave me alone. I wanted to be invisible.

I'd been off work for two days. Not long enough to take it easy even if I knew how. Not long enough either to know whether it would make a difference. Perhaps when I saw the doctor next week, I would find out whether this was the end of the beginning or the beginning of the end.

Ammara, Kate, and Troy were telling me the same thing. Walk away. Let someone else find out who killed those five people. They would say the same thing about Javy Ordonez's killer. I had no illusions that I was the only one who could solve those cases, though I was certain I was the only one who could protect Wendy.

Though I'd yet to find any direct threat to her beyond Colby's probable infidelity, I felt the threat as surely as I did the shakes. It didn't matter that I might be overreacting because of what had happened to Kevin. Taking any chances with her was unthinkable. I would sacrifice anything, including myself, my job, Colby Hudson, or a guilty verdict against the killer, if it meant saving her.

I leaned against the headrest, spent. The shakes had stopped. It was as if they were conducting guerrilla warfare against me, attacking from the shadows and escaping before I could fight back.

There was much I had to do. Talk to Jill Rice and ask her why she was selling her car and house to Colby. Figure out how Colby could afford to buy them even at a discount. Figure out why Tom Rice was so afraid. Find Bodie Grant and ask him whether he was the last man standing. Find the man I thought that I'd seen running away two nights ago. Find Oleta Phillips or what was left of her. Catch the killers. Protect Wendy. Make it all make sense.

At the moment, I couldn't do any of it. I was all over the place and I was no place. The shaking was adding ten rounds in the ring to my day. I raised my hands to my unseen opponent. *No más.* Picking up the dog and going home was all I could do for now.

Ruby raced around the house, sniffing in the corners, flying into the backyard where, to my amazement, she peed and pooped. Pete & Macs had me for life. Back in the house, she followed me from room to room, her eyes delirious with devotion.

The message light on my phone was flashing red. I punched the play button and listened as Joy told me that since I had forgotten to call the radiologist's office, she had done it for me, making an appointment at eight the next morning, ending with a reminder: "It's time for you to learn to take care of yourself, Jack."

I replayed the message, deciphering her voice, not the words. Joy wasn't angry, frustrated, or annoyed that I'd forgotten to call. There was no touch of humor either, no gentle teasing, just sadness, her voice fading away at the end, like she was letting go.

I had buried our shared pain, stepped around our long silences, and ducked her wounded eyes until I was certain that our love had become another casualty of Kevin's death. The truth, though, was in her voice.

Joy still cared, after all that had happened, after all that she had done and I had failed to do. She still cared. That's why she'd come to the house. That's why she'd made the doctor appointments. I listened to her message again, hearing, at last, the rest of it. She still cared, but that was no longer enough.

I retreated to my chair in the den, cross-examining myself in the soft shadow of the lone lamp about what had happened and what might still be possible. I wasn't good at this. I was better at accepting the harsh reality of death, loss, and guilt, lowering my head and pushing on without looking back or wondering whether a second chance lay beneath the wreckage.

I closed my eyes and slept, dreaming that I was suspended in midair, Joy and Kate on either side, each extending a hand, one slipping away, the other reaching out, forcing me to choose. In that instant, a spasm shot through me, arching my back and neck, binding me as I shook, pulverizing my dream in a blast of blinding white light. I opened my eyes. Ruby was standing on my chest licking the tears from my cheeks.

Chapter Thirty-four

Latrell waited until close to midnight before he left home. There was a Wal-Mart two miles from the cave that was open twenty-four hours. No one paid any attention to cars left in that lot. He parked there and walked like he always did, passing through a neighborhood, with few streetlights, of older, modest houses whose residents had long since gone to bed.

He would have preferred to park at the rail yard and take the path behind the storage sheds, but then he would have had to explain why he left his car parked at the terminal building overnight. His coworkers might start asking questions if they saw him disappear into the woods, especially after a body had been found nearby in the Dumpster.

The local news had reported that the victim was another drug dealer. The reporter noted there was speculation that the murder could be part of a gang war that had started with the murders earlier in the week. Good, Latrell thought. Things were coming back together.

Dressed in black jeans and a black T-shirt, he was nothing

more than a shadow. No one saw him slip into the eastern edge of the woods. Aided by the moonlight and the years underground that had sharpened his night vision, and with his flashlight tucked into his backpack, Latrell kept on walking.

Though the night had cooled, the woods were dense, holding on to the day's heat. Latrell heard occasional rustling in the underbrush, night prowlers giving him wide berth. It took him close to an hour to reach the entrance, a thin sheen of sweat coating his skin.

The entrance to the cave was through a hollowed waist-high gash nature had cut into a rocky mound that pushed out from the face of a wooded hillside like a blunt snout.

Concealed with a quilt delicately woven from fallen tree limbs, torn shrubs, and other debris, it appeared natural and random to anyone who stumbled onto it. It was for him a perfect example of ordered chaos, another trick he played on the rest of the world from whom he hid his true self.

Latrell's breath froze in his throat when he saw that his careful camouflage had been shredded, reduced to a pile of rubble scattered around the entrance as if thrown from the back of a truck. He was certain that no animal could have caused such a disturbance. Someone had found his cave. He clutched his gut as if he'd been cut open.

Kneeling in the darkness, Latrell examined each limb, each fragment of tree bark and remnant of bushes and vines, trying to understand what had happened. His mind raced with so many possibilities the woods began to slowly rotate, speeding up until he threw his arms around the base of a tree, holding on with his eyes pinched closed until the earth stopped moving.

Breathing heavily, Latrell let go of the tree, sat with his back to the trunk, and hugged his knees to his chest. He sorted the possibilities like the papers he filed at work until he gained control of them. The exercise calmed him so that he could think clearly.

Whoever had found the entrance may have stopped out-side or gone inside and left or gone inside and stayed. There could have been one person or several—kids drunk or stoned, a bum looking for a cool dry place or, worst of all, it could have been someone who knew, someone who might be waiting inside to ruin everything.

Shock and fear had given way to the fine, hard rage that drove Latrell to put things right. Gripping his flashlight, he shimmied through the slanted opening, crab walking down ten feet of a rough-hewn chute until he came to the first and smallest of three chambers. Standing, he swept the chamber with the flashlight's halogen beam.

The floor of the cave was dirty. Latrell had given up try-ing to keep it clean. Not even he could do that. For once, the dirt was helpful.

There were two overlapping sets of footprints, one com-ing toward him and the other going back toward the interior of the cave, neither of them his. They were large, bigger than his feet, and smooth, not ridged like the athletic shoes he wore. The footprints had not been there when Latrell was in the cave the night before. Latrell stopped, listened for echoes of the intruder's footsteps.

Hearing nothing, Latrell hurried through a floor-to-ceiling crevasse that split the first two chambers, the rock cool and moist, easily picking out more footprints on the floor of the second room with his flashlight. This room, slightly larger than the first, was a humpbacked oval wide enough for a large table but with a ceiling low enough that even he had to stoop. The opening to the main chamber was a long, shoul-der-width vertical cut rising from the base of the opposite wall.

Latrell waited again, pressing against the edge of the opening, listening for any sound that didn't belong, and then, comforted by the silence, he pushed through the open-ing and into his private cathedral. The ceiling was twenty feet above the floor, the walls sloping outward to the edges of a wide basin with jagged alcoves cut into the limestone face. An underground lake lapped at a rock beach, its far shore beyond the reach of Latrell's flashlight.

He stood on the outer edge, cutting through the darkness with his flashlight. The cave was empty, save for him.

Latrell didn't stop to marvel at the limestone formations dripping from the ceiling like melted wax. He didn't stop to light the candles he had left hidden on ledges along the wall. He didn't look for the occasional salamander that crawled out of the ink-black water to lounge on the rocks.

He went straight to the deepest recess of the cave, his most private space, where behind a small barricade of rocks he kept the photograph Johnny McDonald had taken of him and his mother in front of the house when he was fifteen. There, the rocks had been scattered, kicked to the far corners. The photograph was gone. His breath was coming in gasps, his belly churning.

He checked his other hiding place, an alcove Latrell could only reach by climbing ten feet above the floor and holding tight to natural footholds cut into the rock face. That's where he kept his gun and night-vision goggles. They were gone, too. He cocked his head toward the cavern roof, certain that he heard laughter deep in the darkness. He dropped to the floor, spotlighting the ceiling with his flashlight, the beam bouncing back at him from the empty shadows.

Latrell lit every candle, painting flickering images on the limestone canvas, kicking small rocks out of his path, hurtling larger ones into the shallows of the lake. The rest of his things, the canned food, the sleeping bag, the change of clothes he kept neatly stacked and folded, were untouched.

He found more footprints, these coming from the water's edge as if the person leaving them had emerged from the lake. If someone had crossed the lake, how did he do it? By boat? Then where was the boat? Swimming? How could someone swim across the lake in the dark without getting lost or drowning? Latrell followed the footprints from the lake, tracing their route across his cave, eventually coming to each of his hiding places.

He walked back to the water, peering out into the darkness. Latrell had never crossed the lake, had no idea how far it extended or how deep it was. He'd only waded out until the water touched his chin, retreating to the safety of dry rock.

Now someone had crossed the lake, found his hiding place, and stolen his special things and his gun, coming and going through his hidden entrance like they were roommates. He didn't believe such a person was an accidental explorer. No, it had to be someone who had sought him out, someone who had spied on him until he had unwittingly led him to the cave.

What was it the FBI agent had said? That someone always sees something. The agent was taunting him, telling Latrell that he was the one who'd seen something and that it was Latrell he had seen.

This FBI agent who didn't have a badge, who had tried to trick Latrell into remembering a man who wasn't there, he had to be the one who'd followed him to the woods, found the cave, and found a way across the lake in the dark, perhaps in one of those inflatable dinghies Latrell had seen in movies.

This agent who shook so much he couldn't work. That was nothing but a trick meant to throw him off. Latrell should never have given Marcellus's dog to him. He should have taken the agent like he took Oleta when she interfered with his plan. That's what he would have to do now if he were to put things right.

Latrell waded into the water until it covered his ankles. The invisible insects attacked again. He clawed at his flesh until blood ran down his arms, wanting to peel his skin from his bones. Then he dropped to his knees and began to scream.

Chapter Thirty-five

I learned two things at the radiologist's office. The first was that no one would tell me the results of my MRI. Everyone had a friendly smile, offered a helping hand, and gave me the same answer. Your doctor will tell you.

If they had seen something awful on the films, if I only had twenty-four hours to live, or if all was well and I could look forward to being interviewed for my hundredth birthday by the *Today* show weatherman, they wouldn't tell me. Telling me nothing came as easily to them as breathing.

I imagined the radiologist sitting in her office, flipping through films, tossing them into separate piles marked yes, no, and try again later, the medical version of a fortune-telling eight ball. Whatever the news, she would pick up the phone and hand it off to the patient's primary doctor, whose job it would become to break it to the patient while she receded, Oz-like, behind the lead curtain.

My life, my future, had become a digitized entry in the American medical machine. I'd been reduced to a one-dimensional collection of data points, diagnostic codes, and billing schedules. The system knew everything about me, but I was the one who remained in the dark, enlightenment waiting on the other side of the weekend, another version of the neon sign in the bar on Strawberry Hill promising free beer tomorrow.

The second thing I learned was that an MRI made a hell of a racket.

"It's the magnets," the technician explained, her genial disembodied voice filling my headphones as I lay inside an elongated tube that with only a few inches between my nose and the ceiling was more coffin than diagnostic dream machine.

"Just relax," she told him, "and don't move."

"Easy for you to say," I answered.

"That's why we get to say it," she said with a practiced laugh.

My appointment was at eight o'clock. I was finished at eleven. While the MRI was thin-slicing my bones and tissues, relieving them of their secrets, my squad was being x-rayed by the polygraph examiner. I was lying still. I wondered if any of them were still lying.

Kate had left a message on my cell phone that our class in facial micro expressions would begin at seven o'clock at my house. She was, she said, bringing dinner and a toothbrush. I heard the echo of advice I had often given Wendy: "Be careful what you ask for." I had eight hours to ponder the women in my life. That was plenty of time to sort things out, even if I spent part of it chasing bad guys.

Chapter Thirty-six

I pulled into the driveway of Jill Rice's house as the door to her three-car garage was going up. I waited while she backed a Mercedes sedan onto the driveway, braking just in time to avoid crashing into my Chevrolet's grille. She laid on her horn and mouthed something in her rearview mirror that looked like asshole but could just as easily have been fucking asshole.

I was glad to catch her off guard and angry. That made it more likely I would learn something useful. I'd put on an old sport coat and tie that didn't match. My attire was intended to depress expectations, another effective tool in lowering someone's defenses. The more they looked down on you, the more likely they were to underestimate you.

I had slipped my Detective Funkhouser ID into the clear plastic slot of my wallet normally occupied by my FBI credentials. I knew the shelf life on my phony ID was running out, but I needed all the time I could get before Colby Hudson found out I was investigating him. I got out of my car, holding my ID in the palm of my hand, and approached her car.

"Jill Rice?"

She rolled her window down, her eyes obscured by over-sized dark glasses. "Yes. You're blocking my driveway. Who are you?"

"Detective Funkhouser. Kansas City, Kansas, Police Department."

I flashed her my ID. She took off her sunglasses, double-checking my picture against my face.

"I hope this is important."

I stepped closer to her door. "Are you in a hurry, Mrs. Rice?"

"Yes, detective," she said, one arm resting in the open window, the other on the steering wheel. "I'm in a hurry."

She was an attractive woman, forty-plus, her tanned arms lightly muscled, her auburn hair cut short, her pink lip gloss gleaming, and her face unburdened by crow's-feet, laugh lines, or other evidence of natural life. She was wearing a pale green, low-cut tennis top, and a black tennis skirt that was hiked above her well-toned thighs. Rice leaned forward just enough so that her top billowed out, offering me a fuller view of breasts that either defied gravity or weren't original equipment, assuming the sight would either shorten our meeting or distract me from its purpose. I kept my eyes locked on hers until she straightened her blouse, which she finally did, neither of us blushing.

"I won't keep you any longer than I have to."

"What's this about?"

"Your husband, ma'am."

"I don't have a husband, Detective. I have an ex-husband."

"My mistake, ma'am. I apologize. I visited your ex-husband yesterday. He seemed quite worried."

"I'm not surprised. Prison would make anyone worry."

"You're right about that, ma'am. Any idea what he'd be worried about, not counting the whole getting-raped-in-the-shower thing, because I don't think that's what was keeping him up at night."

"I don't know and I don't care. What's this got to do with me?"

"That's what I'm trying to find out, Mrs. Rice. I can't share with you all the details of our investigation at this time, but it appears that Mr. Rice may be under pressure to authorize the sale of certain of his assets against his will."

She shook her head. "Against his will?"

"What I mean, ma'am, is that he may be the victim of extortion, someone trying to take advantage of his incarceration, figuring he's in no position to do anything about it. We've learned that you're also the owner of those assets, so you can understand why I need to talk with you about all of this, even if you are in a hurry. I could have you come down to headquarters and talk there. We'd have plenty of time and no one would bother us. Or we could try and wrap this up now."

Rice let out a sigh. "Thomas doesn't have any assets. I got everything in the divorce."

"Actually, ma'am, that's only partly correct. I checked the court file on your divorce and it turns out that Mr. Rice gets half the proceeds from the sale of your house and he has to sign off on the sale price. We understand that you've agreed to sell the house at a price that's well below market value, which means that Mr. Rice comes out the loser. If someone is using threats to make Mr. Rice sell cheap, that's against the law. Both of you would be victims of extortion."

She tossed her head back, laughing with disgust. "That little shit. He wouldn't know the truth if it bit him in the ass."

"And would you, Mrs. Rice?"

"Would I what?"

"Know the truth if it bit you in the ass."

"Look, Detective. Thomas agreed to give me everything

in the divorce. I thought it was because he felt so guilty, but that's an emotion Thomas is not familiar with. He told me he made a deal that would help him get started when he got out of prison. All I had to do was sell the house and his car at the right price to the right person."

"And you went along?"

"And I went along. He said that if I didn't, he would fight over everything. I went along because I wanted to cut my ties with him as quickly as possible."

"When did he tell you about this deal?"

"Right after he agreed to plead guilty," she said. "He said we'd have to wait six months after he went to jail so my name would be the only one on the papers and the sales wouldn't attract any attention."

"Did he tell you how much to sell the car and house for?"

"He said the buyer would name the price."

I waited a beat before asking the money question, afraid of being right. "Did he tell you who the buyer would be?"

"Not at first. He said he'd let me know when he knew. He called me a few weeks ago and asked me to come for a visit. It was the first time I'd been in a prison. It was awful. I almost felt bad that I had turned him in, but he was the one who cheated on me. So I went to see him and he said someone named Colby Hudson was the buyer. I sold him the car a couple of weeks ago and we closed on the house the other night."

Rice's eyes widened as she said his name, her hand suddenly covering her mouth. "Oh my God, I am such an idiot! He's an FBI agent. I saw that on the forms he filled out. Was I wrong to sell the car and the house to an FBI agent? Did Thomas get me into another one of his messes?"

I sidestepped her question. "I can't answer that, ma'am. Have you talked to Mr. Rice since then?"

"No."

"Had you ever met Agent Hudson before? Maybe while your husband's case was going on?"

"No. I mean there were a lot of agents at our house when they arrested Thomas, but I only met two of them—a man and woman. I'm sorry, but I don't remember their names. Am I in trouble?"

Her concern may have been sincere. It may not have occurred to Rice that her husband was dragging her into yet another scheme until a police detective showed up and started asking her questions. Or, it could all be an act. She seemed too calculating a woman not to have questioned giving a sweetheart deal to an FBI agent so her ex-husband could get a fresh start when he got out of prison. I ignored her question again, sticking to my own.

"When you went to visit your husband, what was his mood like? Was he glad to see you? Was he worried or afraid?"

"He was pathetic. He whined how sorry he was and how much he missed me. All the usual crap. If he was scared, he didn't show it. But then, Thomas was the best salesman I ever saw in my life."

I studied Rice, not saying anything, waiting for her to volunteer something. She tugged at her top again and then checked her watch.

"Can I go now, Detective? I really am in a hurry."

Chapter Thirty-seven

I moved my car to the curb, watching her drive away, wondering if I would know the truth if it bit me in the ass. Colby's story that Jill Rice had called our office looking for a buyer didn't stand up against her version. That didn't make Colby the liar but it did mean one of them wasn't telling the truth. Thomas Rice had offered his alternate reality, that his wife had gotten everything in the divorce and that what she did with the property was up to her. He was careful enough to tell a story that was at least technically true even if it wasn't the whole story.

I called Grisnik to see what he'd found out about who had visited Thomas Rice and who Rice had talked to on the phone.

"His ex-wife came to see him a few weeks ago. Only time she shows up on the visitor logs," Grisnik said.

"That fits with what she told me. Score one for her in the truth sweepstakes."

"Rice have any other visitors?"

"He is one unpopular guy. His lawyer came to see him

once right after he started serving his sentence. No one after that until his wife."

"What about phone calls? Did Rice call anyone after we left?"

"One call to a cell phone."

"Whose was it?"

"Phone belonged to an eighty-five-year-old man lives in an Alzheimer's unit."

"Why would Rice call him?"

"He didn't. Phone was stolen. We don't have any idea who Rice called."

"Let's go back and ask him," I said.

"Too late. He hanged himself in the prison laundry. Happened last night. I just heard about it an hour ago."

"Shit. I just talked to his ex-wife. She didn't say anything about it. She must not have gotten word yet."

"She's the ex-wife, not the wife, which takes her off the next-of-kin list."

"Someone should let her know before she reads about it in the paper."

"You want to volunteer," Grisnik said, "be my guest. Telling the family, even the exes, is the worst part of this job. You can have it."

I hung up and shook. It was a mild ripple, a reminder of the condition my condition was in. I wondered if the news of Rice's death had triggered the tremor, a reaction to guilt over the possibility that my visit had literally scared him to death. If that was the case, I must not have felt too guilty since the tremors were short-lived. I didn't feel responsible for Rice's death. On that, I agreed with his wife. Rice had chosen his road. I was doing my job.

On a purely statistical basis, Rice's death should not have been a surprise. Suicide is the third leading cause of death in prison, which sounds pretty grim until you realize there aren't a lot of other ways to go. The rate is not as bad as in jails, where suicide is the leading cause of death. People don't stay in jail long enough to die for other reasons. They either get out or graduate to prison.

Despite the numbers, Rice didn't strike me as suicidal, even though he ran the gamut of human emotions when I saw him. He was a wheeler-dealer, the kind of person who would never throw in the towel, and the prison laundry was an unlikely place to give up unless he had help.

Of all the emotions Rice had displayed, it turned out that the most honest one had been fear. The only time he was afraid was when I asked him about the sale of his house and car. Though neither of us mentioned him by name, Colby Hudson had hovered over our conversation like a curse that had now come true.

I hadn't learned anything that would convict Colby of a crime, but I doubted that the truth, whatever it was, would set him free. He'd gone on a buying binge that he couldn't afford on his FBI salary. He was the one person who knew about the surveillance camera in Marcellus's house and who matched the description of the man I thought I'd seen running from the murder scene, and who had been sitting at the right hand of Javy Ordonez, late of this world. I didn't know whether he was Forrest Gump, who managed by sheer coincidence to show up at every pivotal moment in the history of this case, or whether he was the man behind the throne, but my litany of suspicion was enough to give any Internal Affairs investigator a blue-diamond woody.

I couldn't separate my suspicions of him from my knowledge that he was cheating on Wendy. Tanja Andrija had neither admitted nor denied having an affair with him. That didn't matter. Colby was having an affair with her even if she wasn't having one with him.

On that score, I realized that Wendy had me dead to rights about my relationship with Kate. I had been unfaithful to

Joy. I shook again, this time from shame. I was judging Colby more harshly than I had judged myself. Truth and righteousness had become silent casualties in my rationalized world.

My cell phone rang. Caller ID said it was Ammara Iverson. I was anxious to talk with her, hoping that she'd been able to get me copies of Thomas Rice's file.

"Hey," I said, "great timing. Any luck with the Rice file?"

"Sorry. I've been jammed up."

"I know you're busy, but the sooner the better. How'd it go with the polygraph?"

"I'm guilty of having sexual fantasies about Denzel Washington. Otherwise, I'm in the clear."

"Good to know. What's up?"

"Have you heard from Colby lately?" asked Ammara.

"Not since I saw him at lunch yesterday. Why?"

"He didn't show up for his polygraph."

"Did you try to reach him?"

"Troy tried his cell and his home phone. When he didn't answer, Troy told Ben Yates. Yates sent two agents to Colby's house. He wasn't there. The lock on the back door had been jimmied. They went inside, where they found some cash and drugs. The U.S. Attorney is getting a search warrant."

"Why? They've already searched the place."

"Colby not showing up, together with the jimmied back door justified the entry into the house. Make sure he was okay and all that."

"Are you telling me that the cash and drugs were sitting out in plain sight?" I asked.

"All I can tell you is what was found inside the house. Now that we can't find Colby and there's evidence of a crime, we've got to do a full search that no one can complain about later, if there is a later."

Ammara let her last words hang, reminding me of our conversation yesterday.

"And what?"

She paused. I could hear her take a deep breath. "I called Wendy before I called you. Just in case Colby was at her place and had overslept."

I started to shake, worse than from guilt, worse than from shame. My heart raced out in front of the tremors. I stumbled over my words.

"Has she heard from Colby?"

"I don't know. I didn't talk to her. She didn't answer at home or on her cell and her boss said she didn't show up to work. I'm sorry, Jack, we can't find either one of them."

Chapter Thirty-eight

There are things we know and things we don't want to know. When what we know is too hard to handle, we convince ourselves that we can box it up, stick it someplace we can forget about, and then, magically, we won't know it any longer. Then we protect ourselves with a lie—what we don't know can't hurt us.

I have never forgotten the pain of losing Kevin. It had hardened into a callus around the unhealed hole in my heart. But I had put away the unspeakable immobilizing fear and the cold rush of primal panic that swept over me when I first learned that my neighbor had taken him. That's what I had hidden in the box that Ammara had just opened and it reentered my system as swiftly as snake's venom.

Wendy wasn't a young child and Colby Hudson wasn't a sexual predator. She might have gone shopping and he might have gone fishing. They might have eloped. Someone might have planted the drugs and cash in Colby's house. Anything was possible and nothing was certain except that I was scared, as frightened as I'd been that day in Dallas.

The disappearance of a child always mobilizes action.

Everyone can identify with the child's vulnerability. There are no gray areas, only outrage and a secret, shameful gratitude of those who join in the search that it wasn't their child.

It would be different with Wendy and Colby because no one knew whether they were victims or suspects, though Ammara's unspoken subtext implied that the Bureau believed that Wendy might be the former while it was more likely that Colby was the latter. Colby's status would be confirmed when the paperwork for his purchase of Jill Rice's car and house was discovered in the search of his home.

It wouldn't take long for Troy Clark to run the same traps I had. He'd find out that I had used a phony ID to visit Thomas Rice and that Rice died less than twenty-four hours later. He'd trace my Detective Funkhouser alter ego to Marty Grisnik, who could only give me so much cover without getting his tit caught in the wringer. And he'd find out that I had braced Jill Rice. He'd lock up Thomas Rice's file before Ammara could copy it and I'd end up answering questions about withholding information and obstruction of justice, shakes or no shakes.

While all that was happening, Wendy would be slipping farther away. She would be only one of several priorities, probably at the bottom of the list until there was hard evidence that she was a victim of something.

When Kevin was taken, I had had the full resources of the federal, state, and local law-enforcement agencies in one of the biggest cities in the United States. They and I did everything we could as fast as we could and it still wasn't enough. This time I was alone and relegated to the sidelines, unable to control the investigation or, for that matter, my own body.

I tried to dial Joy's phone number, but I was shaking so much I couldn't get it right. I slammed the phone onto the car seat, cursing all that was holy and more that wasn't. I hinged forward, smacking into the steering wheel, anchoring my arms around it until the worst had passed.

I raised my head. The street in front of Jill Rice's house

was deserted. It was small consolation that my outburst had gone unnoticed. My breathing slowed, keeping pace with the decreasing aftershocks in my torso. When my hands steadied, I tried Joy's number again, searching for a way to tell her that our nightmare was back.

She answered on the first ring, her voice light, almost playful.

"Jack," she said. "I guess you survived the radiologist."

"Perfect attendance. Do you have a key to Wendy's apartment?"

Joy always said I had two voices, with and without my badge. She hated the badge voice, said it was indifferent.

"What's the matter?"

"Wendy didn't go to work today," I said, taking it one step at a time.

"Did you call her apartment or her cell?"

"I didn't. Ammara Iverson did."

"Why was she calling Wendy?"

Intuitive anxiety had elevated her pitch half an octave, her voice quivering. I imagined her sitting up, spine stiff, running one hand through her hair before grabbing on to something solid.

"She was looking for Colby Hudson. He didn't show up to work, either."

Joy forced a laugh. "Oh, you don't think they ran off and got married, do you?"

My answer caught in my throat, held there by another spasm, escaping with a stutter. "I wish they had, but it doesn't look that way. When Troy couldn't find Colby, Ben Yates sent a couple of agents to his house. They found some things that didn't belong there and now they're looking for both Colby and Wendy."

"Oh, my God, Jack! If Colby did anything wrong, the Bureau can't think Wendy had anything to do with it! That's absurd!"

"No one is saying that she did."

"Then what are they saying?"

"That they can't find her."

Joy let out a low, wailing moan, understanding at last what I was saying. The woman who'd left me two months ago would have hung up, asking the rest of her questions in private, getting the answers from a bottle. She didn't, gathering herself and asking, "What do we do?"

"The Bureau is tied up at Colby's house. I don't know if they've sent anyone to Wendy's yet. I want to get there before they do. But I don't have a key."

"I do. I'll meet you there in twenty minutes."

"I'm on my way."

Chapter Thirty-nine

Wendy lived in an apartment complex on the east side of the Country Club Plaza, a shopping, eating, and drinking district in midtown on the Missouri side of the state line. Her balcony looked west toward the public library and north up Main Street. I could see it as I approached along Ward Parkway, the library to my right, Brush Creek to my left. Her unit was on the northwest corner. The drapes facing the balcony were closed.

Searching her apartment was another calculated risk. If there was evidence of a crime, I might contaminate it without even knowing it. In that event, I'd be adding another count to an indictment for obstruction of justice. Good intentions wouldn't save my career or mitigate my sentence. None of that mattered as much as the precious minutes that would evaporate while Troy Clark allocated his limited resources to finding Colby Hudson. Waiting was not an option.

Joy met me in the parking lot. Her jaw was set, her eyes stony, a thin purse stuck under her arm. She was wearing jeans, a lavender short-sleeved jersey under a tan jacket, and no makeup, her hair pulled back and held in place by a black band. She was bouncing slightly on the toes of her running shoes. She had never been a runner. The shoes were as new as she was. She gave me a hug. I held on until she pulled back.

"Let's go," she said.

Wendy's apartment was a small one bedroom, one bath. The carpet was a rich cream, one pale wall set off by an array of four vibrant prints, each of two women, sitting at a café, strolling on a sidewalk, reclining in a drawing room, and lingering in a garden, their faces blank, featureless, their personalities expressed in their posture. There were prints on the other walls of a fanciful jungle filled with oversized tropical birds, a framed poster from the 1972 Montreux Jazz Festival and another celebrating Shakespeare in the Park. The furniture was modern, spare, and comfortable.

Two dinner dishes caked with uneaten spaghetti, dirty silverware on the top plate, were stacked in the sink alongside two wine glasses, a swallow of red left in each. A colander half filled with pasta sat on the kitchen counter next to an open jar of marinara sauce and an uncorked bottle of wine. Damp towels filled the washing machine, underwear in the dryer. The queen-size bed was unmade, the pillows spread out for two. Wendy's suitcase was under the bed; her clothes still hung in the closet. There was no sign of a struggle or of forced entry.

The stuffed animal from her childhood, Monkey Girl, sat on her dresser. I remembered when I had given it to Wendy.

"It looks like she didn't finish dinner and left in a hurry," I said.

Joy surveyed the kitchen. "Dinner for two."

"This has to be from last night's dinner. Not the night before. That's when she met me at Fortune Wok. As angry as she was, I doubt that she came home and made dinner. When was the last time you talked to her?"

Joy paced the living room, arms folded over her chest.

"Wednesday night, after I talked to you. I called her back so she'd know that we had talked about your doctor appointments."

"Did she say anything about going away?"

Joy shook her head. "No. Remember, I told you that she insisted on going with you to see the neurologist on Monday. She would have told me if she had changed her plans."

"Did you talk about anything else?"

"I told her what you'd said about Kate Scranton. You were right. She was furious with you, but she was too upset about your shaking to deal with that. I told her to give you a break, that you were weak and pathetic like all newly single middle-aged men who had no idea how to live alone."

Joy said it like she was reciting material learned for a test, the humor of her last comment lost until she realized what she'd said, looking at me, covering her mouth.

"I'm sorry, Jack."

I waved off her concern. "You're both right. I screwed up. Did she say anything at all about Colby either in that conversation or anytime in the last week or so?"

"Only that they had argued."

"When? About what?"

"After your scene at Fortune Wok. Wendy didn't say what they argued about."

"Did she say anything about Colby buying a car and a house?"

Joy nodded. "She mentioned the house. What's that got to do with all of this?"

I ran through a quick summary of the Thomas Rice case and the conflicting stories I'd gotten from Rice, his ex-wife, and Colby. When I told Joy that Thomas Rice had apparently hanged himself, the little color in her face vanished.

"Are you saying that Colby had something to do with that?"

"I don't know. I'm trying to tie all this together and I can't make it work. There's too much I don't know."

Wendy's desk was on the wall opposite the balcony. A computer sat on it.

"Go through these papers on her desk," I told Joy. "I'll look at her computer."

"What am I looking for?"

"Anything about Colby, anything about going away, anything that will help us find her."

Fortunately, Wendy had ignored everything that I'd taught her about security and hadn't protected her documents, e-mail, or bank records with passwords. Nothing jumped out at me, but I didn't have time to read much of it.

"I'd take her computer with us, but that's the first thing Troy will look for when he gets here."

"No problem. Back it up with this."

Joy tossed me her key ring. It had a flash bar on it with four gigs of memory.

"You are really something."

"That's the second time this week you've said that. Keep it up and I'll start thinking you believe it."

I looked at her. Her eyes had softened. The corners of her mouth had dipped. She wasn't flirting. She was hoping.

"There's nothing here but bills and junk mail," Joy said.

I finished downloading the contents of Wendy's hard drive to the flash bar. "Let's get out of here."

We had found as much good news as bad. No signs of forced entry. No signs of struggle. No signs she had planned to leave. No signs she was coming back.

Chapter Forty

"What now?" Joy asked.

We were sitting in her car, the engine idling. I wanted to run in a dozen different directions, but I didn't know which one to choose.

"Who did Wendy hang out with? Who were her friends? We should talk with them. Maybe she said something to one of them."

"There's a woman at work she's mentioned quite a bit, Julie Rutherford. I'll call her," Joy said, pausing and then adding, "Isn't that awful?"

"What?"

"Between the two of us, we only know about one of her friends. We don't even know if she has any others. Where have we been?"

"It doesn't matter. We can beat one another up about being lousy parents when this is over. We don't have the luxury of doing that right now."

"What are you going to do?"

"I'm going to talk with Jill Rice again. Tell her about her husband, if she doesn't already know. See if his death refreshes her recollection. Then I'll take a look at whatever was on Wendy's computer. I'll just keep pushing until something breaks."

I fought to get the last words out, my shoulders twisting one way, my neck and head yanking me the other like I was being wound in opposite directions by dueling corkscrews. Joy leaned over, holding me, just as Wendy had, as if she could squeeze the demons out.

"You don't have to do this, Jack," she said, her lips to my ears. "We can leave it to the Bureau."

"You know I do," I managed when the spasm released me. "Ben Yates will make certain that Troy follows standard procedure, which means focus on the high-priority target. That's Colby Hudson. Troy will let things unfold until he knows where Wendy fits into the picture. It's what I would do if I were in his position. But that might take too long."

She let go. I held her hands, looking at them, avoiding her eyes. When Kevin was taken, I had told Joy not to worry, that I would get him back, that he'd be okay. I was afraid to make the same promise again, knowing how hard it would be to keep it. There was too much that could go wrong, beginning with me. She needed to know that.

"I don't know what's happening to me," I said, my voice still wobbly. "And I'm scared that I won't be able to do what I have to do."

"Jack . . ."

"No, let me finish. I've been afraid before. When Kevin was taken, I was crazy scared. But I could do what I had to do then even if it wasn't enough. I haven't been that scared again until today. When I shake, I don't know what I am or who I am. I only know that it can't be me that's doing it. Then it stops and I know that it is me, it's who and what I've become. I don't know why and I don't know if I can do what I have to do."

She cupped my chin in the palm of her hand, bringing her

gaze to mine. Her eyes were full. She blinked back tears, a few escaping across her cheeks.

"We'll do the best we can and we'll live with the rest. We've never had the luxury of doing anything else."

I called Marty Grisnik on my way to Jill Rice's house to let him know that Detective Funkhouser was about to find himself in deep shit.

"You're going to get a call from Troy Clark."

"At last. Is he going to ask me out on a date?"

"He's going to ask you about Detective Funkhouser."

Grisnik hesitated for an instant. "Why would he do that?"

"Troy ordered everyone on the squad to take a polygraph so he could find out if one of us tipped off the drug house killer about the surveillance camera I put in the ceiling fan."

"Including you?"

"Excluding me. Movers and shakers need not apply."

"Makes sense. It's hard enough to tell when someone is lying without all that going on at the same time. But if you're not taking the test, how will Troy find out about Detective Funkhouser?"

"An agent named Colby Hudson didn't show up for his polygraph."

"Any chance he's the same agent who bought Rice's house?"

"Hundred percent. Two agents went to his house to check on him. He wasn't there. They found drugs and cash. Troy is coming back with a search warrant. He'll probably find records showing that Colby bought Rice's house and car. Then he'll find out that you and Funkhouser went to see Rice and that Rice is dead. Then he'll call you."

"What do you want me to tell Troy?"

"Tell him the truth. Tell him that I asked you to help me and that, as far as you knew, I was acting in the course and scope of my official duties."

"You call that the truth?"

"I call that enough of the truth. You helped me out. I'll take the heat."

"Is that all of it?"

"No. I told you before that I had a personal interest. Colby Hudson is involved with my daughter. We can't find either one of them."

"You think she's in trouble?"

"Until I know otherwise."

"Any reason to think she was a victim of a crime committed in Kansas City, Kansas?"

"No."

"Then I can't help you officially, but if you keep me in the loop, I'll do what I can."

"Thanks. You'll know what I know."

"That's what I'm looking for."

I started to tell Grisnik that my daughter's name was Wendy, where she lived and worked, and what she looked like, but he'd already hung up. Either his offer to help was perfunctory, a cop's version of "drop by anytime, we're always open" or he had that information already. If it were the former, I'd misread him. If it was the latter, he was doing a better job than I was.

Chapter Forty-one

Jill Rice came home at four-thirty. I'd been waiting in front of her house for an hour, ignoring the neighbors who'd slowed down as they passed me by. She slowed down as well, giving me a curdled look as she pulled into the driveway. I followed her into the garage and opened her car door.

"We need to talk."

Her makeup was intact, her tennis clothes unwrinkled and unstained by sweat. Her perfume was mixed with wine. My guess was that she'd spent her tennis game gossiping at the net and drinking in the clubhouse.

She stayed in the car. "What about, Detective Funkhouser?"

"My name, for starters. It's Jack Davis. I'm an FBI agent."

"But you said you were a policeman from Kansas City, Kansas."

"It's a long story that will be easier to tell inside."

She drew her lips back. "I want to see some ID."

I knew she would. All I had was my driver's license and a business card I handed to her.

"You can print business cards at Kinko's. I want to see

your badge or I'm calling the police." She reached for her cell phone.

"I am an FBI agent, Mrs. Rice. When we're finished talking, you can call my office and they'll tell you. I'm on leave, so I don't have my FBI credentials."

She edged back toward the center console on the front seat of her car. "I don't believe you. Why should I?"

I reached toward her, extending my hand. "Please, Mrs. Rice. I don't want to make this any harder than it is."

She cringed and flipped open her cell phone. "I'm calling 911."

"Let me talk to you first. I'm not going to hurt you. Inside will be better."

She hesitated with the phone. "Not until you tell me what this is about."

"It's about your ex-husband."

"What about him? I've already answered your questions about him."

"There's been a new development," I said.

"What? Did he screw somebody else?"

"Depends on your point of view."

"How's that?"

"He's dead. He hanged himself last night. I didn't know that when I was here this morning. The prison probably won't notify you since ex-spouses aren't considered next of kin. I didn't want you to find out what had happened watching TV or reading the newspaper. I'm sorry for your loss."

Rice looked at me, looked away, held herself, and shuddered. Her cell phone fell from her hand into her lap. She didn't speak, cry, or moan. She was as silent as if she'd been struck dumb, looking at me again, finding her voice.

"Thomas would never kill himself. There must be some mistake."

"I wish there were. Let's go inside. You can call the prison. Ask for the warden. He'll tell you."

I extended my hand again. This time she took it. Her hand was cool and limp. She walked slowly to the door, slipped the key in, turned the lock, punched in the code that turned off the alarm, and led me into the kitchen.

Copper pots hung in a rectangle above a black marble island. Hardwood floors gleamed. The light was soft, bright, and indirect. The flowers were freshly cut.

The light on her phone was blinking, the digital readout saying she had one new message. She pushed the button to play the message. It was from the prison, a woman identifying herself as the warden's secretary asking her to call as soon as possible. Her eyes were wide, almost wild. She fumbled for paper and pen, trying to write the number down, but the message ended before she could.

She turned to me. "I didn't get all of it."

I replayed the message, writing the number down. I dialed and handed her the phone.

"This is Jill Rice," she said to the secretary. "You left me a message."

She waited a moment and then identified herself again.

"Yes, Warden. This is Jill Rice. My husband is Thomas Rice," she said, retaking her vows.

She listened, slumping against the counter before sliding onto a kitchen chair.

"Thank you. He was a good man. Things just got away from him at the end," she said.

I took the phone, hanging it up for her.

She wiped the corners of her eyes. "The warden said that Thomas listed me as next of kin when he first arrived at the prison. They told him that an ex-spouse didn't qualify. He said he didn't care. He said that I'd always be his wife."

Chapter Forty-two

Death doesn't settle easily or quickly. I'd learned from delivering news of a loved one's death that I couldn't instantly turn a shattered survivor into a good witness. Some people fall apart. Others are brave in public and grieve in private. Others refuse to mourn. They accept their loss as the penalty for their sins or they assign it to God's master plan, something beyond their understanding.

Jill Rice, sitting at her kitchen table in her designer tennis set with pinot noir on her breath, was suffering the death of her husband. Her shoulders were slumped, her chin hung toward her chest. Minutes ago, she had been harsh and unforgiving toward him. It was too soon to tell whether she felt worse for him or for herself.

I wouldn't tell her that he'd brought this on himself. I wouldn't tell her what someone had told me when Kevin died, that he was in a better place. I wouldn't try to justify Thomas Rice's death or her suffering because there was no justification for such things. No one could justify Kevin's death to me because that would have somehow made it okay.

And if we can justify the death of an innocent child, we can justify anything.

So I joined Jill Rice at her table and told her again that I was sorry for her loss. I asked her if I could get her a glass of water or anything else and didn't push when she said no. Then I waited, though I didn't have the time.

After a while she lifted her head in my direction. "What do you want from me?"

"Do you have any idea what could have led to your husband's death?"

"You mean do I know why he killed himself?"

"If that's what happened."

She straightened, a new shock wave rippling through her face. "What are you saying?"

"Did the warden tell you whether Thomas left a note?"

"I was afraid to ask, but he said they didn't find one."

"Most people who commit suicide do it in private. If they've really made up their minds to kill themselves, they don't want someone talking them out of it. If you're in prison, you do it in your cell when your cellmate isn't there, not the laundry.

"What are you saying? That Thomas didn't kill himself? That he was murdered?"

"I don't know. When I saw him yesterday he was frightened of something and I think it had to do with the sale of this house. He wouldn't say what it was, only that I couldn't help him."

"All I know about the sale of the house is what he told me."

"Colby Hudson claims that you called the FBI office not long ago asking if anyone would be interested in buying your husband's car at a great price and that he just happened to take the call. When he bought the car, he said that you offered to also sell him the house for a lot less than it was worth. When he asked you why, he says you told him that you were doing it to get even with your husband. Is any of that true?"

"Not a word of it. I told you. Thomas set the whole thing up before he went to prison. Did Colby Hudson have something to do with my husband's death?"

"Five people were killed the other night in a drug house in Kansas City, Kansas. Two nights ago, another drug dealer was shot to death in the Argentine rail yard. Colby Hudson was working on both of those cases. Last night, your husband either committed suicide or was murdered. Colby was connected to your husband. I don't know how or why, but he is the only common link to all of the victims."

"What does he have to say about all of this?"

"When we find him, we'll ask him."

"I see."

Rice rose from the kitchen table and walked into the den. Bookcases lined one wall, although there were more crystal figurines, lacquered boxes, and other knickknacks than there were books. Photographs framed in silver were interspersed among the other decorator-inspired keepsakes. There was one of an older couple, the woman faintly resembling Jill, another of four small children who I guessed to be nieces and nephews, and others of people whose connection to her I could only speculate about.

She reached for the top shelf, pulling down a photograph that had been pushed to the back where it was barely visible. She brushed the dust from the glass and rubbed the silver frame with the hem of her skirt, holding it up long enough for me to catch a glimpse of her wearing a wedding gown and Thomas Rice in a tuxedo before she pressed it against her chest and turned toward me.

"When we arrested your husband, I'm sure our agents confiscated all of his financial records."

"Boxes of them and the computers he had at the office and at home."

"Did we ever give any of those records back to you?"

She cocked her head, surprised at the question. "As a matter of fact, yes. My accountant couldn't prepare my tax return without them. He told the U.S. Attorney's office what records he needed and they sent him the information. He put it all on his computer and e-mailed it to me. He had to get an extension so I could file my return after April 15th. Everything was finally taken care of about a month ago."

"Did you keep the e-mail with the records?"

"I didn't keep the e-mail, but I did download the records to my computer."

I pulled the flash bar Joy had given me from my pocket. "May I copy those records?"

She pulled her shoulders in close, apprehensive again. "Why? If you're an FBI agent, you should be able to get them from the U.S. Attorney's office."

"Mrs. Rice, I'm not officially assigned to this case. In fact, I'm not officially assigned to anything right now. I'm looking into this on my own."

"Why aren't you officially assigned to anything right now?"

"I'm on medical leave."

I started shaking, not as bad as before, more like I'd just put a quarter in a vibrating bed in a motel that rented rooms by the hour. I closed my eyes, opening them when I'd gotten my money's worth.

Her eyes were narrowed, her brow furrowed. "What makes you do that?"

"I don't know, but until I do and can make it stop, I'm not officially assigned to anything."

"Then why are you running around pretending to be a police detective and asking me all these questions?"

"Colby Hudson brought someone to see your house the other night. Were you here?"

"Yes. He brought a nice-looking young woman. She wasn't wearing a ring, but he was acting like the house was as much for her as it was for him."

"Did he introduce her to you?"

"I'm sure he did, but to tell you the truth, I'm terrible with names."

"Her name is Wendy Davis. She's my daughter and she's missing. I'm trying to find her."

Rice looked at me like she was seeing me for the first time and then returned the photograph to its spot, leaving it near the edge of the shelf where she could see it.

"My computer is downstairs."

Chapter Forty-three

It was close to six o'clock when I left Jill Rice's house. I worked the phone while navigating rush-hour traffic to Pete & Mac's to pick up Ruby.

I called Marty Grisnik to ask if he'd heard from Troy Clark. I called Ammara Iverson to find out when Troy was going to drop the hammer on me and to find out whether she had any leads on Wendy and Colby. I called Joy to ask whether she'd talked with Wendy's friend from work.

I called Kate to make certain she was still on for seven o'clock tonight, not certain whether I was. Wendy was missing and finding her was the only thing that mattered. That Kate could possibly help me by sorting out what I knew from what I suspected was reason enough to keep our date. The earlier promise of the weekend had vanished with Wendy's disappearance even as I remembered how it felt to kiss Kate, hold her close, and imagine holding her closer.

Wendy wasn't the only complication. The anticipation of being with Kate butted heads with my confused feelings for Joy, who'd reappeared, not as the woman I'd fallen in love with or the one whom I'd stopped loving, but as someone else, someone who'd come back to me when I needed her, reborn and not asking for anything in return.

I called Wendy, hoping she would answer, tell me she was fine, and make fun of me for my fears. I'd find a way to tease her in return and apologize for my gaffe with Kate. We'd both laugh and I would stop shaking.

Wendy didn't answer and neither did any of the others. The messages I left were like a net I'd thrown into the water. It was wet and empty when I hauled it in.

Ruby was glad to see me, shaking her short tail faster than I shook on a bad day. I let her in the car and rolled my window down. She parked herself in my lap, front paws on the door, nose in the wind. Of all the things I needed at the moment, a dog that I had to drop off and pick up at day care wasn't on the list. But she imposed a normalcy on my life, making me responsible for her, forcing me to adjust my needs to accommodate hers.

I had never done that with Joy and Wendy. They always had to adapt to me, the city where I was assigned, the hours I kept, the things I couldn't tell them about what I did. I could explain all of that to them and they would acquiesce, but Ruby was not impressed. She wanted to eat, play, and sleep and not necessarily in that order. It was my job to jump through her hoops and I had to admit that even with everything else that had fallen in my lap this week, I liked my new job.

Marty Grisnik was parked in front of my house when I got home. He got out of his car and followed me into the garage just as I had followed Jill Rice into hers. For a moment I had a hollow feeling in my gut that he was going to tell me Wendy was dead the same way I had told Jill about her husband. I started breathing again when he didn't.

"I've been waiting for you," Grisnik said.

"I left you a message at your office."

"I've been out."

"You hear from Troy yet?"

"From him and Special Agent in Charge Ben Yates and that jackleg U.S. Attorney Josh Ziegler and my chief. The only person I haven't heard from is the pope and that's probably only because my line has been busy and there's not enough of my ass left to chew out to make it worth His Holiness's while."

"I'm really sorry. How bad is the fallout?"

Grisnik shrugged. "Don't sweat it. I've got broad shoulders. The chief will yank my chain. I may end up with a nastygram in my personnel file, maybe get a few days unpaid vacation, but that's it. I know where too many bodies are buried for them to bust my chops too bad."

"You're a standup guy, Grisnik. I appreciate it."

He raised his hands. "Don't appreciate so much. I did what you told me. I gave you up in a heartbeat, told them it was all your idea. My chief will give me some cover even if he has to take his shots at me in public, but you've got no friends on your side of the aisle."

"Is that what you came to tell me?"

"Yeah. Figured it wouldn't come as any surprise to you but I wanted to give you a heads-up anyway."

"I appreciate that, too, but you didn't have to drive all the way out here."

"I like the drive. Lets me clear my head. See what I'm missing out here in cupcake land. I did some nosing around with some people I know up at Leavenworth. Word is Tommy Rice was done as a favor."

"Who asked for the favor?"

"I didn't get a name, only that it went with a badge. Sounds like your runaway agent has a long reach."

"The guy who did it, he's been charged?"

Grisnik snorted. "What, are you kidding? They don't know who did it. They only know why it happened. It's going down as a suicide. Plain and simple."

Jill Rice was right. Her husband wouldn't have killed himself. She wouldn't be comforted with the knowledge that Colby had orchestrated his murder. If Colby had Wendy, she was in greater danger than I had thought possible. Knowing who your enemy is gives you a chance. She wouldn't see Colby's betrayal until it was too late. I shook Grisnik's hand.

"Thanks."

"You keep saying that, you're going to wear it out. Anything new on your daughter?"

"Nothing. I don't even know where to look."

"What about your agent?"

"Same story."

"I've got a few people I can tap. Maybe I'll come up with something. Make my day to find your girl and collar a dirty FBI agent all in the same day. Go feed your dog. I'll let you know if I hear anything."

Chapter Forty-four

I had just finished feeding Ruby when the doorbell rang. I looked at my watch. It was six fifty-five. Walking from the kitchen through the entry hall toward the front door, I could see the driveway through the dining room windows. Joy had parked her car there and was ringing my doorbell. I quickened my pace, wondering why she was here, figuring that if she had news about Wendy, she would have called.

I checked my watch again. It was six fifty-six. Kate was astoundingly punctual. She would be here in less than 240 seconds. I had already screwed up my introduction of Kate to Wendy and was on the verge of repeating my mistake with Joy.

I couldn't escape the flushed feeling sweeping across my face. I was about to get caught cheating on my wife even though I told myself I couldn't be cheating if the divorce she had asked for was going to be final in five days and if I'd put my romantic plans on the shelf until I found Wendy. My logic didn't explain the heat under my collar.

I opened the door. Joy had cleaned up. Her hair was

down, her lips shined with fresh gloss, and she was wearing a perfume that was as intoxicating as one of those umbrella drinks that went down easy and packed a wallop you didn't feel until it was too late. She was wearing cocoa-colored linen slacks and a creamy scoop-neck camisole with a matching sweater tied around her neck that showed off new definition in her arms. She was holding a bag of Chinese carryout in one hand and a dog leash in the other. I pointed to the dog on the other end of the leash.

"Roxy?"

"I thought the girls should meet."

Roxy saw Ruby and bolted from Joy's grasp before I could answer. They sniffed, bonded, and raced through the house, tangling in the leash, tumbling across the floor, and scrambling to their feet to do it again.

"Mission accomplished," I said.

"I couldn't stand not knowing what was happening with Wendy. I thought you might have heard something," Joy said.

"You're the first person I would have called if I had heard anything. Actually, I did call you to find out if you'd talked with her girlfriend at work. What was her name? Julie?"

"I was on my way here when I picked up your message. I finally reached Julie late this afternoon. She said that Wendy was at work yesterday and didn't say anything to her about going away or about Colby or anything else that seemed unusual and that she hasn't heard from her since."

Julie's lack of information confirmed my belief that Wendy had left her apartment unexpectedly and probably involuntarily. It was one more piece of bad news, but I didn't want to add to Joy's worry.

"You never know. Wendy might call her. Did you get Julie's home and cell phone numbers?"

Joy reached into her pocket and handed me a slip of

paper. "I learned a few things about investigating a case from living with you."

"Thanks. I'll check back with her."

She looked around and past me into the house. "Are you going to invite me in?"

I took a deep breath before answering and held it when I saw Kate pull up at the curb. Joy turned around. Kate got out of her car. I shook, a quick shimmy like I was warming up for a Michael Jackson moonwalk.

Joy covered her face with her free hand. "I am such an idiot. I should have called first."

"I'm sorry."

She waved her hand. "Don't be silly. I'm the one who should be sorry. Here we are not knowing where our daughter is and I'm acting like a jealous schoolgirl."

She may have been acting like a jealous schoolgirl, but her comment made me feel like Louse of the Year for having a date instead of beating the streets to find Wendy. I retreated to my comfort zone of half-truths.

"That's why Kate is here."

Joy looked at me. "What's that supposed to mean?"

"Kate's helping me with this case. She's an expert in something called the Facial Action Coding System. It's a way of telling whether someone is lying. She's going to help me analyze the evidence."

It was the truth even if it wasn't the whole truth and nothing but the truth. It wouldn't help to explain that Kate and I had planned to screw our brains out all weekend but that, under the circumstances, I had selflessly decided to delay that indulgence.

Kate was standing next to her car sizing up the situation before entering the zone of danger. Joy looked at her again and then at me, embarrassment giving way to rising anger.

"Is that why she's wearing that slinky black dress and carrying a bottle of wine and that grocery bag from Dean & DeLuca?"

Kate was wearing a slinky black dress. She was carrying a bottle of wine and there was a French baguette sticking out of the Dean & DeLuca bag.

"She probably came straight from her office. We're going to work through dinner."

"That's what she wears at the office?"

"It's not her fault. We made these plans before I knew about Wendy. She still doesn't know. I haven't talked to her in a couple of days."

There it was. I had admitted making plans with Kate, redefining the term as a synonym for getting laid. Kate's slinky black dress illustrated my meaning in case Joy had any lingering doubts.

Joy spit out her response. "You could have called her."

"I did. I left her a message. I left you a message. I left messages for half the civilized world. No one answered. Instead they're all showing up on my doorstep."

Joy covered her face again. "Oh my God. I can't believe I'm even having this conversation. Look at me. I brought my dog and Chinese. She brought wine and bread and God knows what else."

Kate began walking toward us. I didn't know what to do. "Stay. We'll have potluck."

Joy tightened her shoulders, held her arms rigidly against her sides, and balled her hands into fists. "You must be kidding! Where's my damn dog?"

She elbowed past me into the house, scooped up Roxy, and came out as Kate reached the front steps. Joy's face had morphed into a flat, cool, closed-mouth smile. She extended her hand.

"I'm Jack's wife, Joy."

Kate smiled in turn, accepting her hand. "I'm Kate Scranton."

"I hope you can help my husband and me get our daughter back."

Kate, her eyebrows raised, looked at me for a clue, then back at Joy. "I'll do my best."

"I'm certain you will, but as Jack will tell you, that's not always good enough."

Chapter Forty-five

"Tell me what's going on with Wendy," Kate said.

"She didn't go to work today. She doesn't answer her phone. Joy and I went to her apartment. It looks like she left in a hurry."

"She's an adult. She can do that. It doesn't mean anything has happened to her."

"Her boyfriend, Colby Hudson, has disappeared too, and he left behind some stuff he's going to have a hard time explaining."

"Like what?"

"Like drugs and cash. Not the sort of thing an FBI agent should leave lying around in plain sight especially when two agents come looking for him to find out why he isn't answering his phone and why he didn't show up to take a polygraph."

Kate set the bottle of wine and the grocery bag on the front stoop, folded her arms across her chest, and stared at the street, lost in thought. She picked up the wine, marched back to her car, left the wine on the front seat, and retrieved an overnight bag.

"Change of plans," she said, when she came back.

The front door was wide open. Ruby found us and jumped on Kate, who picked her up and traded kisses with her.

"You really got a dog. I don't believe it."

"It was your idea."

Ruby spied the grocery bag and squirmed until Kate let her down so she could sniff at the contents.

"Chilean sea bass," Kate said, rescuing our dinner from the dog. "I don't cook, but I do buy."

I took her hand. "I've got to find Wendy and I need all the help I can get."

"Then that's what we'll do. Besides, you've got a dog now."

A black sedan turned down my street before we could go inside. I recognized the government plates before it stopped in front of my house.

"Why can't people just return my phone calls?" I asked.

"What are you talking about?"

"I'll tell you later. Take the dinner inside. I'll be there in a few minutes."

Troy Clark stepped out from the passenger side and waited. Ammara Iverson was his driver. She joined him, leaning against the front corner of the car, the three of us forming a triangle. I took my time walking to the curb.

"I know about Colby and Thomas Rice," Troy said. "What I don't know is why you knew before I did. So tell me."

There was no reason to leave anything out except my conversations with Ammara. She didn't need the aggravation. And the more Troy knew, the better Wendy's chances were, even if she wasn't his first priority. I explained all of it, starting with the man I thought I'd seen running from Marcellus's house. I described my unplanned meeting with Marty Grisnik and how I had learned about Oleta Phillips's disappearance from her brother.

"That's when you called Ammara and told her to check the fingerprints on the cash you found in Marcellus's backyard against Oleta's fingerprints."

Ammara looked at me, nodding. "It's okay, Jack. He knows."

I took a breath and told Troy about almost having dinner with Wendy and Colby and that Colby had told me that he was buying Rice's house and car.

"That's the first you knew about it?" Troy asked, his head cocked to one side, his eyes narrowed as if he expected me to lie.

"Absolutely. Why?"

"Colby was dating your daughter. It was pretty serious from what I understand. Buying a house is the kind of thing a guy talks to his girlfriend about. You being the girlfriend's father and Colby's squad leader, seems logical that she would have told you about it."

Troy's questions reminded me of a lesson in interrogation that I'd failed to follow. The first thing to come out of your mouth was usually the one thing you'd thought the least about and was, therefore, the one thing that was most likely to bite you in the ass.

In fact, I did know about the house before I talked with Colby. Wendy had told me the day before that she couldn't have dinner with me because Colby wanted her to see the house he was buying. It was a little thing but now I had to recant and explain, backfilling against my eroding credibility.

"The day before I talked to Colby, Wendy told me he was buying a house, but she didn't say anything about it being Thomas Rice's house."

Troy nodded, satisfied that he'd made his point. "Good. Now tell me the rest of it."

I told him that I'd gone back to Marcellus's neighborhood

again hoping to find a witness who might have also seen someone running away immediately after the murders. I told him about my conversation with Latrell Kelly and about the dog Latrell had given me.

I told him that I'd talked Marty Grisnik into letting me impersonate a KCK detective named Funkhouser when I visited Thomas Rice, that Rice had been scared and nervous when I asked him about the house but that he hadn't mentioned Colby. I told him that I'd used the same phony ID when I talked to Rice's ex-wife and that her version of the sale of the house didn't match Colby's.

I told him that Joy and I had gone to Wendy's apartment after Ammara told me that she had been unable to reach Wendy and that I hadn't found anything there that indicated where Wendy might have gone. I told him about Joy's conversation with Wendy's coworker and the scuttlebutt Grisnik had heard that someone in law enforcement had put a hit on Thomas Rice, letting Troy fill in Colby's name on the line that said suspect.

I told it in linear, chronological fashion without editorial comment or any effort to justify what I'd done. I was all about the facts and I got through it without a ripple, none of which impressed Troy.

"You're on leave, Jack, because you've got a medical problem no one has figured out. That's why I told you to stay out of this."

"The Bureau can tell me to go home and I have to go home. But you telling me what to do on my own time doesn't mean shit."

Troy's square jaw, already tight, ratcheted down even tighter. His eyes flared and he straightened his shoulders, ready to hit me head-on.

"How about obstruction of justice? You think that doesn't mean shit? You withheld information about an ongoing in-

vestigation. You impersonated a police officer. You entered
your daughter's apartment knowing it might be a crime scene
and risked contaminating the evidence that we might need to
convict her. . . ."

He stopped in midsentence, breaking eye contact, his
head of steam evaporated.

"Convict her? Convict her of what?" I asked him. "Of
having a boyfriend who's an FBI agent who may have
crossed the line? Do you really think I'm going to sit on my
hands while you try to build a case against my daughter
when it's more likely that she's a victim in all of this instead
of an accessory?"

Troy found his voice again, swallowing hard, slowing his
pace, and lowering his voice to regain control.

"I've got to follow the case wherever it goes, Jack. I can't
ignore Wendy's history. You know that. It's still obstruction
of justice."

Wendy's drug use had not been a secret. Things like that
never stay under wraps. I had talked about it openly, proud
that she was doing so well in recovery. Troy was twisting my
pride into his suspicion.

"You want to talk obstruction of justice? How about wast-
ing everyone's time trying to prove that someone on my
squad tipped off whoever killed Marcellus and his people instead of working the hard facts of the case and finding my
daughter?"

I had five inches and twenty pounds on Troy, but I'd managed to set him off again. He stepped up, getting in my face,
biting off his questions.

"Is that what you think I'm doing? You think we haven't
run every bullet through ballistics, and every fingerprint,
hair, fiber, blood sample, and scrap of DNA through the lab?
You think we haven't run down everyone who was a witness
or could have been a witness? Do really think all I've been

doing is sitting around with my thumb up my ass waiting for you to call Ammara to tell her what we should do next while you implicate Colby Hudson in a murder and your daughter goes missing?"

I knew all that but none of it mattered. He had to see the whole picture. I didn't. All I had to see was that my daughter was dragged into something not of her making. It didn't matter why or how. The only thing that mattered was what I was going to do about it.

"Then you know I haven't gotten in your way and you know that I'm going to keep looking for my daughter."

Troy walked around me, hands on his hips, stopping in the middle of my yard. I turned, watching him.

"Damnit, Jack. You've done this long enough to know better. I've got enough to do without looking over my shoulder for you. I don't know what's going on with Colby, but I'm not going to crucify him based on secondhand jailhouse rumors. And, if Wendy is in trouble, we'll find her. If she's mixed up with Colby and Colby's in trouble, well, then she could be in trouble, too, and we'll have to let the chips fall on that one. Don't make it worse."

I would have made the same speech if our positions were reversed. The difference is I would have expected him to do the same things I had and he expected me to be a good civilian and sit by the phone waiting for it to ring with news good or bad. I had to back off him even if I wasn't going to do what he wanted me to do.

"Okay, I'll stay out of your way but you've at least got to keep me in the loop. Let Ammara tell me what's going on. I'm entitled to that much."

Troy thought for a minute, nodded, and let out a long breath. "That's fair. Everyone on the squad who took the polygraph passed. As far as I'm concerned, that's a dead issue except for Colby. The U.S. Attorney is looking at his purchase of Rice's car and house. The warden at Leavenworth said Rice's death was a suicide, but I agree with you that the timing with your visit is a little too neat. I'll see what the warden says about a cop calling in a favor. That's it. That's where we are."

Chapter Forty-six

Troy turned toward the car, emphasizing that our meeting was over. He may have been finished, but I wasn't.

"What about the gun that was found at the rail yard?" I asked.

Ammara perked up, catching Troy's eye. She tilted her head slightly toward me, urging him to answer. Troy stopped. He was holding back. He still didn't trust me, which made us even.

"It's a match, isn't it?" I asked. "The same gun was used to kill Javy Ordonez and the five people in Marcellus's house."

"We aren't letting that out, so if it gets out, I'll know how," Troy said, his back still turned toward me.

"What about Oleta's son? Same gun?"

Troy shook his head. "No. Grisnik sent us the ballistics. Her son was killed with a nine millimeter. The gun found at the rail yard was a forty-five."

"What did you get on the registration for the forty-five?"

He rotated slowly around, hands back on his hips, giving me his hard look again. I waited, letting my silence force him to tell me. He glanced at Ammara who nodded again, tipping the scales in my favor.

"The gun was registered to a dealer in St. Louis," Troy said. "He brought a pair of them to a show in Kansas City seventeen years ago. Reported them stolen along with a pair of night-vision goggles. He filed a police report claiming that a woman distracted him by flashing her tits while her partner, some guy, snatched the guns and goggles. Cops never made an arrest."

"What about the other gun, the mate to the one we found?"

"Still missing."

"Well, that's something."

"But it's not enough, not by a long stretch," Troy said.

His cell phone rang and he walked out in the street to take the call. Ammara waited until Troy was out of earshot.

"I can't get you the files you wanted on Thomas Rice. Troy has them locked up. I'm sorry, Jack."

"Don't sweat it. I put you in a tough spot. I'm the one who should be apologizing."

"Troy's not doing a bad job. In fact, he's doing a pretty good job. He's just growing into being in charge. That comes naturally to you. It's more of a process for him."

"Just don't let him leave Wendy to the last."

"I won't. By the way, I got a phone call from that guy who gave you the dog."

"Latrell Kelly?"

"That's him."

"You find anything else out about him?" I asked.

"Nothing. One of the neighbors says he keeps odd hours, leaving the house late at night, coming home at dawn. That's evidence of someone having a good time, not killing people."

"Latrell strike you as the party-hearty type?"

She shook her head. "Not unless he has a secret identity."

"You better find out if he does. I gave him one of my cards and wrote your number on it. I told him to call you if he remembered anything else. What'd he have to say when he called?"

"Nothing about the case. Just said he had some toys for the dog he forgot to give you. Asked me for your phone number. I told him that I couldn't give it to him but that I'd pass the message on and you'd call him."

"You think he really has some toys for the dog or that he'd just rather talk to me than to you?"

"I don't know. I interviewed him when we did the neighborhood canvass. He seemed like one of the good guys. He doesn't have a record. He has a regular job; his employer vouched for him. He keeps his place up and isn't into the whole hip-hop gangsta bullshit thing. Maybe you clicked with him and I didn't. After all, he gave you the dog."

Managing the information flow is key to any investigation. I had told my story to Troy in the order everything had happened, but that's not how evidence is collected. Sometimes it comes in buckets, like at a crime scene. Sometimes it comes in dribs and drabs, crumbs picked up along the way that don't become gems until something else gives it meaning and context. This was one of those moments.

"Latrell lived behind Marcellus and he worked at the place where Javy Ordonez was killed."

"The rail yard is a lot bigger than his backyard. Harder to make that connection stick."

"It sticks until it falls off."

"What's his motive?" Ammara asked.

"You said he was one of the good guys. Maybe he decided to clean up his neighborhood."

"You saw him. He look like the Terminator to you? Even if he did Marcellus and his people, how does he lure Javy Ordonez out to the rail yard, get in the backseat of Javy's car, and blow his brains all over the leather upholstery? And if he could pull that off, why would he throw the gun away under a Dumpster where it's so likely to be found?"

"It wouldn't have been found for a long time if Javy's body hadn't gotten stuck in the trash truck. Have you found anything to connect Latrell to Javy Ordonez?'

"We haven't looked, but we haven't found anything, either. We've been working the drug angle."

"What about Bodie Grant, the meth dealer from Raytown?"

"Disappeared. We've questioned his people. They think he's dead. If he is, I'd say we're in the middle of an epidemic of dead drug dealers."

"I'd still look for something that ties Latrell to Javy Ordonez."

"I will," she said with a laugh, "but I won't tell Troy you made the suggestion."

"Latrell wants me to call him, I'll need his phone number."

"He said his number was unlisted, and if I wouldn't give him your number, why should he give me his number? So I asked him how you were supposed to get in touch with him and he said that you knew where he lived. Said you could drop by if you were interested. You interested, Jack?"

"Yeah, I think I am."

Troy finished his call, snapping the cell phone shut. "We done here?" he asked Ammara.

"Yes, we are," she said.

Chapter Forty-seven

I wasn't one of those people who could compartmentalize his life, tucking each competing component into a sanitized clean room where it existed independently of everything else. My life was like a teenager's room. Everything was scattered on the floor and I was always tripping over something.

That's the way it was with Wendy, Joy, Kate, and this case. I was consumed with finding Wendy, confused about my feelings for Joy and Kate, and haunted by the images of Keyshon and Kevin begging me not to forget them. It would have been easier to live my life in a straight line—one person, one problem at a time.

"Food first," Kate said when I came inside and found her in the kitchen.

She had changed into faded jeans, a navy blue V-neck cotton sweater and a scruffy pair of Nikes. Her new outfit may not have been a slinky black dress, but the effect was the same—dazzling.

We ate quickly, neither of us suggesting that the wine would have gone better with the sea bass than the tap water we drank from plastic cups. We rinsed the dishes, left them in the sink, and set up shop on the kitchen table.

"Where do you want to start?" she asked.

"I need to know who's lying and who's telling the truth but I don't have a portable polygraph."

"The polygraph isn't a lie catcher's only mechanical option anymore. A lot of research is being done on deception. Some of it involves using an MRI scan of the brain to look for neurological changes associated with lying. The subject pushes a button to answer questions during the brain scan. The MRI picks up changes in brain activity that are associated with lying."

"Does it work?"

"Some of the research suggests that it's as effective as the polygraph, but that's no great comfort if you ask me. The polygraph is limited because it depends on peripheral nervous system activity. Deception is a cognition event that is controlled by the central nervous system. The MRI research has shown an increase in prefrontal and parietal activity when someone lies, but I don't thing a judge is going to admit the results into evidence any time soon."

"I don't see people lining up to lay down inside an MRI. It's claustrophobic and noisy as hell. I'd think that would produce enough stress to skew any results you'd get."

"Have you ever had an MRI?"

"Not since this morning. Wendy called her mother after she saw me shaking the other night when we didn't have dinner. Joy set it up and she also got me an appointment with a neurologist on Monday."

"What about the movement disorder clinic at the KU Hospital?"

"They were happy to see me in two months. I didn't mind waiting, but Joy did."

Kate studied me with the bar-code scanning eyes I'd seen her use in the courtroom, her lids three-quarters open, pinched at the corners, her face flat with concentration. It was like she had X-ray vision into my soul. I imagined a torrent of micro expressions flashing across my face like the ticker at the bottom of the screen on CNN. She leaned forward at the table, her chin in her hand, straightening up when she'd seen what she was looking for.

"You've got a lot on your plate, don't you, Jack?"

"More than I asked for."

"Well, you don't have a portable polygraph or a portable MRI, which leaves you with me."

"I could do worse."

"Yes, you could. A lot worse."

We let it hang there, both of us clear what we were talking about, neither willing to push it.

"Two things," she said, rubbing her palms on her thighs and filling the dead air. "First, the Facial Action Coding System is not a silver bullet and, second, you're probably better at reading faces than you give yourself credit for."

"I'll buy the first, but how do you figure the second?"

"Okay. If you meet someone, do you think you'd recognize them the next time you saw them?"

I thought for a moment. "Yeah. I may not remember their name, but I never forget a face."

"Then you're better at reading faces than the one in fifty people that have some form of face blindness."

"I've never heard of that."

"It's called prosopagnosia. Usually someone with the condition has a hard time recognizing the same set of facial features again and again. It can be so severe that you could show a person who has the condition a picture of Elvis and she will think it's Madonna, anybody except Elvis. In the worst cases, people don't even recognize their own faces."

"That's supposed to make me feel better?"

"Sure. Things could always be worse. Can you tell when someone is angry?"

"Sure."

"How about when they're happy or sad?"

"Of course."

"You make judgments all day long about what someone is really thinking or feeling. You don't do it just based on what they say and do. You do it based on their body language, their facial expressions, and their tone of voice."

"But I'm not interested in their emotions. I'm interested in whether they are telling the truth."

"Then you are definitely interested in their emotions. For most people, lying is stressful. That stress impacts their emotions, and the emotions a liar is trying to conceal will leak. That's when you can catch them in a lie."

"Give me an example."

"Okay," Kate said. "Some emotions just don't go together. It's very hard for someone who is angry to fake being afraid, or vice versa. The involuntary muscle movements associated with anger and fear just don't go together. Fear moves the brows up and anger pulls them down. It's impossible for your brows to be in two places at one time."

"That's it? The eyebrows are the windows to the soul?"

"Just don't pluck them. No single gesture, facial expression, or muscle twitch will prove that someone is lying, but they are clues of emotions that don't fit. That's what I mean by leakage."

"I remember you telling me that some people don't leak."

"Natural liars, sociopaths, actors, politicians, and trial lawyers are all used to convincing an audience of something whether or not they believe it. To varying degrees, deception doesn't bother them. It's what they do. They delight in having duped someone. But even they can leak because it's impossible to completely control facial expressions. Too many of them are involuntary."

"Like the micro facial expressions, the ones that happen so quickly you can't see them."

"Precisely. Genuine expressions don't last long. The duration from onset to offset can be less than a second. Micro expressions flash on and off the face in less than a quarter of a second. If the expression is asymmetrical, stronger on one side of the face than the other, or if the timing is wrong, or the duration is too long, those are all good signs that the expression shown is false."

"But how does that prove someone is lying? I've interviewed plenty of people who it turned out were telling the truth but were scared to death I wouldn't believe them."

"That's why context is so critical. The fear of not being believed is virtually impossible to distinguish from the fear of being caught lying."

"Okay. Since I didn't grow up playing with facial expression flash cards like you did, how do I learn to recognize micro expressions?"

"Practice," she said, rummaging through her purse. "Damn!"

"Don't tell me you left your flash cards at home."

Kate poked me in the arm. "Don't make fun of the teacher or I'll rap your knuckles with my ruler. We don't use flash cards any more. We use images on a CD, which I left at my office."

"So school is out?"

"Not so fast," she said, examining my television. "Your TV has a DVD player with a freeze-frame feature. Do you have any movies?"

"Not anymore. Joy got them in the property settlement."

"Well, at least the two of you settled something. Have you recorded anything? We could play it back and break it down frame by frame."

"As a matter of fact, I've been recording the local news to keep track of stories about the drug house murders. We can take a look at that."

"It's not flash cards but we'll make it work."

Chapter Forty-eight

It turned out that the two news anchors on Channel 6 had issues. In the midst of their happy-talk banter, the male anchor was checking out the female anchor's chest, while she was sneering every time he opened his mouth. Not surprisingly, the weather wonk didn't believe a word of her own forecast. All of that was revealed in the frame-by-frame breakdown of their facial expressions.

"I can see the micro expressions when you freeze them but they blew by me in real time," I told Kate.

"You're a rookie. I'll get you the CD I was talking about. Spend a few hours with it on your computer and you'll pick it up faster than you think. It will change the way you look at people. Let's try a few more."

The next segment in the news broadcast was the interview with Marcellus's neighbors, LaDonna Simpson, Tarla Hicks, and Latrell Kelly. Kate slowed the recording down when LaDonna Simpson appeared on the screen.

"Skip her," I said. "And the next person, another woman. Go to the last guy interviewed. His name is Latrell Kelly. He lives directly behind Marcellus."

"You seem awfully interested in him."

"I should be. He gave me the dog. Play the interview straight through, then go back and break it down."

Kate pushed the play button and Latrell began speaking, his slow, quiet voice now familiar. I mouthed the words as he said again "nobody takes care of a little boy, you see what happens."

Kate gasped. "Unbelievable!"

"What? I didn't see a thing."

She rewound the tape, freezing it as Latrell finished speaking. In that instant, he looked straight into the camera. His placid, respectful, sorrowful face melted away, replaced by a vicious snarl a pit bull would have killed for. His lips were flattened and pulled back, his teeth bared, his eyes trimmed to narrow slits, and his nostrils flared. His devil's face vanished in the next frame.

We stared at him, neither of us saying a word. Kate rewound the segment once more, walking through it frame by frame. There were other micro expressions. I started to ask her what they meant, but she raised her hand, telling me to be quiet.

"Unbelievable," she said for the second time when she finished her review. "Usually, I see ordinary expressions, the kind we associate with guilt or shame or pleasure. And I see a lot of anger and fear. But I've never seen anything like this."

"What's he lying about?"

Kate sat back in her chair, her arms folded across her chest. "Oh, he's not lying about anything. When he said nobody takes care of a little boy, you see what happens, he was absolutely telling the truth."

"One of the murder victims was a little boy, Keyshon. Is that who Latrell was talking about?"

"I don't think so. I think he was talking about himself."

"So who didn't take care of him?" I asked. "His parents?"

"Probably. He could have been abused or abandoned. Whatever it was, he's carrying around a lot of rage."

"Enough to kill five people, including a mother and her little boy, and then blow away another drug dealer two nights later?"

"What other drug dealer?"

"The gun used in the drug house murders was also used to blow away one of Marcellus's competitors. A guy named Javy Ordonez."

"If he was angry enough, but the mother and her little boy are the only ones who make any sense at all."

"How?"

"There's a lot of pain that goes with all that rage. People who hurt that bad sometimes kill themselves because that's the only way they can stop the pain. Other times they kill someone they think caused their pain or someone they think is them, like a mother and a little boy that remind him too much of what happened to him."

"Are you saying you think Latrell is the killer?"

"No. I'm just a jury consultant. I can tell you which version of the evidence the jury is more likely to believe or which juror is more likely to find for the plaintiff or the defendant. I can tell you the odds that a witness is a liar. But I can't tell you if Latrell is a murderer, although there is one thing I can tell you for sure about him."

"What's that?"

She spread her palms flat on the table. "Don't piss him off."

I nodded. "Good to know since he wants to talk to me."

"You? How do you know that and why does he want to talk to you?"

I summarized my trips to Quindaro since the murders, my conversation with Latrell, and his phone call to Ammara asking for my number. Kate peppered me with questions about how Latrell looked, talked, and acted when I was with him, smiling when I told her that I had gone back to the neighborhood not just to find witnesses but that I was also following her instructions to get a dog.

Kate's smile lit up her face, the room, and my heart. I would have freeze-framed it if only I knew what to do with it. She chuckled, watching me watch her.

"You're so busy trying to figure everyone else out, you don't hide much of yourself."

"Actually, I'm a pretty good poker player but I'm not trying to bluff you."

"At the risk of choking on trite metaphors," she said, "you've got to know when to hold them and know when to fold them. Now what do you say we get back on task? Are you going to talk to Latrell?"

"I've got to."

Kate studied me some more, nodding. "I see that. You can't sit back and wait for something to happen even if Latrell had nothing to do with the murders and nothing to do with Wendy. You've got to find out for yourself."

"I can't hide that from you or anybody else."

"So," she said, clicking off her conclusions one finger at a time, "you'll go tomorrow, when it's light out and you've had some rest. And you'll take someone with you. Maybe Ammara Iverson or that detective from Kansas City, Kansas."

I stood and turned off the television.

"I'll go tonight because I can't sit around waiting for something to happen and I'll go alone because if I show up with the FBI or the cops, he won't talk to me."

Kate stood, grabbing my wrist. "Then I'm going with you."

"I don't think so. You're going home."

"You said it yourself. You're lousy at reading faces and you didn't pick up on the micro expressions we just watched. You want to know if Latrell is telling the truth, you have to take me with you."

"How do I explain to Latrell why I brought you along?"

She smiled again. "Tell him that I like dogs."

"And if that doesn't do it?"

"Then tell him that I'm your girlfriend."

She wrapped her arms around my neck, pulled my lips to hers, and kissed me so hard I shook.

Chapter Forty-nine

Latrell knew that Jack Davis would come. He would knock on the door. Latrell would open it and let him in. Davis would walk past him into the living room. Maybe he would turn around and maybe he wouldn't. It didn't matter. Latrell didn't care whether he shot Davis in the back or the front as long as he was dead when he hit the floor.

He held a .45 caliber Marine pistol in his right hand, the mate to the gun he'd used to kill Marcellus. Johnny McDonald had stolen the pair seventeen years ago, bragging to Latrell how he had taken them and the night-vision goggles off a gun dealer with his mother's help, cackling as he described how she had distracted the dealer by showing him her titties, his Adam's apple, big as a grapefruit, bobbing up and down his long neck as he told the story.

Latrell had looked at his mother. She was sprawled on the sofa, the same one that he was sitting on now while he waited for Jack Davis, her eyes closed, smiling that dreamy smile she got when she was high, her lips twitching, the only part of her knowing the high wouldn't last.

Latrell had followed Johnny into the basement, Johnny

asking him did he want to hold one of the guns. Yeah, Latrell told him, asking was it loaded, Johnny saying damn straight it was loaded. How do you shoot it, Latrell asked, Johnny telling him it's simple kid, just pull the trigger. Like this? Latrell asked, and shot Johnny in his Adam's apple, the target so big he couldn't miss even if it was the first time he had shot anybody. Latrell buried Johnny in the basement, adding his mother's body the next day after she came on to him, asking would he get her fixed up.

Latrell kept that gun in the cave and the mate in the bottom drawer of his dresser, never firing it, not even once to see that it worked. He wasn't religious, but he saw the spare gun as his salvation, the way to make things right one last time. So he saved it, keeping it pure and clean, for the moment he would need it. He checked the magazine for the fifth time, making certain it only held two bullets. That was all he would need.

He'd woken up that morning lying on the floor of the cave, hugging his knees to his chest so tightly that when he stretched out he had no feeling in his legs. Soon Latrell's skin started to tingle, his muscles warmed, and he staggered to his feet, bracing himself with one hand against the cave wall, breathing in the moist cool air coming off the underground lake.

The last thing he remembered from the night before was how he had screamed when he discovered that Davis had been in his cave, had stolen his gun and his special things. Latrell didn't remember his screams giving way to sobs or his sobs giving way to sleep, but he knew that's what had happened because it had been that way so many times before.

The candles he had lit had all burned out and the batteries in his flashlight had died. The impenetrable darkness of the cave was broken only by shimmering flecks of green light that dotted the floor and walls, a mysterious glowing mineral that reminded him of the sparks he saw when he squeezed his eyes shut as hard as he could.

Latrell was at ease in the blackness that made everything, including him, invisible. He knew the contours of the cave as well as he knew his own house and could easily navigate by touch and memory. Still groggy, he knelt at the edge of the lake, splashing the icy water on his face, then rocked back on his haunches, thinking about what he had to do and how he would do it.

He was convinced that Davis had followed him to the cave and waited until Latrell was gone so he could sneak inside, learn his secrets, and steal his gun and the picture of him and his mother that Johnny McDonald had taken in front of their house. He didn't know what had made Davis suspect him, but he should have known something was up when Davis tried to play him with that bullshit story about losing his son.

Davis, he was certain, had given his gun to the FBI, who would figure out that it had been used to kill Marcellus, the Winston brothers, Jalise, and Keyshon. Davis would tell them how he'd followed Latrell to the cave and found the gun there and then they would come for him. He didn't know how long these things took but guessed it would be today or tomorrow.

He thought about running but didn't know where he would go or how he would live. He needed a place in the world, like his house and his job, and he needed a safe place away from the world, like the cave. Otherwise he would never survive.

From the instant Latrell had killed Johnny McDonald, he knew that it would eventually end like this no matter how many times he tried to make things right. It wasn't fair. He hadn't asked for the life he'd had. He'd only wanted to be taken care of, and, when he wasn't, he took care of himself the only way he knew how.

It had worked with Johnny and his mother, but it hadn't worked with Marcellus. Latrell blamed Oleta Phillips. She had ruined his plan. That wasn't his fault. It was more of the bad luck that clung to him.

He found his way through the two smaller rooms of the cave, crawled up the chute to the surface, and emerged in the woods. The sun was high overhead and breaking through the trees, the air humid and smelling like wet clay.

The day was half gone, his day just beginning. Latrell thought about walking through the woods, across the rail yard, into the terminal building, and sitting down at his desk as if it was an ordinary day, but he couldn't think of a lie to tell that would explain why he was late, dirty, and still wearing yesterday's clothes.

No one was waiting to arrest him when he got home. Latrell spent an hour in the shower, exhausting the hot water, letting the cold sting his skin until he was numb and clean.

Standing naked in his bedroom, he found the business card the FBI agent had given him. He ran his finger over the raised print that spelled Jack Davis's name and turned the card over, reading the name of the other agent he was supposed to call if he remembered something about the night of the murders. Ammara Iverson. She was one of the agents who had talked to him that night.

He tensed, his shoulders knotting, and dialed her number. She answered. He told her his name, asking did she remember him, waiting for her reaction.

"Yes, Mr. Kelly. I remember. What can I do for you?"

She was polite but unexcited, not acting like he was a wanted man. His muscles eased and he loosened up.

"Agent name of Jack Davis come to see me the other night. He give me your phone number in case I remembered something about the night of the murders."

"Well then, I'm glad you called," she said. Her voice sharpened and he imagined her sitting up in her chair, like he was about to crack the case for her. "What did you remember?"

"That's not why I'm calling you. I didn't remember nothing because I didn't see nothing, just like I told you and him."

"Then why are you calling?"

"Marcellus, he had a little dog. I took it in so it wouldn't get hurt or nothing. Then I give it to Jack Davis, only I forgot to give him some toys I bought for the dog. I was hoping you could give me his phone number so I could tell him to come get the toys."

"I'm sorry, Mr. Kelly. We're not allowed to give out that information, but if you give me your number, I can pass it on to Agent Davis and he can get in touch with you if he wants the dog's toys."

"My number ain't listed. I don't give it out, either. You tell him I got something for him and if he wants it to come get it."

Ammara said she would and he believed her. He started to dial the number for work to tell them that he was sick, but stopped, setting the phone down. It didn't matter why he wasn't at work because he was never going back.

Chapter Fifty

"I'll drive," Kate said.

"Why?"

"Because, in case you haven't noticed, you're shaking."

I was. A few light tremors. Not constant, more like a quick shudder. "That's from your kiss."

She laughed, patted my cheek, and picked up her purse. "I'm flattered, but I'm still driving."

"I can drive."

"I'm certain you can, but my presence will look more innocent if I'm driving. It makes the whole girlfriend thing more believable. And we should bring Ruby. That will show him we believe his story about the dog's toys."

"You've got this figured out."

"It's what I do."

"I thought your job was to find jurors that are gullible enough to vote for your client."

"Of course it is. But gullible isn't as easy as it looks. There are a lot of ways to tell a story. My job is to frame it in the way most likely to convince the jury. You can knock on

Latrell's door by yourself doing your macho FBI thing and hope he spills his guts without trying to kill you."

"Or?"

"Or, the three of us—you, me, and the dog—can make a social call that doesn't scream 'assume the position, dirt bag.' "

"Nobody says 'dirt bag' anymore."

"But you do say 'assume the position.' "

"Not on a first date."

"Cute, but not cute enough," Kate said, crossing her arms over her chest.

"You're not going to let me talk you out of this, are you?"

"No. You can leave me here but I'll follow you. I may even call Troy Clark, tell him where you are going and that you need backup."

We were standing less than a foot apart. Her shoulders were square and her face was tilted up at mine, her lips pressed together in a tight, determined line. I put my hands on her wrists, gently lowering her arms to her sides, pulled her closer, and returned her kiss.

"Okay," I said. "You can drive, but I've got to get something from my car."

A moment later, I slid into the front passenger seat of Kate's BMW 730i. There was a laptop bag and a stack of journals in the backseat. Ruby was in the back with her front paws perched on the center console between Kate and me. She leaned over the dog, kissed me again, and ran her hand around my waist, stopping when she found the gun I had tucked into the back of my waistband. She pulled away.

"Good," she said.

"Good?"

"In case you're right and I'm wrong."

* * *

The last traces of daylight had faded and the sky overhead in Quindaro was a dull black. Ground light had reduced the stars to patchy distant glimmers, the moon too low to make a difference.

Latrell's house was in the middle of the block. The front door was bathed in a soft yellow glow from lamps fixed to the wall on either side. There was a double window to the left of the door, muted interior light leaking through a curtain.

The gang I'd seen playing basketball down the street from Marcellus's house the other day were watching from a driveway across the street. They stood, forming a tight pack, the ringleader at the point, as we glided to a stop.

"Wait here," I told Kate.

I stepped out of the car and waited until the ringleader was looking straight at me. We did the same silent dance we did before. He gave me the same slight nod, agreeing that neither of us was interested in the other's business. I nodded in return as he motioned to the others and they ambled toward the corner.

Kate lowered the passenger window.

"What did you say to them?"

"Nothing, but it was the way I said it. Let's go."

She scooped Ruby into her arms and stepped ahead of me. I caught up to her at Latrell's front door.

"What are you doing?" I asked.

"Leading with our strengths, which are Ruby and me."

Kate elbowed me in the ribs, pushing me outside the field of vision of the peephole in the center of the door. I stepped back, my right hand on the butt of my gun, as she rang the bell.

I'd been on this side of a suspect's door many times, always with a partner or a SWAT team, never with the shakes. My rule was always to plan for every contingency, control everything I could, and trust my people and my training for everything else. That rule was out the window. I had no plan, no backup, and I had let a jury consultant and a dog take the lead. To make matters worse, I didn't know whether I'd be shaken or stirred when Latrell opened the door. I took a breath and said a prayer.

Kate waited, not taking her eyes off the door. A shadow passed across the peephole from inside the house. She shifted Ruby under her left arm, holding her like she was a miniature battering ram, and rang the bell a second time.

Another five seconds passed before the door opened slowly, Latrell standing half in the doorway, his left side hidden. His right shoulder was level. If it dipped, odds were he was pulling a gun. He'd have to step all the way into view before he could shoot us unless he fired through the heavy oak door. That would slow the bullet, distort its trajectory, and tip the odds in our favor for a fraction of a second.

My threat assessment lasted no longer than a micro expression, a product of years of experience and too many doors that opened slowly. I took longer with his face. His cheeks were smooth, his brow relaxed, his mouth slack. Latrell didn't appear surprised, happy, or sad to see us. He shot a quick look at me, then broke a small smile when Ruby barked at him as she squirmed under Kate's arm.

"You must be Latrell," Kate said, putting Ruby on the ground.

"That's right," he said.

His voice was soft and calm. He didn't move. I let my right hand drift from my gun to my side.

"Jack has told me so much about you. We came to pick up the dog's toys."

Ruby ran into the house and jumped up on Latrell, pressing her paws against his leg, her tongue hanging out the side of her mouth, her tail wagging. Latrell hung back, still keeping his left side hidden.

"Isn't that sweet?" Kate said, following the dog into the

open doorway and crouching down to rub the back of her neck. "You must have taken very good care of her. She's so glad to see you."

Kate and Ruby distracted me enough that I didn't see Latrell's left shoulder dip. I caught a glimpse of his right hand swinging over his head, clutching a gun that he slammed into the side of Kate's head. She collapsed without making a sound.

Latrell pivoted, his back to the door, kicking it closed in the same instant I threw my shoulder into it. He hit it low and I hit it high, the dense wood absorbing both blows without moving.

I pulled my gun and crashed into the door a second time, diving over Kate. Latrell was standing in the entry hall just past the sweep of the open door. I heard a gunshot and felt a bullet graze my hip as I rolled on the floor, coming up to one knee, gun in hand. Latrell was holding a .45 caliber Marine pistol to his temple that matched the murder weapon.

"Put it down!" I screamed.

He pulled the trigger but didn't die. The gun was jammed. He pulled the trigger again and the gun still refused to fire. He swung the barrel toward me, his eyes filled with tears, his face twisted with pain as if the gun had fired.

"Put it down, Latrell! Don't make me shoot you!"

He leveled the gun at my head. We both knew it wouldn't fire, but he wouldn't put it down. He had tried to kill himself and me and failed at both. He wouldn't be the first person to commit suicide by threatening a cop, but I wasn't going to let him use me to do it. Then his shoulders caved in and his knees buckled as a high-powered bullet exploded in his chest, tore a hole in his back, and lodged in the wall behind him.

Chapter Fifty-one

I shifted my aim to the front door, lowering my gun when Troy Clark burst into the house seconds after the shot was fired.

"You okay?" he asked.

I nodded. "He missed me and then his gun jammed."

He pointed to my right hip. "From the looks of that burn, he didn't miss you by much."

"Close calls and second chances. That's what keeps it real."

I leaned over Kate. She was lying on her side, a thin stream of blood flowing from a gash on the side of her head, clotting with her hair. I eased her onto her back, cradling her head with my hand. Her eyes were open and she was moaning softly. She reached for my hand and squeezed it tight. All good signs.

"You're going to be fine," I told her.

"You?" she whispered.

"I'm good."

"Latrell?"

He lay at angle to her, his head turned away.

"I don't know."

"What about Ruby?"

I scanned the room. She was hiding under the sofa, her front paws folded over her nose. I whistled and she came running, licked my face, and laid down next to Kate, who closed her eyes and squeezed my hand again.

Troy knelt next to Latrell, his fingers pressing gently on Latrell's neck, searching for a pulse. He snapped an order in to the radio clipped to his bulletproof vest.

"I need two ambulances. Now!"

"Is he dead?" I asked Troy.

"He will be soon. I doubt he'll make it to the hospital."

I left Ruby in charge of Kate and cupped Latrell's chin in my hand, tilting his head toward me. His eyes were fluttering and his breathing was shallow. Troy was on his knees, applying pressure to the wound in Latrell's chest, but I doubted it would be enough to save him.

"Hang in there, Latrell," I told him. "An ambulance will be here any minute."

"That woman you brought messed it up for me," he said, his lips barely moving.

I leaned closer to his face. "How did she mess it up?"

"I knew you would come. That's why I only had two bullets. One for you and one for me. Then you brought that woman and I didn't have enough bullets. She messed things up just like Oleta done."

Latrell wasn't going to live long enough to explain everything. I had to choose which questions I wanted answered, which meant that I had to fill in the blanks first on my own. If, by some miracle, he lived, it would take an army of government lawyers and a deaf, dumb, and blind judge to keep anything he told me in evidence.

"Did Oleta mess things up when you killed Marcellus?"

He nodded, his voice feathery, his words coming in gasps. "She was waiting for me when I come out of the house."

"Where's Oleta now?"

He opened his eyes wide. "Don't matter. You followed me. You ruined all of it."

"I followed you? Where? How did I ruin it?"

"Took my things," he said, his voice rattling for the last time, his eyes open and dead.

Troy studied me. "You got something else you want to tell me?"

"I wish I did. I have no idea what he meant. I haven't followed him anywhere and I haven't taken anything from him. Looks like he's good for the drug house killings, but we may never find Oleta."

I looked around. The house had filled with members of my squad. Ammara Iverson was sharing guard duty with Ruby, one of them on either side of Kate.

"Who's she?" Troy asked.

"Kate Scranton."

"The jury consultant?"

"Yeah."

"What the hell is she doing here? For that matter, what the hell are you doing here?"

"It's a long story and you aren't going to like any of it."

"Well, you aren't going anywhere until I hear all of it."

I gave him a quick and dirty explanation of the Facial Action Coding System, told him about Latrell's phone call to Ammara and why it seemed like a good idea at the time to bring Kate and the dog with me to talk to Latrell. When I finished, he stared at me with openmouthed aggravation.

"Is there any chance at all you will stay out of this without getting killed or arrested?"

"Once I know that Wendy is safe, I'll take a long vacation. You have anything new on her or Colby?"

Troy shook his head. "They aren't using their credit cards. They haven't made any withdrawals from their bank accounts. They haven't made or received calls on their cell phones. Either they don't want to be found or they're in real trouble. I'm sorry, Jack, but I don't know any other way to say it."

We both looked out the door to the street. It was a parking lot of police cars and ambulances. I glanced at Troy, not needing to ask the question out loud.

"From the far side of the BMW," he said. "Sniper rifle."

"You take the shot?"

He looked at Latrell's body, his shoulders sagging. "Yeah. It was me."

"How did you end up there in the nick of time?"

Troy looked at Latrell again. "Wasn't exactly in the nick of time. Latrell had two bullets. He fired one round and the other one jammed. If I'd known that, I'd be reading him his Miranda rights instead of waiting for someone to perform his last rites."

"No way you could have known. If you hadn't shot him, I probably would have," I said.

"Doesn't help much."

"And doesn't tell me what you were doing outside Latrell's house."

"We found a photograph in Javy Ordonez's car. It was of a young boy, probably fifteen, and a woman. Both of them black. Photograph was taken outside a house. You can see the address numbers in the background. We ran the numbers to find every house in Kansas City, Kansas, that matched and then we checked the ownership records. The numbers matched Latrell's address. He's older now and dead, but he's the boy in the picture."

"The photograph doesn't sound like enough evidence to go tactical."

"It's not enough but we got a few decent prints off the gun that was used in the drug house murders and that was used to kill Javy Ordonez. Latrell didn't have a record, so we didn't have his prints in the system, but we caught a break with his employer. Homeland Security requires that all employees at rail yard terminals be fingerprinted. The fingerprints on the murder weapon belong to Latrell. That was enough to go tactical."

"I didn't see you when we got here."

"We staged out of Marcellus's house. Figured no one was using it. Came through the backyard. Left some of the troops in back and I came around to the front. Saw you and your friend knocking at the door, so I took up position behind the BMW."

"That was good work."

"Always is when we get it right, except this one doesn't feel all the way right. There's too much missing," Troy said.

"Like a link between Latrell and Javy Ordonez?"

"Yeah. We haven't found one other than the photograph. Maybe the woman in the picture is the link. I wonder where she is?" Troy said.

"My guess is that she was Latrell's mother and you'll probably find her the same place you find Oleta. Still doesn't explain why Latrell's picture was in Javy's car."

An agent interrupted. "We found something downstairs."

"What?"

"Two graves. One of them fresh, the other one pretty old."

"Oleta and Latrell's mother," I said.

"I'll be down there in a minute," Troy said to the agent, dismissing him. He turned back to me. "Latrell is dead and we haven't identified the woman in the photograph. Maybe she's buried in the basement and maybe she is the link. Maybe she had a thing with Javy that went bad and Latrell is getting even."

"You say Latrell looks like he's around fifteen years old in the photograph?"

"About. Why?"

"Ammara interviewed him when she did the initial neighborhood canvass. She says he was thirty-two. That makes the photograph seventeen years old. Javy Ordonez was what, twenty-five, tops? That makes him eight years old when the photograph was taken. No way Javy's murder has anything to do with the woman in the photograph."

"If Javy was eight and Latrell was fifteen when the picture was taken," Troy said, "there's not much chance they became mortal enemies at that age."

"Maybe whoever killed Javy put the photograph in his car so we would find it and track it back to Latrell."

"Which is a neat way of framing Latrell for Javy's murder," Troy said.

"But it only works if Javy's killer knows that Latrell has the gun used in the drug house murders and if the killer uses it to off Javy. The gun ties the two crimes together."

Troy sighed. "Every circle takes you back to the same place. This circle keeps taking me back to Colby Hudson. He ducked out on his polygraph and his undercover work put him next to Javy Ordonez. And now he's gone invisible."

"Did you talk to the warden at Leavenworth about whether someone put a hit out on Thomas Rice?"

"Yeah. He's heard the same rumors as Grisnik, but they can't prove anything. Until they do, it stays a suicide."

"And until I find Wendy, I'm not backing off."

Troy swept his hand across the first floor of Latrell's house. "You see all this, Jack?"

Crime scene people were everywhere. A paramedic was checking Kate's vital signs. Another was confirming that Latrell was dead. Agents were searching the house. Troy motioned me to the open front door. KCK cops had formed a perimeter, keeping the neighbors and the news crews out of the way.

"There are fifty law-enforcement people all over this," he continued. "There's more where they came from. Every last one of them, including me, will do everything we can to find Wendy and make certain she's safe. I'm begging you. Go home. Let us do our jobs."

"It's my job, too. More than my job."

"You almost got yourself and your friend killed. Next time you may not be so lucky. You're not shaking now, but what happens if you fall apart when somebody's life is on the line? Maybe it'll be yours or mine or even Wendy's. Then what?"

I had held it together since Kate knocked on Latrell's door, but I could feel the breakdown coming like animals can sense an earthquake before it hits. Two paramedics lifted Kate onto a stretcher and wheeled her out. Her eyes were closed. I couldn't tell if she was sleeping, sedated, or unconscious.

"Like I said, it's more than my job."

Chapter Fifty-two

It hit me when I'd driven Kate's car two blocks from La-trell's house. Pressure built behind my eyes, making me blink. I could see, but I was in a fog like my brain was wrapped in a layer of cotton. I didn't remember turning the radio on, but a DJ was rattling on about something. I heard his voice but couldn't follow what he was saying. I pulled to the curb, shaking from the inside out.

I knew the routine by now. I didn't fight it by grabbing the steering wheel. I didn't tense my body as if I was waiting to be struck. Instead, I went limp, letting the tremors have me, opening my eyes when they were gone.

Ruby lay on the front seat, her head up, watching me with her dark eyes. I rubbed her head and she licked my hand.

"What am I going to do with you?" I asked her.

She didn't answer and I didn't blame her. One of the paramedics had told me that they were taking Kate to the KU Hospital. I didn't know how long they would keep her, only that I wouldn't leave until I knew she really was all right. Pete & Mac's didn't pick up. Besides, I had a feeling I wasn't going to be home much until this was over. That left me with only one other option. Joy answered on the fifth ring.

"Did I wake you?"

"No. It's only ten o'clock. I just got out of the shower." She was breathless, her voice pitched with anxiety. "Did they find Wendy?"

"Not yet."

"Are they trying?"

I hesitated. I didn't want to tell her that no news wasn't good news but it wasn't fair to keep what I knew from her.

"They're trying hard. Troy's checked their credit cards, bank accounts, and cell phones. There's been no activity."

"What does that mean?"

"If they had eloped or just taken a last-minute vacation or were just going about their daily lives, there would be electronic and paper trails. Since there aren't any, we have to consider the possibility that something has happened to them or that they have a good reason to be hiding."

"Don't tell me that, Jack. What do we do?"

"Keep looking. Keep trying. That's why I'm calling. I know it's late, but I need you to do me a favor."

"A favor?"

"I need you to pick up Ruby, maybe keep her for a few days."

"Why? Are you going out of town?"

"No. I'm not going anywhere. It's just that I can't be tied down to the dog while I'm trying to find Wendy."

"Okay," she said, taking a breath. "You can bring her over in the morning."

"Actually, I need you to come get her now."

"You're going out at ten o'clock? You must know something. Why won't you tell me?"

"I don't know anything, but I'm not at home and I won't get home for a while."

"Where are you?"

"I'm on my way to the emergency room at the KU Hospital. Can you meet me there and pick up the dog?"

"KU Hospital? What's the matter? Are you hurt? Is it the shaking?"

"No, it's nothing like that. I'm fine."

"Jack Davis, tell me what in the hell is going on or I'm going to hang up this phone!"

I was trying to tell her as little as possible, not just to protect her but to avoid the additional fallout I knew was coming. I realized I couldn't succeed at either and continuing to try would only make things worse.

"We found out who killed the people in the drug house. His name was Latrell Kelly. He lived behind the victims. Kate and I went to talk to him a little while ago. He surprised us and hit Kate in the head with a gun. She's the one in the emergency room. He took a shot at me and mostly missed. I doubt if I'll even need a stitch. Troy Clark shot Latrell. He died at the scene."

I could hear her crying. The sound was muffled. I guessed she was covering the receiver with her hand. She gathered herself, coughing to clear her throat.

"I hate you, Jack, you know that?"

"I know."

"But that's not my real problem. You want to know what my real problem is? My real problem is that I don't hate you all the time."

Joy hung up. I started the car, found my way to Seventh Street and took it south until it turned into Rainbow Boulevard. The hospital was on the corner of Thirty-ninth and Rainbow. I turned east on Rainbow and followed the signs to the emergency room. Joy was standing next to her car when

I arrived. She was wearing jeans and a hooded sweatshirt, the hood pulled tight around her face. I pulled alongside where she had parked. She opened the passenger door of Kate's BMW, put Ruby in her car, and drove away. She never said hello.

Chapter Fifty-three

Emergency rooms are like convenience stores. They're open twenty-four hours a day, but you'd rather get your coffee somewhere else. That was particularly true at KU Hospital, where the coffee was bad, the waiting room was uncomfortable, and the staff was numb from dealing with the daily deluge of crime and accident victims mixed in with the ordinary folks whose string of good living had run out.

I knew that security guards were stationed at the entrance to the emergency room and that I would have to pass through a metal detector, so I locked my gun in the glove compartment of Kate's car. An admitting nurse sat on the opposite side of a counter, keeping patients at arm's length with a sliding-glass window. Access to the treatment area was restricted to patients, family, and medical personnel. The admitting nurse was the gatekeeper, pushing a button that unlocked the door if you knew the secret password.

I tapped on the glass. The nurse, a middle-aged woman with cropped red hair, an extra chin, and giant eggplant arms glanced up at me. Letting out a deep sigh, she reached for the window and slid it open six inches.

"I'm with a woman named Kate Scranton. She came in by ambulance a few minutes ago with a head wound."

"You her husband?"

"No."

"Father, brother, or doctor?"

"No."

"Take a seat."

"I need to see her."

"Take a seat. You'll have to wait until she's released or sent up to a room."

I read her name tag. "Look, Glenda. My name is Jack Davis. I'm an FBI agent. Ms. Scranton was injured during an investigation of one of my cases. I need to see her now."

Glenda gave me a flat stare that said she'd heard that noise before. She stuck out her hand, palm up. "Lemme see some ID."

I showed her my driver's license.

"FBI ID," she said, rolling her eyes.

"I don't have it with me."

"Then take a seat."

One of the paramedics that had taken care of Kate at the scene appeared at Glenda's side. She was solid without being stocky, barely five-five, and her long brown hair was pulled back in a ponytail that stuck out the back of a ball cap. She waved and opened the window all the way.

"Hey, Agent Davis, you should get that stinger checked out."

I gave her my best smile, noting her name tag. "Thanks, Valerie. Just as soon as I convince Glenda here to let me see Kate. How's she doing?"

"They're still checking her out, but I think she'll be fine."

I turned my smile on Glenda, who bit her lip and edged her hand slowly toward the button that unlocked the door to the treatment rooms. Before she could push it, I heard a woman's voice from the back shout, "She's having a seizure!

Dr. Benson is the neurosurgeon on call. Get him down here stat!"

I didn't wait for Glenda. I reached through the window, punched the button, and yanked the door open. Valerie was ahead of me by two steps. I followed her to a room at the back of the ER. People dressed in scrubs were racing in and out. I couldn't tell who was a doctor and who was a nurse.

I pushed my way forward. A man in green scrubs tapped me on the chest, telling me to step back. I started to argue when Valerie took me by the arm and pulled me away.

"Let them do what they need to do," she said.

I stood on the edge of the vortex, catching pieces of shouted orders. There were demands to check vitals, instructions for injections of cc's of some drug I'd never heard of and repeated exclamations of "Where the hell is Benson?"

A moment later, a man burst through the door, also dressed in scrubs, a flowered surgical hat tied around his head. He was tall with a runner's lean build, a narrow face, and intense dark eyes that swallowed the situation in a single glance. He was moving swiftly but purposefully, in complete control. I didn't need a name tag to know that he was Dr. Benson.

He plunged into Kate's room, the noise level dropping to pin-drop quiet. Valerie and I stepped close enough to hear what he was saying.

"She's bleeding in her brain, right side. Get an MRI and then get her into the OR."

He came out of Kate's room with the same purposeful stride. I intercepted him.

"Dr. Benson. I'm Special Agent Jack Davis, FBI. I was with Ms. Scranton when she was injured. What can you tell me about her condition?"

He didn't ask for identification, just glanced at Valerie, who vouched for me with a nod.

"Did you see what happened to her?"

"Yes. She was crouching on the floor and was struck in the right side of her head with the barrel of a .45 caliber pistol."

He nodded. "That's consistent with the injury. Her skull is fractured. I can't tell how badly until I see the MRI and I really won't know how bad it is until I take a look inside."

"How long will that take?" I asked.

"That's a guess I never make, Agent Davis. Best thing I can tell you to do is find a comfortable place to wait. What happened to the guy who hit her?"

"Another agent shot him. He didn't survive."

Benson nodded, a small smile creasing his narrow mouth. "Seems about right."

I watched as Kate was wheeled away a second time, surrounded by people who, if they were worried, didn't show it. Valerie was still at my side.

"Benson is the best neurosurgeon in town," she said. "I've got to go."

"Thanks for everything."

"No sweat," she said. "Take it easy."

The ER was calm again, a steady hum of nurses shuttling in and out of rooms, comforting and soothing the people they were taking care of. I stood in the middle of the floor, uncertain of where to go when I saw Glenda walking toward me smiling like the lead in a Stephen King novel.

"Right this way, Agent Davis," she said, directing me into a vacant treatment area surrounded by a curtain that she pulled closed behind her. "Valerie told me that you're wounded."

"She did?"

"Yes. She did. Now take off your pants."

"My pants?"

"Yes, your pants. And bend over. Let's have a look at that stinger. It won't hurt a bit. I promise."

Chapter Fifty-four

My stinger was more blister than flesh wound, the skin red and tender. Glenda hid her disappointment as she cleaned and dressed my hip. Fifteen minutes later, I had my pants back on. Marty Grisnik was waiting for me when I came out.

"They wouldn't let me in to see you," he said.

"I know. We're not related."

"We're not even dating."

A sign hanging from the ceiling gave directions to the main hospital. I started walking in that direction, preferring to ask anyone except Glenda for directions to the surgery waiting room.

"Where are you headed?" Grisnik asked.

"Waiting room. A friend of mine is in surgery."

"The woman your killer clocked?"

"Yeah. Her name is Kate Scranton."

"You look like you could use some coffee and company."

He was wearing chinos, a short-sleeved polo, and a light windbreaker. It wasn't cold inside or out. The jacket was to cover his weapon. He had the ID to prove he actually was a cop in his own jurisdiction and that meant he didn't have to leave his gun in the car. I knew that he wanted to keep me company as long as he might learn something useful. I didn't mind. Some of my best friends were cops.

"I'll skip the coffee and settle for the company."

We settled into the waiting room. There were two clusters of people and a few solos spread among the chairs, some of them sleeping, some of them watching the television hanging from the ceiling, some of them present only in body. Grisnik tried the coffee, blowing on it before sipping and wincing.

"Hell of a thing," Grisnik said.

"The coffee or what happened with Latrell Kelly?"

"Both, only you can't shoot the coffee."

"You missed all the excitement," I said.

"FBI didn't call us until it was all over. Damn cooperative of them. Not much going on by the time I got there."

"Anybody brief you?"

"Yeah. Ammara Iverson. She and I might wind up friends if a few more of your suspects get killed in my city."

"She tell you the same gun was used on Marcellus Pearson and Javy Ordonez?"

"Yup. And she said that Latrell's fingerprints were on it and that they think it was stolen along with the gun Latrell used on your friend. Know for sure when they check the registrations."

"She tell you anything else?"

"You mean did she tell me about the photograph of Latrell and a woman that was found in Javy Ordonez's car? Yeah, she told me. That, plus the gun, is enough to make Latrell good for doing Ordonez. Ammara asked me to check our mug books for a picture of the woman. Said she'd get a copy to me in the morning. I told her no problem, but that'll take some time."

"Photograph was taken around seventeen years ago. If she's in the books, it's probably for drugs or prostitution.

Start your search back then, crosscheck it against Latrell's address. Go at it that way and I'm betting you get a hit in less than an hour."

"Who do you think she is?"

"Latrell's mother."

"What makes you so sure?"

"After Marcellus went down, Latrell told a reporter that's what happens when nobody takes care of a little boy. He was talking about himself. That's why you'll find her in the system on drugs or prostitution or both."

"So why did he kill Marcellus?"

"I don't know why he went after Marcellus, but he did. Told me so before he died. I think he killed Jalise and her son because they reminded him too much of his mother and him."

"Too bad about the mother and her kid, but he did us a favor getting rid of the others. What about Oleta Phillips?" asked Grisnik.

"Oleta saw Latrell when he came out of Marcellus's house. A real case of wrong place, wrong time. There's a couple of graves in Latrell's basement. Probably Oleta and his mother."

"Somebody like Latrell, they don't usually take seventeen years off between killing people. If they do, they make up for lost time. That's another reason to like him for the Ordonez thing, especially since it was the same gun. Toss in the photograph and it looks tight to me," Grisnik said.

"I don't know. Latrell killing Marcellus and the others makes a twisted kind of sense, but I can't make it stretch to fit Javy Ordonez. Right before he died, Latrell accused me of following him somewhere. Said I took his things. I don't have any idea what he's talking about. Could be whoever killed Javy found Latrell's gun."

"Maybe the guy you saw running from the scene was real. Could have been him," Grisnik said.

"What's the connection?"

"You started out thinking this was a drug war. Maybe you were right. Maybe the guy you saw was planning on taking out Marcellus, only Latrell saved him the trouble. The guy stays on Latrell, gets the gun and the photograph, pops Javy, and plants the picture. End of story."

"Works better than your theory putting Javy on Latrell."

"Hey, I'm just a mule-headed city cop, but I'll tell you one thing. I'd rather get shot than drink any more of this coffee." Grisnik sat the cup on a table and got up. "I'll get someone started on those mug books. If you're right, I don't need the photograph. All I need is to find an arrest record on a woman who lived in Latrell's house seventeen years ago. How hard can that be?"

"You mean you'll have someone else do it?"

"That's exactly what I mean. Hope everything goes okay with your friend. Anything new on Colby Hudson or Wendy?"

"Nothing. They're off the grid."

"That's not good. I've got some feelers out. I'll let you know if I get any bites."

"I appreciate it."

He was at the door to the waiting room when it hit me.

"Hey, Marty." He turned toward me. "How'd you know my daughter's name was Wendy?"

His eyes flickered for an instant and his mouth pulled back in a tight smile. "Ammara Iverson told me. Gave me a description, too. How am I supposed to look for someone if I don't know their name and what they look like? Get some rest. You look like hell," he said, waving good-bye before I could answer.

Chapter Fifty-five

At eleven o'clock, I walked out to the nurses' station and asked a nurse if she could update me on Kate's surgery. She started to say no but then I began to shake and she said she'd be right back. I hate pity, but I'm not above exploiting it.

She returned a few minutes later and told me that Kate's surgery would last at least a couple more hours and that she would be in recovery for another two hours after that before I could see her. I thanked her and went back to the waiting room, sat down, and stopped shaking. If only it were that easy all the time.

I thought about the photograph of Latrell and the unidentified woman. Marty Grisnik believed that it made the case against Latrell for the Ordonez murder. That's what we were supposed to think, but I couldn't make it fit. If the woman were Latrell's mother, it definitely wouldn't fit. Their age differences ruined that scenario. The photograph had to have been planted by the killer to set up Latrell.

I thought again about Kate's explanation of how we read faces. We manipulate our voluntary expressions, choosing honesty or deceit as it suits us. Our micro expressions are honest precisely because they are involuntary, beyond our powers of manipulation. Both are there to be seen, but we settle for what is easier to see, oblivious to what we need to know. Like the person with face blindness, we don't recognize what we're looking at.

The photograph of Latrell and the woman was just one example. If I accepted its presence in Javy's car as proof of a connection between him and Latrell, I wouldn't bother to ask if it made sense. I had to reject at face value everything that had happened since the drug house murders, challenge the assumptions I had made, and disregard my instinctive reactions to the evidence. I had to slow everything down to a freeze-frame and dissect it like it was a micro expression.

Troy Clark had assumed that someone on my squad had leaked the existence of the surveillance camera in Marcellus's house. He seized on Colby Hudson's failure to appear for his polygraph as proof that Colby was the source of the leak. That was the easiest explanation for him and it turned out to be wrong. Latrell Kelly was the killer.

Colby must have had another reason to duck his polygraph. Maybe he was afraid of being asked about his purchase of the car and the house or Thomas Rice's death. Maybe he'd gotten in over his head and was hiding out or had been killed.

Colby had told me his version of buying the house and car, but I preferred the version told by Jill Rice because it fit with my bias against Colby and the intelligence Grisnik had picked up from his penitentiary sources. I was already concerned that Colby had been working undercover so long that he couldn't remember which side he was on. Even if he was telling the truth, I didn't like that he'd taken advantage of Jill Rice's efforts to piss off her ex-husband. And, as much as anything else, I didn't like that he was sleeping with my daughter.

When Colby disappeared and when drugs and cash were

found in his house, I saw what Troy saw—an agent that had crossed the line and taken Wendy with him. It was no different than when Joy went looking for our son Kevin in Frank Tyler's house after Tyler had picked Kevin up at school. When Joy called and told me that Kevin was missing and that she had found Tyler's collection of child pornography, I was certain about what had happened and I was right.

The discovery of incriminating evidence in Colby's house was dramatic and timely, fitting Troy's suspicions and mine, but it could have been planted there just as the photograph of Latrell and the woman had probably been planted in Javy Ordonez's car. Though I had considered the possibility of a frame-up when Ammara first told me about the drugs and cash, I rejected it because I preferred what I saw on the surface.

Troy had reacted in a similar way to my shaking, my body's involuntary expressions, as proof that I couldn't be trusted. He was wrong about me. Perhaps I was wrong about Colby.

If we believe too much too easily, we don't ask the right questions. I realized that I had made that mistake with Colby's story. He had said that Jill Rice had called our office looking for someone to buy her husband's car, but no one had checked our phone records for that incoming call. I called Ammara Iverson.

"How's Kate?" she asked.

"Still in surgery. Is anyone working late tonight?"

"Everyone is working. There is no late."

"Have someone check the records of phone calls made to the office in the last six weeks for any calls originating from a land line or cell phone belonging to Jill Rice."

"Not that it matters since you're doing such a good job staying out of this case while you're on medical leave and all, but why?"

"Colby says that he took a call from Jill Rice and that she

was looking for someone to buy her ex-husband's car. Jill Rice says she never made that call. We need to pick a winner in that liar's match."

"You have a favorite?"

"I wish I did."

"I'll call you when I know something."

"Who did you find buried in Latrell's basement?"

"Black female in the fresh grave. We're checking her prints, but it's probably Oleta Phillips. There were two skeletons in the second grave, one on top of the other."

"One of them is probably Latrell's mother. Anything else interesting turn up?"

"It looks like he was preparing for the end of the world."

"How's that?"

"He had enough candles and flashlights to last a lifetime," she said.

"What about bottled water, canned goods and dried fruit, stuff like that?"

"Now that you mention it, we didn't find any. Maybe he was just afraid of the dark."

"Marty Grisnik stopped by the hospital. Says he saw you at Latrell's."

"Yeah. He wasn't too happy that he was late to the party, but that's the way Troy is playing it."

"You bring him up to date on what's been going on?"

"Sure. Figured that was the best way to get him on our side, but don't tell Troy."

"Not a chance. By the way, you say anything to him about Wendy?"

"Yeah. Grisnik asked for her name and a description. Said he wanted his people to help find her. Why? Is that a problem?"

"No. We need all the help we can get."

"I'll get back to you on the phone records," she said and hung up.

The waiting room felt like it was getting smaller. The walls weren't moving and neither was I. Waiting for Kate to come out of surgery while hoping that my cell phone would ring with good news was a suffocating prospect.

I left my cell phone number with the nurse, who promised to call when I could see Kate. I didn't know where to look for Wendy, but I was certain that if I could find Colby, I would find her.

If they were being held against their will, I could spend the rest of my life combing the city inch by inch and never find them. If they were hiding, at least one of them would have to come out for food, money, or air. That was likely to be Colby. He wouldn't go to his house or to Wendy's apartment because he'd know that the FBI was watching both of those locations, as was anyone else they might be hiding from. Colby would reach out to a friend and I could only think of one person who might qualify.

Chapter Fifty-six

Pete's Place was not the place to be at midnight on a Friday night. There were only three cars parked anywhere near the door, one of them across the street. It may have been crowded earlier, but it was down to the stragglers. The restaurant next door, Pete's Other Place, was buttoned down and black. The nearest streetlight was fifty yards to the north, a ball of yellow that splashed on the pavement and quit, leaving the bar buried in the dark, the faint neon glow in the window a pale beacon for anyone looking for a last stop.

The lights inside the bar were milky, the air quilted with smoke. A heavyset man who looked to be in his sixties, his chin on his chest, was passed out in a chair, his head angled against the wall, an empty beer pitcher on the table in front of him. Tanja Andrija was bent over him, patting his face to bring him around.

"C'mon George. Wake up and go home. I'm not running a bed and breakfast."

George stirred and smiled, trying to grope Tanja. She batted his meaty hand away like he was a child.

"Not tonight, George. You're too drunk to do me any good and your wife would kill us both, anyway."

Two other men were seated at the bar. Both had the broad shoulders and over-the-belt-guts of men who'd spent their lives working hard and drinking harder. They lumbered off their stools.

"We'll get him home, Tanja," one of them said.

They each slipped an arm around George, hefting him to his feet like he was a sack filled with feathers and air. I sat down at the bar as Tanja opened the door and the trio stumbled into the night.

She closed the door behind them and snapped the dead-bolt, came around to the business side of the bar, and leaned against the far wall framed by bottles of booze, the mirrored wall behind her letting me watch me watch her. She was wearing low-riding jeans that hugged her like they meant it and a deep red T-shirt stretched tight across her breasts. Standing with her elbows on the counter, her ankles crossed, her eyes alive, and her mouth pitched at an inviting angle, she promised trouble. If she were on my calendar, I'd never make it to next month.

Marty Grisnik and Colby Hudson had fallen for her. I could see why. Grisnik was probably not over her all these years later. Colby might not get the chance to forget her.

"You came back," Tanja said.

"Is that why you locked the door?"

"We're closed."

"I don't mind."

"I do. Like I said, we're closed."

"I don't want to buy a drink."

"What do you want?"

"I'm looking for Colby Hudson."

She looked around the bar. "I don't see him."

"Doesn't mean you don't know where he is."

"What did he do? Break curfew?"

"I didn't say he did anything. I'm just looking for him."

"He was in here the other day," she said, turning her back to me. The cash register was next to her. She opened it, removed the cash, and stuffed the money into a bank bag. She zipped it closed, tucked it under her arm, and looked at me in the mirror behind the bar. "Same day you were here. He introduced us. You should remember that."

"I remember. You told Marty Grisnik not to bring me back."

"I guess I should have been more specific. I should have told you not to come back. Consider it said."

"You and I aren't going to be friends, are we?"

She held the money bag in front of her with both hands like it was a shield. "I don't think we have enough in common."

"We have more in common than you think."

"Name one thing," she said.

"Colby Hudson. You said he makes you laugh. If you want him to keep doing that, I need to find him."

"What are you, his mother?"

"Colby tell you what he does for a living?"

She hesitated, put the money bag on the counter, and stuck her hands in her pockets. She rolled her shoulders back, her blond hair swirling around her neck and her posture lifting her breasts. I couldn't tell whether she was preparing to attack or surrender. "He's an FBI agent, same as you. Marty told me all about you."

"And Marty told me all about you. He said the two of you used to go out. He's a cop and he's your friend. Colby's an FBI agent and, from what I saw the other day, he's your friend, too. So why are you giving me such a hard time when I'm only trying to help Colby?"

"You're not like Marty and Colby. You're full of self-righteous bullshit, the way you judged Colby and me. What's between us is nobody's business but ours."

I'd never seen Colby look at Wendy the way I'd seen him look at Tanja. I thought again of Joy and Kate. Each time I was ready to condemn someone else, I painted myself with the same brush.

"You're right. It's none of my business, but I still need to find him."

"If Colby wants you to find him, you will."

"Why wouldn't he want me to find him?"

She looked at me straight on, her blank face set in stone. "I don't know. I run a bar. That's all."

I stood. "You hear from Colby, tell him to find me."

"Sure. Next time I see him," she said.

"You do that. Is there another way out of here besides the front door?"

"Why?"

Her eyes widened and her brow arched upward in a flash. In the next instant her face was smooth. If I had blinked, I would have missed her micro expression. Kate would have labeled it a classic expression of fear. It was the kind of fear that could come from hiding Colby in the back of the bar.

"Because you're closed and the front door is locked. I'll just go out the back."

"You don't have to do that," she said, recovering quickly as she smoothed her T-shirt, tugging on the bottom edge. "I'll let you out the front."

I followed her to the door. The breeze stirred her hair. She brushed it away from her eyes. We were inches apart. She was a magnet.

"Remember what I said," I told her.

"You do the same. Don't come back."

Chapter Fifty-seven

I sat in Kate's car on the northbound side of Fifth Street and started the engine. The night had turned cool, the drop in temperature coating the windows with a layer of dew. Tanja was standing inside the bar, peering out over the neon sign promising free beer tomorrow and waiting for me to drive away.

I pulled away from the curb, wondering whether Colby Hudson was standing in the shadows behind her, watching me over her shoulder. Petar and Maja Andrija's house was a few blocks to the north, dark and silent as the rest of Strawberry Hill as I glided past. Glancing in my rearview mirror, I saw a burst of light suddenly flare from their open front door, the porch light blinking on and framing Colby as he flew down the stairs and bolted into the protective darkness surrounding the house next door.

He'd been at Tanja's parents' house, not at the bar. She could have called him by now but, if she had, she would have told him to sit tight until she was certain I was gone. His departure looked more like a jailbreak than a careful getaway.

Either he wasn't supposed to be there or he wasn't supposed to have left.

I stayed off the brakes, not wanting him to think that I'd seen him, knowing that he wouldn't recognize Kate's car and that he'd wait until I was out of sight before he started moving. Advantage mine.

I crested the hill at the intersection of Fifth and Ann in front of St. Ann's Church, which sat on the southwest corner of the intersection, the church and the street named after the same saint. A playground stretched from the east side of the church to the curb. This was where Marty Grisnik and Tanja had gone to school, Marty probably stealing a kiss, getting whacked on the back of his head by a nun for his trouble.

I turned left onto Ann, then right into an alley, where I parked the car. I popped open the dome light and unscrewed the bulb, not wanting to give the edge back to Colby when I got out of the car.

He could have gone in any direction. I was counting on him choosing the only one that gave me a chance. I found a doorway recessed a couple of feet into the damp, limestone wall of the church facing the playground. Standing in the doorway was like nesting in a cave. It was so dark that Colby could have spit on my shoe and not known it. I held my gun at my side, and waited, steady as the rock that surrounded me.

My eyes adjusted to the dark, the shapes of the playground equipment coming into focus. Thinking of the playground as a clock, I was at twelve o'clock, Fifth Street was at six, a swing set in the center. Ann Street was at three o'clock and the jungle gym was at nine. The playground covered half a block and was surrounded by a chain-link fence meant to keep kids and balls in, not meant to keep rogue FBI agents out. If Colby were headed this way, he'd stay close to the church and away from any passing headlights.

Sound travels farther late at night, undiluted by kids playing ball or cars grinding their gears. The jingle jangle sound that chain-link fence makes when someone climbs over it would have been lost in the mix of daytime background noise. In the still of the night, it sounded like an out-of-tune wind chime.

Colby slipped by my doorway, his head down, less than two feet from where I stood. I waited until he'd gone ten feet past me and then stepped onto the playground, my gun aimed at him, calling his name.

He stopped, his back to me. He was wearing jeans and a light jacket. He raised his head, his right shoulder turning in as he reached in to his jacket. I knew he preferred a shoulder harness to a holster stuck in his pants or clipped to his belt.

"You won't need that," I told him.

"Why, Jack? Because you're unarmed or because you're not going to shoot me?"

"Because I won't shoot you if I can help it but I will shoot you if I have to. You pull your gun and there's a lot better chance that will happen. Turn around real slow, keep your hands where I can see them, and talk to me."

He turned around and said, "You don't have to do this."

"Then I apologize in advance. Unzip your jacket, use two fingers to lift your gun out, and put it on the ground. Use three fingers and I'll shoot one of them off. Then kick it over to me."

"Listen, Jack."

"Don't say a word until I tell you. Just get rid of your gun."

Colby did as he was told and I kicked his gun toward the jungle gym, steel skidding hard on the asphalt. I pointed my gun at him.

"You can lay down on your stomach, I can cuff you, and search you for your backup gun, or you can save me the trouble and put it on the ground along with any other toys you're carrying."

"Give me a break, Jack. You don't even have your fucking badge. I'll keep my hands where you can see them, but that's all. You don't like it, you can shoot me, or you can come over here and search me."

I had made a stupid bluff, the kind that always made the other guy bold when he called it and I had to fold. Backing down wasn't an option. That would turn our power struggle on its head.

"Don't push me, Colby. Be a good boy and lay down."

"No," he said, taking a step toward me.

"Don't make me shoot you."

"You won't. In the first place, I'm unarmed and I haven't threatened or attacked you. In the second place, you haven't told me that I'm under arrest. In the third place, if you shoot me you won't get what you really want."

He was right on all counts. My right hand began to quiver. I squeezed the butt of my gun to steady myself but it didn't help. My belly broke out in minitremors. I could feel them but I hoped Colby couldn't see them.

"Where's Wendy?"

"She's not at the Andrijas' house."

"That's what you were doing there? Looking for her? Then where is she?"

"That's not the way this is going to work. You put your gun down and kick it over to me. Then we'll talk."

"She loves you. Now you're using her as a bargaining chip?"

"You're the one pointing a gun at me. Doesn't leave me a lot of choice."

I reached in my pocket with my left hand, removed my cell phone, and flipped it open. "I make one call, we'll have company. Or you can tell me where I can find Wendy and walk away."

"Go ahead. Make the call. That will be worse than shoot-

ing me. Troy and the rest of the gang will show up. I won't
talk until I get a lawyer and the lawyer won't let me say a
word. Besides, they've got nothing to charge me with. By
the time I walk out the door, it won't matter where Wendy is.
It will be too late."

My heart slammed into my throat. "She's alive?"

"Last time I saw her."

"When was that?"

"Last night."

"Where?"

"Her place. We were having dinner. I left. When I came
back, she was gone."

"How can you do this to her?"

Colby ran his hands through his scraggly hair, his eyes
hard but not hard enough to hide a pained wince, too fleeting
to be fake. Kate had been a better teacher than she gave me
credit for. I was seeing things I would have missed.

"I'm not the one doing it."

His question matched his involuntary confession. He was
worried about Wendy, too.

"Then let me help you get her back."

"It's not that simple," he said, looking away.

And then I understood. "So you're willing to sacrifice her
to save your own ass. Just like you did Thomas Rice."

Colby took a deep breath as if he was about to launch a
denial and then dropped his hands in surrender. "Rice was
different."

"Different because you weren't sleeping with him?"

"Different because you think you know what you're talking about but you don't. Wendy's a big girl. She made her
choices, just like me."

He was baiting me, implicating Wendy as an accomplice,
something I wouldn't buy. "When you didn't show for your
polygraph, Troy sent a couple of agents to your house. They

found enough drugs and cash to put you away for a long time. If anything happens to Wendy, that won't matter because I'll kill you before you serve a day."

"The way my luck is running, you'll have to get in line."

"Jill Rice denies calling our office looking for someone to buy her car. She says her ex had it all set up before he went to prison. That it was all part of a deal to set him up for when he got out."

"I guess that's a better story than the one I told."

"You have a good story for the money and dope that was found in your house?"

"Yeah, and this one is irresistible. I'm not that stupid. I know how the game is played. I was set up."

"Why?"

"To discredit me if I came in and told what I know."

"Why would you do that?"

"I needed an exit strategy. The drug business is like every other business, Jack. Everyone always wants a bigger slice of the pie. I took mine and used it to buy the house and car. People I do business with didn't like it."

"Who are they?"

"Sorry, Jack. I'm not making that deal with you or anyone else anytime soon."

"There's a big difference between the drug business and every other business," I told him. "You steal from GM, they send you to jail. You steal from drug dealers, they kill you."

"Except I've got an insurance policy. Anything happens to me, they go down. Long as they don't find it, I've got leverage. They must have snatched Wendy, figuring she gives them leverage against me."

"Except you're willing to let her die!"

He shrugged his shoulders. "It's an ugly world, Jack. You arrest me, they'll think I gave them up and they'll kill

Wendy. You kill me and they'll kill her because they won't need her and can't risk letting her go. Now put your gun down."

Colby took two more steps toward me. I raised my gun at his chest, but my arm began to wobble and then I began to shake. My eyes clamped shut as the fog wrapped around my brain. I twisted and folded in half at the same instant, slammed with contractions that took my breath away. I tried to straighten, but the contractions pulled me to my knees and held me there like chains.

I felt Colby next to me, felt him take the gun from my hand. I opened my eyes. He was standing over me.

I forced my words into a choppy stutter. "What happened to you?"

"I looked around and decided I didn't want to be you. I wanted a life I couldn't afford at my pay grade. I had the girl, the house, and the car. Then you fucked it up. Anything happens to Wendy, it will be on your head."

The contractions eased. My breath was ragged. The shakes were hitting me on and off as if a child was playing with a switch.

"How did I fuck it up?"

"By doing your job."

"What about your girlfriend, Tanja? You running out on her, too?"

He laughed. "That's your problem, Jack. You only see what you want to see."

"My daughter is the only one I want to see. What's happened to her?"

His mouth turned up in a cruel grin.

"Maybe she didn't want to be like you, either."

Another wave of contractions rocked me, arching my back and neck. Colby shoved me on to my side. I watched with clenched teeth as he scooped up his gun and threw mine against the fence. He looked at me, shook his head, turned, and ran away, his silhouette suddenly familiar. I'd seen it once before when he ran away from Marcellus Pearson's house. The fog came again and I closed my eyes, shaking while his footsteps faded in the darkness.

Chapter Fifty-eight

Lewis Carroll wrote in *Alice in Wonderland* that if you don't know where you are going, any road will get you there. My midnight trip to Strawberry Hill would have made the Mad Hatter proud, though I had learned enough to get me back on my feet.

Wendy was alive. I didn't know where she was or how I would find her, but she was alive. Colby had implied that she was as guilty as he was. I wouldn't believe that unless Wendy told me. Even if it was true, it changed nothing.

I focused on what I knew. Colby said that I had screwed up his plans by doing my job. My last job had been shutting down Marcellus Pearson. That threatened Colby because Marcellus would have given him up to make a deal with the U.S. Attorney.

That explained what Colby was doing near Marcellus's house the night of the murders. He'd come there to kill Marcellus, only Latrell had beaten him to it, just as Marty Grisnik had surmised. Colby must have waited around long enough to be certain that the job was finished, letting Latrell kill Oleta Phillips.

With Marcellus out of the way, he knew we'd go after Javy Ordonez next. Colby couldn't let that happen because Javy would also give him up in a heartbeat, so Javy had to die, too. Colby followed Latrell, found the murder weapon, and used it to kill Javy.

Colby must have blessed his luck when he found the photograph of Latrell and his mother. He left the murder weapon beneath a Dumpster where it was likely to be found and planted the photograph of Latrell, nailing him for the murders he was guilty of while framing him for one he didn't commit.

His relationship with Tanja Andrija raised more questions. She had kept her cool until I asked her if there was another way out of the bar besides the front door. I had assumed from her flash of panic that Colby was hiding in the back but, once again, I was wrong, which meant that she was hiding something else in the back of the bar.

In any other case, I would have immediately called Troy Clark and Marty Grisnik, and told them to blanket the area with cops, FBI agents, dogs, and helicopters until we captured Colby Hudson. We'd pick up Tanja, her brother Nick, and her parents, letting Tanja get a look at her parents being interrogated in their pajamas. One of them would turn on the other because that's what crooks, even family, always do.

I would disregard Colby's warning about Wendy, taking my chances that we could find her. But this wasn't any case, it was my daughter's case, and I refused to take the chance that Colby was bluffing or wrong about what would happen to her if he were arrested. I didn't care if he and Tanja got away clean, both of them living to be a hundred and twenty.

Now I knew which road I was taking and that I was taking it alone. It was the road that started at Pete's Place, though I didn't know where it would end.

I left the car parked in the alley and walked down Sixth Street, keeping to the shadows, until it flattened out. A thrift shop and a tire store backed up to the bar and restaurant. Neither the owners nor the city had invested in lighting, leaving their corner of the world dark and deserted.

Both buildings were one story. A forklift was parked on the side of the tire store, the forks raised to within a few feet of the roof. I climbed onto the top of the cab, high-stepped onto the forks and pulled myself onto the flat-pitched roof. The exterior walls rose two feet above the roof. I crouched against the far wall, looking over the edge at the back door to the bar.

The area behind the thrift store, tire store, bar, and restaurant was paved with access to both Fifth and Sixth Streets. A sedan was parked behind the bar next to an air-conditioning tower that was running full out, the rushing air and whirling fan obliterating any other sounds. The back door to the bar had warped, leaving cracks of light along the frame.

I settled in against the wall, the tarred surface of the roof rubbing hard against my knees. Fifteen minutes went by without any activity. Then a light pickup truck with a lid over the bed swept into the parking lot from Fifth Street, the driver backing it up to the rear door of the bar.

Tanja opened the door, the light catching the driver's face. It was her brother Nick, wearing a wife-beater and a pair of jeans. He bulled past Tanja, waving his arms and shaking his head. She waved her arms in reply, giving as good as she got, and closed the door. Though I wasn't able to hear anything they had said, I was willing to bet that the nicest thing was "fuck you."

When the door opened again a few minutes later, they began loading cardboard boxes and bulging garbage bags into the rear of the pickup. They worked quickly, finishing in fifteen minutes. Nick loaded the last box, shoving it into the truck bed and slamming the tailgate shut.

Tanja said something to Nick. He stabbed her chest with the end of his finger. She smacked his hand away and he threw his arms into the air again, got in his truck, and drove away. She stared after him, hands on her hips, and then reached in her pocket for her cell phone, running her hand through her hair as she listened, her shoulders sagging as if the call was another burden she couldn't bear. She locked the door to the bar, grabbed a shoulder bag from her car, and marched toward Fifth Street, turning north when she reached the sidewalk.

I looked at my watch. It was after one. I guessed that the call was from her parents and that she was going to see them, choosing to walk rather than drive either to delay the visit or give her time to cool down from the confrontation with her brother.

I followed her, taking a parallel path between the houses and buildings on Fifth and Sixth, waiting until I saw her pass in the open spaces between them so that I could match her pace. Fortunately for me, the fences I had to climb were low and any watchdogs were asleep.

A small stand of juniper bushes in the Andrijas' backyard provided perfect cover. The kitchen was in the back of the house and the lights were on. Petar and Maja, dressed in their pajamas, sat next to each other at the table, the arms of their chairs touching, Petar's arm around his wife. She rested her head on his shoulder while he stroked the side of her face with his other hand. From the tender way he held her and the way her chest was rising and falling, it looked like she was crying.

Tanja entered the kitchen from the front of the house. One look at her parents and she dropped her bag, raced to her mother's side, and glared at her father as he spoke. When he finished, she took out her phone and punched in a number, resuming her wild gesturing.

She stomped around the kitchen, her parents crouching and cringing if she came too close to them. When Tanja was done, she tossed her phone onto the counter and stared past them into the yard as if they weren't there. I knew that the light would blind her even as she looked straight at where I was hiding. After a moment, she yanked on the blinds, cutting off my view.

Watching them, I was convinced of one thing. Colby hadn't been hiding there. He had broken in. The question was why.

Petar and Maja had probably been asleep. Maja heard something and woke Petar, telling him to take a look. Or maybe Petar got up to pee and heard a noise, turned on the lights, and flushed Colby from the darkness, scaring him and his wife to death. They waited before they called Tanja, doubtless more afraid of her than they were of Colby. I didn't blame them.

Chapter Fifty-nine

Kate was in recovery when I got back to KU Hospital. A nurse told me which room she had been assigned to and that I could wait there. There was a hospital version of an easy chair in the corner of the room. I collapsed into it and fell asleep without a fight.

When I woke up, morning sunlight was streaming into the room. Kate was looking at me, her eyes half dreamy with the residue of anesthetic, the room smelling faintly of disinfectant. I pushed myself out of the chair and stood next to her, her hand in mine.

"Hey," she said.

"Hey, yourself."

"Some first date, huh?"

"Yeah. I got shot. You got conked on the head and we still spent the night together."

"You okay?"

"Just a scrape but the ER nurse said I had a cute ass."

"Damn, and she got to see it before I did."

"I'm giving tours on the half hour. Let me know when you'd like to take one."

Kate took a deep breath. "I guess I was pretty stupid."

"Don't be so hard on yourself. You had me convinced that going to see Latrell was a good idea. How do you feel?"

"Like the inside of my head is under construction."

I looked at the clock next to her bed. It was seven-thirty. "Have you talked to Dr. Benson this morning?"

"He was here a little while ago. He said that I looked better than you did and that I'd be fine. He's going to send me home tomorrow morning if I can stand up without falling down."

She squeezed my hand and tears ran down her cheek. I wiped them with a tissue.

"That's good news," I said. "It's okay to cry for good news."

"I know. I should be grateful but no one understands what it's like."

"What don't we understand?"

"I can't see them anymore."

"See what?"

"Micro expressions. Not yours, not his, not the nurses'. Something happened, some brain damage, I guess. It's like I'm half blind."

She forced her eyes wide open, searching my face, straining to lift her head closer to mine. Exhausted by the effort, she fell back on her pillow, closed her eyes, and turned away. I smoothed her hair, uncertain what to say.

"It's probably just the side effects from the anesthetic. You'll be reading my mind again before you know it."

I kissed Kate softly on the cheek. She nodded and bit her lip, letting me know that she heard me even if she didn't believe me. I told her to get some rest and promised to come back later.

I roamed the halls, looking for Dr. Benson, but couldn't find him. I didn't know much about head injuries, only that football players and boxers were never quite right after they had had too many concussions. Kate, it seemed to me, had suffered more than a concussion.

When my father had a stroke, the doctor explained that it caused bleeding in his brain. Dr. Benson had said that Kate was bleeding in her brain, but I knew that didn't mean that she had had a stroke. She didn't look or act the way my father had, one side of his face paralyzed in a confused mask, his speech slurred, his sense of balance shattered. Yet a part of her brain had been damaged and it wouldn't matter what label Dr. Benson put on it. Whatever the diagnosis, Kate had lost a part of herself.

I knew what would come next. The doctor would order tests to measure and define her condition. He'd prescribe treatment if there was any and apologize if there was none. Kate's family and friends would give her advice and encouragement, cutting out newspaper and magazine articles on the latest breakthroughs, urging her to try holistic cures, acupuncture, Eastern medicine, visual imaging, meditation, and chiropractic. Through it all, she would keep asking herself one question, a silent inquiry made in private that no one could answer: *Who am I now?*

Chapter Sixty

I needed a shower, a shave, clean clothes, and more sleep. I didn't have time for sleep but the rest took half an hour after I got home. I found a pair of jeans that were close to being clean and a polo shirt sporting a day's worth of wrinkles.

I saw the message light flashing on my cell phone when I finished getting dressed. Ammara Iverson had called while I was in the shower.

"It's Jack," I said when I returned her call.

"I know. I've got caller ID."

"Another amazing advance in crime-fighting technology."

"Nights and weekends at no extra charge. How's Kate?"

"She's got a headache but the doc says she'll be fine. Probably going home tomorrow."

"Glad to hear it."

"Me, too. What's up?"

"We checked the phone records. If Jill Rice called our office anytime since her husband was arrested, she didn't do it from a phone in her or her husband's name. That doesn't mean she didn't call. It just means we can't prove it."

"Except she denies making the call. At this point, I give her the edge in the who-do-you trust sweepstakes."

"What's your read?" Ammara asked.

I had to be careful. Ammara would be suspicious if I suddenly stopped talking to her about the case. I needed information I could only get from her, but I wasn't ready to tell her about last night and jeopardize Wendy's slim chances. I needed to know how close they were to picking up Colby, but I didn't want to ask the question.

"Colby crossed the line. He made a deal with Thomas Rice to buy his house and car, probably as a way to launder drug money. I'd look at Colby's bank account. And while you're at it, check the records at Leavenworth. See if Colby visited any of the inmates."

"Like Thomas Rice?"

"No. Someone else. Marty Grisnik already checked on Rice's visitors. His wife and his lawyer were the only ones who came to see him. Maybe Colby used someone else to deliver messages to Rice."

"What about the cash and drugs that were found in Colby's house? You think they could have been planted?" she asked.

"It's possible, maybe even likely. Colby was too smart to leave that stuff lying around."

"Except it wasn't lying around. It was hidden in a floor safe. The U.S. Attorney is pissed. He says the agents who found it didn't have probable cause for that kind of search, which means it can't be used as evidence against Colby. Ben Yates told Troy to bring him Colby's head on a pike."

"Troy will have to figure out who else is playing this game, starting with Tanja and Nick Andrija."

"Who are they and what do they have to do with this?" Ammara asked.

"They're sister and brother and they run a bar and restaurant on Strawberry Hill, the place I told you about where they sell the sausage sandwiches. Colby has something going on with Tanja. It may be connected."

"What about Marty Grisnik? He may know something."

"I'll ask him, but that could be tricky. He's a stand-up guy but he's also close to the family and cops aren't any different than civilians. Everyone gets real defensive about their friends, even the guilty ones."

"I know you'll be diplomatic," she said.

"Do you have anything else? What about Bodie Grant? Did his lawyer cut a deal with the U.S. Attorney?"

"Bodie is still in the wind."

"Running or twisting?" I asked.

"I'll let you know when we find him. Any predictions?"

"Yeah. Bodie's dead."

"Why so certain?"

"I think someone has been cleaning house. First, Marcellus Pearson, then Javy Ordonez. Bodie was cutting in on Marcellus, maybe with Javy's help. It makes sense that Bodie is next."

"You can't put that all on Latrell Kelly."

"I'm not. Latrell had his own agenda. He just did the killer a favor."

There was dead air on Ammara's end. I didn't break the silence. She finally did. "You think Colby . . ." She let the words trail off, unable to complete the sentence.

"I think a lot of things, but the ones I can prove are the only ones that matter."

"And we can't find Colby. We don't even know where to look," she said.

That's what I wanted to hear. "What about his friends or family or the dopers he hung out with when he was on the job?"

"His parents live in Utah and say they haven't talked to him in months. Their phone records bear that out. Turns out he didn't have any friends, at least none we can find. And the dopers aren't talking. It's like he disappeared."

Colby had crossed his line and now I was crossing mine, withholding information that could lead to his capture. "Keep at it. He's bound to surface."

"We'll be there when he does. What are you going to do?"

"Find my daughter," I said and hung up.

I paced around my house, stopping in front of the mirror in the front hall, looking at the man staring back at me who had just thrown away what was left of his career. I'd always thought it was easier to talk about risking everything than actually doing it, but I was wrong. I felt no remorse or guilt over not telling Ammara that I'd seen Colby less than twelve hours ago. If anything, I was too pleased with myself.

I went into the kitchen and opened the refrigerator in the hopes that the food fairy had been there and had left me something to eat. It was as empty as the rest of the house. My stomach was talking to me, demanding to be fed.

I'd left my wallet in yesterday's pants. When I fished it out, I found the flash drive Joy had given me. I decided to read what I'd copied from Jill Rice's and Wendy's computers instead of the morning paper while I ate breakfast. I grabbed my laptop and headed out, looking for food and answers.

Chapter Sixty-one

I went back to the same place where I'd had breakfast the other day. The food was good, the price was right, and the Internet access was free.

The place was full and smelled of bacon grease and fresh-baked cinnamon rolls and hot coffee. The chatter at the two-dozen tables clashed with the sounds coming from the open kitchen of banging pots and pans and orders placed and filled. Harried servers dodged between tables, sweating to keep up, their heavy feet slapping on the hardwood floor, laying down a percussion track.

A few customers wore athletic shorts and T-shirts stained from just-finished workouts. Those who had contented, full faces and round bellies lingered over the *New York Times*. Three couples in skintight, multihued bicycle gear sat at two tables they'd pushed together, shoveling down pancakes and trading jibes about who had dogged it the last five miles.

Two women, perfectly coiffed and made up, sipped coffee and nibbled on fruit, their tennis bracelets catching the light, their rackets resting beneath their table. A cute, dark-haired woman near fifty sat with a white-haired man, the two of them laughing the way a father and daughter should. One man sat alone, hunched over his plate. He looked up as I passed, his red bleary eyes and haggard jowls testament to an ill-spent night.

A corner booth opened up and I slid in as the busboy wiped the table and the server, a woman with beehive hair, pinched eyes, a sour mouth, and a build that spread out the same way the Mississippi pours into the Gulf scooped up the tip the last customer had left, quietly cursing the few quarters she dropped into her pocket.

"I'll have two eggs up, crisp bacon, hash browns, toasted rye, and coffee. Hold the apologies to my arteries."

"Better you hold the jokes, honey. I've heard them all," she said.

By the time my food arrived, I was deep into Jill Rice's tax records. She and her husband filed separate returns, which was common for spouses who wanted to keep their assets separate. Joy and I never did. Neither of us had had more than lunch money when we got married, and what we'd saved since then, we'd saved together. Money hadn't driven us apart.

The records Jill gave me didn't include her husband's return. Hers was pretty simple. She had interest income from CDs and bonds, dividend income from stocks, and capital gains from the sale of an office building she'd purchased ten years earlier. The interest income and dividends totaled approximately three thousand dollars. She made another hundred twenty-five thousand on the sale of the building. Neither amount was a red flag.

I didn't have her returns from prior years, so I had no idea how the income she'd reported compared to the past or whether she'd sold assets to generate cash for living expenses. A lot of wives who depended on their husband's income would do that after their husbands went to jail.

Jill's only other income was from a partnership called

PEMA Partners. There was nothing describing what PEMA Partners was or did. I looked online and came up empty. PEMA was private and quiet, operating below the cyber-space radar, just like hundreds of thousands of other partner-ships all across the country that invested in raw land, strip shopping centers, bamboo farms in Central America, and other can't-miss opportunities of a lifetime.

The only documentation Jill had about PEMA was her partnership tax return, called a K-1, that itemized the amount of income attributed to her ownership interest. Whatever PEMA was, Jill Rice owned 25 percent of it, which threw off $868,000 and some change last year, more than enough to support her lifestyle regardless of her husband's legal problems. She may have filed a separate return just to protect her assets from those problems. That was smart plan-ning and good evidence that she knew enough about what her husband was doing to plan for the worst.

I had been hungry when I ordered but lost my appetite while studying Jill's return. I had staved off my anxiety over Wendy with the certainty that I'd find a lead that would take me to her. When it became obvious that I hadn't, my gut began to twist, optimism giving way to pessimism that soaked my insides with fear. I had been holding myself to-gether with string and chewing gum, fighting the shakes, and trying not to let the memories of my lost son and the damna-tion sure to come if I let history repeat itself and claim my daughter take over all my thoughts.

I took a deep breath. My eggs smelled rotten. I shoved the plate to the edge of the table and opened the files I'd down-loaded from Wendy's computer.

She had e-mail files and photograph files, and other files labeled with every aspect of her life, including work, friends, medical, music, recipes, finances, travel, subscriptions, blogs, yoga, downloads, videos, books, Mom & Dad, MySpace, and one labeled personal, as if there was anything else that could have been left out of the other files. It would take days to study the contents and extract anything useful.

There were software programs that would perform keyword searches of her files, but I hadn't loaded one on to my computer. I logged on to the Internet to find one. When the connection failed, I summoned my server, who told me that the restaurant's system was down.

"It was up a minute ago. What happened?"

"I had a husband used to say the same thing. Like I told him, timing is everything."

"That's just great."

"Hey, it's free. You get what you pay for," she said with a smirk that cost her a tip.

"You got that right," I told her.

I had no choice but to take it one file, one document at a time. I started with Wendy's e-mail files. She used a program that automatically downloaded her e-mail from her ISP's server to her hard drive. That was the good news.

The bad news was she had thousands of e-mails stored, including the ones that promised her long-lasting erections, weight loss without dieting or exercise, and several from former high officials in Nigeria who wanted to split ten million dollars with her because she seemed like an honest American. I looked for e-mail with Colby's name, even though he could have used a screen name different from his own. After an hour, I'd found a handful of innocuous messages confirming dinner plans and other dates.

Frustrated, I closed the e-mail folder and tried her Adobe files. There were hundreds of PDFs, some of them labeled with descriptive terms, many of them anonymous. I scrolled through them, clicking on one dead end after another. When I found a file titled "tax return," I clicked on it.

The file contained a copy of her tax return from last year. She'd filed a Form 1040, not the 1040EZ that I would have expected for someone working a job one step above entry level at a commodity brokerage firm and who didn't have enough deductions to itemize. Wendy's W-2 income was thirty-six thousand.

I skimmed through the rest of her 1040 and understood why she hadn't filed the EZ return. The reason was her eye-popping partnership income of $434,000. I blinked but the number didn't change. I clicked through the rest of the pages to find her partnership tax return, my index finger twitching when I found the K-1. My daughter owned 12.5 percent of PEMA Partners. I started to shake and couldn't stop.

Chapter Sixty-two

Since Kevin died, I had relied on hard facts to tell me whether people were good or bad, guilty or innocent. I stopped trusting my hunches and gut feelings because that's what got Kevin killed. Besides, instinct never convicted anyone. Only the facts did.

Staring at Wendy's K-1 for PEMA Partners, I realized that I'd applied the same standard to my family, demanding tangible proof of their love and loyalty, testing our relationships against only what I could prove beyond a reasonable doubt, afraid of anything that required me to get under their skin and into their hearts. I accused them of their flaws and convicted them of their weaknesses. It made no difference that I applied the same standard to myself. That was only fair.

Joy understood. She showed me her pain because she blamed me for it and concealed everything else. That Wendy may have hidden as much or more was a staggering indictment.

Her ownership interest in PEMA Partners was unmistakable proof of a connection between her and Jill Rice and, by extension, Thomas Rice. I hoped but didn't believe that she had hit a home run in the commodities market and innocently invested her windfall in PEMA. Wendy would have told her mother and me if she had. Instead, she'd kept secret the fact that her net worth now exceeded mine.

Colby was the common denominator between Wendy and the Rices, which meant that unless someone had held a gun to her head, she could be part of everything that had happened. We are all responsible for the choices we make, but life had conspired against her since the moment Kevin was taken, her relationship with Colby spawning the perfect storm that had swept her into the hands of people willing to trade her life for theirs.

When I stopped shaking, I opened my eyes and found my server hovering over me.

"You want me to call 911?" she asked.

I slid out of the booth and dropped a ten on the table, breaking my promise not to leave her a tip, and made my way toward the door. "Forget it."

She looked at my untouched plate. "Something wrong with the food?" When I didn't answer, she got in the last word. "With some people, it doesn't pay to be nice."

Thomas Rice was dead. Colby was on the run and Wendy was probably being held hostage to lure him back. That left Jill Rice as the only person who could shed any light on PEMA Partners. I didn't have to wait for her to come home this time, though she didn't answer the door until I'd rung the bell half a dozen times.

"It's you again," she said when she opened the door.

Her lacquered good looks had crumbled, replaced by a washed-out shell. Her eyes were empty, dull sockets surrounded by dark circles. Without makeup, she had the pale, lifeless look of someone who'd been ill for a long time, her survival still in doubt. She was wearing black pajama pants with a matching shapeless top, though she looked like she hadn't slept since I'd told her that her ex-husband was dead.

Rice clung to the doorframe for a moment, then turned and walked back into the house, the open door an invitation to follow. I expected to find a collection of empty wine bottles scattered through the house but there were none. She was stone sober but tottering on the edge nonetheless.

She sat on a sofa in the den, lost among large, decorative pillows covered in bright floral prints that made her look smaller than she was. The room was large, one wall all glass, two layers of drapes drawn against the sun, the lights turned off, the room and her skin the same shadowy gray.

A decorator's fingerprints were evident in the way each knick fit with each knack, furniture and fabrics blending and contrasting in muted harmony with the wall coverings and artwork. A plasma TV hung above the fireplace, the screen black and silent. It was a perfect, soulless show house.

There were different ways to conduct an interrogation. The choice depended on an assessment of the subject's vulnerability. A good rapport made some people open up. They wanted to talk, to confess to someone they liked or whose approval they craved. A friendly smile, an understanding nod, and a humble acknowledgment that we've all stepped in the bucket at one time or another often opened the floodgates.

The hard way was another way, but it was obvious that I wouldn't have to go there with Jill Rice. She'd already gone there by herself, taken a self-administered beating, and was ready to talk. All I had to do was listen. I sat in a sleek, high-backed, black leather chair angled across from the sofa and waited.

"They won't release Tommy's body until next week," she began.

It was the first time I'd heard her refer to him with any sign of endearment. "That's a long time to wait to see him," I said.

She turned her head toward the covered windows. "I've waited a long time. I can wait a little longer."

"Have you made the arrangements?"

She nodded, studying the drapes. "It will be private. There's really no one else but me. I'm having him cremated."

"Then what?"

She looked at me, a gallows grin creasing her lips. "Then I'll come home and pack."

"Where are you going?"

Rice shrugged. "I haven't figured that part out yet."

"You should talk with someone, maybe a psychologist, someone to help you get through this."

She didn't say anything, this time examining her nails. "Is that what the FBI recommends under these kinds of circumstances?"

"You were divorced, but it's obvious you still cared about him. That's a lot to work through."

She grabbed a pillow and wrapped her arms around it. "I'll tell you what's a lot to work through. Killing him. That's what I did, you know. I killed him."

We both knew that she hadn't, but there was no doubt that she believed she had. "He died in prison, not at home."

"I sent him there."

"He broke the law. It was a risk he took."

"But," Rice said, her eyes red and wet, "I turned him in."

"He was a drug dealer. He deserved to go to jail."

She looked at me like I was a simpleton, rolling her eyes. "I didn't turn him in because he was a drug dealer. You see the way we live. Do you have any idea what this costs? I turned him in because he cheated on me. I caught him screwing our neighbor's twenty-year-old daughter. She was home from college. He was working at home. I walked in on them. She thought it was funny."

"What did he think?"

"That I would put up with it because of the money. That's what he told me. I told him that I wouldn't be his whore. It was all very dramatic."

"How long had you known that he was dealing drugs?"

"From the start. Tommy was very good about business. He put together a pro forma and showed me how it would work. He said it was all about managing the risk."

"That's why he put the assets in your name."

"Not everything. Just enough to take care of me if he ever got caught. He said he loved me and would do whatever he had to do to keep me out of trouble. When I caught him cheating, I was so mad I didn't care what happened to him. After he was arrested, he said he forgave me. He said he'd gotten what he deserved for being unfaithful. Now he's dead and it's my fault."

Jill Rice didn't mind being married to a drug dealer as long as he didn't cheat on her. Thomas Rice made sure he provided for his wife even as he betrayed her. He forgave her for turning him in, but she couldn't forgive herself. Politicians argue about family values. I gave up trying to make sense of them a long time ago.

"Tell me about PEMA Partners. I ran across it when I looked at your tax records."

"I don't know much about it, really. I worked when we were first married. We didn't need my income, so Tommy invested it. I gave him complete control over the account. Then he started putting his money into it. He was good at what he did. Even after he lost his license, he could still invest for me. One day, after he started the drug business, he told me he'd used the account to buy into PEMA. He said it would generate enough money to take care of me if anything happened to him."

"Who are the other partners?"

She shook her head. "No clue. Tommy handled everything. Why are you so interested in PEMA?"

"My daughter is one of your partners."

"Maybe someone was trying to protect her."

Chapter Sixty-three

It had always been my job to protect Wendy. I'd done that as long as she had let me. I cautioned her about strangers when she was little. I embarrassed her in front of her boyfriends when I asked them about their intentions. I called her to ask where she was and why she wasn't home even if it was only midnight and she was over eighteen.

As the anger and bitterness she'd silently harbored percolated to the surface, she lashed out at Joy and me, then drifted away, experimenting with sex and drugs. I tried even harder then, tried to pull her back, tried to protect her from herself. When Wendy finally came back to us, I held her close but not too close, having learned from my mistakes.

When she graduated from college and got her own apartment, I advised her not to rent on the ground floor or near the stairs since that made her a potential victim for burglars and rapists. I engraved her name below the serial number on her computer in case it was ever stolen. After Wendy started her job, I told her to be honest and fair and that she could be disappointed, but not surprised, when others failed to meet her standards.

I spoke the language of modern parents, encouraging her in her education and career, championing her independence. But in my heart of hearts, I was a throwback to my parents' generation. I wanted her married, cared for, and safe, ambitions I kept to myself because she would have heard them as sexist, though I would have wished the same for her brother, had he lived.

Jill Rice's last comment rang in my ears as I drove away. Her husband had put his assets in her name to protect her from him. I remembered my conversation with Colby outside Fortune Wok earlier in the week when he intimated that he and Wendy planned on getting married. Maybe he had protected Wendy in the same way Thomas Rice had protected his wife. Then a greater likelihood hit me.

There are some things a daughter will tell her mother only on the promise that the mother won't tell the father. I was afraid I'd stumbled across one of them.

Joy had moved into an apartment on Tomahawk Creek Parkway in a Johnson County suburb called Leawood. The three-story buildings were red brick with bright yellow trim. A jogging trail wound through the complex. I found her walking the dogs, reining them in from their pursuit of the geese that flocked to the pond at the edge of the complex.

Ruby saw me first and jerked hard enough on the leash that Joy lost her grip. I crouched in the grass, letting Ruby run to me and jump in my face, taking a swipe at my nose. Roxy dragged Joy to our reunion, the dogs climbing over one another for a shot at my chin.

"They could be sisters," Joy said, pointing at the dogs as she picked up Ruby's leash.

I scratched both of them behind the ears, stood, and studied my wife for signs of things she and Wendy had hidden from me. Joy gathered her end of the dogs' leashes to her chest.

"You've got your Bureau face on, Jack. What is it? Have they found Wendy?"

"No, but I think she's alive."

Her arms fell to her sides. "Oh, thank God! What makes you think so?"

"I ran into Colby last night. He told me."

"Colby? Where? How?"

"We were on the same playground."

Joy balled her fists, a leash in each hand, the dogs lying patiently in the grass. "Damnit, Jack! I don't have time for your games. We're talking about our daughter. Tell me what's going on!"

"I came here to ask you the same thing."

Her face tightened. "What's that supposed to mean?"

"Colby went too far undercover and got involved with the people we were investigating. He stole money from these people and now he's on the run. I caught up to him last night long enough to get the gist of things. He doesn't know where Wendy is, but he thinks that she's alive. He made it sound like she went along for the ride."

"I can't believe he would do something like that to Wendy."

"Why? Because they're married?"

Her jaw dropped. I could have knocked her over with a wave of my hand.

"How did you find out?"

"I didn't until just now, at least not for certain. You remember that I copied the hard drive on Wendy's computer onto the flash drive you gave me. I looked through some of her files this morning. She owns an interest in a partnership that paid her over four hundred thousand dollars last year. It's all on her tax return."

"A partnership? What kind of partnership? I don't believe it. She would have told me."

"Why? Because she told you that she and Colby had gotten married?"

Joy crossed her arms over her chest and turned her head away. "Yes, because she told me. After all, I'm her mother."

"And I'm her father."

"Is that what this is about? That she told me and didn't tell you? You've known since last night that she's alive and you didn't bother to tell me, and the only reason you're telling me now is because you're angry that Wendy didn't tell you she'd gotten married."

"You should have told me."

"This isn't about you or me, Jack. It's about her. Wendy told Colby she wouldn't marry him if he stayed at the Bureau, not after what had happened to us. He promised her he was getting out. That was good enough for her, but she didn't want you to know they'd gotten married until after he resigned. She knew how protective you were and how you felt about Colby. She was afraid to tell you, afraid that you'd go ballistic and take it out on him."

"I hope that's true, but it doesn't square with what I know. You should have told me. The fact that Wendy and Colby are married changes everything. It makes it look like she was a willing participant in whatever Colby was doing."

"You can't possibly believe that about your own daughter."

My vocal cords twisted and froze when I tried to speak. Joy watched me, clutching her throat with one hand as if she felt my struggle. I tried to talk through my tremor-induced stutter, but that made it worse, forcing me to start and stop a couple of times before I could respond. When the words finally came out, they were choppy, like a dog's bark.

"The facts are the only thing that matter, not what I believe. Wendy didn't have money to invest in a partnership, not from legitimate sources. Neither did Colby. This partnership was probably used to launder drug money. The least bad explanation is that Colby convinced her the partnership was legitimate and told her that he was putting it in her name as proof that he intended to leave the Bureau."

"If he had all that money last year, why didn't he quit then?"

"Everybody in a deal has to bring something of value to the table. Colby worked undercover. He brought information to the table. If he quit his day job, he'd have nothing to offer his partners. I doubt they would have let him quit even if he wanted out."

"You said Wendy is part of this. How do you know that?"

"Colby said as much. His partners are using Wendy as leverage to get back what he took from them."

"But if Colby is on the run, he can't be of any more use to them. And that means Wendy . . ." She collapsed to her knees without finishing her sentence, weeping and covering her face with her hands. "Oh my God, Jack! Not again!"

Chapter Sixty-four

I headed north on Tomahawk Creek Parkway to College Boulevard, then east to State Line Road, and north again into Kansas City, Missouri, no destination in mind, satisfying my need to keep moving as if that was progress.

Kansas City weather had more mood swings than a teenage girl. Today was cool and getting cooler, the sky a salty seabed, the air tasting like copper rain. A few of the trees had given up, their leaves already brown. I'd blinked and missed the color.

I was used to working out the kinks in a case with my team, sometimes brainstorming until someone shouted out something that made the pieces fit. We'd sit in the center of the war room, surrounded by whiteboards filled with names and dates, questions and answers. Maps, photographs of the crime scene and other physical evidence, forensic reports, and witness statements would be pinned to the walls or spread out on the tables. When we got stuck, we'd walk around the room like we were taking a tour of the murder display at the Museum of Crime, a place that existed only in our minds to catalog the grim work people practiced on one another.

We would challenge each other with theories, shredding some, elevating others to the realm of the possible, even likely. Eventually, patterns would emerge. Explanations that couldn't possibly make sense would become obvious and inevitable.

For me, it was a team sport. I didn't claim to be the best and the brightest, but I prided myself on recruiting a team that was just that and I needed them now.

I was flopping around, bogged down in a quicksand of emotions about my wife and daughter that proved that Ben Yates and Troy Clark were correct in kicking me off this case because it was too personal. It didn't help that I might be falling in love with a woman whom I had almost gotten killed when I let my professional judgment become clouded by my personal feelings or, as my father would have said, when I was too busy thinking with my little head instead of my big head. Toss in an undiagnosed but undeniable movement disorder that could make me collapse quicker than the old Boston Red Sox in September, and I was a mess.

This much I knew. Colby Hudson and Thomas Rice were in business together and they had used the same method of protecting their wives from the risks of their criminal enterprise. That didn't mean their wives were innocent of what was going on. Jill Rice admitted that she knew her husband was dealing drugs. It only meant that their husbands had insured them against that risk.

I had to stop at that. Thinking of Colby and Wendy as co-conspirators, let alone husband and wife, was too disorienting. But there it was. I hung on to to the unlikely prospect that Wendy had been too naive, too in love, or too stupid to have known what Colby was doing.

Thomas Rice had supposedly given up his sources as part of his plea bargain. It looked like the U.S. Attorney had made a bad deal, because Rice plainly hadn't given up his real supplier. It was likely that Rice, Javy Ordonez, and Marcellus Pearson worked for the same person or persons unknown. He, she, or they had been the real target of my investigation of Marcellus and when I got close enough to shake their tree, bodies started falling out.

They say that the definition of insanity is doing the same thing over and over and expecting a different result. I had no choice but to test the definition and shake a few more trees. I started with a phone call to Marty Grisnik.

"What's the latest, big man?" Grisnik asked.

I had pulled into the parking lot at the Ward Parkway Shopping Center.

"Still snipe hunting."

"Catch any?"

"Getting close, but I could use some help."

"That's what I like about you, Jack. You don't hesitate to ask people to waste their time on wild goose chases."

"You might want to go along on this one. The geese are friends of yours."

"How's that?" he asked, his voice tightening.

"Tanja Andrija and her brother, Nick."

Grisnik laughed, deep and long. "You are bullshitting me, right?"

"I hope I am. I just need to be certain."

"The Andrija family has been on Strawberry Hill longer than you and I are likely to live. I spent half my life growing up inside Petar and Maja's house. You drag them down for no reason, you'll answer to me. You got that?"

"Wouldn't want it any other way."

"I assume you've got something solid that ties them in to the bucket of shit you're trying to climb out of."

"Colby had a thing for Tanja. I don't know if that gate swings both ways. Last night, I stopped at the bar to ask her if she'd seen him. She said no and told me to get lost. I said

I'd go out the back and she got real nervous, couldn't wait to show me the front door."

"You're willing to ruin a family over that?"

"Not long after I left, Nick showed up driving a pickup. They loaded it with boxes and garbage bags. They were fighting the whole time."

"You know what would happen you take that pile of crap to my D.A. or your U.S. Attorney? They'd laugh your ass right out of the room."

"There's one other thing, but it's between you and me. Agreed?"

Grisnik sighed. "Agreed—and don't forget the secret decoder rings."

"I thought she was hiding Colby in the back of the bar but I was wrong. He was at her parents' house. I think he broke in, probably looking for something. They caught him and he ran out. Happened just after I drove by. I caught up with Colby a few blocks from there. He didn't implicate Tanja, but he put it out there between the lines."

"So what happened to Colby?"

"He got away."

"That's it? He got away?"

"That's it."

"You still got nothing, but I know you won't leave it alone until you put the parents in the ground. Tell you what. I'll go with you to see them. I'm on my way to my kid's soccer game. It's my weekend. I gotta call their mother, piss her off about having to break her date with the flavor of the month. I'll call you later. Don't do anything stupid without me."

"Don't worry. I do stupid a lot better with you."

My cell phone rang a moment later, the caller ID display showing that it was Ammara Iverson. I grabbed her call like it was lifeline.

"Where are you?" she asked.

"Eighty-fifth and State Line. What's up?"

"Can you come in? Ben Yates and Troy want to talk to you."

It can be hard to tell the difference between a lifeline and a two-hundred-pound test line with a giant steel hook until you've been snagged. I'd been asked, ordered, and threatened to stay away from this case. Now I was being invited back in. I felt the hook anchor deep in the flesh between my ribs.

"Any news on Wendy?" I asked.

"No, but we're doing everything we can."

"Then what do they need me for?"

"They want to go over some loose ends with you. They'll be in the war room."

Forget about the hook. This was a harpoon. Troy must have finally complained to Ben Yates that I was stepping all over his investigation. Yates had the manual tattooed to the back of his eyelids. If Troy had convinced him that I'd become that big of a problem, Yates would forget about my sick leave and suspend me without pay until I learned to sit at home and watch reruns of *Celebrity Poker*. If he knew that I was withholding information about Colby, he'd have me fired and go after my pension.

I was amazed how little I cared.

"Twenty minutes," I said and hung up.

Chapter Sixty-five

I felt like a kid who'd been called to the principal's office as I walked down the hall toward the war room. Heads popped up as I passed cubicles, some people nodding silent greetings that said "tough luck, old buddy, but better you than me." Others chose the safe alternative and averted their gaze so that they wouldn't turn into a pillar of salt.

I took the long way around in order to go past my office. The door was closed. The magnetic strip with my name on it had been peeled off the nameplate. At least no one else had claimed it yet.

I hoped to run into Ammara, but she wasn't in her cubicle and she wasn't roaming the hallways. I guessed that Troy had told her to call me, knowing I'd pick up. Whatever was going on, she wouldn't have liked doing that. It wasn't a good sign that she was avoiding me.

I stopped outside the war room, deciding whether to knock, but didn't because asking permission to come in would have been an act of surrender. I opened the door wide, took two steps inside, stopped, and surveyed the room, hoping I had the rested, confident look of a man who'd just returned from vacation instead of someone who was living inside a Cuisinart running on slice and dice.

Ben Yates and Troy Clark were sitting on the far side of the room. Yates was reviewing a report, his white cuffs expertly shot past the sleeves of his dark gray suit coat, his hair trimmed and well-parted, his face relaxed but intent.

Troy had the haggard look of someone running a tough case on too little sleep and too much coffee. His eyes were puffy and his chinos and polo shirt were wrinkled. He was shuffling through photographs we both knew he'd already looked at a hundred times.

Neither acknowledged my presence. I knew the rules of this game. I'd been summoned, not as a colleague but as someone to be intimidated and interrogated. It was an approach reserved for suspects and subordinates. They were reinforcing the message by ignoring me, intending that I stand there like a supplicant until they could work me into their schedule.

I didn't feel like playing, so I ignored them and walked slowly down the length of the room, taking note of what was written on the whiteboards. The list of witnesses Ammara had started in the hours after the drug house murders had grown, Wendy and the Andrija siblings the latest additions.

I found a list of the evidence removed from Latrell Kelly's house, noting again the large quantity of flashlights and batteries, recognizing them as essential supplies for the secret hiding place Latrell must have had and where he believed that I had followed him.

I grabbed a pen and a pad of paper and jotted down the two things I'd just taken note of, the Andrijas and Latrell's hiding place, adding question marks to both. My gut told me they were the keys to the case. I tore the page off the pad, folded it, and stuck it in my pocket. Round one went to me when Yates blinked first.

"Take a seat, Jack," he said.

The worktables were laid out in the same open rectangle they had been in when Yates gave me the boot. I pushed my way inside the tables and dragged a chair to the side opposite where they were sitting, pulled up to the edge of the table, and folded my hands on the surface, hoping they'd stay in one place. Then I kept my mouth shut and waited because I knew that the first liar didn't stand a chance.

Yates leaned toward me, his hands gripping the table. His eyes were robin's-egg blue, the corners creased enough to be crinkly, not wrinkly. The hard set to his mouth made it clear that he hadn't gotten to where he was on good looks and charm alone. He was the kind who smiled when he stuck the knife in you.

"How are you, Jack?" he asked.

"I'm fine. You're fine. Troy's fine. We're all fucking fine. So can the bullshit."

Troy smiled and rolled his eyes as if I'd made his point for him.

"I know this must be a tough time for you," Yates continued.

"Save it, Ben. You don't give a crap for what kind of day I'm having, so you can skip steps one through seven in the manual on building rapport while establishing power and get to the point."

Yates leaned back, folded his arms over his middle and frowned like a disappointed father. Troy used the pause to jump in.

"Jack, you went to Wendy's apartment what, yesterday? Or was it Thursday?"

"Thursday."

"Where did she keep her computer?" Troy asked.

That she had a computer was a given. I didn't know where he was going, but I could feel the setup coming.

"On a desk in the living room."

Troy nodded. "That's where I would have kept it. No reason to clutter up the bedroom and the kitchen is too small."

He obviously wanted me to know that he'd been in Wendy's apartment. If he hadn't been by now, he wouldn't be doing his job. I kept silent, not because I had anything to hide, but because I wanted to make Troy tell me what this was all about.

"You see, Jack, we got a search warrant this morning for her apartment. Once we told the judge that the daughter of one of our agents was missing, he couldn't sign the warrant fast enough."

Troy didn't add that she was also a person of interest in an ongoing investigation involving murder and drug dealers, though I assumed he'd also explained that to the judge. I pressed back against my chair, forcing myself to stay calm, but I couldn't convince the tremors. They scattered across my body. I put my hands down, letting them vibrate against my thighs, afraid they'd found something that incriminated Wendy. I forced the words from my mouth.

"What did you find?"

"That's the thing," Troy said. "It's what we didn't find that we're interested in. These days, the first things we carry out of any place we search are the computers. You know that. Only Wendy doesn't have one. Which gets us thinking."

"About what?"

"About what happened to her computer. Young woman like her, works at the Board of Trade, dates one of our agents; she has got to have a computer. So we thought we'd ask you."

"How would I know?"

Troy shrugged as if it was obvious. "You just told us. The computer was there when you were in her apartment two days ago. Now it's gone. You were the last one to have seen it. Makes sense we would ask you what happened to it."

"Me? You think I took Wendy's computer? Why would I do that?" I knew the answer but wanted to make him say it.

"Look, Jack. Ben and I both have kids. We'd probably do the same thing. Try to help one of them out if they got into a jam, especially if we thought they got caught up in something not of their making."

"That's what you think? That Wendy is involved?"

It was Yates's turn. He was all ice. "Wouldn't you, if you found out that she was making less than thirty grand a year and had half a million dollars in her savings account?"

Chapter Sixty-six

Credibility is the most valuable asset any suspect has. It can even be more valuable than innocence, as anyone who has spent half his life behind bars for a crime he didn't commit will tell you. It comes from a lot of things, including demeanor, motive, opportunity, and means. It also comes from cooperation and the investigator's ability to corroborate what the suspect says.

Credibility allows the suspect to be heard, to give shape and meaning to facts that, in other hands, would condemn rather than exonerate. I had a story to tell and the way I told it would mean more to Wendy than to me. I began by taking the flash drive out of my pocket and setting it on the table.

"I didn't take Wendy's computer, but I did copy her hard drive onto this."

Troy snatched it off the table, picked up the phone, and summoned a secretary.

"What's on it?" Yates asked.

"I haven't had a chance to look at much of it. There's some routine e-mail between Wendy and Colby. The only thing of interest I saw is Wendy's tax return from last year.

She reported more than four hundred thousand in income from something called PEMA Partners."

"Who or what is PEMA Partners?" Troy asked.

"I'm hoping you guys can figure that out. The only other partner I know of is Jill Rice. Her tax records are also on the flash drive."

"Isn't she the one who turned her husband in for dealing drugs?" Yates asked.

"The same," I told him, adding a quick summary of my conversations with Jill Rice about Colby's purchase of her house and car.

Gina Tomkins, a secretary who had covered my bureaucratic backside more times than I could count, knocked and entered. She was a sturdily built, wide-bodied woman who'd raised five boys on her own and wasn't about to be intimidated by Troy Clark.

"Copy this onto a hard drive and print everything that's on it," he told her, handing her the flash drive. "If any of it is encrypted, get all the help you need to open it up."

She nodded, gave me a wink, and left without speaking.

"What's the connection between the Rice case and this one?" Yates asked.

"I assumed you knew that by now. I asked Ammara to get me the Rice file a few days ago. She told me that Troy had embargoed it. I figured he wanted to review it himself." I glanced around the room. "Isn't it in here somewhere?"

Yates's disappointed-parent look turned into a narrow-eyed glare aimed at Troy, who shifted in his seat like he had diaper rash. Yates let him twist until Troy picked up the phone again and asked for the Rice file.

Yates only knew what Troy had already told him. Even if I told him the same thing, I knew that facts were like food—presentation counted for a lot. I started at the beginning when the FBI put me on the shelf. I told him about my visits back to Quindaro and freely confessed how I'd gained access to Thomas Rice at the penitentiary and used the same phony ID when I first questioned Jill Rice. I finished with Latrell Kelly's death.

Yates didn't move the entire time I spoke. As soon as I had finished, a wave of shakes ran through me. I closed my eyes. He still hadn't moved when I opened them.

"You say that Jill Rice knew what her husband was doing," Yates began, ignoring my condition. "And that he put assets in her name and had her file a separate tax return to protect her. Not that it would have protected her if you and your team had done a proper job tracing Rice's assets. But your daughter doesn't have that excuse."

"Actually, she does," I said. "I think Colby and Rice used PEMA to launder their drug money. I found out this morning that Colby and Wendy were secretly married last year."

Yates leaned forward, dropping his chin, the worry in his voice almost enough to convince me that he was being sincere. "Jack, you have to know how this looks for Wendy."

I nodded, ready to take what was coming, hoping that Colby was long gone by now.

"Yeah, I do. But not in the way you mean. You think she's involved. I think she's in trouble."

"There's not much difference from where I'm sitting." Yates said.

"It makes all the difference. Wendy wanted Colby to quit the Bureau. She grew up in an FBI home and didn't want to grow old in another one. She told me that Colby said he'd hit it big with some investments. He probably convinced her the money was clean and to prove his love for her, he put it all in her name. Only it turns out that the money was twice dirty. In the first place, it was drug money. In the second place, Colby stole it. The people he stole it from want to kill him, except he has an insurance policy."

"Meaning he's probably put everything he knows on paper and left it with someone who will deliver it to us if anything happens to him," Yates said.

"That's the way it usually works. Colby's future former partners snatched Wendy and are using her to cancel Colby's insurance. Trouble is Colby doesn't care if they kill her."

Troy bounded out of his chair and planted his hands on the table palms down, his arms rigid. "How in the hell do you know all that?"

"I saw Colby last night. He told me enough that I could piece the rest of it together."

Troy reached across the table and grabbed my collar, pulling me out of my chair, our faces close enough that I could taste what he'd eaten for lunch.

"You had him and you let him go!"

I wrapped my hand around his wrist. "You can let go or I can break it. Doesn't matter to me."

We stared at each other until Yates interrupted.

"Troy," he said. "Make up your mind."

Troy let go and I gave him back his wrist. Yates nodded his approval.

"I'm waiting," Yates said to me.

I ran through the rest of the story, telling them that I'd gone to Pete's Place looking for Colby, that I'd seen Colby running from the Andrija house, and then confronted him on the playground. I finished with a description of my surveillance of Tanja and her brother and Tanja's visit to her parents.

"Why did you let him go?" Yates asked.

I leveled my gaze at him and took a deep breath. "I started shaking so bad that I ended up on the ground. He got away before I could do anything about it."

"You could have called it in. We'd have shut down Quindaro and the rest of the city. Probably caught him. By now, he could be anywhere."

"The minute you pick Colby up, my daughter dies. They'll assume he cashed in his insurance policy, which makes Wendy a liability instead of an asset."

"Suppose the Andrija family is the aggrieved party. How's it any different if we pick them up?" Yates asked.

"First one to get arrested makes the best deal. The Andrijas can give you anyone upstream of them plus Colby and they can give me Wendy. That gets them the best deal."

Yates furrowed his eyebrows in a quick spasm in the same instant the corners of his mouth turned down. His micro expression was only a flicker but it was enough to pass judgment. He'd wait until this was all over to tell me I was through, but he'd made the decision. For now, he treated my explanation as if it was the most reasonable thing he'd heard all day, moving on with his next question.

"How does this all tie together?" he asked.

"Thomas Rice, Javy Ordonez, Marcellus Pearson, and Bodie Grant were all dealers. I think they had the same supplier. It could be the Andrijas or someone higher up the food chain. Troy was right, after all. There was a leak on my squad. It was Colby. He gave them information about our investigation which was worth as much as the drugs, maybe more."

"Being right doesn't make me feel any better," Troy said.

"Everything worked fine until Jill Rice turned her husband in," I said.

"Why didn't Rice burn the rest of them to save his ass?" Troy asked.

"Rice was a businessman. His wife said he was good at it. He figured he'd take the time and have something to come back to. He and Colby made a deal to run some of the money through the purchase of Rice's car and house. Colby told me that's what he did with the money he stole. I'll bet if you push Jill Rice hard enough, you'll find out she was holding onto her husband's money for when he got out."

"She divorced him," Troy said.

"Paperwork, " I said. "Kept us from pushing. Rice was willing to keep his mouth shut and ride it out. Marcellus wouldn't have done that. Our warrant for the surveillance camera was about to run out. We would have had to shut him down and that would have been it. Colby was supposed to kill Marcellus but Latrell got there first. Then they had to clean up the rest of the loose ends, starting with Thomas Rice."

"The warden still can't prove it wasn't suicide," Troy said.

"And Grisnik's sources inside Leavenworth still say someone with a badge put a hit on Rice. Colby is the only one who fits that description who would have benefited from Rice's death."

"If Colby had Rice taken out, you figure him for the Ordonez hit, too?" Troy asked.

"Hard not to." I explained my theory about how Colby could have followed Latrell, found Latrell's gun, and later used it to kill Javy. "You find Bodie yet?" I asked. Troy shook his head.

"That's some serious corporate reorganization," Yates said. "Take out the people making you all the money. You would have to replace them with new people who are loyal to you and who can control their territories."

It was an expensive way to do business. But it proved my point about the importance of kicking these things around, talking out loud until the holes in the theories were either patched up or grew too big. I got up and paced in the center of the rectangle, studying the whiteboards, stopping when I came to the list of witnesses.

"There's another possibility," I said, as one thread suddenly tied together with another.

"What's that?" Yates asked.

"Retirement. Once things started to unravel, maybe they

decided it wasn't worth the risk anymore. Time to take the money and run."

"So who are we talking about?" Troy asked.

I rose from my chair and walked to the whiteboard and drew a circle around Tanja and Nick Andrija's names.

"Them?" Yates asked.

"Yeah," I said. Then I wrote their parents' names on the board, Petar and Maja, and underlined the first two letters of each. Together they spelled PEMA.

"Them."

Chapter Sixty-seven

"What do you know about the family?" Yates asked.

"The parents are a nice old couple. They live on Strawberry Hill. He sits on the porch and she tends the flowers. The old man used to run a bar called Pete's Place and a restaurant next to it called Pete's Other Place. Now Nick runs the restaurant and Tanja runs the bar. Marty Grisnik introduced me to them the other day. Colby was there trying to stick his tongue down Tanja's throat."

"What's her story?" Yates asked.

"She and Grisnik had a teenage thing. She grew up and moved to New York. Married a guy that owned a restaurant called Mancero's. She says she divorced him a few years ago and came home. Still keeps a photograph of the restaurant on the bar."

Yates straightened in his chair. "What was the name of the restaurant?"

"Mancero's. Why?"

"When I was assigned to the New York office, there was a made guy in one of the families named Mickey Mancero. He bought and sold enough cocaine to melt every nose in the five boroughs and washed the money through a restaurant he owned. Somebody put a bullet in him before we could take him down."

"You think it's the same guy?" Troy asked.

"He had a good-looking wife. Blond, great figure. Except her name was Tina. I'll ask New York if they can find a picture of her."

"Was the wife involved?" Troy asked.

"We never got her on tape, but the operating assumption was that all the wives knew what was going on."

I said, "Tanja told Grisnik she was divorced. Tell them to check those divorce records, too."

"You run any of this past Grisnik?" Yates asked me.

"I talked to him. Petar and Maja are his godparents and I think he still carries a torch for Tanja. He can't be objective but he thinks it's all bullshit."

I didn't tell him that Grisnik was taking me to see the family tonight. If Yates knew that, he'd handcuff me to my chair.

Gina Tomkins opened the door and wheeled in a bookcase loaded with the Thomas Rice file and parked it against the wall. Yates told her what he wanted from the New York office and she left. Ammara Iverson came in as Gina was leaving.

"We've confirmed that Oleta Phillips was one of the bodies in Latrell's basement and we've got tentative ID on the other two skeletons," she said. "We did some more digging in the basement and found a wallet belonging to a guy named Johnny McDonald and a necklace with letters on it spelling the name Shirel."

"Marty Grisnik was supposed to be checking arrest records for a woman living there seventeen years ago," I said.

"I know. So I called him. He found her. Her name was Shirel Kelly. She was a prostitute. She's listed on Latrell's birth certificate as his mother. Grisnik also checked the property records on the house. Johnny McDonald owned it. Both of them were in the system for priors, but they dropped off the radar seventeen years ago. Latrell bought the house at a tax foreclosure sale a few years later."

"If Latrell buried them in the basement, why did he need a secret hiding place somewhere else?" I asked.

"Secret hiding place?" Yates asked.

"Yeah," I said. "Latrell thought I had followed him there. It's got to be a place where you need lots of flashlights and batteries. We need to find it."

"Why?" Yates asked.

"Because that's where Colby found Latrell's gun and the photograph of Latrell. With Latrell dead and Colby on the run, the Andrijas could be using it to hide Wendy."

Troy said, "There used to be a lot of mining in Wyandotte County. Maybe it's an abandoned mine, or a cave."

"Grisnik is a walking history book on Kansas City, Kansas. He told me that Argentine got its start with mining operations. Latrell worked at the railroad terminal in Argentine. I'd start with abandoned mines in that area."

Troy grabbed the phone again and instructed an agent to find someone who could find records of old mines on a Saturday afternoon.

"I've got more," Ammara said. "You asked me to find out whether Colby had visited anyone at Leavenworth who might have had a connection to Thomas Rice. There's no record he was there in the last six months."

"So that's a dead end."

"I don't think so," she said. "I asked for the names of everyone who visited or made phone calls to inmates in the last six months."

"That has to be a huge list."

"It is, and they didn't want to give it to me without jumping through ten levels of red tape even though it's all in a searchable database. So I gave them the list of the people we are interested in and they searched our names against the database and only came up with one hit," she said, pointing to the dry erase board. "Nick Andrija phoned a prisoner named Wilson Reddick five hours after you saw Thomas Rice."

"Who's Wilson Reddick?"

"Homeboy right out of Quindaro. Drove all the way from here to New York City, filled the car's door panels with cocaine, and drove back. A cop tried to stop him for a busted taillight when he got home. Turned into a chase that ended when Wilson flipped the car. He started out serving five years but that turned into twenty-five when he put a shank into one of his neighbors on the cellblock."

"Case sounds familiar," Troy said.

"I thought so, too," Ammara said. "I checked and we've got our own file on Reddick. He was one of Colby's snitches. Less than four hours after Nick Andrija called Reddick, Rice was hanging from the rafters in the laundry room."

"Fits with what Grisnik's source told him. Was the call from Andrija monitored?" I asked.

"No, just the name and number," she said.

The door to the war room sprung open. Gina Tomkins marched in like she expected a salute and handed a photograph to Ben Yates.

"New York e-mailed this," she said.

Yates tossed the photograph across the table to me. Her hair was longer and her face a little thinner, but there was no mistake.

"That's her. Tanja Andrija. Anything on a divorce?" I asked.

"No. The Widow Mancero is still a member of the family and whisper has it she took out her husband," Gina said. "New York says she left town after the funeral and they haven't kept tabs on her since."

Ammara said, "Marcellus was killed before we could

track the money from his operation. Suppose Tanja used her New York connections to open up in Kansas City. She could have supplied the local dealers like Marcellus, Javy Ordonez, and Bodie Grant."

"Thomas Rice could have washed the money through deals like PEMA Partners," I said.

"And Tanja's New York in-laws would take a healthy cut," Ammara said. "Wouldn't have left much for Marcellus."

"I think it's time we talked to the Andrijas," Yates said.

Troy stood. "You and me, Ammara," he said.

Watching them leave, I was numb. Troy had been right that someone on our squad was dirty, even if Colby hadn't tipped Marcellus to the surveillance camera. Troy was willing to look for answers in the dark places where it hurt to be right. My dependence on smoking guns to prove guilt had shut my eyes to crimes masked by human subtlety.

As much as I wanted to believe that Tanja and Nick would use Wendy to make a deal, I knew that it could as easily go the other way, especially if Troy came at them with a lot of firepower.

He wouldn't go after them alone or in a hurry. It would take time to get warrants, map out a plan, and assemble a backup team. That gave me a window in which to work. Yates stopped me as I headed for the door.

"Is this what you wanted from Rice's file?" he asked, handing me an Excel spreadsheet.

The spreadsheet contained a list of people who had invested with Rice but had not sued him. They were the lucky ones, the ones who'd made money with Rice. To his credit, it was a long list. It was also alphabetized. Petar and Maja Andrija were near the top.

"That's it. I saw them sitting in their kitchen last night. They were frail and frightened. When Tanja showed up, they looked more frightened. She must have used them to hide her money the same way Rice used his wife to hide his."

I was finished. I couldn't bring myself to add that it was the same way Colby Hudson had used my daughter.

I took a slow walk around the room, brushing my hand along the wall. The tables, chairs, carpet, and whiteboards were all fungible. You could find them in ten thousand offices in a thousand office buildings. I came to the door and stood for a minute, my hand on the brass knob, certain that I'd never come back. Leaning my head against the door, I felt Ben Yates standing behind me.

"I'm sorry, Jack."

"Me, too."

Chapter Sixty-eight

There is a moment in every case when you can feel the end coming. Momentum builds off a series of breaks, large and small. People pick up their pace, forgetting how tired they are. Phones ring louder. Doors slam. A surge carries everyone to the finish, whatever it turns out to be.

Our computer geeks were dissecting Wendy's hard drive. Wyandotte County officials were being yanked off the golf course and quizzed about the county's underground history. Agents in New York and Kansas City were connecting the dots between Tanja Andrija and her late husband's family while Troy Clark passed out bulletproof vests.

Even with everything coming together, the dull reality was that it might be too late to save Wendy. I may have persuaded Ben and Troy that she was more likely a victim than a perpetrator, but there would be little comfort in saving her reputation if I lost the rest of her to a bullet or a prison cell.

If presented with these facts in any other case, my professional judgment would be that she was most likely dead. Wendy had been missing for two days. She had become a pawn and pawns die unless both sides want them.

Marty Grisnik had promised to call me. I decided to use the time until he did to visit Kate.

It was late afternoon by the time I drove back to the KU Hospital. The day had gotten colder, the pale sky deepening to dirty gray, pressing toward the ground like a flatiron.

Kate's room was at the end of a long hall, voices echoing through her open door. She was propped up in bed surrounded by people I knew but had never met. They were her family, names she had mentioned more than once. I had no trouble putting names to faces.

Her sister, Patty, had the short, frizzy hair Kate had once described as steel wool on a bad day. She stood on the near side at the head of the bed, her features a rough match of Kate's, her face lined with worry as she and Kate whispered to one another.

Kate's son, Brian, leaned on the other side of the mattress, idly playing with a handheld video game, which was a thirteen-year-old boy's way of dealing with the world. His eyes jumped back and forth from the screen to his mother.

Her father, Henry, who had raised her from micro expression guinea pig to professional partner and who Kate had said was nearly eighty, stood at the foot of the bed. He had a thick body, white hair, and blotchy cheeks, his stubby hands clutching at the memory of cigars he'd been forced to give up. Kate's ex-husband, Alan, balding, thin, and dressed in a runner's sweat suit, was next to him, the two men locked in an intense, animated conversation, the few words I caught as I stepped into the room sounding like shoptalk.

It all stopped when they saw me. Kate rolled her eyes and smiled at me, a look that was half happy and half anesthetic hangover.

Her family's faces widened with recognition and then dismay, eyes and mouths narrowing in collective disapproval. Patty turned her back to Kate as if to shield her. Brian straightened, edging closer to his mother. Henry and Alan slid toward Patty, the three of them forming a human barricade cutting me off from Kate.

It was clear that I wasn't the hero of whatever story Kate had told them about what had happened. I knew she would have given them a version unadorned by exaggeration, rich with responsibility for her own actions, and gratitude for mine. But they were her family and were having none of it. There was nothing hidden in their micro expressions. I read in their faces their indictment of me, the FBI agent who'd led their loved one into danger and nearly cost them someone they held dear.

I didn't blame them because it was true, Kate's likely protest notwithstanding. That's the way it's supposed to be with families. Members were to be protected, taken care of. Anyone who threatened one of them threatened all of them. Anyone who failed in their duty to protect one failed all of them.

I couldn't argue and I didn't. No one spoke. It wasn't necessary. I nodded at them, turned around, and left. Kate called my name from behind their backs but I kept on walking.

Chapter Sixty-nine

Ammara Iverson called me as I was leaving the hospital. It was dusk, the air dry and charged.

"We hit the jackpot with Wendy's computer," she said. "The important files are encrypted but we've been able to break into some of them. We're still working on the others. So far we've got some offshore accounts and names."

"Was it Tanja's show?"

"Locally, but she was working for her in-laws. Colby joined up late last year."

"That was when he and Wendy had gotten married. How do you know?"

"He included a confession of sorts, called it his insurance policy, and said he hid it on Wendy's computer. It said that he would probably be dead by the time anyone read it. He says he knows that he fucked up and he's sorry. He also says that Wendy had nothing to do with it."

True or not, Colby had tried to protect her, though he wasn't much of a character reference at this point. I thought of her, wondering where she was and if I'd ever see her again.

"Doesn't help much."

"I know you, Jack," Ammara said. "I know what you want to do and I'm begging you not to do it, especially not in your condition. We're going after them and we'll find Wendy."

My phone beeped with another call. It was Marty Grisnik. "I've got to go."

"I just got a tip from one of my CIs," he said. "It might be something. It might be nothing. We should check it out before we go see Tanja."

I wasn't ready to tell him about Tanja, uncertain how he would take it, wondering whether he would give her a head start, knowing that I'd be tempted to if I had the history with Tanja that Marty did.

"A tip about what?"

"I told you that I'd put the word out about your daughter. One of my guys calls me. Says he saw a man and a woman in Matney Park last night around midnight. Saw them go into a shed back in the woods. Says the man left and didn't come back."

"What about the woman?"

"Never saw her again. Says it was like she disappeared. That's why I'm telling you it might be something and it might be nothing."

"How reliable is this guy?"

"Like most of them. If they bat their weight they're doing good."

"What's he doing hanging out in the park?"

"Getting high. You don't want to check it out, we can let it ride and go have a drink with Tanja. You can ask her if she's the drug kingpin of Strawberry Hill. If she says she is, you can arrest her. If she isn't, you and I go get drunk. Your call."

A tremor hit me in the gut and I bent over, one hand on my knee. It took me a moment to catch my breath.

"Hey, Jack! You there?"

"I'm here and I'm in. Tell me where and I'll meet you."

"You know how to get to Matney Park?"

"No clue."

"Better I come to you. Where are you?"

"I'm just leaving the KU Hospital."

"Wait for me in the circle drive. I'll be there in ten minutes."

The entrance to the hospital is on the east side of the complex. It faces a five-story parking garage. My car was parked on the third level. I retrieved my gun, stowing it beneath my jacket against the small of my back.

Traffic to the hospital flows from Thirty-ninth Street onto Cambridge, which runs past the entrance, where there is a circle drive to drop off and pick people up. A steady stream of patients, visitors, doctors, nurses, and staff flowed in and out as I paced along the curb. A moment later, Grisnik pulled up, his passenger window lowered. He leaned toward me as I opened the door.

"Hurry it up," he said as I got in. "I don't got all night."

"Where the hell is Matney Park?"

"West and north, maybe thirty minutes from here."

He took Thirty-ninth to Rainbow Boulevard, turning north and staying with it as it turned into Seventh Street. He took the ramp westbound onto I-70, chasing the last bit of daylight ahead of us. I leaned back against my seat as a wave of mild tremors swept across my body.

"Still got the shakes," Grisnik said.

"Lets me know I'm alive."

"Amen, brother. Another day on the green side is always a good day."

Grisnik looked like hundreds of other cops and agents I'd known over the years. His eyes were lit up and there was a determined set to his jaw. It was how we all looked when we were on the hunt.

"You ever been wrong about people you think you know?" I asked him.

"Never," he said, "unless you count my ex-wife, and half the people I work with, and I'm not too sure about everyone else."

"If you're wrong about Tanja, what then?"

"Look, Jack. I'm a cop. Just like you. Doesn't mean we don't have family and friends that fuck up. You and me, we've got to do what we've got to do." He was as sincere as a parish priest. "But from what you've told me, all you've got on Tanja is smoke and guesses. What's Troy Clark say?"

It was like I was playing Russian roulette, holding a gun to my head, pulling the trigger until I shot myself with a lie.

"He's like you. He thinks it's bullshit and that I should have collared Colby when I had the chance."

Grisnik laughed. "That's the kind of guy I want covering my back. He'd second-guess what you had for breakfast."

We let it drop and fifteen minutes later we pulled into Matney Park. It was a small stretch of faded grass and hard-packed dirt with a ball field, picnic shelter, and swing set. Home plate had been stolen and the pitcher's mound had eroded to a thin, scarred slab of rubber. The shelter was deserted; the last crumbs had long since been picked clean by squirrels. The bowed swing seats hung empty and still, no memory of a child's soft hands tightly grasping the chains while slender legs pumped hard, reaching for the sky.

We drove past the diamond and followed a gravel road that wound through a stand of trees before dead-ending in a small clearing. A redbrick building twelve feet square with a flat roof, no windows, and a single door facing us stood against the back edge of the clearing, another stretch of woods behind it. Grisnik killed the engine.

"Let's check this out and then I'll take you to apologize to my godparents for saying bad things about their little girl."

I followed him to the door to the brick building. "What is this place?"

"County built it years ago, probably used it for storage."

The door was unlocked. A yellowed lightbulb split the empty room in to light and shadows. A manhole cover six feet in diameter was set in the center of the concrete floor, a tarp bundled in one corner.

"Marty, what the hell is this?"

"An empty room."

"Except for that," I said, pointing at the tarp.

It was blue, made of heavy-gauge plastic. I grabbed a handful and pulled it off the floor. A desktop CPU lay underneath. The side panel had been removed, exposing the motherboard and other components except for the hard drive, which was missing. I stared at it for a long minute, remembering that Wendy's computer was missing when Troy had searched her apartment.

I lifted the CPU, exposing the metal plate where the manufacturer had embossed the serial number. Wendy's name was etched below it in neat block letters, just as I had engraved it. The only surprise was that I didn't start shaking.

"It's Wendy's computer. It was in her apartment when I was there on Thursday. Troy said it wasn't there when he searched the apartment yesterday. The hard drive is gone."

"Looks like my CI has earned his Christmas bonus," Grisnik said. "If the woman he saw was your daughter, that's why she never came out," he said, pointing to the manhole cover. "Give me a hand."

We knelt on the floor, inserting our fingers into slots around the edge and lifted the cover, dropping it on the floor. We stared down a pitch-black shaft that smelled dank and stale. Round, ridged climbing bars had been bolted into the wall of the shaft like a ladder without handrails.

"You know where this goes?" I asked him.

"Down."

We went back to the car. He opened the driver's door,

grabbed two flashlights, tossed one to me, tested the beam on his, and waved it like a lightsaber. I held mine at my side, rooted to the ground by unspeakable fear, memories of Kevin shackling my legs.

"Jack," Grisnik said softly, "we don't have a choice. We've got to see what's down there."

Chapter Seventy

Grisnik took the lead. I put my light on him, and watched
him descend, keeping a couple of body lengths between us.
The ceiling light above the entry to the shaft faded quickly.
Outside the beams of our flashlights, the darkness was ab-
solute. Anyone observing our descent would have thought
they were witnessing an invasion of mutant glowworms.

The shaft was too deep to be part of the sewer system. It
had to be a remnant of an underground mine. I hoped that it
was at the top of the list Troy and Ammara were assembling,
though it was far removed from Latrell Kelly's stomping
grounds.

The climbing bars were made of cold steel and ridged for
traction. Each one was a foot apart. I counted them as I
climbed down, keeping track of how deeply belowground
we were going.

The air got cooler the farther we went. The sides of the
shaft were dry at first but began to show traces of moisture
that gradually increased until the round walls were slick and
wet. My count reached 120 when Grisnik shined his flashlight at me.

"I'm down," he said. "There's a ladder from the bottom of the shaft that ends about five feet above the floor."

They were the first words either of us had spoken since we began our descent. I kept my light aimed at him, the floor quickly coming into view, looking like a flattened moonscape. Grisnik pivoted in a tight circle, pointing his flashlight outward, then turned it off and vanished in the darkness.

I quickly covered the remaining ten feet inside the shaft, emerging into a large, rough-hewn, dome-shaped cavern. The ladder was anchored into the mouth of the shaft. The concrete securing the bolts had eroded and crumbled, causing the entire span to sway like a rope bridge.

"Marty! Where are you?"

He didn't answer. I swept the cavern walls with my flashlight until I found the outer perimeter, and took my bearings. It was a wide-open space, big enough to park half a dozen cars.

I shined my light at the base of the ladder, tracing lines in four directions and hitting the stack of boxes and trash bags I'd last seen being loaded into Nick Andrija's pickup. I continued my survey until the beam spread out like a fan, reflecting off a mirror made of water instead of glass. An inflated raft with a small outboard motor was beached at the edge of an underground lake.

"Come on in, the water's fine," Colby Hudson said.

The echoes in the chamber made it impossible to pinpoint his location and I had no better luck chasing the sound with my flashlight.

A red dot materialized on my shoulder, tracing a path to my heart, where it stopped.

"I've got a clear shot at you, Jack, so unload your gun and drop it. If I don't like the way you do it, I'll shoot you. And that would be a shame because there's someone down here who's dying to see you."

Colby had used Grisnik to lure me into a trap. "Marty! Where are you?"

"Do as he says, Jack," Grisnik answered. "He's holding all the cards."

"Wendy!" I shouted, "It's okay, honey. I'm here!"

She didn't answer. I was suspended in midair, too far from the shaft to climb back into it and too far above the ground to drop and roll. I emptied my Glock and let it go.

"Now," Colby said, "throw the ammo into the water. It's right in front of you, maybe ten feet from the ladder. Then turn off your flashlight and slowly come down the rest of the way."

He tracked me with the laser, using it to hold me in place when I stepped off onto the floor.

"You don't need Wendy," I said. "You've got her computer. You've got Grisnik and me. You can let her go."

"I wish I could," Colby said.

Pale orange light from a lantern, the kind you'd hang in a tent, this one dangling from a hook buried in the cavern wall, spilled into the darkness. Marty Grisnik stood next to the lantern, a pair of night-vision goggles dangling from a strap around his neck. Colby was next to him on bended knees, Grisnik's gun aimed at his head.

Grisnik said, "Now don't get all crazy on me and start shaking like a mental patient. Come into the light, but take it real easy." I closed to within five feet. "Hold it right there. When I was a kid, I always wanted to be a ventriloquist. Looks like I finally got my wish. How'd you like my act?"

I thought of how I had been deceived by Frank Tyler's act, silently apologizing to Kevin again. I heard Kate's voice assuring me that I couldn't have known, not believing her then or now, the props Grisnik had used suddenly becoming clear. He had hidden in plain sight, not disguising his feelings for Tanja, playing me to stay close to an investigation he'd been shut out of, taking advantage of every break I gave him. I wouldn't give him the satisfaction of a good review.

"I've seen better."

"Well, I admit that doing it in the dark with a gun pointed at this dummy's head gives me an unfair advantage, but they don't give style points in a game like this."

"So you never got over Tanja, after all."

"She does have a way about her, I'll give you that."

"Too bad you can't ask her late husband. She killed him and brought his coke business back home, probably did you behind the bar for old times' sake her first night home and never looked back. Had to gripe your ass to see her and Colby bumping and grinding."

Grisnik smiled. "Say what you want, Jack, he's the one on his knees."

Colby stared up at me, his arms handcuffed behind him, his face a bloody mess.

I looked at him without pity. He had betrayed Wendy, me, the people he worked with, and those he was sworn to serve. Colby had treated all of us as chips to be played in a game he had lost. Grisnik was no better, his loyalty belonging to a woman who'd had him by the short hairs since he had his first wet dream.

"Where's my daughter?"

"Ask him," Grisnik said. "Go ahead. I asked him plenty of times. He wouldn't tell me, but he said he'd tell you. I guess that's what family is all about."

Colby may have convinced Grisnik to bring me here, hoping that the cavalry wouldn't be far behind, but I ignored him. Wendy may have escaped or never been captured. If Grisnik didn't know where she was, I wouldn't help him find out. That information would only buy both Colby and me a bullet.

"Wendy can't hurt you. Colby used her to launder his cut,

but he wasn't stupid enough to tell her about you or Tanja," I said.

"Colby was stupid enough to tell Wendy everything and she was probably stupid enough to demand her cut. She and Colby, and now you, are the last of the loose ends. Then Tanja and I are out. Retired, fat, and happy," said Grisnik.

I shined my flashlight on Colby. One of his front teeth was gone and the corners of his mouth were crusted with dried blood, his lips swollen and cracked.

"She didn't know a goddamn thing," Colby said. "She didn't want to know."

"Bullshit! Tell him where she is," Grisnik said.

"Fuck you," Colby said.

Grisnik's face grew hard, blood rushing from his neck to his cheeks, his eyes bulging. "Damn you!" he said, pressing the barrel of his gun against Colby's temple.

"It doesn't matter anymore. It's over," I said, my voice cracking with stutters. "I copied Wendy's hard drive before you stole her computer. I gave it to Troy Clark a few hours ago. He says Colby kept very good records. Tanja has probably been picked up by now and you know what that means. First one to make a deal wins. She'll give you up before the ink on her fingerprints dries. You can turn yourself in and try to beat her to the punch or hide down here for the next fifty years. It doesn't matter. It's over."

Grisnik shook his head, turning his gun toward me. "Listen to you, Jack. You're a lousy liar. Troy Clark is right. You are half crazy."

Tremors began to percolate in my gut, tickling their way into my arms. I didn't have much time left before I'd be on my knees next to Colby. I had to convince Grisnik that he was finished, that Wendy couldn't hurt him. If I succeeded, he'd come to the only other conclusion. He'd have to kill both Colby and me, a price I'd pay to keep her safe.

"This is the way I figure it," I said. "Tanja handled supply.

Rice handled the money. You took care of the KCK cops and Colby played us. Rice went down, but he was willing to do the time to protect his investment. Marcellus Pearson and Javy Ordonez were both going down, but neither of them would take the long view like Rice did. So you decided to close up shop. Latrell Kelly bailed you out with Marcellus."

"I was supposed to do him, but I was only going to warn him," Colby said. "Tell him to get out of town. I was too late."

"Is that what you told Javy Ordonez? Except he said he was staying put, so you killed him."

"I set up the meeting with Javy, but that's all," Colby said. "Grisnik killed him. There's another entrance to the mine on the other side of the lake. Comes out in the woods behind the rail yard. Grisnik showed me. Perfect way to get in and out without being seen. Grisnik used the boat. We didn't know that Latrell used the other side for some kind of hiding place. Grisnik found his gun and the photograph of Latrell and his mother. It was just dumb luck."

I looked at Grisnik. "That's why you put Javy's body in the Dumpster. You knew it would get caught in the sweeper blade, just like the homeless bums you told me about. You left the gun where it would be found and planted the photograph. But you couldn't have known any of that would tie back to Latrell. We didn't find out about him until later."

"I didn't care who it tied back to so long as it wasn't me," Grisnik said.

"And Thomas Rice?"

Colby said, "Rice panicked after you and Grisnik went to see him. He was afraid you'd go after his wife. He called me. I told Grisnik and he called New York. They said Rice had to go."

"And you gave the job to Wilson Reddick," I said. "What about Bodie Grant?"

"In the water," Colby said, nodding at the lake. "That one's on me, too," he added, dropping his head.

"Why?"

He hesitated, choking on his answer. "Tanja," he said.

"She tell you that she'd chosen you instead of Grisnik?"

"Yeah," he said. "Pathetic, huh?"

"You don't know how pathetic," Grisnik said. "I'm a patient man, but I've run out of patience." He stuck his gun in Colby's ear. "Tell me where I can find Wendy."

Colby raised his face toward me. For an instant, a crooked smile flashed across half his face. It happened so fast, I wasn't certain I'd seen it. Then his face and his voice flattened out.

"I threw her body in the Missouri River. She's halfway to St. Louis."

"Well, ain't that the shits," Grisnik said and shot Colby in the head.

Chapter Seventy-one

Colby's head exploded in a mist of bone, blood, and brains, his torso toppling into the lake, his legs still folded on the floor. I went down with him, the gunshot triggering a spasm that coiled me tighter than a roll of steel cable, my head on my knees, and my chin hard against my chest. I braced myself for the aftershocks, using the flashlight like a pylon to steady my feet.

The spasm eased and I tilted my head up, gathering my breath. Grisnik was standing in front of me, arms at his side gun in his right hand.

"If you think about it, Jack, I'm doing you a favor," he said, raising his gun.

"Like hell," I said, and swung the flashlight at him knocking the gun from his hand and launching my shoulder into his gut.

I had the advantage of surprise but knew I was too weakened to ride it more than a few seconds. I drove him backward into the cavern wall, knocking the lantern to the floor. The bulb shattered and the cavern went black.

Grisnik clasped his hands into a single fist and slamme

them down into the center of my spine, putting me on my knees, then grabbed my jacket, yanking me to my feet, and giving me the momentum I needed. Grasping the flashlight, I speared the underside of his chin with the lens, snapping his head against the rock. He let go of my jacket and slid to the floor. I didn't know whether he was down or dead.

The lens on my flashlight was gone, the edges jagged and sticky with blood. I felt around his neck for his night-vision goggles, pulling them over his head and trying them on, throwing them aside when they didn't work.

The darkness was disorienting. I crawled to my right until I found the water, then stood and turned my back to the lake. With my hands stretched out like curb feelers, I walked toward where I hoped I would find the ladder. I missed it the first time, tripping over the stack of boxes from the bar. Coming back, I was certain I'd end up in the water until my left hand bounced off the bottom rung.

I grabbed the highest rung I could reach and pulled myself up. Once my feet made it to the bottom rung, I climbed as fast as I could, knowing that if I stopped moving, I would start shaking and lose my grip.

The first shot came when I was halfway up the ladder. It missed wide, ricocheting off the cavern wall, the sound deafening. My feet slipped and I caught myself after dropping a couple of steps. The red dot from the laser sight on Grisnik's gun searched the cavern for me.

"I know you're on the ladder," Grisnik said. "Guys like you always run."

He fired again, closer but still wide, the air hot with cordite. I started climbing again, the ladder creaking against its shifting anchor bolts. The next shot hit several rungs above me, the steel sparking.

"Getting closer, Jack! I can hear you on the ladder. I'm coming for you!"

Climb and he'd hear me. Hang where I was and he'd find

me. I said a prayer to the god of darkness to hide me and climbed, almost losing my grip when Grisnik grabbed the bottom end of the ladder and rattled it.

"Gotcha!" Grisnik said.

I swung to the outside of the ladder, climbing it like a rope, hoping he'd shoot through the center. Four more shots flew past and I was at the mouth of the shaft. I hung on to the outside of the ladder as he kept firing, swinging back to the center when I heard the dry click of an empty magazine, wondering whether he was reloading. The answer came when I felt the ladder sag with his weight as I climbed into the shaft.

"You're a dead man! I'm coming for you!"

I held on to a rung on the shaft wall, my feet on the top step of the ladder. I locked my feet around the inside edges of the top step on the ladder and started rocking it back and forth. The anchor bolts rolled around inside the crumbling concrete, the ladder groaning against their loosening grip.

I looked down. Grisnik was invisible in the dark, but I heard his heavy breathing and felt him getting closer. He'd stopped threatening, not wanting me to know how close he was.

Sweating heavily, my muscles trembling, I drove my legs harder, the ladder now swinging freely in a growing arc. I pulled my feet back on the rung so that they wouldn't get caught if the ladder came out of its mooring, and locked my left arm around a rung level with my chest. I then leaned away from the wall, bent at the waist, and drove my legs back and forth like a child on the swing set in the park.

Grisnik grabbed my ankle as the anchor bolts slid free. For an instant, he and the ladder were suspended in midair, my shoulder wrenching nearly out of its socket as I clung to the rung on the shaft wall. I kicked loose of his grip and a second later heard the ladder crash onto the cavern floor. He never made a sound.

My left shoulder was ruined, my arm useless. I climbed one handed, keeping my vision focused on the dim point of light at the top of the shaft, watching it grow bigger and brighter until I was near the surface and someone reached down to lift me up, eclipsing the light.

"Lend you a hand?" Ammara Iverson asked.

Chapter Seventy-two

On the way to the hospital to have my shoulder repaired, Ammara told me that the Wyandotte County Surveyor, the District Attorney, and their husbands were having dinner together when she caught up to them. The surveyor started to give a history of the county's mines when the D.A. remembered a case involving the Argentine Mine, explaining that it became a thirty-four-acre underground cave when the mine closed. When a killer was rumored to have dumped his murder victim in the lake, the surveyor led an expedition into the mine through the shaft in Matney Park to search for the body. Detective Martin Grisnik was the lead investigator on the case. The surveyor and the D.A. were there when Ammara helped me to my feet.

I missed my appointment on Monday with the neurologist since I was recovering from surgery to repair the wreck I'd made of my shoulder. Joy postponed the hearing finalizing our divorce. She brought Ruby with her when she visited after I came home from the hospital. The dog raced through the dining room and into the kitchen before jumping onto my easy chair, marking her territory with a wagging tail.

"I don't think there's a future for us," Joy said. "But I'm not in such a hurry for the future, either."

"Maybe it would be better for the dogs if we waited," I said.

She shrugged, giving me a sad smile. "Not too long. Just until we're sure about Wendy."

Despite a massive search of the Missouri River from Kansas City to St. Louis, Wendy's body was never found. The FBI, the police, and scores of volunteers searched the woods in Matney Park and behind the rail yard but there was no trace of her. Joy even hired a psychic, who claimed he saw Wendy's aura in a dozen different places, none of which yielded her body.

I wasn't surprised. At least five times a day and more during the night, I saw Colby's face when he said that she was dead. His micro expression with its asymmetrical, lopsided grin was enough to convince me he hadn't killed her, that he'd lied to protect her from Grisnik, a last grasp at redemption.

Kate said it was possible, but it was also possible that I was finding hope wherever I could. Either way, I said, I'm not giving up on Wendy. We talked about it over dinner, this time at the rotating rooftop restaurant at the Hyatt Hotel, the 360-degree view of Kansas City a more romantic backdrop than the view at IHOP.

Kate was slowly recovering her capacity to read micro expressions. A lot depended, she said, on letting it happen rather than forcing it.

"It's the same with you and me," she said. "We have to let it happen."

"You won't mind if I give it a kick in the ass every now and then."

"Can't see how that would hurt," Kate said, taking my hand in hers.

Tanja Andrija won the confessional race, offering up her

brother and her New York connections that had supplied her with drugs for her retail outlets in return for a new life for her and her parents in the witness protection program. I sat in the back of the courtroom the day she entered her plea. The judge, a white-haired gentleman old enough to know better, did everything but ask for her new phone number. Tanja was a woman of considerable talent.

I eventually made it to the neurologist, who said that he'd never seen a case like mine in forty years of practice, as if I should be pleased to have broken his streak. He declined a diagnosis, sending me to a specialist at the Mayo Clinic in Scottsdale, Arizona. The doctor, a lanky, quiet, and compassionate man, stuck electrodes to my skin and monitored my involuntary movements, telling me with more certainty than hope that I had tics, a childhood disorder that disappeared in adolescence and almost never appeared for the first time in adults although, in my case, it had.

It was, he said, one of the nervous system's unexplained defects, for which there was no known cause or cure. Though he assured me it would neither threaten nor shorten my life, he also conceded it was unlikely to disappear.

When the medications he prescribed didn't work and made me goofy, he told me I had to retire or face worsening symptoms. Take it easy, he said. Do less and take more time doing it.

It sounded like death in slow motion. If living meant shaking, I chose shaking. The Bureau chose retirement and declared me disabled in record time.

Troy kept the case open, pursuing the possibility that Wendy was not only alive but was also the sole survivor of the drug ring. The offshore accounts they had used had been emptied, the money never recovered. Troy suspected that Wendy had made off with the money and was living the high life while her parents mourned her presumed death, a possibility I publicly rejected and privately prayed for.

I didn't want her to be a criminal. I just wanted her to be alive and safe. If she had been involved, she'd be reluctant to contact us. I understood that, trading the nightmares about what had happened to her for the hope she was okay.

Ammara told me all about Troy's theory over coffee, apologizing and saying that she'd asked to be transferred to another squad, adding that Joy and I were being watched in case we received a phone call or e-mail from Wendy or in case the balance in our bank accounts suddenly ballooned.

It was shameful, insulting, and inevitable, but I couldn't criticize Troy. Even now, I couldn't separate the truth from the lies. Each version was layered with shades of guilt, from Colby's confession exonerating Wendy, to his implied indictment of her on the playground, to Grisnik's insistence that she was the biggest thief among the thieves. The version that was missing was her own. Until I knew that, I wouldn't pass judgment.

Either she was dead, her body lost, or she was alive and had left us behind. Whichever was the case, I had failed her.

Three months later I was having coffee at Beanology, one of my favorite haunts not far from my house, laptop on my lap, surfing the web. It was one of those rare winter days when the temperature soared for no apparent reason into the upper sixties. I was sitting on the outdoor patio, the sun at a blinding, sharp angle, Ruby curled on the chair next to me.

A message popped up in my inbox telling me that someone had sent me an electronic greeting card. I clicked on the link and an image materialized on the screen. It was a monkey with an ear-to-ear grin. The caption read *Happy Birthday! Love, Monkey Girl.*

It was my birthday. I'd forgotten, but Wendy hadn't.

AFTERWORD

I have learned about tics through personal experience. My thanks to Dr. John Caviness at the Mayo Clinic, Scottsdale, Arizona, for his kind, compassionate treatment. My thanks to Rabbi Moshe Berger of the Siegal College of Judaic Studies for posing the compelling question whether there is a commanding voice in suffering. The answer is yes. The command is to live well, fully, and righteously. Writing this book is one small step in fulfillment of that command.